The
Heavenly
Realm

NOVELS BY BARRY SWAN

(published by Valley Press)

The Deserted Village

Amerigo Vespucci

The Intelligence Man

The Madness of Eamon Moriarty

The Heavenly Realm
(sequel to *The Intelligence Man*)

http://www.valleypress.co.uk

The Heavenly Realm

Barry Swan

Valley Press

First published in 2005
by Valley Press
Penlan Fach Isaf, Dihewyd,
Lampeter SA48 7QP

Typeset in Horley Old Style
by Martin Noble Editorial, Iffley, Oxford
Cover design by Patrick Swan
Printed and bound in England
by TJ International, Padstow, Cornwall

ISBN 0 9530768 4 9

FOR THE COPTIC THREE

Michael going to bring them, bring them to the Orthodox Church.
No matter what they do, no matter what they say.
Gabriel going to bring them, bring them to the Orthodox Church.
Raphael going to bring them, Uriel going to bring them,
Sorial going to bring them, Raguel going to bring them,
Fanuel going to bring them, bring them to the Orthodox Church.

A nyabingi chant, now incorporated into Orthodox liturgy.

cast

'No matter who you are, or what you have done, here you will only be known as brother.'

SANG

Founding-father, ordained priest of the Catholic Church. A natural-born leader with the inherent weakness such people have of usually making the 'right' decision.

HANS

Founding member, ordained priest with a hidden, dark past he tries to atone for by living on 'the dangerous edge of things'.

JIM MCCALL

Formerly a 'man of the world', a plotter among other things. Gone-to-ground in this community, spending most of his days doing the most boring job of all – office accounts – mainly keeping himself to himself.

GERRY MCARTHUR

Former schoolteacher and fantasist, escaping the trauma of an annulled marriage. In hiding here from his imagined enemies; but finding that his academic talents are welcome in the community.

ALAN   A 'reconciled' malcontent from the days of the original Community of the Nation of Zion (or Jah) before it was incorporated by the Jesuits into the United Church of Jaman.

DAN   Irish exile, who insists that his surname (O'Toole) never be mentioned in the community, doing a lifetime of repentance for murdering his best friend, long ago.

EAMON   Like Dan, an Irishman, who had once been an inmate of a lunatic asylum.

WILBUR ORBECK   Official hermit of the community. Therefore he had to live on the edge of the main enclosure in a hut, bound to the community by an intricate, complicated, abstruse and voluminous series of 'hermit' laws, vows, rules and regulations drawn up by Bro Hans.

PAULO   Formerly a failed newspaper journalist, the scribe of the community, writing a diary, collaborating with Gerry in producing theological and other documents and sending his own musings to his literary agent in Kingstown.

VARIOUS BROTHERS including Alfredo – former heavy drinker, thug and criminal inexplicably drawn to the monastic life – as some have said, by virtue of the shining example of the conversion of his one-time drinking partner Bro Gerry McArthur (who had paid for his drinks in return for 'services obtained').

JOSEPHINE	Founding mother, in charge of the adjoining convent.
SR JANE	Another Irish import and formerly a mother of a very large family; once a confidant of Bro Dan.
SR GLORIA	Sacked from her job and threatened, for her improprieties, by her multiple employers (including the government and US embassy) with death or, at the very least, life imprisonment on the notorious offshore prison. Gained admittance to the community by means of a reference and CV drawn up by Gerry, for whom she had once been a cleaner and confidant.

VARIOUS SISTERS

THE WORLD

chapter
one

The compound of the United Church, situated on gently rolling hillside between the sea and the Blue Mountains, a scenic setting which could just as easily be construed as one from which there was no easy escape, was located in a poor, backward part of the island. The decision to 'set up camp' there was said to have been a deliberate attempt to 'identify' with the rural poor and those on the 'margin of existence'; but it also provided relative freedom from outside interference and plenty of reclaimable, bush land.

In a country plagued by poverty, crime and sometimes dubious management decisions, one might have felt that there was no need to add further to the country's, or indeed the world's, problems. However, Bro Sang, founding father of the new monastic order, managed to do just this in his first decision of the new ecclesiastical year. He made the sorry mistake of decreeing that Induction Day should also be Humility Day.

Perhaps it was a laudable attempt to show what real religion is about – and for the inductees to make a good start in the religious life. But afterwards it was used against him in General Chapter. For on it was blamed the outbreak of offensive graffiti that was first discovered on that same day. This was the moment when –

in hindsight – things started to go wrong, and he first felt his control weakening over his 'tight ship'.

The idea was that for just twenty-four hours everyone would try to be humble. This meant that anybody was free to insult anybody else to the hilt and a person could not respond but had to smile and take it like a Christian. At the same time, they could also say what they really thought of you! For this was the key to humility – to say what you really thought.

It all began at breakfast. The routine was to have a reading from Scripture at every meal, by a monk high above everybody on a plinth where he had nothing to hold on to, and where balance was of extreme importance, with the slightest wrong move meaning a long fall to the floor. To add to the tension, the reader was expected to speak in lofty tones and be very careful not to make mistakes in wording or pronunciation, this being a greater 'sin' even than falling down. That morning's reading was by Bro Alan, whose name had been substituted at the last moment so that the day could begin with maximum humiliation for everyone. Alan, of course, could not read properly. He had done some last minute memorising with the help of Bro Gerry. He immediately forgot all the drilling.

'I read, brethren, dat the firs' mus' be las' and the las' mus' be firs'. All the same thing, yea? If the firs' is las', den it mean dat the las' is firs'. It logical! Like chicken an' egg. Dat's me reading of the t'ing, an'way. When yo chuck me out, I was de firs' in de eyes of de Lord. When yo let me back in, I was de prodigal son come home again. But I was firs' again so now I am las'! It don't mek no sense to me.'

There were two whole pages in front of him, still to be read. He could go no further. He pointed at the window and cried out, 'Ha ha ha he he he! Look dere! Look out de window! See what dere! Lookee!' Everybody in the refectory turned to look out the window, their mouths and eyes agape. Some were hoping to see the devil, or the Second Coming at the very least.

But there was nothing to be seen. Each, in the humiliated privacy of his own ears, heard the despairing, raucous laugh of Alan and smarted with annoyance.

'Nothing dere – at all!' he laughed again.

They finished their breakfast and retired to chapel for morning meditation. Bro Obnoxious tripped up Bro Placid as they made their way along the corridor.

There were no major incidents during meditation, but there occurred one covert 'accident' in the room, not noticed by most but recorded by Bro Paulo for posterity in his *History of the Community*. Bro Alan had let off wind, deliberately and silently, grievously disturbing the meditation of Bro Sanctus who was nearest to him. Paulo had observed this from nearby (his prayer life was being continually distracted by his having to record events around him); and he also noted the embarrassment of the monks as they tried to stifle their laughter.

The monastery surroundings had been much improved upon since the Days of the Great Reform. This was when the two sects, the Jah Brethren and the Society of Jesus (Jesuits), had agreed to bury their differences and join forces. Bro Hans had persuaded Wilbur Orbeck, the main Jah leader, that without help his group was destined for extinction at best, eternal damnation at worst. He said everybody in the world was laughing at them for their eccentric ethnic beliefs and strange, colourful ways. While all the governments of the world, as well as the Mafia, the US military-industrial complex, the international intelligence services, the politically non-accountable megamonopolistic, biotechnological, transnational financial monoliths, the UN and indeed most of the world's population were concerned about the pernicious influence of the Catholic Church, the mere mention of the name Jah produced only incomprehension, or at best howls of laughter. Worse still, they were patronised by well-meaning Western hippies and 'liberals'. Their chief reputation was for irresponsible behaviour, a poor selection of followers, disrespect for authority and boorishness. They were considered a nuisance by Jaman officials concerned for the good image of the country.

Meanwhile the Church – and the Jesuits in particular – were detested and feared by everyone. If you even said the word 'Jesuit' there would be the most profound apprehension and subconscious imagery of woeful authority and influence. Hans said that, unbeknownst to themselves, those very same, powerful world bodies were even infiltrated by those very same Jesuits. If the Jah joined with the Jesuits, their prestige would increase a thousand-fold and the government would think twice about interfering with them. And that lack of organisation and confused leadership that had so characterised them would be a thing of the past.

Brother Orbeck had agreed to go on retreat in a hermitage inside the Jesuits' own compound. Soon thereafter, it was reported that the Lord had given him a private revelation. It was said that He had announced that He would formally withdraw His offer of eventual repatriation to the Original Homeland if the whole Jah brethren did not become Orthodox at once. Soon thereafter, they marched back into their own, specially enlarged enclosure under the sign 'United Church of Jaman'.

One change to the monastery was that there were no longer the armed guards or electrified perimeter fence that had enclosed the former Jah settlement, and which had once been such an eye-catching feature of the place. Gone too was the outer security fence around the open land (although there remained an inner fence cutting off the administrative buildings to ensure a quiet, peaceful atmosphere for the monks' times of prayer and meditation). The open land now grew peanuts (rather than the once lucrative 'holy herb' or cannabis plant) and was worked solely by the monks.

The sisters of the United Church, the former Jah queens and princesses as well as a number of foreigners, had their establishment down the road. They were barred from residing in the main compound after the early experimental period, when a type of communal 'free chaste love' was tried. This broke down when the women found, for one thing, that they always ended up doing the most unpleasant jobs (they always volunteer, was the retort), as well as the heaviest labour on the farm. When an order came from Rome demanding separation and threatening immediate closure, the sisters left for the old abandoned plantation barracks down the road (some with relief). However, they were soon to find themselves being allowed a new role in the United Church hospital, where their services were found to be indispensable with regard to those particularly unpleasant or mundane tasks that the monks found difficult to deal with.

It was *peanuts, peanuts, peanuts* now, Bro Alan commented, full of nostalgia for the old days. These formed the main food at most community meals. Of course new cooking methods were used to vamp up the taste and flavour. Cooking was overseen by Bro Quietitude who was blind, deaf and dumb. As is often the case with such people, he was very talented, in his case with the pots and pans; he could make anything taste good. It was said that he once had to be taken away by Jim McCall and Gerry for cookery lessons. They had used their old CIA interrogation techniques to get through to Quietitude essential information and instructions. Bro Paulo, meanwhile, relishing another challenge to his journalistic skills, noted every exotic recipe down in his heavy tome 'Rules of Strict Orthodox Cooking'.

The farm was a busy place during the day – and they all loved cultivating the peanut now (initially there had been some resistance). Some thought it had a magical aspect, for unlike cannabis its fruit grew under the ground where it couldn't be seen. Sang increased acceptance for it by referring to it as 'our little secretive brother'. They depended on it for their sustenance. The surplus was sold on the market to pay for essentials. Some portion was always left over for the poor, who did not live very far away. It was thus becoming an essential, indeed indispensable part of the local diet.

There was a big problem at the beginning, when Sang had insisted on integration with the neighbourhood and had the outer barrier removed. Landless, poor people flocked in, grazing their goats and pigs on the community land, as well as attempting to steal the peanuts by night. This problem was dealt with by Sang and Hans using a combination of worldly and unworldly methods. The unworldly method was prayer; the worldly method was Bro Alfredo.

In his former life Bro Alfredo had been a criminal thug and his talents were used to keep the peace on the farm and in this he found his true vocation, for the incidents of violence and disruption on the land reduced soon after his deployment as 'doorman'. The great atmosphere of peace that settled over the whole region thereafter had a name – Alfredo's Peace. On his death (to be described later) he was put into his grave with great outpouring of sentiment, the releasing of peace balloons and much clasping of hands by the united community along with the whole population of the neighbouring region. After the burial there was an emotive display by the normally undemonstrative Bros Eamon Moriarty and Dan O'Toole, with whom Alfredo had enjoyed many fights. When they thrust their machetes into the grave-earth it was interpreted as a mime, violent men turning their swords into harmless implements for tilling the soil. A white dove was painted on his gravestone while beneath it was carved:

Evil doers beware
On Resurrection Day
Alfredo will arise

The Induction of the new members was taking place in the Meeting Hall. The system of seating was Roman circus with the whole community staring down at the 'top brass' ensconced at the centre table below. (The unusual construction concealed a secret enclosure underneath, to which entry was barred to all except Sang and Hans.)

As usual, it was a delayed, worried entrance by Sang. He came in eventually, reluctantly.

'Go back a China!' shouted Bro Alan to everyone's amusement; 'we stupid nuff put *you* in charge?'

'Flat face. Have some peanuts,' shouted Bro Gerry, joining in the fun and he threw nuts at Sang, hitting him with a good shot.

Tomatoes, oranges and goat droppings followed from other brothers, most of which hit their target.

Bro Alan had lit up a *cannabis sativa* cigarillo and blew in and out (Jah do not inhale the herb) with great gusto and much thumping on his belly. Paulo was to write in his diary that, for him, Humility Day had the potential to become the most sacred day in the year for it enabled everyone to indulge for a few hours their old vices – a consoling reminder that they had not become improved or different people at all, but were still themselves.

Sang spoke humbly. 'Brethren! I accept your admonishments! As we welcome our newly professed brothers, those little brave souls who have served their noviciate, it is good to know that no one, no matter how high-ranking, or whatever his devotion to duty, is exempt from grievous humiliation, character defamation and hot-blooded embarrassment. These are our life-blood.'

There was more loud, derisive laughter followed by banging of tables and stamping of feet. There were calls to Hans to come out from under the table, where he was hiding in mock-trepidation.

Before the induction, matters of urgent business had to be dealt with. There was a short report on the latest hike in the price of peanuts, the problem of overcrowding at the hospital, the shortage of crucial supplies of just about everything and new 'discipline measures' to replace those that hadn't been working too well. Such minor matters of business got out of the way, it was now time for debating, once again, the big issue.

Sang spoke solemnly and said that he was able at last to report progress on the most burning question facing the church; the one theological issue upon which depended the whole existence and fate of the community. It was a controversy that Sang had put the best brains and most inspired mystics in their midst to work on. (In this way, he was able to keep those same minds and emotions occupied in the never-ending quest for closure on a theological matter (an impossibility), which would otherwise be causing much trouble in other more important, sensitive spheres. Having studied for his doctorate at a top German theological university, Sang had long ago come to realise that theology was a subject of as much practical use as Alchemy. This was why he was able to keep a knowing face, and unruffled demeanour, during the many rows over theology that they had in community. He had, thereby, gained a reputation for great wisdom and a charitable tolerance for a wide variety of deeply conflicting theological opinion.)

He now put on his most persuasive voice, as bespoke deep reflection on the issue, blanking out his personal thoughts and feelings in order to gain that total indifference that they all saw as astuteness. He said that it was a day of great gladness, for he had an important announcement to make.

'You will be overjoyed to hear that the main question which once divided us, and which has spurred us on to seek a solution that will be to the satisfaction of both our brethren and the pope in Rome – the question of the Lord's nationality – has been resolved. On the matter of the ethnicity of the Lord, it is important to remind everyone that we *all* belong to Jah. Many sessions of General Chapter were fruitlessly spent debating whether He is black or white, brown or yellow. But much praise to Bros Gerry, Alan and Paulo, who have put exceedingly great effort into studying Scripture, as well as deep reflection and prayer on the matter. They have examined every single word in the Bible. What evidence, pro and con, they have found they have digested, analysed and debated until finally they came to their inescapable conclusion. It is a conclusion based on accurate data, as sound as that of any physical science.'

They applauded. Of course science would support their beliefs – particularly their way out beliefs – as why else would they have believed them if they were not true?

'It is certainly the case that Jah is multicultural. He is what we have already defined as ethnically mixed. Some brothers were happy to leave it at that. He is not a white man, as was believed for about 2000 years. Born in Judah in the East, the ways of Rome, the wisdom of Greece are also in Him. He ate and drank of the soil of Africa and that land, too, is in His body and blood. Some say that He came to visit this hemisphere, that perhaps he went to other far regions as well. These all form Him, His diet, His opinion of things, His views of the world. He took with Him to Heaven portions of the fragrant soil of many lands. That is the essence both of our problem and our solution.

The learned brothers, however, have found that the mighty words of scripture give us this clear answer:

It ... was spoken of the Lord by the prophets, saying, Out of Egypt have I called my son.'

They all started cheering, stamping their feet and chanting 'true, true!'

'It is now our official Declaration – the Lord is *essentially African!'*

They cheered. Some did so cautiously, suspecting the word 'essentially' and that Sang might still have some sort of trick up his sleeve. For Sang was of the land of China – not Africa.

'At last the long-held belief of our Jah brethren has been approved. Rejoice now too, for the Jesuits have come into the debate on your side. Your patience, brothers, has been rewarded. The new pronouncement has been written down on a formal document. Our declaration is ready to be sent to Rome to be approved by the Congregation for the Doctrine of the Faith.'

The Jah brothers cheered again; and then some new argument began among them. Sang had difficulty restoring quiet, sighing to himself.

'On the matter of the oath of allegiance, brothers, we have also made progress. By a study of the constitutions of other orthodox religious orders, we have at last been able to remove that old, discriminatory privilege that was causing distress. This is the rule whereby the special oath of unquestioning allegiance to Brother Superior could only be taken by senior members of the community. Now all members, regardless of rank, and including new inductees, are allowed to take the oath!'

A cheer went up. It was more important to achieve equality, even if that equality involved a surrender of rights and privilege, than to be in a position of inequality.

They now moved on to AOB.

'Some of you have asked questions about the gentleman who has been living in the room behind the library for some time. He has been keeping himself to himself, reading his books and saying his prayers. He has recently asked permission to use the workshop facilities, for he is a talented craftsman in wood. Perhaps some of you have already come across him in quiet areas of the compound, particularly at a late hour (for he likes to take a walk at this time). He is, or was at one time, a rabbi of the Jewish faith. It is no concern of ours as to why he has had to seek refuge. However, he has let it be known that by insisting on holding to his religious views, he has made a few problems for himself in life.

'He says that the opportunity to read and pray here has been a bonus. Currently, he is awaiting the finalisation of some travel arrangements. We consider it a great privilege to have with us an "elder brother of the Book". A little word of warning. Do not discuss religion or Christianity with him. For one thing, I have found that the subject upsets him a good deal. If you happen to pass him by, bow respectfully and carry on with your own tasks. Remember – our community is only as Christian as it is tolerant.'

They were accustomed to all sorts of people staying at the monastery – but a rabbi!

'Now we have a Jewish dreadlocks!' said Obnoxious.

'Heretic!' shouted another brother. 'If he was here right now I'd teach him a bit of humility. I'd pull him by the locks!'

'Here come the goody-goodies!' shouted Obnoxious as the five new aspirants filed in procession into the hall and lined up in front of Sang and Hans. Everybody silently scorned the naive enthusiasm and piety of the novices. These trainees lived almost in a different world. They were given all the hard tasks to do. They were made to pray in the chapel for long, regular periods. They had to go to bed earlier and get up earlier than everybody else. They were sent out not just to help the sick, poor and mad but were also expected to sympathise with them. They had to teach in the outreach schools, and in reporting the poor results rejoice in the non-educability and indifference of their pupils. They were expected to show the biblical virtues at all times. Yet they seemed to love the hard life! They hated it when their time in the noviciate came to an end and they had to face the more mundane tasks of community life. Receiving the proper portions of food, having rest periods, small luxuries, enjoying the useful, interesting work in administration, organising the arrangements for elaborate ceremonial occasions, attending, and perhaps minuting, innumerable meetings were, at least initially, a severe penance to them.

There were no visitors present this year to witness the ceremony, for none of the candidates could trace a parent, brother or sister. If such relatives did exist, or were alive, they were either deliberately keeping away or they couldn't afford the fare. Some sisters from next door came in now to perform a dance of celebration. The brothers and sisters joined in the somewhat raucous singing of a traditional, native song of induction, full of allusions to the 'heavenly delights' that awaited the inductees, celebrating the passage of the innocent one into the wicked world.

Meanwhile Bro Sanctus was in the chapel, forgotten by everyone and oblivious even to himself. If he had realised that he was missing the year's most important ceremony he would have been horrified, for the very thought of giving scandal would have been the furthest thing from his mind. He had become so caught up in his prayers that he had not yet returned to consciousness. Named Sanctus by everyone, initially as an insult because of his excessive praying, they had come to realise that he had a direct line to the Lord. What else could explain his helpfulness, his self-abasement, his happy, kindly expression, his ability to sort out people's problems by encouragement and concern, his cheerfulness when dealing with difficult personalities? These virtues were interpreted as a true sign of sanctity. He himself, however, knew that these qualities were simply abject, humiliating expressions of his need for acceptance and praise. That he was happy to admit the humiliating fact of his secret, interior emptiness and need was perhaps the truest proof of his real sanctity – he was told in confession.

Sanctus had long ago lost all faith in human beings. He had never known his real mother, as she had abandoned him at birth. Beaten and humiliated by a long line of 'uncles', he was put into child prostitution by his 'aunt'. His final alienation came when the local authorities closed down, without notice, his only home in the world – a cardboard box behind the Kingstown market. He had drifted north and met up with the monks at their travelling school, where he was taken in and, initially, successfully taught to spell the letters of his name. Despite suspicion, cynicism and a lack of enthusiasm on his part, he was eventually persuaded to become a novice with the promise that he would eventually be able not only to spell, but to *write* his name. There was even the prospect that he would be able to read books at some date in the future.

But that background alone, and his overcoming of it, did not explain his great sanctity. For there were many others here with equally impressive upbringings, who were still struggling with stage one of the road to spiritual enlightenment. It was perhaps his very lack of faith in people, in the world, the absence of any feelings, even of resentment and hate, and a total unawareness of any kind of desire that helped explain it. For he was probably the most 'detached' person in the whole history of spirituality. Not relating to anyone or anything, he knew the secret of total dependence upon Providence. He had known this even before he joined the monks. At the end of his second week in the monastery – after completion of all the stipulated Hans-devised 'trials of spiritual strength' – he had woken up one morning and gone forever were the expressionless face, the blank eyes, the lackadaisical posture. In their place was the invisible glow of a mystic.

He was praising God at that moment for the marvellous blessings of all the beatings and mental and physical abuse of the past. However, he was also admitting to God that he was now struggling with perhaps the gravest difficulty that he had ever faced in his life. To his horror, he had been given the worst appointment in the whole community – personal assistant to Bro Obnoxious, the Master of Ceremonies. Despite the revulsion he felt, he now told the Lord that it really didn't matter if he did have to take up this cross. It would only be the ultimate test of patience and virtue.

He would accept his new appointment with a joyful, thankful heart and, unusually, his prayers now were vocal rather than mental as he came back to consciousness, the sound of his voice filling the chapel.

It was at this moment that Snitchus, who had crept out of the

Meeting Hall to see what Sanctus was up to, came along and peered into the chapel. As he saw Sanctus leaving his seat, he gasped.

Sanctus was walking with both feet above ground level, not even looking to see where he was going. His eyes were raised to heaven! When Snitchus went back to the Meeting hall and told everyone what he had seen, there was much awe and wonder.

But then something happened that was to change their whole attitude to Sanctus. After *this* incident, he would be treated as somebody who should, perhaps, be carefully watched.

With the induction ceremony over, the rest of the day had reverted again to the celebration and anarchy of 'humility events'. After the sisters had left, the bad manners and mutual insulting recommenced in earnest, making life particularly difficult for the newly inducted members. But it was not any of this that called into question Sang's judgement – as well as the integrity of every single member of the community.

It was somebody's idea that day to start writing graffiti in various, unusual places. It appeared in curious little spots, such as under kitchen tables and above doors. It was in places no one might be expected to reach with any ease. The graffiti expressed complaints about aspects of life in the community. But even these would not have been too remarkable (for Humility Day), were it not for one particularly disturbing, offensive piece of graffiti. It was, as Sang sorely pointed out, political graffiti. It was an insinuation that there was something bad about peanuts. It had been carved with a sharp implement on the ceiling high above Sang's door. It read: 'Peanuts bad food dat kill innocents'.

It could only have been put there by someone with wings.

two

That evening Sang was ruminating over the debacle of Humility Day. The experiment had been recommended to him by a highly reputed psychologist who claimed that the outcome would give him some measure of how the community was progressing spiritually.

And now here was yet another brother standing before him, complaining about his duties!

Why was it that the first vow they forgot after leaving the noviciate was obedience? Rivalry and grumbles over jobs were a greater problem than anything else – so much for humility and submission. Even so, in this particular case he had to show sensitivity, for it was Bro Asissy who had come to complain. Asissy said that he had had enough. The last thing on Earth he needed now was to be taken off his duties as assistant master of ceremonies and sent to the farm. (He helped prepare the chapel for services and made public areas look presentable with flowers etc. Bro Obnoxious's role was to oversee and issue instructions.)

He told Sang now that he had been thinking about his personal problem for a long time. His effeminate nature, which had been given to him as a special gift by God, was his most treasured possession. However, it had caused him all sorts of problems in life. He had originally fled to the safety of the monastery after being pursued there by a stone-throwing mob, incensed by his wearing of 'lady's clothes' – a colourful dress and an original-design woolly hat. There had been a reasonable degree of acceptance here, despite the disrespectful name he had been given. He loved, in particular, wearing the attractive, comfortable habits and robes.

'Father, you know I have lived a good, honest life here and have done my best at the washing, laying the tables and arranging the flowers. But I can't go back to work in the fields again. For I have been bearing a heavy burden for some time. I think, now, it is in my nature to be a woman. Each day I dream of dressing up again in a lady's dress, putting on makeup and having my hair plaited with beads.'

Sang mused: sex was not such a problem here in the Third World, as it was in the developed countries. They had the common-sense way of handling lawful or illicit, natural or unnatural desire. Don't talk about it, accept it, it nearly always goes away.

'Bro Asissy. You have done great and good work here and your gentle ways are appreciated by every member of the community. But if I let you dress as a woman – that would be bad enough in itself. As it is, the word out there in the media is that we are a religious cult, dealing in everything from guns and drugs to pornographic material. They even say that we bury our poor victims in the peanut fields! You can imagine what ordinary people already say about us – a bunch of males living together, without women, dressed in frocks! You know, I have heard that some even accuse us of using the sisters as sex slaves. And that is not the worst. I could show you some of the hate mail we get! In fact, between you and me, Asissy, appearing a little bit iniquitous or ridiculous is probably good for our image in certain quarters, especially with those who would destroy us if they ever saw us as serious rivals for power. But a monk in make-up and plaited hair? We do not need that publicity!'

'The saints were often different to others. They were called all sorts of names. Some were nudists.'

'They were saints. Some of them could get away with anything.'

'Couldn't I just be put in charge of the choir? You know I have a sweet voice. I find it impossible to quench this *thing* in myself.'

'It's only sex.'

'No. It's not. It is what I call a person's intuition of highest beauty. It's ultimate desire. It is infinitely above sex. What they teach in theology class – when they talk about chastity and so on – doesn't even begin to explore my problem. I can't find any reference to it in a single book in the library.'

Ah, when people confuse sex with 'beauty' – that is where the trouble starts, thought Sang to himself.

'Write it all down. It might help you and others struggling with the same problem. Work through it by means of artistic expression. Some of the great artists had tremendous problems in that field! Because you have this problem – you can help humankind gain new insights.'

'I sometimes experience thoughts so deep that I can't even explain them. Not even in confession. I am not even sure whether they are sinful – or holy. Neither does the confessor to whom I have related them.'

He paused, took a deep breath and asked in a pleading voice, 'If I cannot have my way with my dress, at least let me remain as assistant master of ceremonies.'

'It has all been leading up to this,' thought Sang.

He was not an inhuman superior, or a harsh 'director of souls'. Some scorned him and said that he was more Buddhist than Christian what with his apparent cool indifference in the face of problems, many of which he would refuse to acknowledge even existed – at least in the terms that they were presented to him. Now, it was true that monks were forbidden to show emotion or too much empathy to a fellow brother – especially in an unashamedly physical way. This was in order to encourage self- and-God-reliance. But he felt it was incumbent upon him now to demonstrate that he, too, was a companion in the perplexities of existence, an equal bearer of the burdens of life and love. He laid a hand in blessing on Asissy's head. The monk sank to the floor in tears.

It was such minor, heartfelt actions that perhaps, while dis- playing the stuff of leadership, were also the seed of disaster in this superior's tenure. It was certainly true that such displays of humanity had helped him maintain control over his varied com- munity, despite some grievous errors in policy and administ- ration. But what works at the collective level can frequently be disastrous when dealing with individuals. Sang did not under- stand human nature sufficiently to see the dangers of demonstrat- ing or practising love.

Asissy felt deeply humiliated for having 'bared his soul' in Sang's presence. He kicked his feet and hit his fists on the ground. This was what he hated most – finding himself in a situation where he couldn't help but appear lacking in all self-control. Tears had always been his greatest weakness and shame.

How they had flowed during that time of joining the nov- iciate! That memory was still the greatest humiliation of his life. Unbeknownst to him at the time, part of the induction routine was to tell each candidate that they were totally unsuitable for such a life, and quite unfitted to be a monk. Then they would be called back as they walked out the gates, or were even very far down the road. Asissy hadn't been able to bring himself to leave the building. As a last resort, he had claimed he smelt the 'odour of sanctity' and could see angels. He fell to his knees and implored him to let him stay. This was observed by the whole community. It went on for a number of hours. When the novice master assessed that he had been sufficiently debased, he was told that he would certainly have to leave now for having made such a fool of himself. He took his leave, wordlessly. He had in fact gone a good mile beyond the bend of the road when a messenger was sent to bring him back.

Now here he was, crying helplessly again. He felt like saying something rude to Father Sang for making him feel such a ... weakling.

Yet even as he lay on the floor, he began to put into operation a plan that would see him get his way.

All he had to do, after all, was to persuade Sang to make the 'right decision'. There were two ways to influence a decision, the carrot and the stick. Now what did Sang want most of all? A strong peanut market? A peaceful community? Good public relations? None of these. He wanted a *holy* community above all. At least he was forever saying so. Now, Asissy knew that once a person was in community, it was extremely difficult to get thrown out. Hadn't Bro Gerry, in particular, tried that often enough? But if Sang decided that Bro Asissy was *sinning*, then he could be on his way to success. If he could persuade the worldly-wise, yet 'unworldly-unwise' man that the only way he would ever attain holiness would be to go around attired in a harmless skirt and plaited hair, and exempt from all tasks of manual labour for which there was enough manpower already – then that certainly could be interpreted as God's will? It was worth a shot.

His tears had stopped and he had a relieved, if thoughtful smile on his face as he left Sang's office.

The next day saw another 'bad turn' in Bro Eamon. He was in his usual place hacking away at the tough red earth on the slopes over on the east of the farm. A machete was in his hand (he was never without one these days). It was his favourite tool and when he had come over from Cork, Ireland after his release from the asylum (as part of the Care in the Community programme) he had taken to life here as a fish to water. He had become a hard-working individual, and this formerly uncommunicative character was now unusually erudite about farming and other matters relating to the soil. The social services department that had arranged for his transportation to the Indies had claimed, in his release papers, that he would never be a completely cured man or useful to society in any way. This was not evidently the case. Eamon had long since proved that he was a hardworking farm labourer, outdoing the others in enthusiasm and sweat. He loved to tackle the extra hard bits of digging, and to weed in pest-infested places that the other brothers shied away from.

It was a mystery how Eamon had come to know so much about farming in the tropics. Indeed his zeal could be awkward, for he had opposed the introduction of modern technology, such as heavy machinery, on the farm. The somewhat frightening vehemence of his opposition to such improvements in farming methods had made the community very wary of introducing any changes whatsoever. It was Eamon who had threatened violence at the suggestion of getting a tractor. He had railed for weeks against what he called dangerous 'dragons'.

Yet the worth of his simple wisdom was later to be realised by the monks. For the soil had much red laterite in it, an iron product of the chemical weathering that made it very sticky and impenetrable in the wet season. The soil was liable easily to become compacted. Paulo, the scribe, discovered one day in the library an account of the expensive fiasco of the great East African groundnut scheme. Heavy tractor wheels had compacted the soil, causing it to be eroded and making it unworkable. Eamon had saved the brothers from a costly mistake. Of course, in writing it up, Paulo got all the credit for the fortunate discovery and the cancelling of the tractor-plan. Eamon's flashes of wisdom, his peasant genius and knack for problem-solving in a difficult environment were considered just part of his sick, irrational mind.

He was happiest when put to work on the infertile slopes far away from the easy, level areas of rich soil. This also meant that he usually worked in some isolation from the other monks, (though he had a regular working partner in his friend, Dan O'Toole). The main group of monks toiled at a steady, regular pace, praying silently or singing loud hymns of praise in rhythm with their work. Eamon would only ever mutter or groan to himself. Could the likes of Eamon pray? Some wondered. He and Dan were still being taught (by Gerry) in special lessons on how to say basic, simple prayers. Dan was never seen to pray at all. This was due, it was said, to a mental block. In fact, Eamon said that he had never heard of God before he came here. This was a marvel to the community, as Eamon had grown up in what was, at that time, the most religious country in world.

It seemed to suit him to work only with basic handtools, especially where progress was slow and difficult. It allowed him to concentrate all his emotions on stubborn patches of ground, giving him a feeling of 'release' when he eventually moved a stubborn rock or cleared out a deeply rooted, malignant weed. He loved to work in the high sun of the day, just when others were taking refuge in the shade, which was strange considering that he came from mild, rain-beaten Cork. But then perhaps, when one considered the lack of sunshine in that Irish climate, it was not so strange. There seemed to be some chemical lack in the fellow that caused him to bear his naked flesh to the sun. His skin originally burned red, then developed its present dark blue hue. This man produced good fruit – it was well known throughout the region that Bro Eamon's peanuts, from the scrubby patches with all the weeds, were the tastiest of all the community's output. There was even a black market in them.

It was discovered, not long after Eamon's arrival, that he would have 'bad periods'. He would be found gibbering and hiding in remote places such as in the thorn bushes, under the kitchen table or in the pigeon loft, always clutching his now never-to-be-without machete. Much patient coaxing by Sanctus was the only course of action that would succeed in calming him down,

and eventually persuade him to return to his cubicle. These attacks at first had come about once every three months or so (therefore he was not, as some in community had been claiming, fully cured after all). Disturbingly, these bad phases appeared to be becoming more frequent and intense recently. The chief medical orderly Bro Capricious, together with his assistant Bro Malicious, asserted that the man's condition was actually deteriorating, and would end most likely in a relapse into total madness.

The only hope for him then (and for the safety of the community) would be to have him officially re-declared insane and admitted to the community hospital. There he would certainly benefit from the cures that were taking place. Sang suspected that there was some vested interest here – the two medical orderlies barely concealed their enthusiasm and desire to get their hands on Eamon.

Capricious and Malicious were, despite their nicknames, well-meaning, all-round experts on everything to do with physical and mental health. Their 'popular names' were based on the jocular supposition that the two were to blame for every case of ill health and death that occurred in their dispensary. Conventional wisdom had it that they displayed a devil-may-care attitude to their work – the antithesis of their true attitude. Each failure to bring about a full recovery, each death, while always deeply mourned, was celebrated by universal opinion in the community as always a direct result of their unorthodox and unreliable methods. There was no malice in this; it was merely an established, even superstitious, way of ensuring that the 'lightning' of blame and guilt did not strike the innocent, uninvolved brother.

As regards Eamon's treatment – he was eventually brought to them after his most recent 'bad turn' – their attitude was businesslike but fatalistic.

'Those treatments they used in the hospitals over there are the cause of all his troubles,' Capricious said solemnly. 'They made him worse by making him think about his problems. The only cure is to get him not to think. If he tries to think, he gets worse.'

'We will have to try our natural cures,' said Malicious.

'True,' Sang had agreed, 'and we will just continue to pray for him. He is so happy here, most of the time, it would be a pity to have to send him back to Cork. The weather suits him here.'

The progressive policy of amalgamating religious sisters and brothers in practical, day-to-day living and work in a unique 'ecumenism of the sexes' was proceeding again smoothly after the initial, disastrous 'free-chaste love' experiment. The leading figures had all known each other in pre-community days, and had previous practical experience of the world. They knew just how far to go. The brethren enjoyed each other's company at those regulated times when they came together in work or song. However, there was now a problem with one of the sisters. Sang himself had to come over recently to discuss tactics to prevent a possible scandal.

Sr Gloria, a simple woman from the squatter precinct of Kingstown had claimed, under Jah rules – whereby it was sufficient for a couple to declare themselves man and wife – to be 'married' to Bro Gerry. Josephine (and her assistant Jane Wood) had recently interviewed her for final profession. Gloria had demanded, to their great surprise, visiting rights to her 'husband' over at the monastery. Josephine and Jane had once been women of the world and they had responded with laughter. On a number of occasions Gloria had, indeed, been found wandering the monastery grounds at a late hour. However, this last time she had had to be removed from Gerry's cubicle; shouting and creating a scene.

Gloria's own religious practices had their origin in Street Pentecostalism. By means of song and high spirits, the members of this often frowned-upon Christian sect were known to raise up the despondent and sinning at street-corner vigils. It was claimed that, at some of their more esoteric rituals held during the early hours in secret locations, the dead were raised up. Their sessions took place only where insalubrious and uneducated folk were to be found, for it seemed that sensible or prospering people could not be helped by their methods.

Attired in white, these apostles of the highways-and-byeways put their mainstream brethren into the 'also-rans' for enthusiasm and spiritual determination. It is true what the street preachers say – that all sinners who come across their candlelit activities on a night feel very uncomfortable – and will pretend not to be the least bit bothered by it – may even laugh aloud at it all. But if the 'writing on the ground' ceremony takes place, with revelatory chalk markings that none can resist interpreting in their own, private fashion and when, inevitably, they *do* see all their sins there, it is time for them to step forward for pardon, or to get away fast. Later in the night, as the frenetic dancing, speaking in tongues, fainting and flying-about start, then few indeed are the hardened sinners still there observing – sagely or otherwise.

It was one such night that an inebriated, expatriate teacher working in the district, Gerry McArthur, came upon the spectacle. He was astonished to see Gloria, his helper woman (she did his clothes, although he also knew that she was paid by the Americans, as well as police intelligence, to spy on him) there in the company of her brethren. Her head jolting up and down, her eyes in a trance, her body swaying backwards and forwards, she seemed to be moving effortlessly forward until she was almost lying backwards, her trunk forming a right angle with her legs, her back horizontal with the ground. In this fashion she and her companions moved in a circular dance around three candles fluttering on the pavement, their eyes now fixed heavenward. Hands clapped as the spirit-possessed achieved weightlessness and the fainthearted swooned. As well as surprise, he felt awe at the many-faceted character of Gloria, his seemingly harmless, inept washerwoman; especially now as she passed in front of him and, even in her rapture, mouthed 'Hello Gerry!'

Gerry, a spiritually and emotionally diffident Irish American, whose higher sensibilities were long ago made frigid by the cold religious rituals and dogmas of his strict upbringing, suddenly felt drawn into the spirit of the thing. Before he knew what was happening he was grabbed by Gloria and soon he was swinging, his arms and body hopping about in that ecstasy of chanting and spirit-jumping, as though he had done it all his life. He began to feel he was being released from all his old inhibitions. As the tempo increased, Gerry experienced an even greater input of metaphysical energy. Gloria now held him in a tight embrace as they careered about the street corner. The thought came to him at that moment, ludicrously, that there was something to religion after all!

Inhibitions of false respectability, hypocritical decorum and so-called self-respect had been dispensed with. His clothing had been discarded, although he did not know the how or the why. He shouted out all his past sins with great pride. He felt himself being taken over by a great, overpowering pseudo-religious force; that force that had enabled – and continues to enable – many, even mediocre people to rise to positions of great power and prestige in the world – shamelessness.

He finally collapsed to the ground. The others continued to dance around him, chanting. It was as if they were celebrating a great victory. Gloria was beaming, her gaze seemingly everlastingly fixed on the inert figure of Gerry.

The next day Gerry was unable to remember clearly much of the night. Had he just dreamt that he had dispensed with his old inner identity? He felt drained, not of his bodily strength but of his soul. That normal morning heavy headiness, the grumpiness of minor melancholy that was ameliorated by a prospect of a mug of coffee and which was the strongest, most enduring mark of the identity of the old Gerry McArthur (at that time of day), was absent. Instead, he felt light-headed and dizzy. He kept mumbling 'Gerry McArthur' to himself. The name sounded foreign, even bizarre. If he had made an exhibition of himself (he somehow thought he might have), how would he face everybody when he went to work? Word travelled fast, and far, in that community. He indeed remembered that he had shouted his sins from the rooftop. Did everyone in the country now know all about his past? Those many, personal sordid misdeeds that he liked to pretend had never happened? He remembered now, too, that he had felt gratification and pride in recounting all those squalid acts and fantasies!

He put his head in his hands as he sat on the edge of his bed and wondered what on Earth had come over him. The shame! Hadn't he been warned, even as a child, to reveal his sins *only* in the comforting shadows of the confessional? Then, at least, providing he had expressed real contrition and 'firm purpose of amendment', he was rid of his vices forever. That ritual had even given him the perfect excuse for not dwelling on his sins – lest he commit them again! But boasting of them in public! And here he was reliving his sinful past again this morning, almost relishing the thoughts of those misdemeanours once more, as though they had never been forgiven or forgotten. As if his crimes were still the best, most vital part of him!

Soon thereafter Gloria appeared at his door, stepping inside without waiting to be asked. She was no longer the warm, if over-familiar individual who was always ostentatiously friendly and 'relaxed' in his presence. On those occasions it was as though being with Gerry was the same as holidaying at a luxurious hotel, picking off the fruits in the bowl on the coffee table, helping herself to 'treats' from the fridge, examining all the various, exotic bits and pieces expatriates usually have around their home. Now, in contrast, she looked serious and began preaching to him in a loud, domineering voice. It appeared that she considered that she as good as owned him, body and soul. Her accounts of his inadequacies and failures as revealed the night before, made him feel he was in the presence once more of a possessive wife, or a strict, pious schoolmistress.

What was worse, even those faintly romantic, excited notions that he had sometimes entertained in Gloria's presence seemed to have disappeared, with the advent of her new religious persona. Before, she had only been at worst a bit of a nuisance. Now he felt strangely sad at the thought that the old Gloria was lost to him forever, because of religion.

It was only much later, with hindsight, that he realised that this indeed had been the dramatic beginning of his spiritual journey to this present (occasionally contented) life in a strict, if unconventional community of people.

Afterwards, Gerry had to leave town (after losing his job) and Gloria herself was also banished from the neighbourhood, sacked presumably for her failure as a trustworthy spy as rumours of her unprofessional 'liaison' with Gerry got back to certain quarters. She, as did Gerry, made her way north where the Nation of Zion eventually came across her trying to convert American tourists, under the pretext of giving exhibitions of native singing and dancing, now for ten dollars a time.

Gerry and Gloria found themselves sharing their lives again – this time the spiritual life – albeit in different establishments.

Sr Gloria showed no sign of the virtue of humility or reticence in her pre-final profession of vows talk with Sisters Josephine and Jane. She and Gerry were now both dedicated to the Lord and living good lives, she said. She had brought him to the Lord, but she was in love with Gerry as well as with the Lord. It was wrong now that the only time she ever saw Gerry was during cross-community meetings, perhaps at peanut sowing or harvest, or at the occasional choral event. She was not allowed to work in the hospital. That was deliberate sex discrimination. Even when she did see him she was not supposed to speak, touch, or even to *look*

at Gerry! Gloria was adamant: The work of the Holy Spirit, she
was told, demanded a dedicated, sacrificed life. But what had the
Holy Spirit – and she had certainly experienced the power of the
Spirit many times – to do with *not* loving a man?

She knew in her heart that Gerry wanted to spend more time
with her, too. What was wrong with two people being in love
anyway? It was natural. Sometimes it was as if they were kept
prisoners in this place. No, she would not leave either, as the Lord
had put her here. Josephine explained to her that they all had to
keep away from men in that way – emotionally and physically. All
sisters had to take that vow and no exception could be made, not
even in Gloria's case. That was the end of it. Gloria thought for
some moments:

'Ah no, ma'am, me tek de vow. Don't worry. Me leave Gerry
alone now.'

She laughed loudly, giggled and began to sing a hymn with
much joyful expression as she went out without waiting to be dismissed.

That was the same old, unchanged Gloria, sighed Josephine.
The Gloria who never sang in tune or in time with the choir; who
shouted out ejaculatory prayers during times of silence or meditation, who never arrived for meals on time or finished eating with
the others, who never accepted any ruling, or law or custom. She
was such a character!

She pondered the problems of 'culture shock' that they all
faced in the community. The ideal of selfless love, for one thing,
seemed to be alien to the local culture. There were some brethren
who still thought that the theological virtues of faith and hope
meant that a fellow brother or sister would, and should, always
get their comeuppance. Charity meant not striking someone too
hard, but perhaps just smacking them where it hurts but no real
bodily harm is done. The strictures on humility and equality they
found particularly difficult. Everyone in the community seemed
to assume that they already had their ticket to paradise. By simply

signing up to the terms and conditions of the community rules, and making a half-hearted attempt to keep them, their entry into heaven was guaranteed. This was what 'allowed' even the most well-behaved, best-intentioned brother or sister to commit the most grievous of offences on occasions against their fellow brother or sister.

Often, when the sisters were getting on each other's nerves, she had to indulge in extremely cruel retorts and harsh disciplinary methods in order to control them. The only thing that seemed to calm them down was punishment. Punishment had to be increased in severity on every successive occasion. They were even beginning to call her a tyrant now!

How contrary to her previous liberal, progressive beliefs was all this! If, long ago, she had seen herself as she was now, doing all those bureaucratic things, thinking up new punishments for infringements of petty rules, propping up the current establishment by whatever means necessary, she would have been filled with horror.

That young hippy Californian, straight out of university, had, in those days, seen in the tyranny of power the root of every evil.

She had set out to abolish all religious and political systems. In the end, after meeting a certain Hans (plain Hans, as he was calling himself then), she had decided to change the system from within. She joined Hans's new Third World religious order.

She had first come across Hans while lying on a sun-bleached, tropical beach. She was taken aback at how cool and clued-up this obviously well-educated, middle-aged person was. It was not every day that you meet a Jesuit tanning himself in swimwear in a heathenish luxury resort, talking about the pros and cons of 'pot' (he did not initially reveal that he was a 'man of the cloth'). When she said that she had a great desire to change the world, he began talking about a new religious order that St Francis himself – not known to be a snob – would have been proud of. When she discovered more about its offbeat constitution and membership, she knew immediately that this was the place for her.

Reflecting on it all now, she had no need to be apologetic. None had taken greater risks, especially with their pride and self-esteem, that she had when helping to set up the United Church. She had not disdained to involve herself when necessary in cleaning up 'scenes of crime'; placing herself in situations that were serious 'occasions of sin', being in the presence of what was legally 'criminal', drinking, dancing, cursing and smoking with the worst of them. All just to bring the really big sinners to the Lord!

And what was she going to do about her assistant, Sister Jane? The Irishwoman was so busy 'organising' everything that Josephine wondered whether she actually saw herself as Mother Superior! The trouble was that she was a highly disciplined, practical person whom it was difficult to fault or criticise. She took even the spiritual aspect of life as just one more chore to be accomplished. Her characteristic, dismissive 'ha!' was often heard during ser-mons whenever references to contemplative mysticism or even old hippy ideals came up. She was the kind of sister who, having experienced the hard life in the old country, knew exactly what to do in every situation. The best/worst sort of sister.

Jane disturbed the 'spiritual feel' of the place with her go-and-do-it-now attitude and constant frenetic activity. Everyone felt with her that they were walking on a treadmill, concrete results being the only criteria of even spiritual progress. In her presence everybody, including Josephine, felt inferior. She was always on for more and more sacrifice. According to her, they all had it easy here. She had a thing about what she called toxic drinks. Her strictures had now extended even to coffee, a natural, economically valuable product of the local highlands.

She was aiming to have it banned in community.

Sr Josephine sighed and wondered if she was being just too soft with them. She bet that the sensible, capable Father Sang didn't have such awkward people over in his place. *He* would not tolerate such nonsense. Perhaps she should make herself more obnoxious, and become a real tyrant. That would keep them in their place! She tried to imagine what a harsh, despotic ruler would be like. She now, closing her eyes and breathing deeply, tried willing herself into becoming that person.

Yes, she would definitely tighten things up. Even if the thought of confronting Jane still made her tremble.

There came much shouting down the telephone line – it was a personal call from the Archbishop of the Indies, John Da Souza, for a 'senior man' to attend an urgent meeting at his palace in Kingstown. The United Church had always kept a discreet distance between itself and ecclesiastical authorities, nearly always failing to send a representative to various circuit meetings. This blasé treatment of higher authority had obviously trod on sensitive toes. The Archbishop's voice was adamant, even strident.

Da Souza was a member of the country's most elite ruling family, the Da Souzas (of the Puerto Rico clan), a cousin of present and former prime ministers and presidents. As is the way of the world, having a big name counted far more in his life and work than any personal characteristics, talents or practical achievements. There was a saying: nobody slighted a Da Souza to their face; and this was true even in the case of Sang's community, who were always careful to communicate only by letter or, at worst, telephone.

The archbishop liked to claim that he always, like the Lord Himself, had the long-term interests of the church at heart; which meant he thought in terms not of today (and its problems and issues) but of those 2000 years ahead. It was an impressive line that, along with the grandeur of his regalia and his authoritative personality, usually worked its purpose in getting his way with overawed peers.

Furthermore, Da Souza hated 'religion' – and religious 'sects' such as the United Church in particular. He liked to preach about

State and Church working closely together, as 'a great team under the patronage of the Almighty'. A lover of glamour and glitz, his sermons always studiously avoided banal matters of spirituality and theology. They revolved instead around the magnificent, worthy and never to be exhausted subject of national achievements and the great and glorious deeds of famous personages, dead and alive. Many of these heroes were his own relatives, and quite a few were old friends. The holy shibboleth of national unity was the eternal, underlying theme of salvation theory. How he hated political division! That was the unforgivable sin mentioned in the Bible, for it was a sin against that unity that is revealed in the Trinity. He foresaw a country with only one political party, one people, one faith and, most importantly, one frame of mind as regards all things unapproved. His favourite, most repeated sermon was on how respect for the flag, allied with properly staged church ceremonial, instilled in the lower orders the virtues of self-respect and pride. The acquiring of these qualities guaranteed the eventual abolition of crime, delinquency and all social problems. Although his words never seemed to be matched by events on the ground, nevertheless his standing in the community was very high, perhaps due to the very fact of his unworldly beliefs, which were at variance with what life is really all about.

To say that he had always been extremely wary of The Community of the Nation of Zion in Association with the Society of Jesus, aka the United Church of Jaman, was perhaps the truest, most accurate and unreserved statement that could be made about his beliefs and attitudes. It was, as a religious order, essentially outside his everyday, direct control. Some independently operating Jesuits had taken under their wings the theologically dubious Nation of Zion, through a mysterious legal arrangement that was still undergoing examination in Rome. It concerned itself mainly with its own affairs, never sending representatives to the various church meetings or to those held semi-annually at the archbishop's palace. This was most unusual for the Jesuits, who usually never failed to poke their noses into everything that was going on. They hardly ever came out of the place at all. Instead, it seemed that they enticed people in. It was all very suspicious. There was the troublesome matter of the local parish priest. This man had resented the monks' strong influence on his own flock, who were always going up to the monastery for part-time work, handouts and even to attend the new Native Music choral sessions. But what was more worrying – and which was why he had demanded to speak with them – the local Member of Parliament had complained to him that his constituents were also going up to the monastery for their help, rather than his.

Sang went around asking everyone 'who would like to represent them at a meeting at the Archbishop's palace in Kingstown?' The offer of promotion to senior status for the duration of the visit was the enticement, or carrot. There were no takers. After many long, fruitless arguments, held over several days, they eventually found it necessary to hold an official emergency meeting. (Sang wearily noted that the people who objected most to such time-wasting and pointless meetings, were the same ones who always prolonged the debate!) Sang had opted out at the start, saying that he was too busy. Hans was finally 'selected' by default, as being the only one who had not absolutely refused outright to volunteer.

The whole exercise of course had been a cynical charade whereby Sang and Hans were able to assure the brothers that there was 'consultation' – that they were all equal. Hans had known from the start that he was the one destined to go. Apologies were made by Sang over the phone to Da Souza's assistant for the delay, stating that the cause of the problem was finding a brother who was not too tired to face the long, difficult journey by public transport after the exhausting work in the monastery. So it had all been left to poor Hans to do again.

Dressed in the community's more 'dressy' brown, seamless

habit, Hans set out. Once on the bus, he was able to think clearly and breathe easily, for the first in a very long time. He had long ago given up his old routine of wearing unkempt, lay clothing on such outings, for there was kudos to be gained from going around in a monk's habit. In the past, disguising his role as a religious had been necessary for the accomplishment of his tasks. He felt some nostalgia now for those days when there had been a sense of excitement, the thrill of danger as he had gone incognito about his work. Now, wearing the clerical gear meant that he was subjected to continual obsequious greetings and approaches from all manners of people with all kinds of ulterior motives. He was not to be fooled. The days of genuine religious faith and deference to the clergy were long gone from that country, as everywhere else. These approaches were usually covert requests for money or aid in kind, especially as the reputation of the monastery for success in business matters had spread.

He thought to himself – it would not be a bad idea to bring back the medieval tradition of sending monks out to beg! They would beg from both the rich and poverty-stricken. That would put a balance back into things!

He was fed up with the ways of the world. To hell with worldly power, money and influence! As he had got older, he had become more attracted to that precious, yet impractical ideal of financial and spiritual poverty. He and Sang had often discussed this. They felt guilty over their dependence on the financial input of their benefactors – which they could not do without. Despite a healthy bank balance, they had lately taken to insisting on whole-sale economies throughout the community. (For reasons not clear, this is the normal, universal course of action with institutions when they find they have plenty of money.) What earned most approval internally and externally was the stipulation that they utilise only cheap, local products and ingredients for all their requirements. The hospital orderlies were instructed to employ local herbal remedies in their care of the sick and diseased. Bro

Eamon's farming methods were highlighted and presented as the height and width of all good practice. They made contact with 'medicine men', local cannabis growers, mountebanks and hucksters of all shades to see what good there was in their activities. All this was positive for the image of the community. People now did not necessarily see them as a greedy, prosperous profit-making outfit in cahoots with metropolitan suppliers and agencies.

The bus was rickety and noisy. Passengers on such journeys were always in an argumentative mood, a safety valve for the mental and physical rigours of the drive. Hans did his best to keep his head down, but it was no use.

'Why you men live locked up in dat place wi' no women or pickney?' asked a suspicious man beside him who, from the elaborate cross around his neck, was evidently a member of another, competing Christian flock.

'It not natural.'

Hans muttered, more to himself than to his interlocutor, 'The lord sent them out two by two, in sandals, without extra shirt or money bag ...'

'Yo cheeky blackguard! Answer me question! Or me mash yore face up.'

'Wherever you are welcomed, stay ...'

'Bad man! How you dare read Scripture to me! Me can tell dat de devil here speak. Giv' me one minute an' me put yo off de bus.'

The man got up and went to stand at the back near the door, loudly proclaiming with curses that he would no longer seat himself anywhere near the anti-Christ, the Whore of Babylon, the man in khaki who was the devil himself.

But Hans said a prayer of forgiveness. He also felt that he had scored one over the righteous fellow, at least in terms of correct Christian behaviour. And how religious people hated scripture being quoted at them! They always claimed that it was the devil doing it!

Then he suddenly realised that he was congratulating himself, and gloating at the man's discomfiture. So he was sinning again after all! He would have to confess his pride in confession. His pride! There was no getting away from it! The original sin. He should really get up and beg forgiveness from the man, both for his own pride and all the sins he and his people had committed in the past.

But he could not stretch virtue that far. After all these years of practice he was still at stage one, if even that.

Hans carried a great burden with him wherever he went. The possibility of a clear conscience would always be something he could only dream of – and never possess. He continually told himself that his 'big lie' was for good motives. It was necessary for the good of the community, of the Church, of mankind.

This virtuous 'Dutchman', co-founding father of that dedicated, evangelising community was in fact German and as a young boy a member of the Hitler Youth. His father, who had held a high position in the Nazi party, was renowned for his dedication to the cause. 'Hans Senior' had been hunted all over the world after World War II. He was never caught; but Hans had known of his whereabouts – and had never told. Nobody ever suspected his background (not Sang, not even Jim McCall who knew every secret). Full of guilt, he had very early in life set out to do only good in the world. He told himself that it would have been an impediment if the past had become public knowledge. This was so especially in the sensitive work he, the Jesuit, had to do, not least in international relations in the period before he and Sang had set up the monastery.

Thus, by means of a lie, he was able to do great things everywhere he went in the world.

The hateful glare that his interlocutor gave him as he got off the bus was taken by Hans as a well-deserved rebuke, and he (inwardly) thanked the man.

The bus trundled into Kingstown and Hans spotted the First Class, a bar frequented by Gerry and Paulo in the old days. It was situated in a poor neighbourhood – and as part of his noviciate Gerry had famously had to go and proselytise in the same bar and crime-infested area. He had some success, for he had gained two new brothers, Alfredo and Paulo, in the process. The First Class, after all its history, still looked like any other dingy bar. He saw that none of its once characteristic neon lights were working now. It had gone down in the world. It was certainly hard to associate it with any idea of vocations to the religious life. But then poverty explained a lot of apparently inexplicable things in the world.

He was greeted warmly at the Episcopal Palace by the Archbishop's assistant, Fr Jaime Da Souza (a cousin). The palace was an old wooden house, trumped up with the national flag and yellow and white papal colours. Once most likely the home of some colonial official with dreams and aspirations beyond his means, it was now succumbing to rot caused by the ubiquitous wood-boring beetle.

'You should have had your taxi drop you off at the door. It's a long walk up the avenue carrying that case,' the assistant said, showing concern at Hans's intense perspiring.

'I have walked here from the bus station,' replied Hans, 'due to poverty.'

'His Lordship is waiting for you in his office. Take my word for it, he is not in a good mood today.'

'Thanks.'

'It's you, is it, Hans? I suppose Sang couldn't make it again. The roads too bumpy for him?'

Da Souza came into the sitting room and gestured to Hans to sit in the huge, red velvet and satin-lined throne seat. He himself sat on the hard, plain wooden chair normally reserved for visitors. Hans felt very uncomfortable in the archbishop's seat, but realised that this was a tactic – the sort of psychology that he himself would have practised in the old days.

'It seems like it's been a long time, Hans. Where have you been? Hiding out in the backwoods? I would be a lot happier if I had more hard facts to confirm the serious complaints about you lot. Not a word comes out from there about your activities these days, except the moans from that bothersome parish priest and rumours galore. You're all as quiet as mice.'

'Oh,' laughed Hans, 'it ees not smooth riding all the time. We have some queer characters in our place. I would not say it ees a quiet monastery at all! Even times of sacred silence are quite tense with all kinds of disconcerting undercurrents. And Humility Day! It ees a shambles at the moment. I don't think we have quite got the hang of that yet. It ees one of our innovations.'

'Humility Days, eh? Very interesting. I am impressed. You decry your own great institution, Father Hans. That is suspicious. Look. We just want you to pull out of the power trip. Don't do so many "good works". We all know how simplicity, self-abasement and "good works" are the subversive's route to real power. You will end up as a great success and turn into another worldly organisation, beholden to people's respect and deference. You will find yourself having to devise a multitude of petty, bureaucratic rules that you despise in order to control the whole thing. You will become a rival to everybody, including us here at the Archdiocese. Get back into the ordinary business of a church. Saving souls. That is a harmless activity.'

'We only go by the book, Your Excellency.'

'That is the problem. I am not saying that I believe all the rumours that are going about. It is sour grapes mostly. But the very lack of solid evidence for wrongdoing is what bothers me! Believe me, various people have tried to dig the dirt on you, but nobody has yet come up with anything satisfying. It is very disconcerting. This absence of information is probably responsible for exaggerating the amount of good that is being done there. The reputation that you have for practical Christianity – that sounds so seditious! – is not good for the Church, the country or the government.'

John Da Souza now stood up and commenced pacing up and down.

'It's a form of ...' he struggled with the word, 'of Marxism! As head of the Church in Jaman, I have to show the government that I am taking action. Begin by cutting out all those activities that are no part of the business of a church. Reign in your commercial activities. Beg from rich businessmen instead. The devil worshippers you shelter there – convert them properly or disband them altogether. They must publicly repent of their heretical past and abandon all their old ways.'

His tone was bullying. He glared at Hans. 'You have enemies in the government here, you know.'

'We know. We'd be worried eef we hadn't. '

'Ah, I'm fed up beating about the bush. You are influencing the people too much. This is not the Middle Ages. The days of superstition, idealism and simple belief are over. My God, Hans, it's 2000 – two millennia after the Crucifixion!'

'Your Excellency – you know that we are orthodox and don't espouse any of those modern heresies – Liberation Theology, New Age spirituality, Modernism, or indeed anything that Rome disapproves of. We are truly faithful to Mother Church.'

'Indeed, but that is not the point ...'

He paused, stuck for words.

'There is one thing that has always bothered me,' he eventually said, brusquely, his solemnity and decorum slipping. 'How the hell did you convert those Jahmonks?'

Hans paused a while, shuffled in the big chair, sighed and put his hand over his heart as if to deny any duplicity.

'In long discussions weeth them I introduced to them that great work of St Thomas Aquinas – the Summa Theologica. We know that these people have a great respect for old, venerable books. Brother Orbeck was very impressed, in particular, when I read to him how Aquinas definitely proves that the Jah movement ees part of Divine Providence.'

'How does he do that?' asked Da Souza, eyebrows raised.

'It was a tricky problem as Orbeck's bishopric is not part of the Apostolic Succession. But I found where Thomas Aquinas says words to the effect that "So far as something escapes the order of a particular cause and are casual or fortuitous as regards the universal cause outside whose range nothing can happen, they are said to be foreseen by Divine Providence."'

'You said that to him?'

'I assured him that this covers his case. He was overjoyed to hear that the Church could recognise his movement. For he ees in awe of the power of the Catholic Church. He liked, in particular, the mysteriousness of Aquinas's words, for it is one of their beliefs that if anything can be understood by the mind, it is false and not worth knowing. They are very spiritual – and that is the key to their conversion.'

'One thing I have never understood about you Jesuits, is why you go after the most unlikely converts. Some of your best men wasted their days in the remotest corners of the Earth where there was not even one Christian. No wonder the popes were suspicious. What you are telling me is not the full story. You were dealing and conspiring with them long before you came to any so-called discussion on theology. There was something going on at that time with the Americans. I remember it all – crooked goings on.'

'It was to get rid of their drugs. They loved to use drugs and meditate on many fantastical ideas een their religion. We discovered the key to all this. We translated their important sayings into Latin for them. In the process, we redrafted some of their doctrines and liturgy, giving the whole a more orthodox setting. Een that way, even the words they once understood became no longer so understandable to them, and hence more meaningful.'

Da Souza shook his head in bemusement.

'What ees it you require us to do?' asked Hans politely.

'Stop your monks going to those local schools, giving the young people ideas and skills above their station. Close down the hospital and peanut farm. Turn your hand to more modest enterprises that are not so brazenly successful, such as nursing the dying. Succour the sick by prayer and spiritual encouragement alone – give up all these experiments I hear you are up to. Kick out those who are capable of surviving, which might be about three-quarters of those you are looking after. That is all I ask. What harm will come of that? It will save you expense, and the destitute cannot be made any more miserable. Create that holy aura of failure and imminent departure from this life that people are comfortable with – and normally expect – from religious institutions.

'There is no need for special cures or complicated methods of treatment for the poor. A government minister has complained to me that your so-called medical centre has returned cripples, psychotics and incurables to the world where they make greater nuisances of themselves than they even were before. Apparently they are all brainwashed by you lot into that old heretical belief – equality. They insist on their rights, think nothing of approaching and interrogating those who are their betters, and even demand jobs! Finally, make sure that your monks undertake plenty of penance – good, old-fashioned mortification. That will keep them in their place. Above all, you must show that you are working with – and not against – the government.'

'Those are some great ideas you have suggested to me, Excellency. I will pass them on to Father Sang.'

'Listen,' said Da Souza in an impatient voice, as he went over to his desk and picked up a sheet of paper, 'I am going to carry out a Visitation on the monastery, at the behest of the Papal Nuncio. My assistant and I will come for three days and do a full inspection. I have prepared a list of our requirements. Our quarters must be apart from the main community. Our food must come from that American hotel near your place. You will provide an ample supply of bottled water. Nobody may approach us on their own initiative. It will take place in three weeks' time. That is July 22nd to the 24th. That is all.'

'It is a great honour that you are coming to see the mighty works being done in the name of the Lord. I will make sure that the brothers have the place tidy and get the bookwork up to date – we have nothing to hide.'

Something inside had gripped Hans's innards, a nightmarish, indeterminate fear, triggered by his last five words.

Later that evening Hans changed his habit for an old suit he had taken out of his case. It was a suit that he had kept from the old days. Checking that nobody was watching, he headed out into the night. His expression was that of a determined, almost medieval missionary heading out on a bleak mission of evangel-isation. He headed for Three Quarter Way Tree, a neutral zone between downtown and uptown Kingstown where the denizens of both districts were accustomed to mingle and do business. He went into the La Cucaracha Hotel and was recognised at once by the staff there, even though he hadn't been around for some time. He was led into a smoke-filled backroom, where a large group of people sat around a table playing cards.

'Bedamn but it's Hans,' shouted one loud man, a fat fellow smoking a cigar who was the boss of Upper Kingstown.

'Hi Hans,' everyone shouted, 'where have you been, you old gangster?'

'Hi. I am een the land and property business, up on the north coast.'

'I heard that,' said Luis García, the fat man, 'but nobody could ever contact you. I miss you at the poker games.'

Hans's heart sank. He did not like being here. He felt guilty. These criminals and heathens were far higher in the sight of God than he. They were not guilty of concealing who they were. They accepted that they were greedy, good-time louts. They were proud of their tough, merciless reputations. He wished he had been born in the slums, like them, and worked his way up by bribery, threat and blackmail. He wished he had been an ordinary, proper criminal. They were not guilty of World War II. He did not deserve to be in their company. It was no wonder that he felt the 'torments of the damned' whenever he took their money from them in a game of poker. He would have preferred to lose. And he wished that these guys weren't so stupid that they made it so easy for him to win their cash. A part of him was hoping now – though not praying – that he would indeed lose everything in this game.

'May I join the game, gentlemen? Eet has been a long time since I have played. I am very rusty.'

'You know, Hans, you have been here too long. You have lost your quaint old European accent. You speak like us now,' said Dr Underwood, the country's only anaesthetist.

'Ho ho, true, I am a man of the Indies now!'

For a moment he felt relief from the existential pain of being who he was.

He accepted a cigar from one of the other men and lit it from Luis's proffered butt end.

'What have you got, Hans? Cash, bills of exchange, keys to a car, property?' asked Luis, turning serious all of a sudden. There was no mercy, much less charity, shown in these games.

'A beet of cash and the title deeds to a very large property and farmland on the north coast,' was Hans's reply.

Hans had been given the task of bringing to Kingstown, for lodging in the prestigious Commercial Bank, a generous cash donation from a recent delegation from the Canadian Leprosy Fund. He had also been given the title deeds to the whole monastic property, acquired at last through the generosity of the McCall family, for putting in safe keeping in the same bank. He had hated carrying all this material wealth with him, this overt dependence on the capitalist system. It went completely against the early Christian spirit, when disciples had set out in their slippers with no baggage. If only they could really live from hand to mouth, day to day – how simpler life would be! Still, he would have to continue to sup with the devil using a long spoon; the Leprosy Fund cash alone would pay for medicine for the dispensary for a whole year – and here was a chance to increase it.

And now he was putting faith on the line again; faith in Providence, faith that the monastery, the farm, the educational programme, the hospital and holistic services, would not be allowed to go down the plughole due to an unlucky hand in cards.

But he was still as wise as a serpent. He had a foolproof, or near foolproof, method for winning this game. For it was based on something beyond logic and rationalism. He had observed the phenomenon over the years of beginner's luck. It had been a long time since Hans had played so he was, in a sense, a beginner. It was not only the phenomenon of the newcomer often pulling the best hand. He had noticed something more. It was often – more often than chance would ordain – not the first decent hand that won but the very first hand, however mediocre, that the beginner got. It did not have to be a high hand. A seasoned player would never place everything on these cards but the newcomer would think he was flying and put down the lot. And win. A three of tens, two pair jacks high would do.

He knew what he had to do. And nobody there could resist the temptation of following him when he put down his stake. As well as the leprosy cash there were real-life *land and property title deeds* on the table! That was when the saliva would dribble and hearts thump all round. It was also a matter of timing and facial expression. The professional (who is never a beginner) always gives the impression of just relaxing himself into the game with a few initial, relaxed runs. People are often caught off guard when the big stake goes in. But the trick of the 'newcomer' is to sweat, look worried, let the hands go rigid even at the start, with only a small sum at stake.

Of course, it might be argued by the cynical, or non-superstitious, that someone else might have a better hand. But that was the point – they never did in a newcomer's game. He had seen it so many times!

'Well, I am really rusty. Let us start with a small stake, gentlemen. I must feel myself eento the game again,' he said quietly. He was already perspiring in that airless, smoky, poorly lit room.

They dealt the cards somewhat listlessly, for they had lost the impetus of the previous games. That had built up into a sort of 'vendetta campaign' in which mutual antagonisms and enmities had come to the fore and the temptation had been to take great risks just for spite and regardless of cards dealt. A few snide insults, rivalry over a big commercial tender, and the previous loss of some hefty stakes had soured the atmosphere.

Now they had to start all over again, but it had been a welcome interruption for the release of tension it had allowed. Hans looked at his hand. After a few moments he was holding two pairs of sixes and eights. Better than might have been expected! He was on his way. Nobody seemed to be paying much attention to him and when Hans put down all the cash he had in his possession (one thousand dollars) it appeared to take them some moments to realise what he had done. From their unguarded, careless expressions it was obvious that they had not expected a high stake in this round. (Hans, like most poker players, could tell a genuine careless expression from a non-genuine one). They had clearly been expecting the game to go a few more rounds. Except Luis across whose mind, Hans sensed, a fleeting thought had crossed. That was the only little worry. Luis was, indeed, the only person who proceeded to pay to 'see' his hand. Then Hans reached inside his jacket, pulled out some papers and put them down on the table.

'Some title deeds, Luis, to a large property on the north coast, worth a million US dollars,' he said casually.

Luis calmly took the deeds and studied them carefully. He

took out a cheque book and said as he wrote, 'One million dollars US.'

The others laughed and stopped puffing their tobacco. The smoke in the room ceased rising and slowly began to settle over them, as if the whole world were coming to a stop. The silence was, as is said at fraught moments, audible.

'OK,' said Hans.

Just before he showed his cards Hans thought deeply. What was he doing? Was this faith? Or was he putting God to the test? There was a more down-to-earth question. Where did gambling fit into the system of ethics? He had long since forgotten most of the complex, intricate points he had learnt in philosophy school. He racked his brains.

There was the Motivationist theory – which holds that the rightness and wrongness of an action depends upon the motive from which the act is done. So he was all right on that one, as he had the future financial security of the monastery at heart and Kant himself would have agreed with him. For there was his famous statement: *Nothing can possibly be conceived in the world, or even out of it, which can be called good without qualification, except a Good Will.* But the Motivationist theory had too many holes in it, as bad things were done through good motives.

Then there was the Consequence theory – which holds that it all depends on the good or bad consequences an act has. Now here he was in the same boat with the Utilitarians, who hold that the greatest happiness for the greatest number was the point. Wouldn't a large win help a far greater number, if indeed he did win? Whatever the consequence, if he lost, of his committing sins of anger and despair – and causing consternation to a great many innocent people, the monks, those destitute who depended on them – these were, nevertheless, of a much smaller number than the greater majority (the whole country's population perhaps) who would be helped by a win.

He remembered a third theory – called the Deontological

theory – which claims that the morality of an act depends solely on what kind of act it is. This card playing was pretty harmless. Who got hurt?

So put simply, the big question was whether what he was doing was morally right. Well, he seemed to come out on top as regards *all* the ethical theories. He considered it his duty to further the economic viability of the monastery. And what better source of funds than the richest, most crooked men in the country, all done in a perfectly legal way? It meant that they would not have to badger the poor for funds any more.

So he was in the clear, on every front!

It was all very interesting, these academic speculations, he thought as he prepared to put his cards down on the table and doubt filled his mind again. But ethics was a very murky subject. Like every other discipline taught in the seminary, it was full of contradictory ideas. Yes, he was trained always to follow his conscience. That seemed OK on the surface, but it was also the case that the conscience, too, can be misguided.

So it was all up to him in the end. Gambling was a queer one. He would have to see the outcome before he could decide whether it was good or bad! Well then, I guess the Consequencists win, he concluded, at least on this one.

'Two pairs, sixes and eights. There you are.'

Luis put his cards down; it was two threes and two sevens. He had guessed Hans's strategy but had slightly underestimated beginner's luck. He would now have to think of a way to win his money back, but for the moment Hans had that cheque, signed and drawn on the Commercial Bank (which Luis owned), as well as the precious title deeds, in his hands.

Hans was now also, suddenly, feeling sick due to the cigar smoke and the straight whisky he had been imbibing – refreshments that he had not tasted for some time. He ran from the room clutching his stomach, retching loudly.

As he threw up on the flowerpot in front of the gambling parlour he thought, 'I feel worse. That wasn't faith. It didn't feel like it. It was just … a gamble. What sort of a religious person am I?'

He continued to retch painfully into the flowers, feeling like Peter when the cock crowed for the first time.

Yet he had won, and everyone would benefit. It was a strange, anomalous situation.

He did not go back inside but headed for the palace, occasionally feeling the cheque, cash and documents hidden inside his clothes and wondering what lie he would have to tell the bishop or his assistant should he happen to run into one of them – having to explain why he had been out in the dead of night in the wrong clothes. A monk's life was no paradisial tryst, he ruefully thought.

Finding all the doors locked and the lights out, he looked for some way to get in. Eventually he decided that he would have to squeeze through the aluminium louvres of his bedroom window. It was a tight squeeze and to his horror he found that he was stuck, his body half in and half out. It was in this position that he was found the following morning. The archbishop himself came to inspect and direct the rescue operation.

'You Jesuits like to get into tight spots,' he said, more sarcastic than friendly.

'I was out late fundraising,' replied Hans truthfully.

After depositing Luis's cheque in the uptown bank an hour later, Hans took the same crowded, noisy, uncomfortable bus back home again, even though a little quiet voice told him a comfortable private taxi would have been more sensible.

chapter
three

Down on the swamp, the thunderous afternoon rain was falling not as drops, sheets, lines or waves but in that manner characteristic of the tropics – bucketfuls. The sun's harsh glare had now become tempered and cooled by masses of black-blue clouds. But the rain was shifting everything in front of it as it swept up the swamp and the outlaws eventually moved their rafts to the shelter of the low-lying mangrove trees. There was the odd thunder crack or two, flashes of lightning and then darkness came over the land.

Dagga – he liked his underlings to call him Don – the leader, a youth in his early twenties with the slim, short build of a jockey – took out his ratchet knife and cut a small piece of cane off its stem with one movement of his thumb and began to chew it angrily as he considered his next move. He felt with his free hand the beloved AK47 in his lap; he had been promised a heap of new, even better guns if he would consider working with Doctor Wesley. It could be a trick.

The doctor man's name and voice he had often heard coming out of the radio. But what he stood for, or what he had ever said about anything, Dagga didn't have a clue. The one thing about Dr Wesley, he had heard, was that he had been born with a silver spoon sticking out of his mouth. That was a strange thing. Someone had told him that the brainy man wanted to save the working class. This would mean, probably, that he wanted to give them money. For people save money? He was also told that Dr Wesley's parents had sent him abroad to get him a good education. Education means money, he had once been told, and he must have that education stacked away somewhere. And some of it could come in useful to him, Dagga. Especially if, as he had also heard, the police never arrested people who had it. Or if they did arrest a person with education, the courts hardly ever sent them to prison.

This fellow was now being picked up by Dagga's deputy, Dog, at Tin Hut City with a batch of new guns and a much-heralded plan. A plan sounded good, because the police knew, now, that he was in the swamp and they were sending a helicopter and a patrol boat on regular sweeps. He would soon have to move elsewhere.

Dr Wesley was brought to him by the eerie light of a carrota – a long stick with the bark peeled off the top, whose kerosene-soaked sap burned like a candle. For once Dagga felt himself inadequate, for he was unsure what words to utter. It would have to be in the 'Babylon language' – Standard English. The thought made him sweat a little.

However they both squatted on the ground like equals.

'Jus' *one* gun an' *no* bullets?' said Dagga, disappointed.

'It a H&K MP5! An' it got a nighttime light to shoot by.'

The intellectual zealot was thin, ascetic-looking and wore spectacles, which made Dagga despise and fear him. His eyes had the sharp, bitter look of someone who was always determined to get his opinion over against all opposition. He was full of so many ideas, principles and beliefs that these were always getting in the way of each other. He often found himself having to jettison one belief for another due to lack of room, then reinstating the discarded one later when, or where, there was space or time. Yet he scorned all ideas unless they could be put into action. It was his failure here, of putting his ideas into practice, that gave him his great bitterness.

Wesley was trying to talk the slum dialect, to put Dagga at ease and in order to show that he, too, was streetwise.

'The police after yo, Dagga. It only a liddle time 'fore they ged yo in shootout. I have *big* friends – who can give yo many more guns. Dis one jus' fe look an' see. But yo mus' hear Dr Wesley plan.'

'Plan?'

'I de new leader.'

'Jus' cos you can't win election, you wan' us,' said Dagga's suspicious deputy, Dog, a thirty year old who had respectability and seniority in the gang, having been a criminal in a big city overseas. He was reputed to have done a number of shooting jobs in Miami.

'Listen, you guys. You go 'round robbing and murdering your own people. You are jus' criminals. You have no plan of action. You leave the rich alone, behind their high gates and security grills. You see those mansions up in the hills with de big satellite dishes and swimming pools? The uptown employer class and their foreign puppet masters are your enemies – not the poor, hardworking shopkeeper downtown. Although he, too, is a bit of an exploiter, in his own small way, and deserves the punishment he gets, for he would be a bigger exploiter if he could. Now I have a political plan – a plan of political action. You direct your guns at *political* targets dat I will select. That is de only way you can become important, powerful men. I will be your voice. I give you respectability. There are foreign powers that will send us help an' support us. Remember our brothers in Taran. How they fought and won against overwhelming odds?'

'Can you get us lots more o' dese submachine guns an' more bullets?' asked Dagga quietly.

'Yea, man. And I will show you how to mek explosives. You know – bombs, big bangs! But yo will have only special targets.

You must learn discipline. Yo mustn't go round killing everyone. Anybody who disobeys my orders will be executed.'

'*Dat's* what dey call discipline? Me do practise it all de time,' said Dagga proudly.

Lacking a father figure in his own life, he was now unconsciously taking to this doctor fellow as a child to a parent.

'Good,' said Wesley, 'but now it is I who give orders. I promise police an' army keep well away from yo once yo become political.'

'De army, you say? Me don't like de army. De police – they bad, bud w'en dey come in we fight an' kill dem. But if army dem come in – we run. Dey brek de whole place down las' time. But I don't say me scared o' dem.'

'We do all right up till now widout you,' said Dog sourly.

Wesley ignored him.

'What did dey do in Taran?' asked Dr Wesley rhetorically, his tone that of a great expert.

'Me nuah care wad they do in Taran!' replied Dog.

Wesley and Dagga both stared disapprovingly at him. The doctor answered his own question.

'They dig underground! Nobody find dem or get at dem dere! The Taranese Liberation Army built their headquarters underneath the enemy's biggest military base! Yo, too, will dig out tunnels and live under the earth. Dat is the way forward. Dat is the future! Yo will be safe as mice.'

'Whee ...' said Dagga; marvelling at the thought of a place where nobody could ever find him.

'We moving out of dis area altogether,' said the doctor. 'We going north where we dig a big underground headquarters, from where we terrorise de ruling class.'

'Sound good to me,' said Dagga.

'And where do yu think is the safest place in the north to build an underground base, Dagga?'

'Wha? Me know? Yo ask me question? Me know de answer.

But me no say.'

'There is big-big religion place up dere. Dey own a massive big land. Many foreigners dere. Dey called monks. It de last place in de world police or army or government think of looking for gunmen ... no, liberation fighters yo call.'

Because he didn't understand much about Dr Wesley's plan, though he caught the general drift of things, Dagga replied, 'Yo very clever. Me call yo Shaft! Daddy Shaft.'

Dog's face was crunched up in thought.

'But won't monks find out we dere?' he asked.

'Daddy Shaft' Wesley looked at Dog with disgust. Was he afraid of the monks? he asked. This big bad guy was scared of some little holy people who only practise magic and harmless incantations! What was this big brave man afraid of?

'Superstition! The curse of humankind!' Wesley thundered. Thank God *he* had never been guilty of that weakness. He was no cringer. He had often commented on those shameful, national traits, superstition and stupidity, and had made efforts to eradicate them. They were even to be found in his university students! There was really no point in correcting their essays, they were so dumb. He would always mark their written work with a red zero, and sign off with some brilliantly sarcastic comment – all without reading a single word! It was not necessary.

This detachment and nonchalance he liked to think his students respected. He actually found that he preferred to socialise with uneducated people! When he gained power, he would employ all the sciences for the liquidation of superstition, stupidity, and in particular that right-wing reactionism they call 'free will' – the greatest enemy of human progress. Religion and the political establishment exploited the so-called free-will theory to justify all the great crimes of history. It allowed the government, for instance, to tax each individual person in the country. It enticed people into working as slave labour under the misconception that they were working voluntarily. It allowed authority to place much of the blame for great historical injustices on the injured parties, the poor and oppressed, by claiming that it was due punishment for their sins or backwardness.

And he would not make the mistake of the communists – allowing personality cults, for these had always prevented the completion of the revolution. He would, when the time came, install a complete nonentity, Dagga himself, as head of state, and this would certainly discourage any undue hero-worship.

At the end of Wesley's speech Dagga clapped his hands in approval, although he had not understood any of it. He continued to listen uncomprehendingly as the doctor laid out what would hopefully be the foundations for a successful revolution.

The communists were outdated. Their methods had proved faulty. Even he had been taken in by their false political methodology. Their mistake was to confuse Communism with Marxism. Marxism was the true religion – for hadn't it provided the only foolproof analysis of history?

Dagga nodded. He knew all the answers.

'There is no better explanation of your own predicament, Dagga, than that which Marxism provides,' he said to the open-mouthed bandit.

Wasn't it the case that Marxist concepts had been acknowledged by the greatest thinkers in history? Democritus (no accident that name) and the classical philosophers had 'discovered' atomism and dialectics long ago. All matter coming out of nothing. You see Marxism all around you, people dialecticing all the time without their even being conscious of it.

'Dagga, you Dog, all your men act dialectically, unawares. Even the village idiot – the unfortunate who everybody laughs at, who makes a nuisance of himself in front of passing traffic and places the public at risk with his wild antics – is to be respected. He is worth something. He, too, is involved in some kind of thesis, antithesis and synthesis, even if it might only be in the accident that he causes.

'In the contemporary sphere, there is the conventional wisdom always promulgated by the so-called middle ground. There is a false doctrine of a watered-down socialist agenda with its critique – a fetishism of rampant consumerism (opium of the people) and a proposed intensification and diversification of wealth creation through altered spending power by means of a progressive rate of taxation; allied to an equally false, contradictory doctrine of putting the so-called moral improvement of the masses before the goal of a 3.5% real growth rate. These do-gooders got it wrong. Economic growth, in conjunction with exploitation of the masses, are as inevitable as sunrise and sunset. The anti-revolutionary mindset is as much a fact-of-life as procreation. Pro-creation, itself, is just another word for economic growth ...'

He paused and looked for assent in their faces. Dagga and Dog stared back expressionlessly.

There was nothing new in time or space. While it was all very fine for rich, erudite, liberals to indulge in all this highfaluting talk about *EC VAL = QL, given soc av conditions of prod, av soc intensity + av skill of L employed* in seminars or fancy restaurants – the irony of the fact of the cleaners or the dishwashers being underpaid always escaped them. Political idealism was very fine for the political/social cliques, but who of the common people could understand that kind of obscurantism?

He had thrown away all his textbooks after his disappointing election loss. Who of his colleagues and social circle had ever *experienced* social alienation such as had Dagga, or even Dog here? Education of the masses was always the main task, and a formidable challenge. What did they think?

They did not know what to think. All Dog could see was a gun held up to the head of this brainy man, and then his brains shooting out in dirty, mixed colours. Dagga's mind was a blank. He knew, though, that there was a magic power in big words, and Daddy Shaft had many of those.

'Me afraid de monks,' was Dog's comment.

'Man, what are they!' said the doctor testily, 'yo don't believe dat they have any power over yo? What sort of fighter are yo, Dog?'

Daddy Shaft was already working on Dog. He wanted rid of him.

'Dem sort people mek strange magic, me hear Obeah man say,' said Dog glumly.

'Yo go now, Daddy Shaft. We have t'ings to do,' said Dagga quietly. 'Bring us more guns yo say yo get and den we work out next stage. How yo dig tunnel?'

'Leave dat to I. Me know engineer expert at the university. The important thing will be to get in *under the monks*. We infiltrate their ranks. Put we in position an' take over de place. Den we extirpate them. If the police an' army ever find hideout, dey are not allowed to go in there anyway! It protected by international law!'

'Extir ...?' said Dog.

'Inter ...?' said Dagga.

'Police and soldier do not enter religious place. If crook hide in church, police no go in.'

Dagga and Dog looked at each. This was wonderful information. How was it that they had never heard it before?

'What are yo going to do with dat man yo have tied up over there?' asked Wesley.

'Him prisoner,' said Dagga. 'He use' be number three in we gang. Me don't know what me do wi' him. He mek eye at me gal.'

Daddy Shaft knew it would be a strategic mistake to plea for the poor man's life. It would give the impression of 'particularism' or favouritism. It would be best to offer a political solution.

'Try not to get a reputation for pointless cruelty, Dagga. Yo must show people that you have a *method*. Yo must act like a business man. Has he had a trial?'

'Trial, Daddy Shaft – what yo mean?'

Dog knew the answer to this one. He bent over and whispered in Dagga's ear. They both burst out laughing.

'Why yo want do *dat* stupid thing?' Dagga asked.

'Everybody we capture from now on must be tried by a people's court. Yo have one representative from the local community and one of your own men sitting on the panel. Then any execution will be legally OK.'

'Me get it nuh, what yo say,' said Dog slowly. 'If we kill him with no proper court den it look like murder, but if we kill him legally like in an execution den it *political!*'

'Yea, man. Right! You call him a hostage and dump his body with a warning pinned to it saying he's a traitor, a hireling of the foreigner. But before that, arrange for him to have a trial. Have a practice one now. You can forget about the local representative on this occasion, as no one is immediately available. In emergency situations some rules may be dispensed with. As they say, justice should be swift.'

Soon after, as Daddy Shaft was being slowly punted back to 'civilisation' on the flimsy raft by a lowly gang member, he heard a shot accompanied by a loud cry.

There would be a lot to do before these folk get the message, he thought.

A little later Dagga was muttering to himself:

> *'De swamp, de swamp, de dirty swamp,*
> *Sweet home to me,*
> *We bury de dead an' hide de loot,*
> *Nobody find it dere ...'*

'What you hum, Dagga?' asked Dog, worried about the strange, intense look in the don's eyes.

Dagga stared back at Dog's concerned face and continued his

song:

> *'Swamp it full o' bad, an' slimy t'ings,*
> *Mangrove duppies an' weed,*
> *Smell o' death, an' strange warning,*
> *Swift strong vengeful devil's breath ...'*

He stopped humming suddenly and looked at Dog.

'But we leave, Dog. We leave as de doctor man say. It time to go. Me feel de devil's breath come over de water. It better we hide under de ground. Me like de idea of underground, especially under de rich monks' castle.'

'OK, we go, Don. But we mus' watch out for de monks' magic. You wait 'n see. It powerful.'

'Me fear more de police an' army gun dan magic,' said Dagga scornfully, proud of his disdain of the weaker man's fear. He was a brave, strong man himself. Daddy Shaft had more or less said so.

'But dey have God on their side,' said Dog, persisting. 'God and all de angels in heaven ... '

'Me believe in de devil only,' said Dagga glumly. 'Dat is why we leave dis here sweet swamp now. Me hear him coming after me. But *me* believe in God? No. *Who* is God, anyway? He what de preacher man say?'

'No, Dagga. God is God and devil is de devil. Yo no play 'round wid God. Me 'fraid of de devil, but me more 'fraid o' God.'

'Why *yo* play 'round with dis God den? If yo say yo believe in him, why yo go rob, shoot an' kill? Whaa ...? Yo have no fear he will ged yo?'

Dog got very angry, jumped up and waved his arms. 'God most powerful of all. Me show him respect, den he show me respect.'

Dagga spoke in a harsh voice. 'Maybe he powerful – but he

don't care what me do. He let me fall in pond one day, but it meself pull me out! He only do t'ings like mek big explosions in sky, mek de moon an' stars an' t'ings. He sometime mek joke on people like w'en rich man fe get robbed or policeman fe get shot. Hee! What he do wid me? Do he mek me? It me mama an' some man dat mek me. Do he give me job, big house an' car? No! What *me* care 'bout him den!'

Dagga had clearly been thinking about God, too. Dog looked at him more warily.

'If yo say you believe in powerful God, Dog, why den yo no go work for him? Dat only sense! He pay yo much more money than me.'

Dog sensed a trap.

'*Me* work for God? Me have no boss 'cept yo, Don. Nobody tell Dog what do, 'cept Don. Nobody! Dat is law. An' yo know more than God anyway. How can he see all things dat happen? W'en we hide money *nobody* find it. Do he see what we do nex'? Can he stop bad men like we? No!'

'Only *me* tell *yuh* what to do,' said Dagga sullenly. 'Me only worry 'bout devil for he real, not like dis God. Me see devil once, looking a' me when me rob bar wi' Cockroach. He scare de life out o' me, me tell you! Hee. People see me run like bullet! They think me run from cops!'

'What he look like?'

'He ... big black magga dog. Him hav' shadow, shadow bigger than *him*!'

'Was he master devil or small devil?' asked Dog.

'Him master devil! He come fe bite me. Me tell you Dog, he frighten me. Worse dan police or army—'

'W'ich of us,' asked Dog thoughtfully, 'is the baddest man?'

The question, being as they were in a metaphysical frame of mind, did not carry an air of competitiveness or one-upmanship, as it might otherwise have.

'Before now, me say I,' said Dagga; 'but now me think yo,

Dog. For yo say you believe in dis God.'

'Me no understand.'

'Me better dan yo for me no hypocrite. What yo think 'bout dis Wesley revolution?'

'It sound bad plan. Wad money we mek from dis politics?'

'Is not de politics why we leave, Dog – is de devil,' said Dagga.

There was an uncharacteristic urgency in his voice. 'We mus' leave de marsh. It bad here now. Me smell it. We leave as de man say. It time a we go.'

He suddenly felt the back of his neck with his hand and shouted in a shrill voice that startled even Dog: 'Me feel de devil breath on me neck *right now, a'ready!* It better we go under dis ground quickly. It better plan even dan more guns.'

They dumped their former colleague's body into the water and then went off to visit their girlfriends to boast that one day soon, when they had set up their new headquarters, they would be very important and powerful political people in the island.

The government cabinet was in another emergency meeting to deal with a matter of party funding, as well as to discuss the latest security and public image problems to hit the country. The government had been getting a bad press both locally and abroad and this was very bad for the country. Last month's upsurge in the crime rate downtown (blamed on the small but ruthless gang that was congregating under the leadership of the notorious Dagga, self-styled Don) and the need to prevent the spread of such lawlessness uptown, was top of the agenda. Then there was the World Health Organisation report on the huge rise in malaria, typhoid and other diseases in the city swamps and garbage dumps wherein resided half of the city's population. Also an Amnesty International condemnation of the police shoot-to-kill policy; another seasonal hurricane approaching from the south; the missing World Bank education funds; and a major US tourism agency criticising the country for the rise in the number of poor people who were congregating in the tourist resorts and inexplicably harassing the visitors with requests for money.

'First item on the agenda,' said Prime Minister Raul Umberto Sr, 'is the little matter of the snide remarks being made about me behind my back by members of this very Cabinet. A little bird has told me that the backbiting by some of you has reached the fine audacity of being mentioned on that cheeky radio-phone-in programme. Now if it doesn't stop there will be repercussions. I know who is behind it.

'Second item. The ministerial cars. That old perennial! How many times do I have to tell you – *book them in and book them out!* We cannot have the spectacle of ministers quarrelling in pubic about who has which car, and when. It all gets to the media, you know!

'Third item. My—'

He was interrupted abruptly by Erico Mauris Sr, Minister of Internal Affairs, who had something urgent to say, and knew that now would be his one and only chance to get their attention before they all got off on their hobby horses.

'Can I just butt in here for a moment to say that there is a very important crisis coming up regarding the Working Party on the 1995 Riots. The Chair is threatening to resign over the change in venue for their meetings, from the ground floor to the third floor, without *proper consultation.* He feels devalued and the whole committee along with him. At the same time other members are also expressing their dissatisfaction at the lack of any progress, and the failure of the Working Party to come up with a report, or even recommendation, after five years. Some of them have not been paid their proper allowances for this year, either. Then—'

'As you all know,' said the prime minister, annoyed, 'we spent a good part of the last Cabinet meeting' – in fact it had taken up one minute of Cabinet time – 'discussing the Riots Working Party. We cannot allow this matter to impede the progress of this meeting as well, which I may remind you, is an *emergency* meeting, called to deal with the matter of party funding.'

The deep thinker of the government, and the most verbose, the Minister for External Affairs, Mr Sandy Mann, former high school teacher and once a famous headmaster in a remote rural district, spoke.

'I disagree with the Prime Minister on a point of procedure. What use is this *emergency* anyway? A big fancy word. Being *government* is about more than emergency. It is about *decision* – about what really matters – today, not tomorrow or yesterday.'

He continued as the other ministers leant back, yawned and prepared for a long *spiel*. 'Well, they would not have stood for this in Victorian times. And nobody was more Victorian than my father! He, too, stood in the long line of volunteers and hostages to the fortunes of the times. Including two world wars. To him an *emergency* was something he had to learn to live with day in and day out. There was the *emergency* of the struggle for independence, the memory of which still resounds in the family histories of many of my good colleagues here at this table—'

Prime Minister Raul banged the table and said in a loud voice, 'Third item! The acquisition of my personal jet, exclusively for the use of myself and members of the Cabinet. Essential for security reasons. Does the Cabinet approve?'

'Approved.'

'Fourth, the final and equally important item. The lack of funds and donations to the party. We should hit those foreign bodies wishing to set up in our country a bit harder. I guess we've bled the local businesses enough – they're bone dry. What about the churches? Some of them are doing very well, I hear. I am told that many very rich preachers from Texas and Florida and such places are coming into the country with loads of vehicles and cash these days. Why aren't we getting our small contribution? I am asking the Minister for Internal Affairs to approach these preachers about whether they possess proper licences.

The Minister, Erico Mauris Sr, excitedly stopped Raul in his tracks, for he had an item of gossip.

'You have all heard about this United Church that is making a name for itself up in the north. I don't know if you have heard what I have recently.'

For no apparent reason, as if it were necessary even in the privacy of the cabinet room, he lowered his voice to a whisper, his tone becoming strident.

'It is a cult, a den of thieves, a gang of drug dealers and sexual perverts. Well, last night I heard something else, from a source at a big poker game in town. They are religious fanatics, who are also bent on *converting* the whole nation to their evil, superstitious beliefs. One of their leaders almost cornered the bonds market, saying that it was part of his prayer for the conversion of the people.

'Converting ...? Well, I am shocked!' said Prime Minister Raul loudly. There was unanimity and an equal degree of shock around the table. They stared at the Prime Minister in expectation of a significant statement. Here was something they felt they could definitely 'act on' – and enlist popular support as well.

The Prime Minister was triumphant. 'This we will not tolerate at all! We are a Christian nation! Nobody is going to convert us! Religious sects are the worst of all. They have the mentality of fanatics. I want Archbishop John to come and see me. Make a note, secretary.'

There was a short silence as they waited for the Cabinet secretary to write the last instruction down. The secretary whispered something in Raul's ear. There was even more impatience in his voice now.

'The secretary has just reminded me that the head of the Civil Service *must* have a statement on our recommendations for solving the problems we have before us today. He has to face a barrage of questions from all those nuisance committees we have set up around the place, as well as the press. Can we do that now? As Prime Minister, it is my responsibility to see that there are *decisions* made on these matters. Here are my proposals.

'The WHO report. The Ministry of Health is to set up a Working Party on the feasibility of spraying the whole diseased area with anti-pesticides and any other strong chemicals that they can lay their hands on.

'Amnesty International. I want the Riots Working Party to extend the time of their remit for making an inquiry into their expressed concerns.

'The hurricane. An immediate Emergency Committee to be formed by junior ministers with the brief for giving the alert and a list of suggestions for the nation on how best to defend lives, homes and possessions before, during and in the aftermath of the disaster.

'The missing World Bank funds. A Financial Fraud Working Party will be set up comprising a police representative, an approved accountant and our good colleague here, the Minister for the Economy, Mr Raul Umberto Jr.

'The hassling of tourists. Courses in craftwork and teach-ins on how to be polite to foreigners will be conducted on a country-wide basis as soon as we have the funding. A Working Party will be set up to look into that whole issue by our good colleague, the Minister for Culture, Mr Erico Mauris Jr.

'The criminal element. Shoot up the whole damn shanty town. There! A very positive meeting. Do you all agree?'

'Yes,' they replied in unison, anxious for it all to end and to get on with their private affairs.

They had long ago realised that the important issues of national and international government were as minutiae compared with the pressing needs at the local level of family, friends, colleagues and enemies. Politicians had to keep a constant eye on the small, petty details of life, scrutinising the intents even of people closest to them, for there was always someone looking to stab them in the back, and fill their place. Serious crime, impending natural or human-made disasters and international politics always sorted themselves out, regardless of what governments did. It was a comfort to know this. It saved sleepless nights. The human system is such that it is only able to bear a single set of worries at a time.

But at the back of all their minds, or more correctly deep below in their subconscious minds, though none considered religion to be of any consequence in the real world, as they trooped out of the room was an unspoken disquiet and anxiety about what they had heard concerning the United Church. If they could have put words to their angst, it was the statement that a sect was bent on *converting the whole nation!* Each found it disturbing, in an indefinable way.

'Wesley sure let his family down badly failing to win his father's old seat, didn't he?' said Erico Mauris Sr smugly in the privacy of the Prime Minister's office later as they discussed the private agenda (the agenda that only this 'inner circle' of government ever got to consider). 'And he has made a complete fool of himself trying to set up a second political party. A megalomaniac! We are not good enough for him! I wonder what he will do now. Join the Opposition party?'

'Hopefully leave the country, to lecture and philosophise from afar, as political failures do,' said Raul Sr, 'but he has always been a troublemaker with big ideas. He is a disgrace to his family. He has let his brain and academic qualifications go to his head with all those big, pompous ideas. Ideas are what rot people's brains. He doesn't believe in the ordinary things, like democratic government, respecting one's relatives, standing to attention and singing the National Anthem, attending the Rotary Annual Charity Ball in morning suit. Where would we all be without these national symbols?'

'Where for true,' said Erico.

'I would have had him arrested years ago for subversion if it were not for his family. His father was a close acquaintance of my own pappy. They served together in putting down the Jah insurrection in the early days. He made his money later in the importing and exporting business. His son can't forgive him his great success in life. Wesley has always been trying to outshine his daddy. He feels guilty about his family's wealth. He thinks he must achieve power in order to undo the great damage he says his daddy's generation has caused. But really, all he wants is to equal – if not surpass in power and success – his pappy. He wants to be more powerful than his daddy ever was. He wants absolute power. He is always on about redressing inequality of wealth. But if he ever did become prime minister, he would soon realise how soul-destroying so-called political power is. As a former Chief of the Armed Forces and Prime Minister for the last fifteen years, I can tell you that I feel absolutely powerless in the face of all of our problems. I have achieved nothing. There is not enough wealth to share around; that is the first lesson for any would-be egalitarian. There is no solution to our problems, bar the process of natural elimination and the survival and domination of the fittest. That is the meaning of democracy.'

He shook his head sadly.

'The only way to keep your head up is through faith. I always say, Erico, *have faith! Have faith!*'

'Faith?' asked Erico.

Umberto answered, in his best philosophical voice. 'Yes, faith in your government, in your country, in your beliefs, in your hopes, ideals and above all, faith in yourself.' His mood became practical. 'Now, Erico, as Minister for Internal Affairs, let us address our two most pressing problems. How are we going to pay for my personal jet liner? And will you find out, for heaven's sake, which cabinet minister has embezzled the World Bank funds.'

Gerry, official community theologian, Paulo Costello, community scribe, and Alan the Jah Recalcitrant were sitting in the meeting room discussing a follow-up letter (nothing had been heard back on their first communiqué) to Cardinal Rice, Head of the Congregation for the Doctrine of the Faith. Alan, as usual, came in a bit sulky. He always felt deep down that he was invited along to these meetings merely as a token representative of the ethnic population. He had always believed that the amalgamation of the two 'sects' had been an unnatural event. He would not have gone along with it only for the extraordinary mystical wisdom of Brother Wilbur Orbeck.

Wilbur had a vision in which it was revealed to him that the Jah was destined to take over the Church of Rome, dominate all religion and conquer the whole world. This victory would represent the triumph of the common man over the theologians and doctors of official religion. It would represent the winning out of basic, simple beliefs over the absurdities of elaborate tradition and incomprehensible dogma. It illustrated the importance of the simple, anonymous, ignorant human being over the greatest, highest powers of corrupt civilisation.

It had also been intimated to Alan by Orbeck that it was he, Alan, who would one day become the first Jah pope! In his imagination Alan had started preparing for that now! He saw himself, in the native garb of the African plainsman, appearing on the balcony of St Peter's as the Lord's representative on Earth. No more would the world treat his people with that old contempt, or adjudge their history as consisting only of the memory and shame of slavery. In the meantime, he would have to put up with these annoying people here, as it was the will of the Lord that he keep a low profile until the Day of Jah when He, too, would appear in all His Africanness.

Alan, after revisiting his dreams, was now more at ease and he listened to Gerry with interest.

'His Eminence the Cardinal is probably still considering our letter and petition,' said Gerry.

Accompanying their letter had been a petition, signed by the members of the community, calling upon the Vatican to proclaim the validity of the African revelation, the unique charism and prophetic gift that had enabled the Jah to foresee the rise of the original Chosen People and their crucial role in the approaching End Times.

Gerry, despite his best effort, was speaking in a strained, somewhat aggrieved voice. For one thing, he was badly missing the illicit cigarettes that an alert Brother Malicious had confiscated from his bedside drawer earlier in the week. But more importantly, he had a feeling that there was a likelihood that their missive to the Vatican might have been actually ignored by those to whom it had been addressed. Yet he dare not admit this openly, or to Alan, whose hope resided in the certainty that the Vatican was taking them seriously. Only the visit to the island from Africa of the Chief Jah Prophet, many years ago, had caused in Alan such an emotion of anticipation and satisfaction as the sending of that first communiqué. He had even insisted that the envelope and its contents be ceremonially blessed with incense before being handed over for posting. It had seemed, then, a far cry from the days when every buffoon in the country had laughed at their over-colourful dress, weird beliefs and futile hopes. It was at moments like those that Alan lost even his resentment at being in the company of these 'foreigners'.

Gerry sighed. He was feeling negative these days. His excitement at 'discovering God intellectually' had long since worn off. Perhaps his conversion had consisted mainly in the hope that he might be able to turn his life around, to save something from the 'debris' of the past – his failed job and marriage. Maybe he could even become a somebody here, at least in the unexciting, noncompetitive field of theology if nothing else. He had indeed had some quite original, even strange ideas about the nature of God (later a community-appointed psychologist was to tenaciously pursue him on some of these 'ideas' of his; of God as a 'drunken spirit', a 'wayward firebrand', a 'ghost in the brain'). He was sure that some of these might be of interest, even to those idle theologians at the Vatican, who never seemed to do any work. They hadn't changed, added to, or improved upon theology since the Resurrection.

'The way forward is by outmanoeuvring the Vatican and in particular, the cardinal,' said Gerry grimly. 'And it will not be easy. We must be careful with the magisterium. It has not for nothing spent twenty centuries combating heresy of every shape, size and description. And they know that the worst ones always originate with good, religious people. But I have previous experience in dealing with powerful institutions. They usually have unspoken, unwritten codes and motivations. These subtle signs hold the most crucial pieces of information about the institution. They are known only to a handful of intimates. If you can crack them, you are on your way. When I wrote the letter, I was surreptitiously addressing that code that is overtly known by most of us as "there is only one truth".'

Gerry smiled with his cryptic knowledge. Alan was impressed. Paulo was making notes.

'Let me assure you that they take a very broad view at the Vatican. All we have to do is keep on the right side of them. I deduct from the fact that we have heard nothing back, that they are happy for us to continue to pursue our line of enquiry into the Lord's origins.'

'Others, too, are showing interest in our theological research,' said Paulo. 'I have been sending reports of our discussions to all the avant-garde publications via my literary agent in Kingstown. He says that he has had acknowledgment of receipt of my articles. There are a number of important left-wing periodicals around the world, he says, that have expressed an interest in the outcome. He says that they are especially curious about Rome's response.'

'The matter has assumed immense importance in the outside world, with all the different religions and cultural blocs looking to us for enlightenment,' said Gerry;

'When the Vatican has officially declared the Lord to be of African nationality, I estimate that the balance of power in the world will change. The United States, Europe and the other world powers will find themselves at loggerheads with a newly empowered and emboldened Organisation for African Unity. Africa, at the head of the Third World, will stride ahead in its new role as the "chosen land". All the defamation, persecutions, misfortunes and problems that once bedevilled her, that greatest and most varied of all continents, will end. The Chinese, meanwhile, will lose face at taking second place to Africa as chief spokesman on Third World issues, and will resolve to make Christianity part of neo-Confucianism and an exclusively Chinese religion—'

'True,' said Paulo, and Alan clapped his hands.

Despite the lack of feedback from the Vatican, the trio were feeling unaccountably elated. For Alan, it was similar to that ecstatic mood he sometimes achieved when they played the drums and incense was burned. For Paulo, the prospect of having his work appear in international periodicals outdid even that of dying and going to heaven. For Gerry, there was the paradoxical buzz that he always got when he knew that he, or some plan of his, was facing insurmountable odds. Each felt that his dreams and hopes were imminently, impossibly, about to be fulfilled.

Sang was interrupted in his prayers in chapel by Obnoxious barging noisily in. At that very moment he was, at long last, about to 'tune in' again to what he considered his own special spiritual wavelength, after kneeling there fruitlessly for an hour fiddling with worldly 'distractions'. Sang had a spirituality somewhat different to what is the norm in the West. It was more of an impersonal, 'non-material' nature. Yet it was also more practical. For instance, he not only prayed to Ignatius of Loyola, founding father of the Jesuits, but had over the years actually made contact with him on a person-to-person basis. He took advice from him directly, and not via some half-witted, vague 'this is what he would have done' methodology. He had lost touch with the saint lately, what with all the problems in community. He was now, somewhat desperately, attempting to make contact again in order to ask for instructions on a number of critical problems, and while he was at it, for some general advice on how to run a religious order. It was this delicate procedure of contacting a saint directly – without breaking proscriptions against raising the dead – that he had just completed when Obnoxious disturbed him.

The brother announced that there was a very important letter awaiting his attention in the office. No other interruption could have been guaranteed to annoy Sang more. Had Obnoxious appointed himself his personal secretary? He was poking his nose in again. And there was that sardonic smile on Obnoxious's face. Sometimes it seemed a permanent feature of the man's countenance. His own people were Buddhists – he himself was brought up on many of their precepts. Yet none of that old, classical philosophy – the sense of the Void or the proper regulation betwixt and between species – had a chance of working in this environment. Obnoxious's smirk was precisely the opposite of that of the Buddha's supremely spiritual smile. He imagined that were it not for that stoical upbringing – and the understanding that to practise Christian love (something that no other religion attempts) had the paradoxical effect of bringing out the worst in those who attempt it – Obnoxious would by now have had more than a flea in his ear.

On this occasion, what had amused Obnoxious was the sight of his superior spreadeagled in a vain effort to communicate with heaven! It always made him laugh to see people praying. He himself knew that there was no need to pray – God was omnipotent and knew everything already. He himself just pretended to pray, for he would be in trouble if he revealed his non-committal attitude to what was always proclaimed as the monk's first duty. When, in fact, everyone around him was intoning the liturgy he himself would be mumbling or concocting rude lyrics about his fellow brothers. He was sure that God, too, laughed at his jokes, for wasn't the world full of practical jokes? These were surely more acceptable than all the pathetic pleading, begging, recriminations and hypocritical requests for forgiveness that He had to listen to all the time.

'I must interview Obnoxious about his spirituality one day soon,' thought Sang. 'He never seems to know when to do the right thing. Or even what the right thing is.'

He knew that it wouldn't be sensible to delve too deeply into the monk's psyche – or to ask how he ever came to be a monk. But it was his duty to 'appraise' his children spiritually once in a while; he would soon have to have a go with Obnoxious.

'It's from the government!' said Obnoxious. 'Some Ministry wants to hold an enquiry into our operations. Peanut farmers around the country have sent up a petition about our unfair practices. They accuse us of using "cheap slave labour". We are also "poisoning the ground". Hans is back, too, looking worried about something. By the way, the water-carrier has just been shouting that there is some trouble over on the farm.'

Obnoxious was well nicknamed, he thought.

'How did you ever come to be a monk?' Sang suddenly asked him.

There followed a long silence on the part of Obnoxious, and there was surprise on his face. Clouds seemed to pass over his features and his whole demeanour changed. He sat down on the bench and spoke in a low voice.

'I am so glad you asked me that. Nobody ever shows an interest in me or in what I think. They all hate me. Even my confessor, Fr Hans, can't wait for me to get out of the confessional. He never asks me *why* I commit my sins. Oh, I wish I could open my heart to someone. I have never been able to reveal my ... inner torment.'

Obnoxious went down his knees, his head bowed in 'humility', a virtue he knew Sang prized.

Sang observed this newly obsequious behaviour on the part of the monk with distaste. He thought to himself – couldn't they all do with some old-fashioned, time-proven, oriental indifference! Instead of this, he remained true to the Western way and comforted Obnoxious by placing a hand on his head and telling him that his unpopularity was of invaluable benefit to the community, as it taught members the habits of tolerance and forgiveness.

'You will probably be responsible for more saints in this monastery than anybody else. You will have your own reward for that.'

Obnoxious appeared fortified as he left the room and he listened with care to Sang's advice as he went out the door.

'Just make sure that you don't bare your soul to anyone else just yet. It is not time for that.'

On the farm Bros Eamon and Dan were working away at the hard, tacky soil with their machetes. The two of them had just made up after a fistfight over the right to dig a particularly rough patch of earth (the same 'trouble' that was reported earlier by the water-carrier). Dan was talking about the old days in Bailedecoinin in his native Wicklow; about how they had much harder-to-dig soil there and that this stuff was just like putty compared to what he was used to. Despite these occasional rows, they really enjoyed their common enthusiasm for matters agricultural. They discussed items of interest in conversations that were, seemingly, conducted in long, quiet grunts. Eamon said that he had always been more of a stick-gatherer than a farmer, but he now found farming to be a most enjoyable job. The strange noises in his head, and the weird things he saw on the ground, such as immensely long snakes that seemed to have no end, giant insects with hund-reds of legs, and one monster of a thing in a shell whose tentacles had stung him in the leg, had been spoiling life for him a bit with the pain. But it beat anything back home.

'What goes on in your head, Eamon?' asked Dan sympathetically.

'I see and hear weird things.'

'Does prayer help?'

'Da only way I can do dis prayer is look up at da sky and curse an' swear. Dat is why I am forbidden to open me mouth in chapel.'

'At first I, too, didn't know anything about prayer, but I think I am starting to pray now. Malicious has been working hard on me. It began to work when I made up a little prayer for my best friend, who I killed long ago. Now I don't feel half as bad. That is what prayer has done for me. I don't even regret killing him now, for hasn't it given him the great grace of being able to forgive me for a serious sin against him? That will win him great benefits in heaven. Still, I fear the day I meet him again, even if it is in heaven.'

'Why did you kill him? Were you queer in da head too?'

'No. I had too much to drink, and the porter had run dry. I was frustrated. But that's no reason to kill a friend. I wish I *was* mad like you. Then I'd have an excuse.'

'It's not nice being mad, Dan. You don't know what is going to happen from one minute to the next. I t'ink I'm fine and den I find meself walking in some queer spot, sitting on a thorny bush, or drinking some horrible t'ing like ditchwater.'

'Why don't you pray for a cure, Eamon? God will cure you. He can cure anybody. They cure people all the time here.'

'I'm afraid to ask for a cure, Dan. I t'ink dat if I was cured, something worse would come to me.'

'That is true,' replied Dan.

'Having all dese fearful noises inside me head makes me feel happy. On the quiet days I do miss them. It's so quiet dat I think something dreadful is going to happen. Then I feel really scared. Den da scary noises return and I feel happy again.'

'There's a sister I know over there in that building – Sister Jane. She is great for sorting out people's problems. She might be able to help ye.'

'Trying for a cure only makes t'ings worse. She'd put me into a bath of cold water. Or make me eat grass. Like they did in the asylum. They exorcised me once dere. Dat had no effect either, even after three weeks of prayers and fasting!'

'I feel sorry for you when you are put out of prayers for making too much noise. You don't even seem to mind dat. You must be as thick-skinned as an elephant. You probably don't even notice all the insults and humiliations that are heaped on you. Would ye ever go back home?'

'It's better here than in the asylum. At least I am allowed out in da open. I can use tools and work on the land. Back dere I was kept locked in. I was allowed out only for a short walk on a Sunday, once a month, when I was guarded by two huge men.'

'Being in dis place keeps me off the drink, anyway,' said Dan. 'In any case, if either of us did leave, there is a huge ocean between here and home.'

'Dan?' said Eamon quietly, his voice suddenly full of a pointed awareness that caught Dan by surprise.

'What?'

'Dere's something I know. I can always tell.'

'What is that?'

'Dat Bro Gerry. He is like me.'

'Like you?'

'Yes. Mad.'

chapter
four

Paulo Costello, sitting at his cubicle desk, was writing down Bro Gerry's words with the composed air of an Old Testament scribe. Some weeks before, Gerry and Paulo had decided to write the community memoirs, incorporating in them their reflections on everyday religious life. Paulo had volunteered to transcribe Gerry's particular ruminations.

'I found an interesting quotation in a book of church history in the library. It will please Alan very much,' said Gerry, as he began dictating.

'*April 2nd (Feast of St Mary of Egypt) Year 2000, The Monastery – Study time.*'

'*Nice to note that we are celebrating another African saint's feast. They seem to be multiplying by the score these days, what with multitudes of holy men and women in that continent martyred each passing week. We are all proud of the Mother Continent's rise to superstardom in the Church. Even the Americans in this community are "African" these days, with their assiduous expression of soul and lack of adherence to the old, Roman discipline. Rome will have a problem approving our new constitution. There are troubled waters ahead – reminding one of those words of the council in Carthage to the Pope as long ago as AD 424:*

'"*Never interfere in Africa again, lest it seem that we are in-*

troducing the blinding pride of secular dominion into the Church."

'Now as this same Africa arises from dust and announces the Second Coming—'

'The world never changes, does it?' said Paulo, interrupting Gerry in order to rest his hand.

'I will bring that quote along with me to the next assembly,' said Gerry. Paulo, pen in hand, waved his writing arm around to limber up for more of Gerry's words:

'This monastery is a hive of activity, as everybody gets his act together for the official Visitation tomorrow. Yesterday's foolishness is behind us. Even holy people seem to believe that they must always indulge in the most extreme tomfoolery on April 1st. At the start of breakfast Bro Obnoxious told Sanctus that Jesus was up on top of the hill, asking for him. Sanctus rushed out and up the hill. He returned, disappointed, to Obnoxious's cry of 'April Fool'. This annual escapism is a sort of religious poetic licence, a necessary holy foolery that sinful souls must partake in en route to spiritual advancement.

'Purgatory, one may argue, is possibly a Holy April Fools Day on the timescale of eternity. Each soul, still full of pride and self-importance, is made to undergo one long series of terrible April Fool jokes, such as "You're not dead – only dreaming" and "Heaven will be yours if you pray hard, non-stop for the next 300 years." However, April Fool jokes do have the benefit of showing up our tendency to nurture illusionary hopes.

'Everyone prays of course that he – or she – will receive a private interview with the Archbishop. This is in the hope that they can get to express their "personal view" on what is happening in and around the monastery and indeed in the world at large. The urge to "tell all" is the result of having emotions and words pent up for so long. And such is the vanity of human nature that some will even expect to impress the Archbishop with their inside knowledge of this and that, and may perforce tell a

few fibs in so doing, excusing their exaggeration as a fruit of their zeal.

'Yet there is a wonderful joy – an atmosphere of faith, hope and charity in this community that is the surest mark of Divine approval. Any number of good works get done here and in the surrounding area.

'What is it that makes us all hold together – such a disparate lot?

'The answer may lie in the fact that everybody seems full of faith in some unspoken, imminent parousia, an approaching apocalypse of some kind.

'I often wonder what makes us feel such a strange, mad happiness in this remote, rudimentary place. Even the raucous behaviour of some of the Church of Jah with their get-togethers and chanting, not to mention their burning incense in secret and total lack of enthusiasm for agricultural labour (a throwback to the association of agricultural work with the enslavement of their ancestors), does not jolt the steady rhythm of the place.

'As I said the other day to my old friend Jim McCall, "What are we doing here, Bro Jim? How did we ever convert to religion?"

'"I can only repeat your own words, Gerry," he had replied; "it is Providence. No matter what happens now or in the future, tomorrow or at the end of our days, it was all meant to be." McCall is a sage these days. Those were the first words he has spoken to me since I joined the community. This man – whom I once venerated as a hero – is scarcely ever seen about the place. With that preoccupied, knowing look he always seems to have, I wonder if he does have a private line to some outside source, some secret, powerful confidante.

'Yet, we have only to look at Sanctus to know that all is well in the world and eternity.'

As Gerry stopped for an intake of breath, Paulo took the opportunity to rest his arm.

'*Are we divinely inspired? The scribes had Divine guidance as they assiduously and laboriously wrote down the words of the prophets. They were not conscious of being inspired. They were only tools in the hands of the Almighty, writing in the way that He wanted. It was as if they were intoxicated, drunk. But what they wrote was the testimony of ordinary folk – even of the likes of our Dan and Eamon. All has its parallel in Scripture – the outrageous behaviour, the black moods, the petty, unwarranted interferences such as cigarette snatching, the embarrassing lack of tact of a Sister Gloria (only last evening her loud, raucous singing of a "love" song and calling my name, could be heard in the monks' dormitory), the holy antics of Sanctus ...*'

Gerry paused a moment to recover his composure.

'*We ignore each other's differences, expressing our unity of purpose in the planting of each new season's crop. The task of cultivation, of "making love" to the earth, is a great therapy for us, inspiring us in strangely sensual agrarian exercises that absorb and consummate all our physical and mental energies. However, it is a fallacy that the tropics are lands of fertile abundance, or that it is possible to squeeze three crops out of the ground each year. Alas, we only bring to birth this new life by a strenuous effort of interior meditation and the exercise of all our limbs in a deep intercourse with Mother Nature. There is no such thing as a pain-free mother-womb, a happy paradise of easy reproduction. Instead we must put all our effort into our work; consume ourselves within the burning intestines of our labour, drawing together through sweat and tears the barren, rough and resistant elements of nature, forcing them against their will to co-operate in a joint push and heave to bring forth at least the seeds, if not the fully fleshed fruits of goodness.*

'*We are subject, even here in the tropics, to the ups and downs of the seasonal aberrations; the earthly rhythms of night and day, dry and wet, cloudy and sunny, the great perspiration and panting followed by a slow cooling down of the body, the* draining out of wastes, physical along with metaphysical ills and forebodings, counterbalanced by the intake of the hopes, fulfilments, wiser em-otions and trials of the perennial bodily rhythms.

'And what about our "little chats"?

'These are all the rage now. It all began with a protracted, on-going argument between two brothers over whether it had been right to use the mules one Sabbath to ferry over supplies to the sisters. Their arguing carried on even into meal times and during prayers.

'Eventually open forum was declared and everybody had to come to the meeting room for a long-drawn-out debating session. It appeared that Hans, as chair, was deliberating, prolonging the boring and pointless debate, but there was method in his mad-ness, as everyone later discovered. The two men discussed their opinions to the point of mental and bodily exhaustion. Whenever they ran out of ideas or clammed up, Hans would bring in new points and suggest new ways to pursue their arguments. He intr-oduced maxims and case studies that neither the two unfortunate monks, or anybody else, had ever heard of before.

'After many hours, it was suggested by the chair that the problem – namely the inability to come to any conclusion – was a matter of a lack of training in rhetoric. Thereafter every sentence, phrase and word that passed from their mouths were examined meticulously by Hans. Praise or criticism was offered in relation to appropriateness and logic. Hans took them into the world of oratory, with long accounts of the role of rhetoric in ancient, classical learning. He encouraged, indeed forced, them to carry different arguments to many different conclusions, some sensible, some ridiculous, simple or abstruse. The two were so exhausted at the end that their spirit was broken. They had no more stomach for any argument. And everybody else had had enough of the subject too, as was evidenced by the whole room more or less having fallen asleep from fatigue and boredom.

'It had felt like we had been there for ten hours (afterwards nobody could be dissuaded from the belief that they had spent a whole afternoon and evening in the room). I checked a wall clock and it had only been 45 minutes! This was Hans's genius at work.

Adept in the art of manipulating individuals and crowds, he now introduced his master stroke, with the introduction of what was to become famous as the "little chat". He suggested that the two go with a neutral brother into a small room and come to an agreement. After only a few minutes the miracle of reconciliation happened! For whatever reason, this previously intractable argument that had separated the two in a long-standing civil war was settled. They came out smiling and made up, glad to get it all over with, looking at everyone sheepishly.

'We all marvelled at how it was possible to come to such a quick solution to what had seemed an impossible problem. Another strange thing was that neither the two disputants, nor the rest of the community, were able to remember much about the whole argument subsequently.

'We all reflected on how this change of heart had been achieved. Sang came up with a proposal for holding such sessions regularly, as the means to solving all problems or conflict that arose in, and even outside, community.

'Combatants face the ordeal of debating their differences interminably, with a moderator chosen from a cadre of specially selected, trained monks, in a confined space – something between a confessional and a very small room. The exhausted protagonists are given no respite, until the time comes for the little chat. Then a drink of lemonade or even a cup of tea is offered to lighten the occasion. Success is guaranteed; one reason being that people always put personal comfort before principle, even in the most resistant of cases, and foremost in the minds of most normal protagonists is the wish to get out of the room. The whole procedure has quite quickly become streamlined. In recent sessions, with a very skilled moderator, the long-drawn-out initial debating stage *has been completely dispensed with.*

'Furthermore, anyone who comes to the monastery with a problem of any sort, even a purely "personal problem", is guaranteed a little chat. Nobody and nothing is outside the scope of the little chat. All sorts of intimate, complex matters are dealt with.

'We have started to use this "method" as a treatment where psychological causes may be at play – for the sick, the lame and for those labouring under grave illusions or uncontrollable, destructive urges. We are beginning to see many sick, disabled and mad people coming in from the surrounding countryside. They congregate disorderedly and noisily around the grounds, many believing that their condition can be ameliorated, or cured, by the little chat.

'Eventually people from the wider world – politicians, warlords, participants in long-standing vendettas – will be coming here for the cure. Even our own community must become more peaceful soon, with every dispute and problem ending up in the forum and disputant and sufferer alike experiencing that all-healing, truth-establishing, miracle-facilitating little chat. There is an air of excitement and happy chaos in the community. Are these the End Times?'

'That's it for today,' said Gerry and Paulo put his pen down with the pride of one who 'knows' that his transcriptions, all things being equal, would eventually be placed in that category of writing called 'inspired prophecy'.

Despite the existence of miracle-producing cures and world-problem-solving facilities, the monastery still seemed to have many problems with its own personnel, some of a disappointingly familiar kind.

'It's Malicious's turn to preach at supper tonight,' said Sanctus sadly to Gerry later. 'I suppose people will twist his words as usual. I pray for him all the time.'

Everything Malicious said or did always had the worst possible interpretation put on it. It was a natural result of his physical appearance, his shambling walk, his devious face and his unconvincing, insincere manner of speech. This most positive, well-meaning of monks (his many good deeds – done always anonymously – were never noticed) looked and sounded like a crook. Sometimes even Sang and Hans found it hard to bring themselves to give him the time of day. His grim face bespoke a lifetime spent in crime, subversion, mockery of virtue and the murder of everything innocent.

There was a legend explaining why he had been accepted into the community in the first place. He had failed his interview (it was said) and Hans was showing him the door when Malicious grabbed a passing cripple and demonstrated his medical skills. By sleight of hand he adjusted a bone in the man's bad leg and the fellow threw away his crutch and walked away effortlessly. For someone with a reputation for doing harm rather than good to his patients, this 'cure' of Malicious was very suspicious. He had conned no less a person than Hans, it was generally agreed. It was said that the lame man had either been an accomplice, or that Malicious was a practitioner of the black arts. There was no underhand skill or trick that Malicious was unaware of; but he usually kept this criminal aptitude hidden behind a facade of ineptitude and ill will.

Aware of a problem with his image, and always keen to give a good impression, Bro Malicious had selected the most harmless of topics he could think of, for his talk.

'De growing of peanuts,' he said quietly after he had taken the rostrum with a humble bend of body and slowness of pace that was taken as sullenness and cunning stealth by his brethren, 'is a lesson in de spiritual life. What is mo' simple, mo' insignificant, mo' 'umble dan a peanut? What food, nut, fruit, root crop or cereal mek one give out a laugh in the instant of its mention mo' easy dan a peanut?

'"It's peanuts," de wit says.

'Dis wit has revealed to us something very important. Id is de wish to decry, to denigrate dat which is small, simple and pure. It may only be de heartfelt dream of some poor soul, something precious dat the arrogant detractor wishes to destroy! Dis man take the name of de peanut in vain. He tells de poor soul id is a self-illusion; de insidious purpose of dis man—'

Malicious stopped to get control of himself. He clearly loved the peanut, his words coming over in waves of emotion.

Those listening felt uneasy, as if each one there was being blamed for the recent anti-peanut vendetta.

'Id a humbling thing to do – to bend down and carefully put a tiny little ol' peanut in its narrow grave and dismiss it with a covering of earth. As if to say goodbye forever and ever. And den, praying all de time for the Day of the Lord, carefully tending that pathetic grave over the weeks, keeping it pure from weed, insect, predator and human devilment in all its forms in de hope that eventually, after nature has done her work, something new will spring up out of de ground!'

He was shouting now.

'And lo – it happens, every time! How den, brothers, if de Lord can do dis to a simple peanut, can he not do it to you an' me, after we have been put in the ground?'

Some were interpreting this now as Malicious implying that they themselves were worth no more than peanuts. The whole talk was an exercise in sarcasm. For didn't he have 'that look' on his face again – superior, contemptuous, a smug smile.

Once again, Malicious's enthusiasm had been taken as mockery. The spiritual ambience that is so necessary in a spiritual talk, the soulful look, the voice moist with sympathy, were just not there. It all sounded so earthy, practical and ironic, satire at its most primitive (and probably best) level, despite Malicious's sincere efforts. Rumblings of discontent and anger were now being heard over the peanut paste and water.

Hans thought to himself that, with Malicious on the rostrum, supper times were going to be embarrassing and overly taut occasions this week. Malicious's spirituality was very peculiar, he thought; an instance of where good intentions only ever bore bad fruit. He wondered why it was that Malicious was destined to be hated by others, no matter how much he wanted to do good or be liked. Not even Obnoxious, in his most offhand moments, aroused the same hatred.

Yet, Hans also mused, while Malicious was the scapegoat for nearly everything that went wrong from day to day in community, when that major disaster occurs – that lay ahead of them as surely as Judgment Day itself – he bet it wouldn't be Malicious on whom retribution would fall. It would be some other unsuspecting, tragic scapegoat. Some poor wretch caught completely unawares on whom everyone will turn for no good reason or purpose. Such were the ways of the world.

As regards his own dealings with Malicious, he had always found the brother to be an approachable, well-meaning chap, even if he seemed to go about things the hard way. The strange thing was – in private other monks said exactly the same about Malicious. Incidents such as his recent cigarette-removal exercise that had so annoyed Gerry showed Malicious's dedication to the well-being of the community of which no other brother was capable.

Others were thinking less charitable thoughts.

'We'll get you for this,' they muttered, their feelings of inadequacy and negativity unaccountably brought to the fore by Malicious's preaching. 'We'll see if we don't make you pay for these insults.'

Obnoxious was gloating to himself. 'I bet I am more popular than Malicious. They tease me with the name Obnoxious, but they really hate Malicious. He should be removed from the rostrum. He is a troublemaker. He does not understand how to talk about godliness or holy things. His choice of a profane, earthy thing, a mere vegetable fit only for eating (if even for that) in a sermon, is so ... blasphemous.'

And as he looked around at the others' irate expressions, he knew that they all agreed with him.

Malicious sensed now that, once again, things were not going as expected. There must have been something wrong in his choice of topic! He decided now to speak impromptu, from the top of his head, or was it his heart, in the hope at least of persuading them of his goodwill and sincerity of purpose.

'Potatoes,' he said, in a determined tone, 'what are we to say about dem? If a brother talks about potatoes an' not peanuts, do *dey* cause hostile thoughts? Why are folk prejudiced against the peanut? Dey are prejudiced against the peanut because it is a weak, tiny thing. We are prejudiced against the peanut because it gives us our living! But de potato is, like rice – I use big words of Bro Gerry here – culturally assimilated. Id is one o' us. Society does not look down on de potato for id is a traditional crop! Potato is revered. If, for instance, I said that potatoes mus' be outlawed, dey would say me mad. But not if I said dat about de newcomer – de peanut! Some call for end to peanut. Many wan' return of more brown or white rice. But ... popularity is not de same as sanctity – so Gerry say.'

He paused. Gerry felt a little uncomfortable hearing his name spoken out here.

Still, it was a wonder someone remembered his sayings!

Sang and Hans's ears pricked up: this sounded almost like a call to protest! Even rebellion. What was the fellow going on about!

Everyone put their heads down for they knew that, with all this talk about peanuts, cunning eyes would be looking out for some giveaway sign on the face of the anonymous graffiti artist.

'Is id not time we stopped cussing de peanut? We mus' no mo' confuse, as I say, popularity wid sanctity, virtue wid respectability. We mus' be ready to root out prejudice, dear brothers – wherever id occurs.'

As Malicious continued speaking, arguments between some of the more excitable brothers broke out below over the comparative advantages of peanuts and potatoes. They, of course, broke the rule of silence at meals.

Some marvelled that the fellow up on his rostrum showed no nervousness at all, apparently more or less oblivious to the effects of his words. He seemed to sway deliberately in rhythm as he spoke, enjoying himself, with that fearful danger – the possibility of tipping over and plunging to the ground below – apparently not occurring to him, at least.

'Crap,' said Wilbur Orbeck. 'All dis theology an' books 'bout seven different mansions is hokus pocus to me. Me send letter to Big Man Sang an' tell him dat mysticism a fool.'

He had been given a book on the spiritual life by Hans entitled *The Interior Castle* to help him develop his spiritual reading, during his isolation. He was told that this was written by a famous mystic named St Teresa, and to follow it would ensure his attaining paradise even before he was dead. He was told that the book was the highest exposition of the spiritual life ever written. But it aroused only frustration and bewilderment in this famous founder of the Church of Jah.

Originally, Wilbur had been sent by Sang on a retreat of 40 days. This had been then extended to 40 weeks, which became 40 months. It had recently been suggested to him that 40 years might be the 'great idea'. Orbeck was a man whose interpretation of religion had once been far more exciting, revolutionary and controversial than it was now. It was he who had first announced to the poor that Jah had come down and lived among them. They heard his message with joy, astonished that it was the first time they were hearing such stupendous news. People had not recognised Him, due to the lies of bad men. He had gone back to Africa Heaven before they had known who He was.

Orbeck had been His right hand man. He had told him that He would return again and this time take His followers back with Him to paradise. This was believed to be not just 'in Africa' but 'was Africa' – the state of highest spiritual being. Orbeck's estimation of the Church of Jah's success, in former times, had been based on its social and political power with large numbers being entered in the Book of Membership each year. A sure sign of Divine favour was the fact that the Church had frightened off most of the respectable and learned in society by means of its exotic costumes, scarifying rites and raucous celebrations welcoming the imminent Day of Africa Judgement.

Confirmation of Divine approval was shown by the many poor flocking to its ranks, anxious to be taken away from their present, poverty-stricken existence. Just when excitement was at its peak and the Day of Arrival was about to be announced, Orbeck suddenly realised (in a dream) that the Day of Judgement might be a long way off. Fortuitously (he put it down to Divine guidance) he was approached by Sang and Hans the very morning after the dream, when the two came on a goodwill visit bearing the gift of an ancient African book (what they called a real African book) – the Confessions of St Augustine. They had a long talk. Orbeck found the story of the African, Augustine, to be irresistible. There was a need for another Augustine, he was told. (Later, Hans was to suggest that this long talk was the 'moral precursor' of the 'little chat'.)

As he listened to Sang's and Hans's arguments there came on the ken of his horizon the vision and prospect of having at his disposal the power of the Church of Rome, plus international fame and respectability. It was a revelation. This clinched the deal.

The move to a hermitage had been necessitated by Orbeck's inability to let go of *all* his worldly ideas. His initial insistence, for instance, on a march to Rome by the whole United Church to confront the 'imperialists' over their scandalous abandonment of 'real religion' became a cause of division in the early community.

Now he was all by himself, with nothing but prayer sheets and this so-called *Interior Castle-in-the-Sky* book, compulsory reading as an indispensable guide to his spiritual, if not indeed his bodily, liberation.

He looked askance at the pages now. It was just another instance of the obscurantism that he found permeated the Catholic Church. It was all talk about the supernatural afterlife in some mythical land of the spirit. In his opinion this so-called 'theology' only contrasted with the simple, pure teaching of the Church of Jah. Jah had promised a paradise whose delights were real, normal, human. Where would his body be in supernatural paradise? He could not imagine himself without his body. Africa he knew for certain existed, in all its exquisite colours, abundant earthy, red-blood life.

When he had first opened the book he thought that there was no point in starting at the beginning. *He* was no novice to the spiritual life! The book talked about seven mansions. Sure hadn't he been taken up into the *seventh* heaven many times in the old days?

About halfway through would be best. Pick up the threads from there. The first part of the book was all about reptiles and dangerous, devil-things that plague a person at the start of the spiritual journey. A simple exorcism had done the trick for him many years ago! He had all those creatures put down into hell with great gusto during the great mass baptism in the river at Mobby Bay. Many came up glorious while those 'who were not to be saved' went down in the waters taking the unclean spirits with them and never came up again. Oh, how he well remembered it all! Joyous times! Never to come back again.

He opened the book again and looked at the different headings. Here and there he dipped into the text. This Christian mysticism all seemed to be a very vague philosophy to him. Mainly concerned with strange thoughts of no real consequence. These thoughts tend to come into your head when you are doing nothing very much. Their main purpose is to lead you astray, the book says. They begin by tempting you to the worst sin of all – to give up reading that same book!

This spiritual life is hopeless! This God keeps hiding himself all the time! He is always calling his followers – some say they hear his voice – and when they answer he goes silent, pretending not to be there. He plays hide and seek! Just when you have worked out where he is, he goes off somewhere else! And when you think you are doing things right, you are certain to be doing them wrong. And when you are certain you are wrong, you are probably right!

They say you must 'surrender' to this God. Well, hadn't he surrendered everything. His headship of the church, his old way of life? How many others would have given up the perks of the top job so easily?

Yet giving everything to God didn't seem to be enough either! You must hand over everything you didn't own as well! You must give up the *world!* This God is a tyrant!

He is not like Jah. Jah does not hide away like a shy bride, but takes pride in body. He sports golden locks of hair, his skin reflects many colours of the sun, his flesh emanates perfumed essence of the bountiful Earth, his breath the sweet blessing-carrying winds from the four corners of the Earth. He is good-looking, strong, handsome God who smiles on his people and tells them that they are great! He does not make people cringe in his presence. He tells them to take pride in themselves! He orders them to get up off the ground and shed their bondage. He comes of a proud race from a holy land that is at the centre of the Earth. His people are his children, offspring of his loins, heirs to his throne. He speaks as a lion; His roar is heard all over the world.

Orbeck started to shout out his thoughts. 'Me here two years now! Mysticism whole heap o' contradiction. What Sang trying do to me? Me sit here day an' night on stool in dis liddle wooden hut. Me forget all de t'ings dat go on in de world. An' me pray, pray. Me pray in de morning an' me pray in de night. Me pray at midday. Not a moment me don't pray.'

Suddenly there came over the air the sound of beautiful singing to the accompaniment of a light stringed instrument. Wilbur became quiet and listened in wonder. He seemed to fall into a deep sleep.

Some time later he found himself slowly and laboriously writing a letter to Bro Sang. He was writing under some compulsion, experiencing emotions he couldn't comprehend.

Dear Bro Sang, Straynge ting appen wile ago wen me outside sittin on rock. Me wos jus tinking how wikked you an church mus be to keep me lok up here. Me lissen to de silence at firs. Nottin bud silence. Me try to get reddy to shout at you agen in litter. Sudenly me here buttyfull music me tink frum far away in derektun of chapel. Me sid an lissun and me fill wid joy. Me in extasy. After wile it go, bud me still in extasy. Me haart stay full ov joy and happiness till nuah. Me nuah no id true wot you say – heven is not of dis world. Me beleev nuah, Bro Sang. Me showt at you in litter no more.

Me no care wad happun in dis world nuah. Me no care bout Rome or de top job any more. Me kare no more bout Africa.

Me rite no more. Me doant care wad happun nuah. Rite me an led me no wad I mus do.

Signed: Wilbur Orbeck, bro

Gerry was disappointed that his old pal, Jim McCall, seemed to have deliberately gone incommunicado. It could hardly be the case that it was because he had taken such a liking for contemplating the infinite that he didn't wish to talk to his old buddy any more! He outdid all the normal regulations of silence, annoying ordinary brothers with his know-nothing know-everything face. When at work in the office he surpassed the zeal of the most recondite practitioner of the art of self-composure. One would have thought that here was a candidate for the hermitage! Paradoxically, for someone who had always been self-willed and an adventurer, Jim was the most self-disciplined of all the brothers. He was never seen drinking, smoking, speaking out or sucking up to Sang, Hans or important visitors.

Jim's self-absorption, Gerry reasoned, would be seen by his superiors as the qualities of confidentiality and discretion, the very merits that ensured that he would be given privileged access to all important, inside information. Knowing how Sang's mind worked, it would have been incumbent upon him to keep Jim in the midst of administrative affairs and at the centre of power, as that was clearly the job the Lord wanted him to do (for those very qualities of prudence); and therefore was for his own spiritual good.

Gerry marvelled at his self-assurance. This, along with his superior knowledge, charm, always smart physical presence and strength of character (Gerry had never seen him show distress in any situation), was probably in his family genes, not to mention a product of his education in the best schools. The McCalls, an old East coast family, were influential to this very day in Washington DC. They had served the state. Their name was their bond. They had done business (as commodity dealers) with all the major international brokers. Fact or myth – it was never denied by Sang or Hans – it was believed that their money had funded the United Church. This was accepted by everybody as a good reason never to slight the man, or subject him to any of the indignities imposed on the other brothers.

Gerry presumed that the McCalls were probably relieved that their wayward son (aka the black sheep of the family) had somewhat late in life given up on his illegal and errant ways and entered the safer confines of a monastery. They could claim that their kith and kin was now doing great good in the world and was no longer on the run from the CIA, FBI and various international agencies. They could proclaim that his previous ill doing was a Providence-guided preparation for the virtuous, holy life. They were also probably relieved to be able to offload some of their surplus wealth on the United Church of Jaman by endowing it with a portion of 'tax saved'. This they did, in particular one supposed, to ensure that Jim was able to stay in the monastery.

McCall was lost in thought now as he walked along the pathway between the admin block and the meeting room, his hands in his slacks, his head bent downwards, his face a sphinx-like mystery. Gerry hailed him loudly, sounding as cheerful as he could, hoping to bring Jim back to his old self.

'What's the matter, Jim? Two years here and you have barely spoken a word to me. Do you remember the old army days when we cocked a snoot at the top brass? When we were called the Young Turks. You wouldn't think that now! Ha ha.'

Jim looked up. He seemed to be pretending that he was seeing Gerry for the first time in his life.

Everything that Gerry knew about him told him that Jim was up to something. McCall would never be satisfied with anything less than the top position. But it might not be the top job here! To him that would be small potatoes. There was only one other job around that would be worthy of Jim. Knowing him of old, Gerry was certain that he was aiming at something more important than any ordinary position or job in the church, no matter how elevated.

This was control of the Vatican state itself, its levers of power and its finances. That would be achieved by the means in which he had been trained – infiltration at an initially low level. Something noteworthy and impressive would be done in the vicinity of his present post – the boss is impressed and Corporation Head office comes headhunting!

That was it! Hadn't Jim once said to him that he knew all the inside workings of the Vatican? All of this business of being a dedicated religious was simply another means to an end!

Gerry suddenly found himself ruminating ... a doubt entered his mind. His surroundings, when he looked around him, made all his conjectures appear unreal. The deep countryside setting, the chirping and cheeping of innumerable birds and insects accentuating the sense of human isolation, the high heat and immobility of the hottest time of year, the absence of other visible human beings (one took, on faith, that they were all at that moment diligently going about their duties), under a silvery, glaring, overpowering sky made his imaginings about McCall influencing global events, or changing the future of the Church or world, absurd. For a moment, it felt as if nothing could ever change, or would ever change here in this beehive of monkish tedious toil, of repetitive bodily, mental and spiritual exercises.

This was perhaps all just fantasy – a nostalgia for the excitement of the old, carefree days that would never return. After all, life was so ... peaceful here that at times you could say it was ... monotonous. No wonder the imagination got up to its old tricks.

'Wha ...' Jim muttered now at Gerry's interruption.

'How's it going? Haven't spoken to you for a long while. I expect you are thinking about things a lot.'

McCall's shook his head slowly and his eyes opened wide. It was as if he were awakening from a deep, long sleep. He raised his head and looked at Gerry.

'We are changing the world,' he said heavily, with great strength of feeling.

'How is that, Jim?'

Gerry was used to McCall's penchant for outlandish, controversial statements. He would have expected nothing less.

'The mad people yesterday who stormed the compound. It is a sign of the times. Before long, the whole world will be coming to our doorstep.'

Ah, the same old Jim, thought Gerry – thinking on the grand scale!

The previous day there had been a great fuss and commotion when many sick, mentally unbalanced and distraught people attacked the fencing around the compound in an attempt to enter the monastery. Every available brother had to come out to help control and calm the situation. Hundreds of ill-clad (some indeed not clad at all) folk struggled to gain access to the monastery. It was said that the supposed 'cure' of one of their number was the cause of the whole thing.

The cured man had left the place smiling, walking normally, dressed up in a new outfit and promising to help 'spread the word' of his little chat back in the world. The message had gone round that the monks had a new cure. Many did not even bother to try the gate but threw themselves at the wire. Cut, bruised and otherwise injured, climbing over each other or running around chaotically, they finally brought down the fence through sheer force of numbers.

This had the result of an immediate confrontation with the hard men of the community – in particular Bros Alfredo, Dan and Eamon. Fist fighting began, and in the case of the more aggressive intruders it had to be said that both monk and intruder were enjoying themselves immensely. This unexpected excuse for uninhibited behaviour was, in contrast to all the spiritual stuff, welcome to the three brothers not least because of its old familiarity. For a while, it looked as if there was to be no easy – or Christian – solution to the confrontation.

'You cure Catch. Cure us!' they cried. 'Mek us whole again. Show us how you fix Catch.'

One man sank to his knees in front of Eamon and pleaded, 'De doctor fix me brain wid block o' ice. Den he put me in his palace for he also great king! After w'ile he try fe mek me king an' offer me golden crown. Me refuse an' run away, for he mad! Save me from mad doctor.'

Eamon asked, 'Did he have a telescope on his face and show ye faraway moons where da little people live?'

'Yea.'

'And did he stick da ice pick in your head?'

'Yea!'

'Den you were right to run away.'

'You boys an' girls ged out of here now or me shave yore heads,' shouted Alfredo, threatening them with the worst punishment possible in that culture – baldness. (So accustomed were the people in that region to all the deformities of natural vice, disease and abnormality that it had been necessary for human wisdom to introduce the 'natural abnormality' of baldness as the only acceptable taboo – and as the surest sign of God's displeasure. Only a small minority of bald-headed people existed in the island; other exceptionally strong genetic features perhaps having enabled them to survive the early persecutions and pogroms.)

'Move off,' shouted Dan, in good humour.

Great spiritual and psychological progress was evident in Dan O'Toole. This was due to the fact that not only did he not try to hurt anyone, but he was more concerned to comfort the distraught and to control the aggressor, especially by taking the many blows that came his way with a fixed smile and muttered 'prayers'. For the guilt of the crime of murder, that had so long haunted him, was slowly being replaced by the firm resolve to do penance in this life. It was Hans who had advised him that his Purgatory might be reduced to a less extravagant block of time if he could show willingness, while still alive, to accept strong punishment.

This fracas was a golden opportunity for him spiritually, for lately he had been feeling that there just weren't enough punishments about, and had been looking for more ways to suffer. He had found, to his disappointment, that whatever suffering he inflicted on himself, it could never match the suffering and regret that he still felt over the killing of his friend. Now he was finding deep satisfaction in taking the blows of the fellows around him. He did not want this free-for-all to stop – ever.

As he took yet another vicious swipe to the pelvis he prayed (this was, unbeknownst to him, that which was so commended in sermons – a 'first' pure prayer) that the fight would go on forever.

Eamon was in an emotional muddle. He perceived in this multitude those whom he took to be fellow sufferers. He wanted to bring them into the community with him. But, as he was leading a group to the safety of the inner enclosure, he objected now to their walking all over the peanut plants. He saw red and felt much emotional distress as he sought for a way both to love these fellow sufferers and at the same time to punish them for destroying the community's precious peanut crop. He grabbed the nearest fellow and began strangling him, as the others ran back to the perimeter in a great stampede. He was eventually pulled off the unfortunate fellow by Dan who, disappointed that the fighting had now stopped, had some recompense in the almighty kick that Eamon gave him in the stomach.

Sanctus's voice suddenly rang out, reverberating in all directions, like the call of God.

'My beloved children! Stop now. I am here.'

Everyone had the distinct perception that Sanctus had been addressing them alone. Whether this was the result of hypnotism ('devil's device') or some psychic ability was not clear. Each soul, both monk and afflicted, was made aware that he really was the most important person in the world. Each felt astonished and baffled by the strange impression that a holy voice had spoken in a uniquely personal way, such as he had never experienced before. Yet a number claimed that it had not been Sanctus's voice, but that of someone else, the voice of some unknown speaker who had been standing near, or behind Sanctus as he spoke. (It was a moment that was to become highly significant later in community folklore.)

'Give your name to a brother,' the voice continued; 'I will see to it that you have a little chat before the next full moon. And do not speak of the cure to anyone. In the meantime just wait your turn in the queue.'

They all turned and went back to their allotted places, each (monk as well as afflicted) believing that he would soon indeed be really cured of all earthly ills.

Sang and Hans, arms waving and shouting in unison, arrived belatedly on the scene, flushed and flustered. They immediately began exerting their 'control' over the situation, telling the departing crowd that everything was now OK. But even as they were speaking everyone had departed.

Jim McCall had observed the whole series of events from afar. He had watched intently as those powerful words had taken effect. Here was something, he knew, that needed controlling – and exploiting – for positive ends.

He now made the gesture of 'confidante' towards Gerry, touching him on the shoulder, sighing as though he had come to a decision finally to unburden himself of a great weight.

'I've been thinking. We need stronger leadership. I've observed the way we do things here for over two years now. I've said nothing. I've seen the beginning of the decline. Sang just lets things happen. He hasn't the least bit of control over anything. And Hans? He's just an organiser. He thinks that as long as he has a tidy office and task schedules are completed on time all is OK. The more I watch him the more I think there is something odd about his dedication to trivia.

'The other day he spent an hour arguing with Sr Josephine over the collection time for the washing. When I first met him his talk was forever of great spiritual concerns, heaven and hell. Now he goes on about paperwork. He is constantly complimenting me on my filing! I asked him once if God would have kept the paperwork on everything he did when creating the universe. His reply was that he wouldn't be surprised if he had! Neurotics like that – I make no apology for using the word – are always hiding some dreadful secret.'

Gerry was disappointed with Jim's lack of spiritual mien. Many in community did indeed hide a terrible secret from the past. For a while, it had been quite fashionable for a monk to hint, with barely concealed anguish, at some secret that was too dreadful to reveal. That is – until one day Malicious called for the attention of everyone in assembly and revealed, in all good faith, that he truly loved Obnoxious! It became unfashionable after that for anyone to claim to have a secret!

'Jim,' said Gerry softly, 'we all have ulterior motives for being in this place, but it is what we make of our time here that counts. Don't you think it's a bit hopeless to expect anything from this world? Those old grandiose plans of ours – to do away with all bad governments and rule the world ourselves – what presumptuous *pride*. I now find fulfilment in studying theological matters. It is my humble hope that soon I will crack the nature of God, as Einstein cracked the nature of matter. Please God I will put an end to all those existential dilemmas that have wracked man-kind's collective brain. I will end the mystery of existence. I keep it all written down in a private notebook. It is amazing that I can get greater pleasure now out of meditating on death, thinking about what it will be like to be completely free of the human body – able to think and feel freely without the "human" encumbrance – than I ever did get out of wine, women and song. I do feel that all these arms, legs and bodily things are a hindrance to clear thought. Don't you?'

McCall shook his head in exasperation. He gave Gerry a quizzical look.

'I don't think intellectual concepts appertain to anything that is happening in this place,' he replied. 'They are an ordinary lot here. The quality of the instruction is not strict enough. It doesn't even begin to compare with our military training. Yes, I have some ideas of my own about how we might improve the personnel. But at the moment the priority is for good quality leadership. May I say charismatic leadership?'

Gerry laughed loudly.

'Charismatic leadership! The last thing we need is some mad guru leading us like Gadarene swine to the abyss! I am quite happy with the eccentricity of Hans and honest dim-headiness of Sang.'

He laughed again but with a hollow laughter. This man McCall showed surprisingly little improvement in character or self-development, despite his time in the monastery. Gerry was even beginning to think that Jim, too, might benefit from a 'little chat'.

'I've just seen how the simple words of a holy man controlled a disorderly crowd. That is the sort of charisma we need.'

'No way should that saint be troubled with rudimentary business matters or the day-to-day affairs of the world. He is the spiritual powerhouse without whose intercession we would all be lost. In any case, do not meddle with the Holy Spirit, Jim.'

'I agree. Indeed, the power of his words did not come from him. He was inspired to speak them, by an even more powerful voice that belongs to someone else. Anyway, I could have my chap installed in the top job in no time. Forget about any elaborate election in General Chapter. It wouldn't matter. But that is not my plan.'

The same old Jim, thought Gerry again, ruefully. 'What's your plan?' he asked.

'My plan must remain a secret for the moment. But I will say one thing to you – and to you alone. One day soon we will indeed be the New Jerusalem. All roads will lead to this godforsaken spot. Our edicts and remits will go out to the city and the world.'

'I thought you came here to find inner peace – and to abandon ambition? Oh, I wish we could all just be like Sanctus, or even Orbeck. Jim, I think you and I are holding back this community from true holiness.'

'Well, at least we are sinners, Gerry. It could be worse.'

Gerry wondered. Surely Jim wasn't here under false pretences, pretending to be a man of God? That would be too much! After receiving a rare dispensation for ordination in only two years (ordination was something that Gerry himself would probably never receive) ... that would amount to ... a sin against God Himself.

Feeling emboldened by Jim's talkativeness, he made an attempt to obtain more information. 'Why is the rabbi here?'

'He's a guy – no pun intended – who has few friends in the world. He was in a big financial scandal. Corrupted an important tax official, it was said. He has also lost his licence to preach. He is related (distantly) to one of the world's most famous banking families. So I suppose he is the black sheep! I had some dealings with him myself in the past. He is presently a pawn in a game of political and financial chess. But he is here at my behest.'

He chuckled to himself. 'It sure shows his devil-may-care attitude to religion, though, that he chose to live with us!'

Gerry thought: Jim has sure retained at least one past conversational trick – that of leaving a person with the feeling that somehow he was still not in the full picture. When Hans and Jim had brought him in, Rabbi Fogelman had all the appearance of a down and out. Or was that also some sort of subterfuge? Thinking about it now, it looked more like he was a prisoner!

Gerry departed with relief, feeling that weight of men's affairs that had descended on him as he had spoken with Jim, lifting again.

If only he had looked behind him, he would have seen a surprising sight. The bold Jim commenced to hide his face in the white hood of his habit and started to weep uncontrollably. The man's choking words, when they eventually came, were bitter.

'Oh Lord, Lord, help me ...'

five

'The Archbishop ees with Sang right now,' said Hans to Gerry a little later on the grassy area in front of the main building, a tinge of excitement in his voice.

Gerry had gone to see Hans feeling, after a long period of peace, the return of a worldly disturbance. It was the talk with McCall that was now causing him more doubts about his vocation. For one thing McCall had never once complimented him on – or even mentioned – his important work in the field of theology. He doubted now that there existed any respect for him at all as a theologian. He spoke in an agitated voice.

'Has he asked to see me? You know – about my theological writings?'

'I don't think he knows about them, Gerry. He has more pressing things on his mind. He ees on a mission to curtail our activities. He claims that we are too preoccupied with ill-conceived socio-economic projects, while neglecting the Church's main business – preaching morality to the masses. Een particular, we are giving scandal by our great economic success in cultivating the peanut. We have put mammon before God. We have set up an alternative state, with our health care and educational services. We have a Bro Poison Pen, who apparently has sent a letter to his Grace, which he flouted on his arrival this morning. In it we are accused of malpractice. Health & Safety issues are being raised concerning the chemicals it ees claimed we are putting into the ground and which, apparently, would explain the abundant harvests of our poison-food! And for good measure, he says, the government claims that we are plotting their overthrow.'

'Well, what defamation!' shouted Gerry with anger and disbelief, his own worries temporarily forgotten. 'Who sends them all this information?'

'No idea. All the same, we have nothing to worry about,' said Hans, 'as long as they do not discover our big secret.'

'Our big secret? What do you mean?'

'The physical presence of the Spirit. A few brothers are in the know. Most have an inkling; some suspect.'

'What do you mean – physical presence ...?'

Hans looked at Gerry with surprise.

'His presence is detectable to the five senses, smell, touch ... Surely, Bro Gerry, you know about the Holy Spirit?'

Gerry was embarrassed, but defiant. 'I have heard a lot – read a lot about it.'

'It is by eets power that we are doing great things. And we will go on to do greater things! Why do you think multitudes of people are coming here looking for help; indeed many wanting to join the community? They sense there ees something here, even though each individual puts a different interpretation on what they are feeling. If it ever gets out that we possess the greatest power een Heaven and on Earth, all the evil forces and malign influences in the world – in the universe – will make a beeline for this place and descend like a thousand furies to drive it away from us. Eet will be the end of all our grand plans.'

'I am sure that if we said to Archbishop Da Souza that we are all filled with the Holy Spirit, he would not bat an eyelid.'

'True. But if he really believed you, then he would be heading straight off to file a report and begin proceedings to close us down.'

'I ... never noticed it. I will certainly have to keep my eyes open in future.'

'Not your eyes alone, Gerry.'

Hans sighed, as if despairing of a dim pupil. His tone became more down to earth, even jocular. 'John Da Souza and his assistant are going to end up doing our bidding – without their realising it. We have put them een the clutches of the sisters! Ha ha ha. Sr Jane will confiscate their cigarettes and see to eet that they are given water instead of coffee or alcohol. Josephine will make sure that they are not treated like nobility!

To make sure that they understand all the workings of the community, they will be called upon in the middle of the night to get out of their beds and lend a hand with the emergency cases at the hospital. Josephine will devise some onerous chores, such as cleaning up the bed mess after a patient has passed away, or giving Winston his medicine. They will be kept there working into the early hours under the pretext of letting the sisters get on with more important jobs, or to catch up on their sleep. And they will barely have fallen back asleep again when they will be awoken by the call to early prayer with extra-strong, long ringing of the bell! Then they will be taken on a long tour of the farm een the heat of midday by Bros Eamon and Dan. They will be impressed by our simple methods and back-to-earth technologies, to which they will be invited to lay their hands by those two demanding taskmasters! Ha ha.

Meanwhile, the bishop's assistant has been taken een hand by Malicious, whom I have appointed as his valet. He is dosing him up on our extra strong bush tea. The fellow has an unspeakable complaint that was noticed immediately by Malicious. Apparently, the Archbishop forbade him the native, traditional cure on the grounds that eets origins are pagan. So the fellow is in our power already, for he is extremely grateful for the relief he ees finding.'

Hans lowered his voice. 'You see, whatever happens during this inspection, we must ensure that they don't get wind of our real work. They must not suspect that the peanut farm ees just a cover for secret, hidden, supernatural activity. Let them think that we are, indeed, all politics, practical projects, controversial lines in liturgy and ritual, heretical ideas and so on. Let them think that the peanut harvest is not a miracle but a commercial fraud. Long may they fume at our debating the colour of the Lord's skin and our gratuitous tinkering with the Trinity. They will feel greatly justified when they ban such things here – and all will be well with us.'

Gerry walked away full of thought. Although still not sure about the meaning of Hans's words, he felt pleased that at least he was being given some inside information.

Da Souza had proceeded carefully, not betraying any impatience or bad temper, but coolness and firmness.

He declaimed that he found too much introspection in the mentality of the Jah brothers. 'Your introversion is not good for the public image of a responsible church in the civilised world,' he told the open-mouthed gathering of Jah brethren. 'After all, we have a reputation to uphold.'

He had not been impressed by the open-air concert put on for his benefit by these folk. At first he had simply been greatly relieved to get away from the sisters, who had dropped down very low in his estimation. Disgust was not too strong a word for what he felt after a night spent in their company (and one more still to go!). With all that uninhibited bossiness and over-familiarity that they apparently liked to distinguish with the term 'sharing', he was quite tired. He now had a headache from the loud music and asserted that these 'locals' were devoting themselves to folksy carry-overs when they should be praying and doing penance. He had not been swayed by the bright costumes, soul singing, smiling, clapping, drumming excitement of dance and ceremony as they celebrated what they called the 'ethnicity' of the Lord.

This obsession with the racial origin of the Lord was becoming a bit of a problem. It seemed to have taken over from normal doctrinal and pastoral concerns as the great new issue in some parts of the church. He had heard that Rome was ignoring the 'controversy', considering it just one of the 'fads' of the times. Such heresies had the potential to cause serious division among the different hierarchies and peoples representing the five continents. Each world region would begin to assert 'ownership' of the Lord, claiming that He had manifested Himself to their people in a special way. This made them a 'chosen people', without any need any more for a hierarchy as such, or for obedience to supposedly obsolescent traditions or rules. Salvation would be theirs merely by being the people they were!

After the Resurrection – it was being claimed – the Lord had taken on a new version of his body. Some were saying that he had the body of an African king, others a Native American. There were numerous rumoured sightings of the Lord as an Asian, an Arab, a European. Accusations of racism were being made, with each church party claiming that the Lord's true nature was being distorted or falsified by this or that faction. Spirituality, theology and metaphysics did not matter; they had gone out the window.

At the last meeting of cardinals at Rome there had been an ominous incident. Much surprise and upset occurred when many, rejecting the uniform of red hats and vestments, had turned up in native, traditional outfits, speaking and singing praises to *their* Lord in a myriad of languages. One cardinal was observed tap dancing his way into St Peter's. A German cardinal came dressed like a tramp, while the head of the church in China, sporting a beard, ponytail and bobbles, making him indistinguishable from an orthodox rabbi, actually demanded that the papacy be moved to Beijing which he was calling the 'original Jerusalem'.

The Church was going to pot again and the rot started in

places like this.

'It's not real prayer,' Da Souza commented now to his assistant (who was actually enjoying the concert spectacle). 'It's more a
cover-up for a lack of seriousness, a non-acceptance of the strict
rules of religion. You don't honestly think that the Lord – up on
His high throne in all His majesty – would lower Himself to listen
to the likes of that?'

He shook his head, secretly pleased that he would have much
to condemn here when he reported to the Prime Minister.

The assistant meanwhile, fast recovering from his previous
malady, had summarised in his own mind his impressions of the
proceedings as being 'good for religion'. It had a definite attraction, he thought, especially for bringing back into the Church all
those spiritually dead, numb or jaded people, like himself, who
had given up on religion.

He was now feeling such warmth and peace in this community that he thought to himself – who cares about such irrelevant things as work, prayer, seriousness or the future of religion
in the world any more? He would welcome death now – even,
especially his own death – and he did not care any more whether
or not there was life everlasting. His sudden lack of concentration
made him stumble and he collided with Sister Gloria who was
dancing nearby. Da Souza was so busy officially scrutinising the
'overall' proceedings that he failed to notice the strange exuber-
ance of his deputy.

Alan had harsh words for His Excellency in reply to the
Archbishop's criticism:

'You – Archbishop – Chief Priest and Scribe – are de problem,' he shouted in front of the assembly. 'For you say body don't
count. You say dat we leave de body behind w'en we die. Dat de
Resurrection body *maybe* de same body but dat it won't look like
de firs' body. Dat is stupidity. Dat is blasphemy! What is de
glorified body if not de human body? Well, we say de body is de
body. No God even can change it. We celebrate body because

God *mek* it like it is. Why do de Lord live to dis day in de same hAfrican body – Lion of Judah?'

'That man was shot years ago,' Da Souza replied angrily, reminding them of the somewhat insalubrious demise of the Emperor of Ethiopia, whom some had seen as God on Earth.

'So heretic say. He still with us today. An' some say dey even see him in dis place.'

Da Souza knew there was no point in pursuing the discussion. The Jesuits would relieve them of their fantasies and misconceptions in time. It took not centuries but millennia to sort out some heresies. He would be strict with them. Their leaders had somehow brought them into mainstream Christianity, mainly through the persuasive theological arguments (and possibly other dubious shenanigans) of the Jesuits Sang and Hans.

He had even heard a preposterous rumour that this auspicious decision was made at the end of an evening's drinking and dominoes-playing session. The silly tittle-tattle claimed that submission to either Jah, or the Roman Catholic Church, had depended on the final score line, having been agreed by both parties that this would be taken as a sign of the Divine will! He had never heard anything so outrageous. But there must have been some element of truth in it for such a rumour to arise. It just went to show the profanity matters of religion fell into when they were in the hands of people such as these. There were certainly forces at work attempting to make the Church look ridiculous in the eyes of the public.

He turned to address them with as much authority as he could muster. 'The benefits of respectability which you now have in the United Church must be accompanied by the duties and responsibilities of Christians. You will all be confirmed by me into the Holy Roman Catholic Apostolic Church.'

'Wha ...? No ... Not till Rome accept Lion of Judah!' shouted Alan.

'Heresy! I knew I would find heresy here!'

He reflected bitterly. 'It was all too good to be true. Those glowing progress reports from Sang and Hans – all that helping the poor, infirm and outcast, the wonderfully expressive liturgy and the rest of it, are the stones under which all the little worms hide.

'Your status, then,' he pronounced, 'will remain that of lay brothers and sisters!'

There was a riot on the campus after the delivery of this edict. The visiting party was surrounded by the crowd of singing, swaying Jah brothers and sisters who, without using any undue physical force but more by the sheer impress of their combined weight, escorted Da Souza and his assistant to the car port and sent them forthwith off the premises without their luggage, formal goodbyes and with many fists and a few stones banging on their vehicle.

'Yo don't tell *us* what fe do! Yo leave now! Go back to yore palace! We throw yo out!'

As the assistant drove the car at speed out through the gates Sang and Hans appeared on the scene, their cassocks askew with the effort of running. They kicked themselves that, once again, they were too late to intervene in another major 'incident' on the ground.

Later in Kingstown, in an urgently called conference in the residence of the Papal Nuncio, Monsignor O'Delly, Da Souza did not hold back the full force of his fury and delight.

The Nuncio himself had just returned from reporting personally to the Vatican on alarmist reports of the rising threat of Fundamentalism in the hemisphere. The Secretary of State was alarmed and passed his concern on to the Pope. However, the pontiff, accustomed to hearing doom-laden reports of imminent disasters of every description in every part of the world, only worried these days if he got a report of good news. That would be the sure sign there was something wrong; and woe betide the prelate who brought him such bizarre tidings.

He was relieved to hear that that was all it was: that religious orthodoxy, and indeed orthodox politics were being undermined by a fanatical Bible belt, business-orientated and extremely well-financed group bent on corrupting the scriptures and achieving world domination. Its clandestine plan was to take over the entire, democratically elected government and imbue the country, and eventually the universal church, with its own weird brand of Christianity. He was intrigued to learn that it was one of their own religious orders – calling itself the United Church and already known to Vatican officials on other accounts – that was successfully playing the others at this game.

The Pope and secretary made alternatively smiling and serious faces to reassure the Nuncio that they were taking it all seriously as they hunched together and each one made the very same comment: 'what a world!' A little niggling thought made the Nuncio wonder if the matter had justified his coming all the way back to Rome. What the Pope had really thought about it nobody knew.

'I tell you, Monsignor,' the bishop went on now to O'Delly, 'it is a fact. I have definite evidence of heresy and mismanagement there. My assistant now tells me he wants to resign his position at the Palace. He is besotted with them and wants to go back and join them! I asked him what made him want to do this and he says 'they must all be happy there, for what else would make them stay?' The man is sick, I tell you!'

They sent to the waiting room for the Archbishop's assistant, Fr Jaime Da Souza, a cousin, and the monsignor asked the now dreamy faced man if his hoped-for apostasy from his comfortable ecclesiastic duties, in order to spend the rest of his life with a mendicant order specialising in hard physical labour, penance and mutual soul-tormenting, was true.

'It is true, Monsignor. I can't wait to get back there.'

That was enough for the Nuncio. He dismissed the assistant and said to Da Souza in a profound tone. 'It is either all good or all bad. I will have to visit them to see for myself. In the meantime you may inform the government that the Vatican is going to strictly monitor and curtail the activities of the United Church.'

Da Souza left the Nuncio's house, feeling that in the matter of the politically sensitive activities of Sang's crew the big wheels were at last beginning to turn. He would be able to show the government that he was acting on their concerns. He knew that it was the sect's economic success in particular that worried the government, for it only showed up their own incompetence in such matters. He wanted to persuade the government that the Catholic religion was really a harmless activity, that in fact it was a bonus to the government, through fostering the virtues of allegiance, respect and sometimes, let it be faced, fear in people. And after all, at the end of the day he, the Archbishop, and nobody else, was God's representative in this country. The ruling powers would trust him because they knew that he (a cousin as well!) was on their side.

Little did Da Souza realise the real reason for the Nuncio O'Delly's desire to visit the monastery. Due to a number of factors, including a curiosity about what the Jesuits were 'up to now' – and not least a degree of envy of the assistant's discovery of inner peace and joy – O'Delly was intent on finding out what was the attraction that called the assistant back there.

His spiritual antenna had also been raised – quite a dangerous development at the best of times for those who might have something to hide, and even more worrying in these circumstances because it meant that Rome might soon, indeed, be taking a more serious interest in matters. He had been struck by the assistant's happiness because it was a condition so rare in life, in any sphere, that its presence was always to be noted. The whole affair had somewhat diminished Archbishop Da Souza's credibility in his eyes ... how could the fellow not only have allowed his right hand man to fall for some monkish spiritual *pâté de foie gras*, but not even have noticed anything different about the place? Whatever it was, it had all been right there before Da Souza's eyes and, despite his authority and experience, he had failed to recognise it or its potential danger.

What this cultic secret was he must certainly discover – and quickly – for himself.

Meanwhile back at the hospital there was extreme frustration among the sisters over the fact that the most unpleasant work, such as dressing the patients' wounds and washing the clothes, was continually being left to them while the brothers got on with more 'important' tasks such as cures and decision-making meetings. What with all this bickering and conflict over areas of responsibility (with Jane's increasing defiance of Josephine adding to the tension) people were overwrought. The fact was that the unsanitary, inadequate conditions were lately being made worse by the massive new intake.

The hospital was a former steam-powered sugar factory. Sang was always holding out before the sisters the big promise – years now in the offing – that all the factory paraphernalia would *very soon* be removed and the building smartened up leaving them with a spic and span hospital. Meanwhile the patients lay on *bagasse* or cane waste mattresses wedged in between the rusting heat exchangers, flywheel gearing, broken liner pipes, cracked vacuum pans, multiple-effect evaporators, clarifying tanks and gutters that once, instead of blood, carried juice crushed from cane.

At every turn were flapping pieces of corrugated iron that were meant to be walls but whose tendency to fly through the building in strong winds injured as many patients and staff than any disease epidemic or domestic violence at Christmas time. The early-industrial grandeur of the old mill seemed to have gone to some brothers' heads, and a time-and-motion study which had been launched with such great fuss and corporate optimism meant now that there were precarious climbs up slippery ramps for staff and walking-wounded alike to beds on higher levels (also considered to be the most sanitary part of the hospital), with some patients in this overcrowded Home of Healing resting on platforms high up in the rafters.

To the deafening background noise of the ancient, fume puffing paraffin power generator the sisters had to take themselves and their blind, crippled or otherwise incapacitated patients along a perilous route by the steam engine, doing their best to dodge the rusty spikes and protruding nails, ducking under the very low ramps that led to the elevated areas of final repose. Here, more long-disused equipment such as syrup tanks and centrifugal separators overshadowed everything but their own shadows. At the same time, this scene of mechanical chaos represented for the patients a sort of assurance that they were in a place which had once possessed some importance for mankind.

In order to overcome the problem of the difficult ascent to the top of the building, Bro's Capricious and Malicious had lately devised a most shaky but grand mechanical system. Pulled by milling wheels reconditioned by these same two all-round mechanics, dubiously reliable but still-functional chain pulleys that had once ferried heavy equipment skywards to the molasses separation section now dragged up there (and perhaps out of greater harm's way) the more serious spine, neck and limb injured patients with as much stability and ease of motion as possible.

'It was like some medieval torture chamber, making Christian ministry at that place appear to be the very lowest circle of Dante's Hell.' Such was the description used by a shocked visiting journalist in a cosmopolitan newspaper. He had reported back to New York, with the zeal of a recent convert to atheism aligned to the need for a good story, on the activities of the dubious 'charity'. It was due to this reporter's dedicated campaign to 'expose the truth' that the story began to circulate in the civilised world of a slave camp using diabolical machinery run by a sadistic, enclosed sect; where guileless, superstitious peasants were 'inculcated' with the bizarre ideas of a mad, futuristic belief system using medieval (and modern) instruments of torture such as punishment racks, confinement cages, water immersion tanks, electrical shock equipment and so forth. 'Sect dupes sponsors with false display of humanity to further their obscurantism and sadomasochism' and 'Worse than the worse days of slavery' were their sensational headlines.

The surgery (the former factory manager's office) was a very busy place these days, with occasional visits from an 'always-greeted-with-immense-relief' qualified surgeon from distant Kingstown – with most of the minor surgery being done either by the sisters themselves or some very keen brothers (Capricious and Malicious were the most frequent volunteers).

Now they also had to deal with the new intake, not to mention all those who were also disturbed in mind and spirit. They were having to find space to contain them all while they awaited their particular treatment. For it was agreed that it would be therapeutic for everybody if all the sick people were kept together in the hospital. The mentally disturbed and physically injured or diseased would find peace in helping to care for each other. The overspill could sleep on the floor, or even outside – all were free to come in and out of the hospital and enjoy the freedom of the monastery grounds.

This they were keen to do; it was noteworthy that while outside, instead of casually wandering about they all seemed to seek out some favourite spot where they would sit quietly, sniffing the air as if sensing some mysterious 'whiff of fragrance'.

Bro Obnoxious had found a new vocation in ministering to the sick. He had, in fact, now been appointed as hospital registrar, to solve the problem of Sanctus having to work with him, to keep him busy and to get him out from under the other monks' feet.

He decided straight away that a tiny office was too small for his important job, and sensing a new challenge in the increased numbers, demanded that he have some of the building's 'wasted space'. He had always believed that his powers of estimation were far more reliable than the laborious, and notoriously inaccurate job of counting. He was particularly scathing of all the records that had been compiled to date. He dispensed immediately with all current, most likely 'misleading' data, sending the papers to the incinerator. To put his 'computing' skills into full effect, he would have to be out and about much of the time, which would give him the opportunity to oversee other brothers' work and shortcomings.

He was also giving Mother Josephine the benefit of his wisdom on holistic matters.

'Saving the soul is much more important than all this medical stuff,' he declared.

He had spoken crossly, not seeing what could possibly justify Josephine's rudeness and impatience with him. These unfortunate people were clearly far more in need of spiritual redemption than bodily health (why else were they crying out to the Lord for mercy all the time?). Spiritual regeneration was by far a more worthy task than looking after bodily needs – however many graces difficult, smelly, off-putting jobs might obtain for one. He would, he said, spend his shifts counselling the patients; particularly those undergoing serious operations. After all, he would hate to have been somehow responsible for even one poor soul among them going to hell.

'All *you* have to do is feed, wash and give them a few medicines while they wait for their turn to go for the real cure; a little chat with a brother. That doesn't call for a great exercise of ability,' he said, keeping up the pressure.

'The sisters,' said Josephine to Capricious, ignoring Obnoxious, 'would really like to access some of the secret funds of community. Investment money seems to be available for farming, for I heard about that expensive scheme to get in tractors so that you men could bask in the sun. Oh, if it had not been for Eamon and Dan downing tools and threatening self-mutilation the community would probably be bankrupt by now.'

'Bask in the sun!'

Obnoxious pretended he was outraged.

'Meditate and contemplate you mean! I believe that Thomas Aquinas says women are incapable of that!'

'Not true – he only said, following Aristotle, that they are inferior. Anyway, taking care of the sick is a sacred obligation. It comes before meditation, contemplation or even cures.'

'Saving their souls is the most sacred obligation,' interrupted Obnoxious again. 'Curing their bodies is an easy thing. I have already cured some people here of their ailments simply by my presence. I have walked into the sickroom and a diseased or demented person has immediately got up from his bed and walked out. It happened this morning! Words weren't even necessary – simply my attendance. Wait till you see – they'll all be out of here in no time – including the shirkers.'

'Look,' said Josephine, 'what has a "cure" got to do with this poor old man? He is breathing his last now. I can feel the life going out through his gangrenous arm even as I hold it. It is more important to die than to live. Ask him if this is not the greatest moment of his life. We have had a long conversation and he has begged me not to try and cure him. Good health only keeps a person tied up in this futile human existence. Life comes through death. Have any of the dead ever come back – moaning about how much they miss it all, pleading to be allowed to stay in this world? Only the Lord ever came back. But he didn't stay around for too long, did he?'

'You are a heretic, Mother Josephine! He cured people. The

diseased, blind, dumb, paralytic, the possessed, the dead. He cured them all. *And he did not use a single medicine!* He just gave them faith. I will show you. I will cure their souls and their bodies will cure themselves.'

Obnoxious loved taking the high moral ground. His face glowed with self-righteousness even as his eyes held the glint of spite.

Josephine spoke with Christian patience. 'Attempts to defeat death and disease will always fail. Our Lord was showing us that we should improve our lives – but not avoid our eventual going. Of course quality of life is improved by alleviating the symptoms – by postponing the dire effects. I am all for that. Which is why I say give us some money to clean up this place and to get some vital supplies.'

'Ah, minimalism! Another sin!' said Obnoxious; 'It's no wonder the newspapers say horrible things about us. And Sister Jane certainly would not agree with you! If it were not for her all your patients would be dead by now. Isn't she famous for getting Dan O'Toole off the drink?'

'Yes – she is famous for that miracle. Seminars and articles about Dan O'Toole's cure from the drink abound in learned journals. But if Sister Jane gets her way, we will become the Spare Bits and Pieces Biotechnological Hospital Incorporated, everything spic and span and breaking records for innovative brain surgery and efficient body–soul transplants. But you can't do even one of these things without having the incurable and the dying in the first place, both to provide, and to be recipients of the parts. So we will always need to have the hopeless cases with us.'

Capricious interrupted their talk.

'Let us see what we can do for that poor man with the gangrene. I think the arm will definitely have to go. Maybe the leg.'

He sighed in pretended exhaustion. 'Another day's work!'

The jollity reflected his optimistic approach even in the most pessimistic of situations.

Josephine reminded him that they had run out of anaesthetic.

Capricious was upbeat. After all, his name was that of someone of unpredictable ways, a person never bound by the rules and always positive, even if sometimes a taker of unnecessary risks.

'There is that new serum derived from the Great Bloated Fish the fishermen catch in the bay. The Jah assure me it has been used for generations by very old women for the worst medical cases. I wonder if we should give it a try? They say it induces a trancelike state in the subject and allows one to do what one likes with the patient.'

'Isn't that the zombie drug?' asked Josephine, concerned.

'Yes. Of course it has probably been used for evil purposes in the past. But I guarantee that, given a positive result here, the chemical giants will be flocking in and taking it away to their laboratories. We are in the front line of the war against incurable diseases – the cutting edge of medical advancement.'

Josephine shook her head. She knew there was no stopping Capricious who, even if he was impetuous, never retreated from the most difficult, painful or unpleasant of situations.

Josephine gave another of her morale-building sermons, which usually covered a multitude of (methodological) sins.

'Well, anything that will make Sylvester feel better. He could not be worse off than he is right now. You see, that which is most awful is usually the most productive of good. In fact that is why God allows evil. The cruelty of nature, the killing of the weak is what creates the beauty of the world. The very worst things are the most beautiful of all. The sinner, the murderer, the plunderer, has the deepest insight into beauty. The sadistic torturer does his job most thoroughly as he observes the integrity and splendour of his victim.

'Bro Gerry enlightened me about evil when I went to him once with a theological problem. He explained it beautifully, in his own way. I have remembered every word to this day. He defined evil as the breaking of things asunder from their original, natural state. Violence is a wonderful force, he said. The attack of the sperm on the ovum, followed by the destruction of zillions of microbes and cells creates new entities that eventually bring forth the most beautiful creation of all – a newborn babe. And with what self-sacrifice does nature herself – in the clash and annihilation of com-peting life forms – advance that same babe to become the white-haired, wise, intuitive, peacemaking old man or woman. This elderly sage has attained his or her dignified, glor-ified state not by means of silence, peace, inaction and hands-off, wishy-washy Ut-opian ideals, but by the degenerative processes and ravages of ruinous, twisted yet wise nature. The experience of the All-Won-derful which, we are told, mystics such as Bro Orbeck find in "nothingness", is the result not of peaceful inactivity but of a painful disassembling and destruction of their inner selves.'

She sighed long and deeply, rolled up her sleeves and almost shouted, 'So let us attack Sylvester's arm with gusto and confid-ence, for Providence will bring order out of chaos.'

Obnoxious had been listening carefully. He was extremely pleased that he now had clear evidence of the proliferation of heresy in the community, emanating from its official theologian, Gerry. There was nothing he loved more than bringing instances of careless theological talk to the notice of superiors. He spoke uncharacteristically carefully, making sure that he had got all his facts right.

'What you are really saying is that even if Sylvester is not cured, if his last state is worse than his first and he is turned into a complete zombie by our treatment, it will be a better Sylvester than the one who existed before? That is the sense I am getting from what you are saying – that evil is really good. '

'Yes,' answered Josephine defiantly, 'he will experience the stark truth that not only is he very ill, but also something that he and many do not fully appreciate – that such conditions as good health and personal happiness really do exist. He will then acknowledge in the depth of his being, as never before, the beauty of good health and the marvels of the properly working human body. His consciousness will be deepened. It is the first step on the long journey of spiritual perfection to knowledge of the Absolute Good – who is the Perfection of all States, by the slow, tedious path of imperfection. Yes, evil serves a good purpose.'

The operation on Sylvester took place soon afterwards, with the Bloated Fish serum having the positive effect of making the patient, while remaining awake, completely compliant and inert. Capricious was joyous as he held the diseased leg aloft after what had been a surprisingly easy procedure. For a triumphant moment it was as if only the leg – and not Sylvester – existed. Sylvester meanwhile stared nonplussed at the leg and muttered that he would miss it terribly. Capricious asked him if it had hurt.

'I felt all de pain, bud me feel somet'ing better than pain – me feel me go through damnation an' high water and back. Me fear de pains o' hell no more. Me free now. Nobody do de wors' on me 'gain. Me stronger than the strongest man in de world! Me *giant*! Me heap-up warrior, me champion of the downheart. Me move all injustice from de Earth! You lot 'ere – you doan' do t'ings de right way at all! Here – clear hup dis mess. *Me* give de orders now!'

'He'll be back to his old self in a little while,' said Sister Josephine, taken aback by Sylvester's apparent complete cure, as well as his profound coherence and new, uncharacteristic attitude of rebellion and assertiveness.

It was Gerry's turn now to preach at meals. Suppertime would be grim for the brothers this week.

'It is forever the intellectuals against the boors,' he said, somewhat flippantly.

He had lately been experiencing a heightened intellectual restlessness. He had decided that he was going to use this opportunity to stir things up. He was becoming more and more antipathetic to the *pious* ethos of the place. He was fed up with the lack of intellectual activity, the pervasive atmosphere of mental stagnation that some liked to call prayerfulness and closeness to God. And when they were not praying they were usually preocc-upied with mundane physical activities that, however useful and praiseworthy, belied any worthwhile questioning of the meaning of life.

Many times, even while under the code of silence, he would question things with facial grimaces and sign language, but would never get any response! He could not make out what they thought of him or his theological reflections. That is, if they ever thought about him (or anything) at all! He mused that probably – as far as the rest of the community was concerned – he was just another 'intellectual', given to wild, meaningless flights of fancy that were quite irrelevant to the doing of good and the 'saving of souls'. But – in a strange kind of way – such incomprehension was for Gerry a life-giving encouragement, spurring him on to make a definite mark, however ephemeral, on the stupidity of the world.

They all sighed deeply as he spoke in his terse voice. The Jah were trying to drown it out, drumming rhythms of imaginary tunes in their heads; some ex-pats looked up at the rusty tin ceiling and mulling over schemes of building improvement, while others indulged idle daydreams of escape from this way of life they had inexplicitly chosen.

'The only trouble is, *who* are the intellectuals and *who* are the boors?

'We all know that the Baptist and his crowd were considered the boors of their day. The administrators and respectable clergy were the intellectuals! But it is always the boor who has the new ideas! The uncouth are the ones who are not tied to formal ways or are afraid of offending. They live in the wilderness, eating bad food and – let us admit it – sometimes taking what legally is not theirs. They dress like criminals, speak in a rough manner and for a considerable length of time hang about conspiratorially in the desert or in the undergrowth where they fashion their revolutionary plans. They are accused of many things – murder, banditry, threatening rich people, witchcraft. Ordinary people live in great fear of them and many myths and legends tell of their terrible deeds. Folk worry that they will move into their district – even into the house next door. They are, in fact, just like we were in the old days ... And now I ask you, who are *we* afraid of? Are we afraid of the intellectuals? Or are we afraid of the boors ...?'

He went silent and there was a spluttering as someone caught his food in his throat. Who, or what, was Gerry getting at? The damned intellectual was always coming out with contentious, outrageous statements, raising hackles. Here he was now, disturbing their prayers and trying to make them think 'politically', stirring up class warfare and probably hoping to set brethren against brethren in the pursuit of some personal agenda.

'Jezebels. Jeremiahs. Whores of Babylon!' his voice thundered across the hall. He banged the podium, making everybody jump in their seats and proceeded to decry 'right-wing, fundamentalist, religious fascisti', wolves in sheep's clothing undermining the good work of the 'true, invisible church'. Clergy were the pawns of those 'principalities and powers' that controlled society – as well as the United Church!

Sang looked at Gerry and an old suspicion came back. The man was perspiring all over; his hands shook and there was a look of paranoia in his eyes. He remembered when Gerry had first presented himself for interview. He had the same feverish look then, talked incessantly about the 'mysterious reality' that was (the) 'Ultimate Being'; this 'being' (God was not 'a' being) controlled all his 'higher thought' and in fact determined a great many of his actions. Sang, even then, had wondered not only about his theology, but about his state of mind.

Gerry was a monk who would never settle into the monastic spirit of peaceful silence. They had always given him his head with his avant-garde intellectual ventures, believing that all talents should be used according to the old Jesuit motto *Ad Majorem Dei Gloriam*. This devout open-mindedness had been severely tested lately as another recent project of Gerry's had caused unease.

It was an 'experiment' that Gerry performed alone in the privacy of the meditation room. It involved co-joining in his psyche the 'spirit-possession' of traditional Pentecostalism with a purely intellectual concentration on the eternal dogmas of the Church. He had claimed:

'We intone the articles of faith; we sing praises to them; we even 'meditate' on them – but we don't really believe them.'

His induced, trancelike state united the two roads to the divine – the emotional and the cerebral. As he prayed in the spirit, he chanted aloud all the doctrines of the church (in Latin) from memory. In this way, uniting the innate and instinctive with the abstract, he would reach the point of 'religious saturation'. He would thus be able at last to divest himself of all the unnecessary mental and emotional paraphernalia of religion. By expunging the emotional and mental garbage of the old-fashioned religious experience, he could enter into the 'real spiritual world'.

His experiment – which he officially called The New Spiritual Exercises of Gerry Of Jah (or 'the method') – would also eliminate, by a process of attrition, all those 'bad and incorrect religious attitudes' – always to be found in the faithful – caused by their predisposition for having 'beliefs' and 'feelings'. Forever rendered redundant would be the tendency to divide truth into its multiple subdivisions, ignoring the fundamental unity of all truth. As he had put it to Sang, it would help to develop in the religious person 'the emotionally purified, intellectually honest rationality and humanism previously the prerogative of the atheist'. It would be the end of mysticism and of philosophy. The practitioner would enter into that state, so rarely achieved by anybody in this life, of a real, utter belief in God without the need for thought, reflection or any conscious effort.

(He had appealed to Sang to be allowed to partake of a harmless intoxicating substance while entering these uncharted territories, as a 'safety net'. This was how he was allowed to smoke cigarettes again, whilst praying in the 'new way'.)

Although Gerry insisted that the experiment was going well, the 'method' had begun to cause concern for his physical as well as emotional health. Much damage was inflicted on the furniture in the meditation room. However there were some positive results. To Sang's satisfaction, the Jah folk were now showing interest in something other than their own obsessive rituals. They had heard stories of Gerry's esoteric methodology and were trying out some of his techniques. They were impressed in particular by what they believed to be accompanying paranormal phenomena. Often there was a strange, inexplicable light on Gerry's face when he emerged from meditation. There were those impressive scenes of chaos and broken, thrown-about objects within the 'room of peace', as though Gerry had been joined by some spirit of (creative) destruction. The Jah folk now, Bro Sang enthused, wanted to learn Latin too!

But how everyone hated it when Gerry gave his long, intellectual diatribes at mealtimes. They closed their ears completely, the Jah brethren concentrating as a last resort on their newly learnt Latin phrases, intoning in their heads ambitious attempts at Gregorian chant.

They were all suddenly surprised by another breach of the rules of silence as Eamon interrupted Gerry, shouting:

'That day is nigh upon us! They are coming in their sinful multitudes to inhabit da land. And da place below da earth. They will come forth from da bowels of da earth to do their dirty work. And we will gnash our teeth and remember Zion!'

He shook all over as he said these words and there was a great strain and paleness on his face. He collapsed into a heap on the table and appeared to go to sleep.

Bro Sang looked up at Gerry and nodded. The spiritual talk was over. Eamon had obviously been receiving – in his literacy lessons – too much biblical language for his own good.

Asissy and Sanctus had gone into the tool shed for a private talk.

'I am going to sin,' shouted Asissy.

They had not realised that the rabbi was there, quietly working away on his woodwork project.

The presence of this particular guest was something of an unspoken community secret. It was as if there were some taboo in talking about the fellow. This was probably as much due to social embarrassment as the difference of religion. He was from 'out-of-town'. He appeared well educated, possessing an air of sophistication not found in any of the brethren (not even in Sang or Hans). Whenever he appeared 'in the open' he had a calm, unhurried manner that contrasted with the average brother's busied look of prayerful determination.

Perhaps he had, indeed, been dismissed from his post as rabbi in some respectable community. In such cases, it was often a very shameful incident. It meant that he couldn't go back to face his own people. It was possible, also, that he was a financier or tycoon of some sort; that he had been in a position of influence and had double-crossed powerful people. In that case, a Christian monastery would be a very clever choice of hiding place.

There were other speculations. For instance, that he had millions stacked away. There was a rumour – originating from a conversation a brother had had with him – that in his youth he had resided in one of the world's wickedest cities, observing its fleshpots. He would have mixed with various con artists there, himself perhaps picking up some of the talents of the confidence trickster.

One instance of his 'skill' was his ability to make every monk he happened to have a few words with forget that he was even talking to a Jew. Monks, apparently, let down their guard in his presence and would proceed to chatter away with him as if he were a fully fledged member of community!

As time went by, many began to wonder why he hadn't moved on. Other such temporary 'guests' – people whose situation was usually euphemistically described as being 'on retreat', 'partaking of rest and recuperation' and so on – always disappeared after a limited period of residence. He was beginning to be seen as a long-term guest, even as a sort of prisoner. Was he being kept there against his will? Indeed, most sinister of all, was pressure being applied on him to convert; to become a member of the United Church?

Yet Asissy and Sanctus – when they had gone into the shed for their supposedly secret conversation – did not feel discomfited or in any need to become silent when they saw him.

He was aged about forty, wore a navy corduroy smock, and had a small, rotund middle and brown beard. His aura was that of a friendly person, one well versed in the ways of the world and people. Yet there was a twinkle in his eye that suggested an ultimately disinterested attitude to worldly or material things.

The shed was filled with artefacts he had made. There were all sorts of useful objects. Some had been commissioned by the community, but many were of his own inspiration and were mainly for use in the hospital and schools. They were noteworthy for their simple, innovatory excellence. For the local schools there were tiny, portable tripod tables for pupils to put their work on and small, fold-up stools which, as with the tables, allowed double the maximum number of pupils to take their place in the classroom. These also lent themselves to being taken home to assist in not only doing the homework but as useful, additional pieces of furniture around the house, such as dining tables etc.

For the hospital he had made ingenious portable toilets for the disabled that converted into admirable wheelchairs. There were cheap, pliable bamboo crutches with a spring in their step that even the totally incapacitated would find easy and enjoyable to use, as their elasticity propelled the invalid along. There were very attractive, colourful begging bowls for the blind, deaf and dumb that guaranteed a good income if only because of their eye-catching design that, through a myriad of colours, bespoke love, openness and generosity. There were various religious artefacts, miniature arks, an original, wooden temple, carved animals such as a ram, whale, fishing boats, shepherd's crooks etc.

All these items the rabbi had been exhorting Sang to display to local unemployed craftsmen who, he said, could reproduce them using the monastery's name as a trade mark for extra selling clout. That would go down very well indeed with foreign tourists, keen to acquire something associated with a real, genuine monastery.

'I am telling you – I am going to commit a sin. It is the only way! Will you tell Bro Sang that I am going off the rails? Then he will have to let me dress in a skirt! At the very least, he can leave me in my old job. I know it is blackmail. There is no other way. He has to take my spiritual well-being into account. I am desperate. Many sins are committed out of desperation. Who can blame me? I did not make myself. I will sin and it will be Bro Sang's fault.'

'Asissy, man, cool it,' said Sanctus.

The rabbi put his smoothing plane to one side. He was somewhat hesitant to intervene in an internal Christian dispute, but he obviously felt that he too had to help soothe the excitable brother. They both looked at the rabbi now as he began to speak to them from another, seemingly distant world, his thick, rolling accent immediately pouring oil on troubled waters.

'Bruthur Sunctus us unly tryung tu hulp, Usussy! Hu us pruvunting yo frum mukung purhups thu buggust mustook uf yur luf. Lustun tu hum, hu pruys frum thu hurt.'

His words made them wonder. They seemed to say much more than their literal meaning. It was as though he was speaking to them in a code. He was saying something far and beyond what their ears were hearing. This mysterious message – if they could decode it – they knew would go to the very depths of their souls.

Asissy spoke, more subdued now. 'It's not my fault that I'm like this.'

The rabbi laughed, softly. 'Thut us u spurutully ummuture wuy uf tulkung! Lustun tu yur unnur sulf.'

Asissy stared at him. The man's words resounded in his ears. It was an incomprehensible message, bespeaking a long forgotten, purer motivation – a reassurance and a warning.

Sanctus spoke urgently. 'Asissy, man. Yo need to go for swim in de sea. It feel *no* better after yo sin than before! Yo feel de urge more after! W'en me sin wid me hate for rich man in de past me feel no better, only mo' bitter. So me give up hate an' resentment! Dat is how me reach dis stage. Yo feel good an' happy after yo resist sin!'

'Only purtly tru, Sunctus,' said the rabbi, his voice suddenly become downbeat.

The strangely spoken man was now leaning on the bench. His whole frame seemed to constrict under a heaviness that came over him. He raised his head, his brown eyes dull with an old, familiar gloom.

'Ut us ulso u questun uf lurnung tu luv tu full bud. Thu cuuse uf ull thu surruw un thu wurld us thut puple chuse uftur buty ruthur thun uglunuss! Wu shuuld umbruce thu ugly, thu unluvuble, thu uvul. Us suun us wu uwuke, thun ull duy lung, thun us wu gu tu uur nughtly rupuse wu shuuld tuk tu ur hurts thu bud. Thun wu wull sue thut thu ugly us butuful und wu wull sun nu mure.'

The two monks stared at him. His words were the strangest, yet truest (no matter that they had not fully comprehended them) that they had ever heard in their lives!

Sadness now appeared in the man's eyes and he spoke in such a low voice that they had to strain to hear him.

'U cure fur thu prude uf munkund – thut us whut thus luf us. Ut us thu pruce wu puy fur lufung. Wu shuuld tuk uthurs' fulurus us ur un. Thu must shurt, unfulfullud, wrutched luf shuuld bu whut uttructs ur udmurutun; surruw shuuld bu ur durust hup. Ut us un uxpuruncung und studuing u shurt und dusullusunud luf thut wusdum us lurnt.'

He sighed again, like someone who had experienced a great failure or disappointment, whose hopes and dreams were no more.

It was now that Sanctus and Asissy realised that they were talking to someone who inhabited another reality. He was some-one who was not a Christian – and yet they reflected with rever-ence on his words. They had listened to him with an intensity and seriousness that they never experienced even when listening to Sang's personal saint's Feast Day sermon.

Asissy, for some reason known only to himself, but mainly because he knew that this man had seen through his shenanigans, saw fit to insult the rabbi as he stormed out of the room.

'You are a blackguard,' he shouted at him, to the horror of Sanctus.

'Don't pay him no heed,' said Sanctus, trying to make amends,

'He is bad example of a Christian.'

A new rumour about the rabbi began to go the rounds because of what happened after the conversation in the workshop. The whole community had known about their talk almost immediately. This was by the means that not even the most secretive of illicit enterprises or cryptic of espionage codes can circumvent – the ephemeral, disorganised, haphazard yet infallible process known universally as 'did-you-hear'.

The word now was that the rabbi was a subversive. Worse than a crook, he was a religious oddball pursuing some obscure, personal agenda. For he was not above stooping to manipulating the most feeble-minded members of the community. The biggest offence, it was said, was that the rabbi had *influenced* Asissy and Sanctus. The carpentry (a rather odd occupation in that day and age) was clearly a cover for something more questionable, less wholesome.

Asissy had immediately requested to be taken off his vestment/flower duties. He asked to work with the pigs, feed them, and muck out the sties. All this had, apparently, the added attraction for him of working with the smelly and dirty Brothers Eamon and Dan. (Hans once said that those two's lack of personal hygiene had been the only discernible sign that they might at least be at the beginning of the long road to sanctity.) The community regime had agreed with alacrity to Asissy's request, impressed by the new man. They were astonished to see the monk going around in the following days covered from head to toe in dung and muck, and smelling like nothing on Earth.

The phenomenon of uncleanliness spread amongst the brothers. It was as if dirt had become the new fashion, a craze. Over a period of weeks there developed a total lack of bodily propriety, neatness and hygiene in everyday aspect of living. People would spill fluids, drop food and have any number of other unpleasant accidents (always creating a huge mess) in places both sacred and profane. It was not only Asissy who was smelly now, but all the monks. They began to dress slovenly, to omit bodily washing and to use coarse language during recreation periods. The novelty of the initial phase, when it was considered 'wonderful to see a new sort of asceticism flowering', gave way to alarm on the part of the administration when the whole monastery appeared to be slipping into the ways of a slum tenement. Now 'asceticism' became transgression in the eyes of authority.

Concern increased when Sanctus, too, began to display uncharacteristic behaviour. He started to let his hair grow back into unwashed dreadlocks. He became less happy. He was agitated. No longer was the world 'lovable'. He muttered about great injustices. He asked who were the 'real' sinners. He spoke of millstones around necks and the appropriateness of cutting off 'sinning limbs'. Brother Obnoxious – Sanctus's chief tormentor – found to his wonder that his snide remarks to Sanctus now brought forth not silence or blessings but uncharacteristic, 'unholy' rebuffs.

The fathers, already concerned over the breakdown in standards of hygiene, were even more dismayed to see this 'relapse' of their only for-definite saint. His sanctity, once displayed as a proud trophy to important visitors to the United Church, had imploded in the throes of some interior crisis. The deprivation he had endured in his childhood was clearly making itself felt again. His prayer life had probably been only a means of repressing bad memories. There were suggestions that he had been a fraud all along. That his reputed supernatural powers and 'holy' deeds were merely the sublimated products of a suppressed, psychopathic nature. He had abused his supernatural powers. How else – other than by levitation – could those calumnious and offensive suggestions have appeared high up on walls and ceilings out of human reach? And how else, other than by telekinesis, could the leaking of complete dossiers of information to the Kingstown media about everything that happened in community be taking place?

What caused even greater suspicion was Sanctus's proposal, made during assembly – to *remove* all the graffiti from walls and ceilings. He said that it was about time somebody did something about getting rid of the insulting scrawls. This was obviously a sinister use of his telepathic powers. It proved to them that he *knew* that they had been gossiping about his graffiti antics. He was also showing them, in a twisted way, that there was nothing they could hide from him.

All this bizarre behaviour, the puzzling conduct of Asissy, the unsaintly acts of Sanctus, the obsession with 'self-improvement' through dirt, 'inner truth' and disregard for etiquette, was now being officially condemned as 'antisocial activity'. Official disapproval began with casual, then strident, and finally authoritative admonishments at meals.

That a number of positive developments had taken place that might be due to the rabbi's 'chat' was never conceded at all. For instance, Asissy seemed to have forgotten all about that stated intention of his to 'sin'.

Some time afterwards Sanctus said to him, 'Bro Asissy – what were yo going to do dat time when yo said yo was going to sin?'

'Sin, Bro Sanctus? Did I say I was going to sin? Ah, if only I was pure enough to be able to sin! Only a holy person can sin. No, I am an unclean person, Sanctus. I am dirty. I rejoice in my disgusting nature. I am too dirty now to be *able* to sin.'

He lowered his head and struck his chest a severe blow, which sent him falling backwards to the ground. There he lay for some time, embracing the earth, kissing the dust.

When he arose he spoke in a joyful voice. 'The man in the workshop made me forget about the problem of my body. I once thought that I had aimed high – for pure spirituality – for beauty. But it was a hopeless delusion. I realise – especially from working with Eamon and Dan – that nothing is beautiful. Now I have a real and proper pride, not in bodily allures but in life's dirty and disgusting things. I can no longer commit a sin of the body, for the body has lost its attraction for me.'

He struck his chest again, this time less hard. His voice became quieter. 'Oh, how I love dirt, sin, vice. Even pride! I am proud to be a dirty fellow. I hate humility now, for to have humility you have to be clean and pure.'

Sanctus had been listening dispassionately. After that chat with the rabbi he, also, had been analysing his own motives. He realised that, like Asissy, he had been clinging to the Beautiful, the Pure and the True. But that was to neglect the essential ingredients of real life – unattractiveness, rejection, scapegoating, banishment. And just as Asissy had once clung to bodily beauty and now chose the opposite, he too had now decided to cling to something equally, or even more attractive than ugliness and dirt – sin.

He would cure his tendency to luxuriate in feel-good emotions. He had told himself that just as Asissy was now experiencing his 'bad' body, he would practise feeling 'bad' emotions and 'bad spirituality'. He would gain the contempt and hostility of the community. This would be achieved not by bad deeds, but paradoxically by doing positive acts, 'good deeds'. These always, if carefully chosen, can rub people up the wrong way. He would find some deep-rooted, near-at-hand injustice and confront the community with it. He would challenge the 'powers' of the community. That could lead to a final, catastrophic humiliation for him and his reputation. It would put paid to his previous image of being a 'nice guy'. He would even end up hating himself, like Bro Asissy.

Asissy walked away, dragging his feet and kicking up dust.

Sanctus sat down and closed his eyes. After a short prayer he was able to see the old sugar mill where the sick were healed. At that moment, as he found himself looking down from a great height, a dishevelled man of about thirty with one leg was running with a sort of hopping motion towards a group of people at the outside gate. They must have been relatives or friends, so eagerly were they awaiting him. Another satisfied client!

Then he turned his eyes towards the building at the end of the mill where the mentally ill received their treatment. All was quiet and calm there, except for the low hum of monks having 'little chats' with various disturbed people. Looking down through the roof to a corner where one such session was in progress, he was able to see that the patient – Victor Jimenez – was at that moment realising that his madness, which had made him an outcast in his village, was caused not by any personal fault but by his gifts. It was his own extraordinarily insightful, rational and sympathetic nature that had been the cause of all his troubles! It was the folk back in the village who were really mad. He was feeling better already!

He floated over to the admin office. Sang, Hans and McCall were in conference. He could see and hear them discussing a notification that had come that day from the Ministry of Internal Affairs. Another inspection was in the offing! This time it was a Health & Safety inspection. He had never heard of this kind of inspection. Apparently, legislation had been brought in the day before ordering the immediate closure of all institutions not complying with the new requirements. One of these was that every member of staff employed in residential institutions had to present their qualifications and certificates for the work they undertook. So – for instance – Sang would have to produce a Senior Management Course diploma; McArthur a teaching certificate (even for his lecturing in theology – though everyone knew that he had no academic qualifications in the subject); Dan and Eamon would have to pass physical fitness tests; the brothers and sisters in the 'hospital' would have to prove that they were qualified doctors or nurses; while those employed in the 'psychiatric' unit would be expected to have psychiatric and psychology degrees – and so on.

Dey have a point, thought Sanctus, wondering what certificate they would ask him to produce.

He now moved in a westerly direction and observed the Jah group. They were holding their daily 'reasoning', a heated discussion of some important matter while seated in a circle on the grass.

Bro Alan was speaking:

'Africa – it de *Roman* name for homeland!'

'Africa, Africa, African*us*,' they all intoned.

'No, African*we!*' corrected Alan.

The introduction of Latin into their terminology seemed to have raised their consciousness of things spiritual and legal.

Sister Gloria shouted, 'An' Rome non instigatus concession for confirmatum. Requestus Bro Orbeck investigatus conumdrum. An' why Orbeck incarceratum? Habeus Corpus!'

'Lie-berat-us, lie-berat-us, lie-berat-us,' they intoned.

Another perplexed brother declared, 'This old religion is jus' babble on! An' de Grate baby Lion, de what man, dis I land govern man, de Gray Teeth bare! All hokus pocus!'

'Is jus' babble on, babble on,' another intoned in his disillusionment.

Some proceeded to pray that their erstwhile leader, Bro Orbeck, might soon come back and lead them, finally, to the Homeland. But even as they dreamed, some remembered the rumour about Orbeck – that he was already in 'the seventh heaven' of the new religion and scarcely likely to want to return.

The Jah are treated as second class citizens in their own community! Sanctus thought to himself. *Their leader is imprisoned.* Here was an injustice! He would bring it to the leadership's attention.

It was an issue of equality, of civil rights denied!

As he moved back in an easterly direction to rejoin his body, he began to develop a headache. He could not make out anything clearly, but there appeared to be a problem directly down below him, where the old ruins were, though he could see and hear nothing.

It was the previous night that a strange phenomenon had first been noticed by locals living in the proximity of the compound. Hearing unusual noises during the early hours, they went out cautiously at first light and found that huge piles of earth had appeared at the sides of the lane, in ditches and even outside some front doors. Rumours started immediately. It was said that zombies were going about their night time business. Consequently, on following nights no person dared to go outside to investigate the sound of scurrying feet, strange grunts and whispers that continued to be heard.

Shadows were seen moving by the light of the kerosene lamps, proving to the terrified householders that, beyond any doubt, evil beings were doing their work.

chapter
six

In Kingstown the Cabinet was in session, eagerly awaiting the last, but most important item on the agenda – a motion 'that this capital city of Kingstown be renamed President Eddie City' (in honour of the famous politician who got them all their jobs).

But before that there were some vexatious matters to be dealt with. First off there was the cessation of activity by the city's largest criminal gang. This was not good for security. For ever since Dagga and his cohorts had apparently vanished, there had been not one report of any major crime in the city. This meant that people now had other things to think about – such as the government's record!

Prime Minister Raul Umberto Sr spoke. 'Our old friend Dr Wesley was spotted in the swamps recently. When questioned by police he said that he had gone there on a peace mission, as well as to conduct research for his annual seminar at the London School of Economics. He would not be the first politician to use these misfits to bolster an academic or political reputation. He has been depressed by the poor sales of his *The Socio-dynamics of the Underclass and the Demise of the Political System*. These have been zero, apart from what he sold to his students, having made it a compulsory part of the curriculum.'

They all laughed. Umberto Sr coughed loudly in exasperation.

'This government, comrades, is – I must insist – the *only* body that can be trusted to properly control and channel the activities of such dangerous gangs for the overall common good. We should be greatly concerned that Dr Wesley might indeed have persuaded them to give up crime. Then where will we be? The criminals will become respectable members of society. No longer will they be greedy for loot or for the sight of blood. Instead they will seek power and political prestige. In return for giving up crime they will be sitting in Parliament. Even here at the cabinet table. They will turn us out. That must be prevented at all costs!

'Secretary, you may record – officially – that the government intends to confront crime with all the resources at its command!'

'Hup, hup,' everyone went.

He paused momentarily, then continued, 'Do not minute what I am going to say now. Pass the word down to party officials. It's official policy – now – to encourage crime in the downtown area. That's the *best* way to monitor national security.

'Next item, comrades: Church and State. There is no doubt that this new cult calling itself the United Church is undermining not only established religion but the state itself. And more insidiously than we first suspected. Disturbing reports of a new, rival state-within-a-state are coming in. Just when it began to appear that we had got the whole country under control, some group of cowboys made up of local outcasts, American hippies, gamblers, drug dealers, crooks, even lunatics, set themselves up where we can't get at them – to dedicate themselves to that very suspicious objective called "doing good".

'It is really a challenge to our system. Do you know that numerous mad people, who were hitherto safely kept under lock and key or confined within some local place where the damage they could do was limited, are now restored to sanity and freely wander the country? They now go around speaking of matters that would never have even occurred to them before, suggesting all sorts of remedies for the country's problems, claiming that it was not man but God who had made them whole and that no one should have to bother again with mere human agencies such as government, public authorities or the established powers of this world. Some of them have come here to the capital, where they speak in joyful voices, their faces and whole bearing showing cheerfulness, confidence, lack of fear or hesitancy of any kind – sure signs of extremism and fascism!

'The cult is also curing the bodily sick in what they call their hospital. The way we are going there will be no need any more for a national medical service, for hospitals, doctors or clinics in this country. They won't even stop there – they will go on with their Utopia to make our educational service, our police, army and naval services redundant. Their experimenting with crafts and trades, encouraging the people to do their own thing and create their own employment, will render our economic programmes a thing of the past. They will certainly end up controlling the whole country, enforcing *their* standards of "right" and "wrong"; everyone to be judged, by the way, not by our decent, accredited judges whom we all know and respect, but by some airy-fairy judge sitting on a cloud up in the sky! Now doesn't that sound very suspicious! Comrades, I tell you. They, more than Dr Wesley or other political upstarts, are the ultimate obstacle to our achieving a total political victory.'

'Harrumph, harrumph,' they all shouted.

'Our special agent,' said Umberto, pulling out a sheet of paper, 'has sent us a copy of the diary notes of one Paulo Costello. Remember him – the young fella who used to write satirical articles for the anti-government newspaper under the pseudonym of "The Real President"? That stuff did so much damage to the morale of the country by making people laugh at us. Now he writes on such invidious matters as, listen, the "approaching apocalypse, a new vision, new life, divine inspiration, sovereignty of the common folk and ... Heaven. Very weird but dangerous stuff! Promising folk even more than we politicians do. As you would expect with these cults there is pornography galore. Listen to this filth from his diary – *sensual agrarian exercises, deep intercourse with Mother Nature, happy paradise of easy reproduction, great perspiration and panting.* What's that all about? They also hold ideological indoctrination sessions for malcontents and subversives called "little chats". These sound more intimidating and frightening than anything our Special Branch interrogators have ever come up with.

'If only they would stick to straightforward, old-style religious programmes – for godliness, law and order, public morals, condemnation of sinners! With them, according to this Paulo, it's a strange, subversive methodology they call "imaginative meditaton", "self-realisation", the exploration of "alternative states of mind". Imagine if we introduced that into government! We would be laughed out of town.'

'There is evidence, confirmed by our good friend and colleague Bishop Da Souza, that they are on some kind of drug,' said the Minister for Culture, Erico Mauris Jr. 'Elation, dedication to "doing good", indifference to what is going on in the real world – are sure signs of intoxication.'

'However,' said the Prime Minister, 'reading bits and pieces from this diary, it is obvious that there is also a lot of reassuring worldly ambition, internal politicking, backbiting and sexual tension pushed under the carpet there. Some of them aspire to high office in the Church and will do anything to achieve their ambition. Their leader Sang's work is clearly cut out trying to keep them all under control.'

'The day will come,' said Erico Jr, 'when one ambitious empire builder among them will make the first application for a government grant. That will be when we begin to get them in our grip.'

'Young fool,' said Raul, 'it shows how much you know. It will be one of them who will come and make us an offer we can't refuse (as the man said)!' He sighed. 'Well, at least I suppose they keep the Jah troublemakers out of circulation.'

'I am sure that those ragamuffins are totally brainwashed by now,' said Erico Mauris Sr, Minister for Internal Affairs. 'The archbishop tells me that their morale is so low they have begun learning to read and write. Contrary to modern theory, education reduces the likelihood of revolution. Clear action gives way to confused thought. When they were ruffians, they held the respect of the uneducated, illiterate populace. There was a real possibility that, under their leader, Wilbur Orbeck – that madman whose oratory enthralled the masses with talk of a politico/religious utopia – they would have taken over the country. He was only brought to his downfall by a complete, innocent faith in God! And the Jesuits!'

Loud laughs greeted his words.

'The peanut situation is being continually monitored, due to the threat to our tax revenue on imported peanuts,' said the Minister for the Economy, Raul Umberto Jr, determined to put his mark on what was his first cabinet meeting. 'I am reliably informed that these peanuts come with a secret political and religious agenda. They represent a real threat to the nation. Their particular brand is being pushed island-wide. They have even reached Kingstown markets. If the people continue to eat these peanuts, I am certain that the country will sicken and die from some as yet unclassified, deadly disease. They must be banned for Health & Safety reasons.'

'Action now, action now,' other ministers intoned, banging the table.

The Prime Minister beamed a smile. 'We are already turning the screws on this so-called United Church. Da Souza is cooperating very well. He is more than just on our side. He hates and fears them too. He says they are fundamentalist fanatics and that their insistence on this so-called doing good is not only dangerous for society – it is against true religion and bad for Christianity. In any case, comrades, the Health & Safety team will have the place condemned by next week. Court action will follow.'

'Hear hear,' the Cabinet concurred.

'Dr Wesley. What are we to decide about him?' asked the Prime Minister. 'I think it is time we had an official government policy on Dr Wesley and his activities. We need to deal with this pest once and for all. He is worse than the Opposition Party (for at least they agree with us on most things in private). An assassination might be too obvious. A character assassination campaign would be the thing. We need to bring before the public the unpatriotic, immoral nature of the man and his politics.'

'Call him a pervert. He's not married and doesn't keep a woman,' said Erico Mauris Jr.

'A peacenik,' suggested Raul Umberto Jr.

'An intellectual,' ventured Sandy Mann of External Affairs, who considered himself the country's official philosopher and detested any potential rivals in that field.

'How about all three?' asked the Prime Minister – to general acclaim.

'Now,' Raul continued in a businesslike manner, 'progress reports since the last cabinet meeting. The bad press about the crime rate. The national media have already picked up on the fact that the main criminal gang seems to have disappeared. The army's latest "trawl" through the slums certainly helped to give us some credit for that. Erico Sr, can you send out the improved crime statistics? These are always a great source of consolation, especially when they seem to contradict everyday experience.

'The WHO report. Our expert at the university assures us that the increase in disease is down to excess population. He suggests that we let typhoid, cholera and malaria continue to reduce the surplus population. In that way the exponential rise in disease rates must inevitably disappear.

'Amnesty International. The police and army have assured the media that there never has been a shoot-to-kill policy. Hurricanes. Bring home to the population, through a mass education cam-paign, that there were far more hurricanes during the colonial per-iod than under self-government. We are confident that this sit-uation of reduced hurricane frequency will continue, for God is watching over us.

'Riots Working Party. I am glad to announce that it is back in full harness and rearing to go.

'Now – a few things off the record.

'Snide remarks. These may as well stop now because I know who is behind them.

'Donations. On the up! Erico Jr has also suggested the marv-ellous idea of creating a whole series of new offences – punishable by heavy fines – as a way to raise funds. More new laws will be brought in, such as the latest Health and Safety bill, to fine people. Government is just a great way of raising money, isn't it? Sure, we even print our own money!

'Ministerial cars. Disregard the previous instruction to sign in and sign out. That crash involving one of our limousines caused serious fatalities.

'Finally, my personal jet. Thank you, comrades, for approv-ing its funding from the Defence budget. As a result, we need to merge the army and the police. They have the same job to do, after all. It's not a question of national pride – we are only a small island so why do we need a separate army and police force?'

After the ministers had left the Prime Minister got together, as usual, with his close confidant Erico Mauris Sr for sensitive dis-cussions on issues that he considered should not be raised in cab-inet so as to (his new catch phrase) protect the 'confidentiality of government'.

'Fogelman's in the monastery?' said Raul, whispering again in that sound-proof, private room.

'I'm sure of it. Paulo mentions some foreigner professing an exotic religion who, apparently, has been interfering in their affairs. I am going to make surreptitious enquiries. Not a word to anyone, mind you.'

Even Umberto Sr was whispering. 'Meanwhile,' he went on now in a more normal voice, 'we need a *comprehensive* policy for dealing with this problem. You know how over in Taran they have banned all religion? It works a treat, as the money of the poor is not siphoned off to supposed "good causes". And President H'ard Casa assures me that they look upon him now as God. He is the father of his people; he feeds them with good things and shows them the way to salvation. Unfortunately, the people of our country still love all the old hooha that goes on in church. No – to get the people to turn against the United Church we have got to think up something better than all our previous efforts and suggestions. Circulating salacious stories no longer causes scandal, but are a source of amusement and even toleration to our people, accustomed to seeing all the latest sensationalist trash from Hollywood. It leaves us with just one thing – the one unforgivable sin.'

'What is that – writing books?' asked Erico Sr sheepishly.

'No. Witchcraft, man! Black magic. It still has the power to scare the pants off even our most intelligent and sophisticated colleagues.'

Erico went quiet. He would never say it to Umberto Sr, but the subject made him very apprehensive.

'That is one thing they would never live down. Their supporters will have nothing more to do with them. Everybody wants to believe that their neighbour has the devil in them, don't they? It's a fundamental human trait. And who are more different, odder than monks? We just need to put it out that that the devil is a frequent visitor to their monastery. That he goes there for secret meetings and revelry. They will believe it all.'

He lowered his voice again to a whisper; Erico Sr noticed an uncharacteristic uneasiness in his eyes.

'It's important that the source of this rumour is untraceable. For the devil himself might come after us if he gets to hear of this ... libel against his name.'

Erico Sr, for once, said very little, grunting only in what might have been acquiescence, or might even have been dissent.

'A great plan,' he said, preparing to leave, 'I will leave it in your capable hands, Prime Minister. See you later for that drink.'

He went out the door thinking, 'Now I have something against Raul that I may use one day, when I go for his job.'

Dan was explaining to Eamon about God but was not meeting with much success.

'Ya mean God is everywhere, all 'round us and dere is nowhere where he ain't?'

'Yea,' said Dan, becoming somewhat unsure of his own meaning when his words were flung back at him like that.

'Yet ya can't even see him. Not even a little tiny bit o' him!'

'No, he is invisible,' replied Dan.

'Who told you dat?'

'Sister Jane. She says it's in all da books. Dat is why we can't see him.'

'How do dey know in da books?'

'Dose book writers have big brains. They know.'

'Is he in da sky?'

'Yea.'

'Is he unda da ground?'

'Yea.'

'Are ya sure?'

'Yea.'

Eamon's brow creased with some private thought or worry. He stared at the ground and mumbled something.

O'Toole suddenly remembered the strange words he was made to learn off by heart when he was given preparatory tuition in Ireland, on his first applying to join the monastery. He could still remember them (through rote learning) and uttered them now in a heavy monotone.

'God is *one* in the absolute sense that there cannot be another, and in the relative sense that there is not even *one* God. True in that he does not even have to exist to exist. Living in that he knows that *you* are alive; omnipotent in that he can do anything that can be done; eternal in that he has no beginning, no end and no now. Immense in that we cannot measure him in any way; incomprehensible in that he is neither here nor there; infinite in that he has no limitations; unique in that he is the supreme essence. Pure spirit in that he is *being*; simple in that he is not made up of bits and parts; unchangeable because he has told us so. Transcendent in that he is distinct from the world; perfectly happy in that he does not need anything for his happiness; sublime in that he is better even than anything that we can imagine.'

Eamon stared at Dan, as though he were seeing a wonderful, glorious being, an angel, standing before him. Then he thumped O'Toole on the back and exclaimed, 'I undastand now, Dan! Why didn't ya say dat before?'

He laughed with a loud cackle.

Dan thought to himself: No one will ever know what goes on inside Eamon's head.

Eamon came up close to Dan and whispered in his ear, 'Don't ya tell enybody, bud I think I've met him. Ya know – God. I know where he is hiding out.'

'Where?'

'Come and I'll show ya.'

'The Health & Safety Inspectorate are due this morning,'

announced Sang solemnly, a certain amount of irritation in his tone. 'Be courteous, helpful, accept all censure, and we may get away with severe criticism rather than total condemnation.'

He then disappeared for the rest of the day.

Three solemn-faced individuals, two men and a woman, duly arrived at the appointed time and after a quick handshake with Hans, presented their credentials. They proceeded at once to examine the Visitors' Reception area. Their eyes darted hither and thither and their brows creased in disgust.

They proceeded immediately on their tour of the establishment, heads held high and a slow, astute stride to their step. Monks were interrupted as they went about their work and questioned. The woman made a beeline for every sister she saw, with a seeming obsession for checking if hands were clean. Such an eerie atmosphere settled over the compound that, in the subconscious minds of the brethren, it was Judgement Day when all are silent and alone with their sins.

Some monks suddenly became conscious of the real possibility that the chores in which they were involved – and most certainly their motivation for doing them – were impure and immoral. A few now began to feel that they were conduits of evil in the world. These guilt-ridden brethren approached their tasks for the rest of the day with renewed dedication, reciting acts of contrition and being overly careful to follow all the rules. Only later would it become apparent to them that the opposite attitude would have been more conducive of results, as their own condemnation by the inspectors exceeded that of the slackers.

Dan and Eamon, however, seemed unaware of the inspectors' purpose. When the officials arrived at the farm they saw O'Toole and Moriarty pushing Sanctus and Asissy into pig muck, amidst shouts of great laughter and glee, the two assailants following the two ecstatic monks into the mire.

Later, the inspectors found themselves unwilling partakers in the community midday meal – to them an unconventional mixture of peanut soup and boiled chicken feet. It was immediately after the meal that the two men, somewhat hesitantly strolling near the 'little chat' room, came under physical and verbal attack from those clients patiently waiting their turn, who had assumed that the strangers were queue jumping. In the course of the afternoon they also found themselves being roped in to help in 'emergencies'; such as assisting brothers in holding down patients who were unwilling or unable to take their prescribed medicine or some other appropriate treatment; holding back quite large numbers of unruly destitute who were impatiently waiting for scheduled handouts; and having to introduce themselves – and explain their business – to satisfy the curiosity of, it seemed, every single mental patient in the compound.

It appeared to them at one point that they would never be allowed to escape, that five o'clock would never come, that normal life would never come back again. At the very end of their inspection they were astonished to be asked to act as guinea pigs for a new, untested herbal medicine. So demoralised had they become from the rigours of the day that they had not the strength of mind to refuse. They were quite willing even to accept that they might begin to feel some uncomfortable side effects in a matter of weeks, if not days. In order to appease these insistent, all-powerful, God-like tyrant-brothers, and finally to get out of there, they made formal vows to 'report back' assiduously on whatever side-effects might occur. They were only just too happy to help out in a good cause.

Their colleague had an equally hard time of it over with the sisters, for Second-in-Command Jane had taken her in hand and spent an inordinately long part of the afternoon haranguing her on the dangers of intoxicants – specifically those found in tea and coffee – too much drinking of which was going on in the community. The danger signs were already there, she said, in quite a few of the brethren, whereby the 'inevitable next step' – hard drugs, specifically alcohol – was just around the corner. In her younger days she had seen the ravages caused by those 'little pleasure givers'. (The only criticism the inspector was later able to make was that it was bad for Health & Safety that the workers were deprived of adequate liquid refreshment.) Jane's firm grip on the inspector's arm, allied to long lectures on cleanliness, the different ways various parts of the body should be cleaned out and other such topics, meant that the visitor had little chance to pursue her own schedule, being more or less rendered speechless from exhaustion by the five o'clock deadline.

To the astonishment of everyone, including a very relieved Sang, the inspectorate trio came to him at the end of the day smiling broadly. The men were giggling for no good reason and the woman laughed her head off at every seemingly innocuous remark by Sang (such as that they looked tired after a hard day's work, wasn't the weather very humid, and wouldn't they like some peanut soup before they left?).

A little later, bemused monks saw the team departing after much hugging and kissing between them, Sang and Hans.

The official report, when it did eventually appear, carried the required number of mandatory criticisms (to show that they had done their job) but gave the establishment a 'pass'; which meant that the inspection team would not have to return.

A further auspicious event of that week was another riot by the Jah. Sanctus appeared to have taken over the leadership of the group from the now even more disgruntled Alan.

He addressed the brethren on their 'rights'.

Bro Paulo Costello translated it later for his diary. He had shed the burden of holiness, he said, and was possessed now of the belligerence of 'a new broom sweeping away all refuse before it'.

Sanctus claimed that he had never really been holy. When he had joined the community he had of course detected the 'odour of sanctity' in the place, as they all had done. Through imbibing of this sanctity, he had experienced an artificial joy. His joy had been easy, pleasurable, with no misgivings. It had enabled him to do foolish things – things of which he was now ashamed. He had been able to work 'little miracles'; but he now realised that these 'gifts', so-called feats of physical wonder such as walking where no one else could – or would – and the ability to work out what others were up to, were from the devil. His holiness was just a very good disguise for his sinfulness.

Real joy came only with sorrow and hardship. Striving for holiness was the cause of all the trouble in religion – in the same way that idealism, of whatever ilk, was the cause of all the world's troubles. He was happy now that he had become a troublemaker and was debauched. He was happy that many in community were not washing themselves these days. Dan and Eamon were the standard-bearers of authentic religion. He hoped and believed that the United Church – and all its works – would one day be held in total, universal contempt. They should all forget about keeping up appearances – such as learning Latin for instance or other useless educational projects. The Lord did not wait until people had a particular academic qualification, or the correct dress or appearance before *he* accepted them. If their heart was right that was good enough.

'Are yore hearts right?' he asked.

'We heart is right,' they shouted back.

'Den de time of salvation *come*,' he exclaimed.

They began shouting, dancing and jumping around.

'Sanctus has now started a riot!' said Hans from across the way, viewing the scene through his binoculars.

'Better to let them get on with it,' said Sang; 'A good old fracas is what more religious people should enjoy every now and then. It lets off steam. It prepares them for real combat. Good for Sanctus – he's so holy he can't put a foot wrong. Even when he tries to be a nuisance, he only ends up doing good.'

'Oh, my ... it's Orbeck! Where did *he* come from?' said Hans. Orbeck was standing in the middle of the rioters.

It was said later by some that he had appeared out of nowhere, his hands raised in blessing and calling for calm. Others claimed that he had only seemed to have come suddenly out of nowhere because he had been hiding in the big berry bush all the time. A few insisted that he had just simply walked over from his hut after hearing the uproar; that they had, in fact, clearly observed him doing so. The latter theory, being the most obvious, was the one most thoroughly rejected.

Jah respect for Orbeck was still greater even than that for Sanctus, for hadn't he – alone of all his tribe – been inducted by the Jesuits into the secret rites?

'Listen, brothers,' said Orbeck.

'Amen,' they replied.

'Is true that Bro Sanctus learn de ways o' God naturally. Me go in de secret room wid dis high-filuting theology book. Dey think theology harmless activity dat confuse, an' mek quiet, dangerous mind. But they wrong, for me learn dis t'ing call "meditate". W'en I meditate I go in ecstasy. No confusion, no sorrow, no pain. I throw book 'way. I never come out of ecstasy. Bro Sang say me sick an' call doctor but me still in ecstasy. Me see visions. Me hear great music. I find I in Seven Heaven an' even converse wid Bro Sanctus dere! Me see den dat Lord Almighty fe call de good an' bad from all ends of de Earth in dis place for reason. Aiyee ... I no believe before how many bad men and women here! He bring we all here for *big* announcement!'

Clapping and shouts of triumph greeted his words. Their own brother Wilbur had not only mastered the secret ways of the Jesuits but now – like Sanctus – was able to communicate directly with God. Orbeck and Sanctus held hands and danced as the others watched and clapped.

Then Orbeck raised his hand again for silence. 'Brothers and sisters, the Lord Almighty announce Second Coming! Second

Coming of Lord *now* ...'

The silence of diminished expectations – of disappointment – greeted this announcement.

'Jus' like we say *all* de time.'

'No, brothers and sisters. It *really* coming dis time!'

'Amen!'

'For me have great vision of messiah coming through cloud o' smoke.'

'Amen!'

'Me hear he voice now as me speak.'

'Halleluiah!'

'He voice says: *Go tell dem – dere is One among you—*'

'Aaah!'

'Who is Lord?' Alan interjected.

'Aiyee!'

Orbeck was suddenly finding it difficult to speak. He was choking on his words. His face turned purple. He couldn't get any more words out. He spluttered.

'Who is he? Where is de Lord?' they demanded to know, concerned at his sudden incoherence.

'He *African*? No African – no messiah!' shouted Alan.

'I see he through mist. He face hide in cloud that mek it hard to see ... He hide he name. He ...'

Orbeck was straining. He had sat down. Sanctus laid his hand on Wilbur's head, trying desperately to impart psychological and moral support.

'Aah, then he be *false* messiah! Messiah who hide African-ness,' Alan shouted.

'Brother Wilbur. Dey poison yore mind,' another voice proclaimed.

'No, no, brethren. For messiah mus' deny his messiah in public. I see he now ... Jus' hol' a minute ... Maybe he glory in disguise ... He definitely have humble face, but when he time come he have face o' majesty. No locks on he head now, but w'en him comb hair on glory morning there be flowing, golden locks like *Lion*! Him eyes look not too good now, but dey fe shoot fire when he prophesy on day. He poor now, have no job an' no proper home. But he King of Heaven when Glory come. Nobody wan' him now. He hold no place in church, no friends in his lonely hidey place, no human speak to he day or night, no praise or power in high places—'

'Brother Orbeck *too* humble to say it *him! He* de Messiah! We see now!' someone cried out.

They began clapping and dancing again, chanting, 'Lord, Lord, we praise thee, all praise to Brother Orbeck.'

'No, no,' shouted Orbeck as they surrounded him. Many hands grabbed him.

'No, do not touch I,' he shouted as he fell beneath the multitude. 'I lose ecstasy.'

Surveying the scene through his binoculars, straining his head to hear what was going on, Hans said to Sang, 'They're only talking about the Second Coming. Harmless talk. Nothing to worry about.'

He looked more closely and tensed up. 'Looks like they're beating up Orbeck and Sanctus ...!'

Sang took a look through Hans's binoculars. 'Well, I suppose if those two are holy prophets, they'll prove their worth by suffering their persecution gladly. If they are rogues, they are simply receiving their punishment and cleansing. The community is obsessed these days with this idea of the Second Coming. Apparently, he has to be in ethnic garb! It always comes around every one thousand years! This millennium is no different.'

'Isn't eet strange that nobody ever sees the Lord as someone with power, authority and respectability in thees world, like you or me?' said Hans. 'With these people he always has to be "one of them", a sort of outlaw. He ees not someone who bears the burden of power, who has a track record een recognised achievements. These dreamers take the high moral ground, while we donkeys get the blame for everything that goes wrong. We need practical, unromantic heads to run an outfit like this successfully – not mumbo jumbo. We have to deal with the real world. Do these idealists ever think about financial viability, hostile politicians, the ruses of vain bishops? The peanut – not de millenarian vision – ees the star of our show. We will start to worry only when the peanut market takes a dip.'

'Will the Jah ever be fully integrated?' asked Sang, musingly. 'There is one mysterious thing that has always made me wonder. The way they get along with Bros Eamon and Dan. They seem to tolerate them very well. I have seen those two wild men haranguing them to go work in the fields. They even forced Alan to accompany them one day to the pig farm. That is quite an achievement, considering that pork is taboo in Jah diet. It is almost as if they enjoy being pushed around and bossed about by those two.'

Hans nodded and said it was queer how it was the most oppressed who always both handed out, and accepted, such treatment.

Sang continued in a businesslike manner, 'Meanwhile, Hans, you and I had better have a word with Rabbi Fogelman. I cannot state definitely how it is so – but I feel that his finger has been in some of the problems we have lately been having, especially with morale and discipline. At the last count, only Obnoxious, Gerry and Paulo Costello continue to wash themselves! I know that he has been talking to more than one or two brethren. Most likely he does not realise how childish, how isolated from outside influences monks are. I believe that they take every throwaway remark of Fogelman's and turn it into an article of faith, simply because he is not a Christian. He probably has the very best of intentions. Gerry says that he explains scripture like no one else, enthralling them with local colour and detail, especially the Judaic backdrop to every biblical story. He claims that Fogelman said that Jesus was just like any other man, afraid for his life, and depressed that his preaching career had hit the skids. I'm not sure that the brothers should be hearing such demoralising talk. Especially as – after all – we believe as Christians that Jesus is God. The man has, I'm afraid, become a problem.'

Hans sighed and said, 'I suppose that this ees the sort of talk you would expect from a rabbi – getting at the human truth underneath all the theology. I am sure he has no intention of undermining our faith.'

They reminisced on Fogelman's arrival at the monastery.

'When you and Jim went proselytising, and met him in that Kingstown brothel, he must certainly have been in serious trouble,' said Sang. 'For such a person to be hiding in such a place necessitated great desperation.'

'God knows why he had gone there to hide! Eet must be the most public place in Kingstown,' said Hans. 'I thought he was a tourist at first. He had all the appearance of someone sightseeing, or at least "slumming". He had been moving around a lot, he said, and he mentioned quite a few places where hees travels had taken him.'

'Fogelman's desperation certainly showed itself in his willingness to listen to all your arguments for the Christian religion in that house of ill repute – you not realising his previous station in life! I suppose a brothel is as good a place as any to seek souls. Indeed, they are noted places for philosophical discussion. Anyway, your explaining scripture to him – a rabbi – in that brothel was a good joke in community that cheered us all up for a long time. His own good humour, when he revealed that he also was a man of the book, commended him not just to you but to all of us.'

'Then Jim came een,' went on Hans, 'and I said, "Jim, this ees another Jesus we have before us." At first, neither of them recognised each other. Then suddenly they were all over each other, greeting one another as old friends. "Oh yes, it *is* you," and

"I recognise you now" they both kept saying excitedly and happily. When they had finished their greetings, Jim started asking him, "Why, when, what brought you here? And to a brothel, of all places?" There was some surprise, or embarrassment, in Jim's voice.

'Jim took me to one side and said that we must help him. They had met before. Een Egypt, McCall said. Then he comes up with another of his tall tales. He said that he had infiltrated an arms dealing operation. There was a double-cross. This Fogelman had suddenly appeared – out of nowhere – and whisked him away to safety. He never saw him again. Well, Jim, as we know, ees full of marvellous tales! He said that Fogelman's life was een danger. It was not ordinary criminals who were pursuing him, he said, but a respectable authority! He asked me if we could put him up for a night or two, and that Fogelman would see that we were recompensed for living costs.

'On the way home, he kept such a tight grip on Fogelman, as though he had, indeed, found a long lost soul mate. He was being over-solicitous, protective. You would have thought that Fogelman might try to run away, or was a bit ... weak in the head or something.'

'He has a queer way of talking,' said Sang. 'The brothers often take him to mean the opposite of what he says. In that way, they tell me, they believe they can somehow understand some special, covert message he is giving them. Obnoxious asked him – presumably to embarrass him – if he was happy living in a Christian monastery. He replied crossly that he was quite comfortable with being a Jew. He said that he whom Christians adored as the Lord and Son of God was a Jew like himself. Obnoxious says that Fogelman became angry and shouted that the Jews did not reject the Lord. That was a lie, the result of a great cover-up. It was the Christians who had rejected him, by rejecting his people! It was not the Jews who should be accused of heresy. Obnoxious says that he became so angry he was in tears.

When Obnoxious protested that he himself was right and that Fogelman didn't understand the first thing about Christianity, he told Obnoxious that he was an obtuse, unlearned monk. That was enough to send Obnoxious on his way, fuming!'

They both laughed.

'But we'll have to go and ask him what he's up to,' Sang continued. 'And if he is thinking of leaving soon.'

'I am already working on arranging a safe passage for heem,' said Hans. 'I have told him that his physical safety is uppermost een my mind.'

'What did he say to that?'

'He looked at me een a queer way. He gives me that look whenever we meet. Sometimes I think ... he is trying to figure out what I'm thinking.'

Hans looked down, biting his lip, as if upset over something.

'Emergency meeting tomorrow,' Sang went around shouting soon afterwards.

Everybody gathered in the assembly room after morning chores. Outside there was a continuous, heavy downpour, creating a thunderous noise on the corrugated roof. The brothers appeared half-asleep, their heads resting on arms outstretched on the benches. In the oppressively humid air one's consciousness, Gerry had observed, tended to revolve around particularly morbid thoughts. Perhaps it was a survival strategy of evolution – the only way that the mind can continue to subsist under such oppressive, tiresome conditions is by clinging on to the dark debris of semi-consciousness.

As their thoughts and hearts succumbed to gloominess, he sensed hordes of small devils coming out of the black ether emitting malign, suggestive thoughts. These – according to his spiritual advisor – were 'diabolical obsessions' (there was no accusation here of deliberate sin), which set about provoking vulnerable individuals to acts of minor violence or, perhaps, severe uncharitableness. It was as if everyone relapsed into the state of original sin. If it were not for the pervasive lethargy, he reckoned, quite a few more unconscionable acts would undoubtedly be committed on these occasions.

Once he, too, had suffered terribly during these periods of suffocating, humid weather. On one occasion, he had gone into a room and torn up the collected notebooks of the English class. On another occasion, he had thrown a rock from a concealed position at the back of Hans's head. Eventually he had found a way to counteract this mood. It was on the last occasion (after three days of uninterrupted heavy rain), that he had taken a hammer to smash the venerable podium – where he had been due to give the week's talks – that he had first used 'reasoning power'. He had suddenly 'realised' that what he was about to do that was of no practical advantage to him or benefit to the community. The deed – while supercharged with primitive emotion – was pointless. It was a liberating moment. He could now, whenever the occasion arose, pour scorn on and verbally abuse those devils even as they intensified the ferocity of their attacks – simply by the use of 'reason'. He proceeded now, once again, to argue with and chide these assailants for their 'irrationality', mocking them for the unreasonableness of their behaviour.

His agitated entrance into the room, with much grimacing and gesturing, was observed and commented on.

As they all awaited the (as usual) delayed entrance of the top two, a mood of ill-defined antagonism persisted. Gradually, the monks came back to their senses and more or less sluggishly began to take in their surroundings. A murmuring started. The absence, indeed late disappearance of Eamon and Dan, was the main gossip and controversy. They were nowhere to be found. They might turn out to be the first monks ever to abscond successfully – this possibility created much excitement. But nobody could under-stand why they should have run away. Both had appeared content in their own way. Furthermore, as Irishmen unaccustomed to the tropical environment, there would be hardships and dangers out-side the perimeter. Surely they could not have reached as far as the end of the lane before being picked up by some authority – official or otherwise? Had Sang called the meeting to make some announcement on the matter? A few had already made up a 'ballad' celebrating the duo's escape. They began to sing it aloud.

Sang and Hans detected the heated atmosphere even before they entered the room. They were already somewhat unnerved as a result of their meeting with Rabbi Fogelman. They felt that, for the first time in their long careers, things were beginning to get on top of them.

Elsewhere, there were strange goings on. At the corner of the compound was the remnant of an old stone building. This had once served as a punishment block for recalcitrant plantation slaves. It was said to contain a dungeon in which dwelt the ghosts of former inmates. Needless to say, very few people ever ventured near the ruins. Except for Eamon and Dan – for whom it was a favourite place of repose.

Eamon had first come across the 'desperados' the night he had dragged an unwilling Dan along to a soiree with the 'gods' of the ruins.

'They're not gods, they're ghosts,' Dan had told him.

They first believed that the noises and vibrations below were the ghosts behaving badly. But the spectres had not appeared that night. Instead, it was Dagga who popped up out of the ground, his silhouette jittery against the pale moonlight, the gunman fearfully chattering a spell (some ghetto curse) to ward off all danger. He saw before him a sight that terrified – Eamon holding up two machetes in the form of a cross. If, instead, the machetes had slashed out attempting to behead him or to amputate some limb, he would have felt much better. Even happy. Instead, they bespoke an evil enchantment. He had been warned by Dog, his second in command, about this place, about the strange ways of the monks. He became even more unsettled now at the sight of Dan's dark presence in the corner. Eamon spoke in a strange, guttural voice that weaved its own spell over Dagga (who by this time had been joined by Dog).

'I have been waiting for ye. I knew ye were coming. Me friends, the ghosts, told me about ye. The divil is with ye ...'

'Wha ...' said Dagga, his eyes wild with anxiety.

'The divil is yer leader. He is yer master. Yer power is very small compared to the divil's. He never lets ye have peace. Ye must run with him day and night ...'

The two criminals sat down (collapsed would be more accurate) at Eamon's feet, as much out of nervous exhaustion than anything else and Dagga said, 'We listen. Yo talk.'

Within the hour, after listening to Eamon hold forth loquaciously on topics as varied as the 'troubles' of the ghosts, his old home in Ireland, the fairy world and the best reputed spells for warding off evil, Eamon had been accepted by Dagga and Dog as friend, confidant and well-nigh spiritual leader.

The two community leaders had found the rabbi a tricky customer. He was not the reserved, humble man that they had previously assumed. He did not even appear to be the same man that had first come to the monastery. He stated that he saw it as his God-given mission to save the community from itself! Being a complete outsider – and from talking to the monks – he could see what was going wrong. For one thing, the brothers were overworked. Prayers offered to the Lord were the empty platitudes of tired men and women. Such prayers were not good enough. He could teach them a few tricks about prayer – and would welcome the opportunity.

He informed them – in reply to Sang's initial comment that his presence was now having an unsettling effect on the monks – that there were other, more important things than that to worry about. He said that they had been misled by their desire to appear always hospitable and Christian. For they had inadvertently given sanctuary to the devil himself. *His* unmasking was a task fraught with danger and would require the uttermost tact and skill. Fortunately, he knew the ropes here, for they studied these things in rabbi school. But they would have to listen carefully, stop acting as if they were sole lords of their own domain, and take his advice.

He had spoken authoritatively. His criticisms, initially unwelcomed, Sang soon realised had something to them. He felt admonished, confused and anxious. He began to feel as though the community he had founded was no longer, now, even under his remit. He was an innocent, even ignorant blunderer in a world of spiritual complexity and conflict he did not understand.

Hans, meanwhile, was also uncharacteristically floundering. He had never before met quite such a formidable 'opponent'. He felt that the rabbi was – in some unspoken manner, as if just by looking at him – demanding obedience and compliance. It was a weird sensation, like temporarily losing one's willpower, almost like being hypnotised.

As they slowly walked from their office to the meeting, nerves taut, Sang did indeed sense the Adversary's invisible, threatening presence. It was coming ever closer, the atmosphere filled with foreboding. His mind struggled with the effort to remember who else had visited in recent times – to whom else they had offered hospitality. He recalled now the visit some months previously of Dr Wesley, the intellectual from Kingstown.

Sang and Hans had been over the moon at the visit of the country's best-known media commentator, Marxist and atheist. That such a prominent thinker could take them seriously was one for the books. They might even get a slot on radio or television.

And to come and spend two whole days in the monastery discussing a whole range of issues affecting society, the world and life in general – as if their views were worth taking into account – meant that they must be doing something right.

Dr Wesley had complimented them on their success in appealing to the masses. He praised their health programmes in particular, commenting that the significance of the power of suggestion and the will to believe should not be dismissed; that in certain circumstances not even the correct suggestions or beliefs were necessary.

Sang glowed with pride. They *were* getting somewhere! Even if it ever turned out that there was no God – only the devil – they were at least still achieving something – something that was worthy of praise by a complete outsider and respected intellectual!

As Wesley was escorted on a tour of the establishment and its facilities he was talking non-stop, like a man with an all-consuming mission. 'Instead of bandaging up people's wounds and preaching forgiveness, you should be calling out for the overthrow of that unjust system which is the cause of all poverty,' he was saying as they passed the long queue of supplicants (the scene aroused Wesley's contempt).

'Ah, so true,' Sang glowed.

'You paper over the cracks,' went on Wesley, his voice denoting impatience, 'which is of no service. In fact you act as counter-revolutionaries.'

'Oh, that is a great insight,' Sang enthused.

Wesley was exasperated by Sang's asides. His hackles were raised even further by Han's words. 'Amen!' he said. 'We hear about your famous political campaigns. But you fail to take into consideration the other side of the political coin. The spiritual. That ees your great failing.'

Hans never ceased trying to convert people, even as antagonistic or unpromising as Wesley.

Wesley was filled with anger. But a little voice told him to be very cautious now.

'What . . .?

'Do you *love* the poor?'

Hans's voice was gentle, even soft. Wesley decided to keep his cool and play Hans at his own game. He would answer his question with another question.

'What do you mean ... love?'

'Let me ask the question een another way. Who – or what – do you *hate?*'

Hans's voice now was more resolute, becoming didactic. Wesley glared at him.

'I don't ... *hate* . . anyone.'

He went silent. He had sounded almost apologetic, excusing himself.

'One cannot hate without also love,' Hans said.

A Jesuit trap, thought Wesley.

'Love ... That is just church talk. I gave all that up in childhood. You ... exhort from on high what you call the "spiritual virtues". You claim the high moral ground as your private property. What is "love"? The only word in the language that has no meaning. That is why it appears in not one of the great scientific treatises. What sensible ruler, what genius, what great man of history, what famous political speech or dissertation ever talked about love? It's a nonsensical word. It doesn't belong in the real world.'

Trevor kicked himself for losing his cool. And in an argument with a ... cleric!

'What other world is there apart from the real world?' asked Hans. He went on, in what was almost a triumphant voice. '*Indifference*! That is what is een your heart, ees it not? Love and hate are *good*. Indifference ees bad. I have observed, today, the way you look at the poor. There ees no love in your eyes!'

Wesley threw all caution aside. 'Well! That is a fine one from you – a Jesuit! Crooked operators on the grand scale, in cahoots with the CIA, Mafia and every major criminal organisation. Gamblers who do not deal straight! What have you done with all the money you yourself, Hans, have embezzled or blackmailed from many well-known people and businesses in Kingstown? And what about all the dollars you make from the peanut business? I'm sure it doesn't go on feeding these poor, starving monks. Without mammon, you would have no power. And look at them!'

He pointed at the Jah brethren in the distance, who were sitting down having another 'reasoning' session. His words continued to gush out. 'Many are the scandals of your so-called 'conversions' – look at the Jah. Everybody is aware of your notorious brainwashing methods. You have enslaved an entire people. You enticed them out of their cultural and spiritual homeland with false promises, to a sad exile in Babylon. I *hate* you.'

'Aah,' said Hans, 'at last, the truth! It ees true – you do hate! That ees *good!*'

Wesley silently cursed his own outspokenness. He had come here determined to win the trust of the monks – so as to be better able to use them for his own purpose.

To his astonishment, Hans now slapped him on the shoulder. 'What you say about *me* ees the truth! I am even badder than you think. I am so bad that I can never change my ways. I am reconciled to being of the crooked frame of mind. I am a bad man, from a family of bad people. It was to escape just retribution for their criminal acts that my family sought refuge in a far country. There! I am telling you things I have told nobody before. Not even Fr sang here. It ees true that I – and the church – hypocritically always take the high moral ground. But I am not damned yet. I need only a leetle more time to ensure that I am damned. In hating me, you have proved your wisdom and integrity.'

'It is no good trying to convert me, Hans!'

Wesley was kicking himself for leaving himself open to these asides. He should have been more cool, more cunning. He thought to play it all down again. He suggested that they sit and discuss a proposition he had to make. He had only argued with them, he said, because he knew that the Jesuits loved to argue. He had learnt from their healthy debate. They sat in chairs on the veranda and Quietitude brought them orange juice (tea as well as coffee now being off the menu).

'As you know, the crime rate has got out of control,' said Wesley, 'and I am advising the government on how to develop proactive schemes to counteract the problem. I am offering you an opportunity, a great challenge! The criminals are the ones most in need of conversion from their aberrant ways. They are as pitiable, if not more so, as the poor and sick you already have here. I have been using political and psychological methods to persuade them to give up crime. I have already succeeded in getting the main gang to call a temporary halt to their activities. If only I could get that most notorious group, headed by a psychopath called Dagga, into a safe, secure place – we would be as good as there. Their minds can then be taken off crime and subjected to new ideas. I believe that there are aspects of your philosophy that could work with them. For they are extremely superstitious. That is where Stalin and others went wrong – not incorporating some kind of superstit... sorry, folk religion into their scheme of things.'

'Your cause is a good one,' said Sang solemnly (Hans also nodded enthusiastically), 'but I am not sure it would work having them living inside the perimeter fence. I doubt, too, that they would come here willingly, or with the correct intentions.'

'I saw that old derelict building over the fields, well away from your living quarters. It would make an excellent isolation block.'

'Well,' said Sang, 'who are we to judge others? Ask them and see if they would like to come here and we could have a few chats with them.'

'Is it true,' asked Wesley, seemingly as an afterthought, 'that the police and security forces may never enter a religious establishment. Even if the most wanted criminal in the country happens to be hiding inside?'

'That is correct, 'said Sang. 'This is God's private property. We have given sanctuary to some desperate characters here.'

They went indoors, Dr Wesley still enthusiastically discussing the gang-conversion scheme, the two humouring him as they might an over-zealous, naïve novice.

It was, then, as they made their way to the Assembly room weeks later that a second, uncomfortable realisation slowly began to dawn on the two. It had always been part of the official *raison d'étre* to be open to all sorts of people. To engage fully with whoever asked for help. To turn no one away. If they failed at that – they failed the Lord. Yet here they were now, questioning their response to two people who were 'up to their eyes' in different sorts of trouble; hesitating, dissembling their 'Christian charity'. Here were two non-Christians, Fogelman and Wesley, each attempting in his own way to solve the problems that touched all humanity. They were offering their help to an institution that they had no part in; indeed one that was alien to their ways and culture. Yet here were two, supposedly, charitable men thinking about the possibility that one – or both – of these visitors might be the devil, or in league with him. Yet they also had to ask themselves – who was fooling who here? As a result of their tête-à-têtes with these two individuals, they felt that they had, in a way they could not quite understand, allowed control over the United Church somehow to slip out of their hands.

chapter
seven

Their entrance into the hall was greeted with banging of tables and loud hooting. This had the paradoxical effect of soothing his nerves and Sang used his usual method – raised hand and a blissful smile to calm things down.

His first announcement was that there were to be no more days devoted to specific virtues, in the light of the disruption caused by Humility Day. Next Monday's Obedience Day was therefore cancelled. Such 'dedicated days' gave vent only to a pernicious form of hooliganism as 'smart alecks', under the pretext of testing the virtue of others, experimented with the boundaries of tolerance.

'The main purpose for the meeting was the problem of monks going to Rabbi Fogelman's room for chats. It was not so long ago that they were calling for his expulsion! They had to be more careful about having 'little chats' with just anyone. These were meant to be for special occasions, with proper, controlled procedures. Not free-for-alls. He could assure the community that he was not going to send the rabbi away immediately – at least not until he himself was ready to leave. Therefore, there was no further need for the brothers to threaten strike action, as he had heard some were doing.

He would be failing in his duty if he did not warn them that the rabbi was not a Christian and therefore likely, simply by giving opinions on theology, to undermine their own faith. He was not decrying Judaism. But this particular man was probably not a qualified rabbi. In particular, his comments on Christianity could not be trusted. Once you undo one tiny thread of Christian doctrine the whole thing begins to unravel. His reported criticism of the community's great success in the world (he had decried the prevalent 'work' ethic) sounded like that old favourite of religious purists – justification by faith alone. The man had certainly cast a spell over everyone with his persuasive style of speech. The rabbi had a few oratorical tricks. Part of his trade. Well, they had known false prophets before. Just think back to recent times when Bro Alan had seen himself as a messiah and martyr, before he realised the error of his ways.

Bro Alan, sitting sullenly at the back, was nodding his head at every remark of Sang's. He had become a changed person after having recently experienced a revelation of Hell. This happened at about the same time that Sanctus had started interfering in Jah affairs. While sitting in the library, trying hard but failing to successfully read a primer, he had observed the pages burst into flames. He saw multitudes of lost souls in the fire, burning, writhing and screaming. His ears were in agony at the din of awful noise. The faces glared back at him with murderous hate, resentment, hopelessness.

He had decided (despite Hans's attempts to put him right on the matter) that their displeasure was due to his trying to read the book, by doing something that none of his ancestors had ever attempted. That he had, thereby, been breaking some unwritten law. He had slammed the book down with a determination never to read again. Alan never really spoke coherently on the subject of books again. However he had, now, in the eyes of his brethren, joined that select group of brothers who had been privileged with a private revelation. When word came out that 'Alan see Hell' he became a hero – held in an awe and respect that he discovered to be even greater than the prestige that he had once held as leader of the Jah recalcitrants.

And why, asked Sang, was Brother Orbeck in the throes of a nervous collapse? It was due to this solitary man having being dragged back by his brethren to be caught up again in the craze of the Second Coming (the very sort of religious mania that Orbeck had originally been sent away to recover from). And why was Bro Sanctus unable to pray any more, claiming that (or at least very soon) there would be no further need for prayer? Such millenarianism was a noted psychological phenomenon. It reared its head particularly every thousand years. Putting a specific time and place to the Second Coming (and the end of the world) was a heretical interpretation of Scripture that had been condemned by the Church. 'The Lord will not come until the Church says so!'

'You all get carried away talking about the Lord, as though he can appear at a whim. As if all the arrangements of the cosmos, heaven, hell, all the events of world history that must be in place before the Apocalypse happens can be simply set aside. That "He" could walk in here any day as "one of us", sporting African dreadlocks, speaking the Jah dialect and leading everyone in folk music and dance up the road to the heavenly banquet!'

For the first time ever, they saw anger in Sang.

Well, he had better warn them right away – that kind of language has been heard before. It was the language of the cult. It ended in ruin, fire and death.

'No more, no more of this nonsense! I plead with you, brothers.'

Bro Gerry spoke up (everyone put their hands to their ears). 'Speaking intellectually and theologically, I agree with Bro Sang in decrying the emotionality of some people in regard to religion. I prefer to analyse belief in a detached manner. In fact, I once had a very bad experience myself when I was inadvertently caught up in religious emotionalism. I was supposedly "in the spirit", made a complete fool of myself, singing and shouting crazy, even obscene words that I had never heard before in my life – from where they came I did not know.

'I believed that I was God; that the world was my own creation. Suddenly a voice spoke to me. It informed me that I was a person of no consequence. I was *nothing*. I collapsed on the ground. What desolation the truth brings! Oh, brothers ... there is no word in the language that can describe that despair. If this is real religion, I told myself, I want nothing to do with it.'

He paused, evidently reliving some traumatic emotion. He continued in a slower, deeper voice.

'Since the Great Illumination, as I call it in my notes, I have been careful to avoid intense prayer. It does not do any good for the soul. However, I always ensure that I listen to the voices in my head. They have become my friends and regular counsellors. They have given me the key to life, directing me to work through detached reasoning alone, bypassing all emotion.'

Now his voice lightened and he cheered up again. 'However, I must admit that I, too, went to the rabbi's room. I had heard that he was against most things in religion, which gave me confidence. He told me that *Waiting on the Messiah* and the *Second Coming* were both great misunderstandings. Whatever forms the Judeo-Christian heritage takes the same confusion arises, he said. It has been the cause of great errors. The matter of dates, times, eras or that which lies in the future is based on an illusion. Have you ever known, he asked me, a time in your life that wasn't just *now*? The Coming of the Messiah, His Second Coming, has been, is now and forever shall be. At least that is what I think he said for his speech is very hard to follow.'

'Heresy', shouted Obnoxious.

'I must say,' said Sang quietly, 'that the rabbi does not even appear to believe in his own creed.'

'Neither does Bro. Gerry,' shouted Obnoxious.

'I, too,' said Hans, surprising everybody by intruding into a 'brothers' debate', 'at times question the reality of the spiritual world and the goodness of God. I doubt that I can do anything good ...'

They were taken aback. Nihilism in Hans? Impossible!

'Me too,' shouted Bro Malicious, relieved at last to be able to admit a long-kept, pent-up secret. 'I stay here only because I, also, have learnt to live with despair.'

Immediately there was the banging of tables again (now become an established ritual whenever some communal emotion was expressed). This was followed by shouts of disbelief, nihilistic statements, cries denigrating all things religious, confessions to all manner of offences and pessimistic thinking. Everybody, it seemed, was speaking their thoughts.

Something that Sang had once encouraged them to do!

Bro Paulo Costello that evening wrote his own account of the meeting's denouement.

Major event at emergency meeting today. Bro Gerry was accused of heresy when he declared that he did not believe in the Creed – that 'He will come again in glory to judge both the living and the dead.' He was certain that the Lord was not coming back. The many in community who awaited Him were wasting their time. This caused an outbreak of undisciplined behaviour, with every brother trying to outdo the next one in declaring unbelief. Even Bro Hans said that he had doubts! Bro Obnoxious demanded that Gerry be tried for heresy – and for leading the whole community astray. Bro Snitchus, who normally keeps very quiet, spoke out for the first time ever in a meeting, and said that he had often heard Bro Gerry say he didn't believe in God. He said that Bro Gerry also sometimes talks to himself. One time he heard him having a loud argument with someone and when he looked in the door Bro Gerry was waving his arms and threatening to assault this person. But there was nobody else in the room!

As all this was going on nobody noticed the door opening and a silent figure in black habit (black habits are normally worn only during Lent), head in cowl, enter the room. This person stood at the back and it was some time before even I noticed him. All the shouting was still going on, everybody enjoying themselves as usual, mocking and accusing one another, until eventually there came a noticeable decrease in the volume of noise, with this one and then that one dropping out of the shouting until at last there was total silence in the room and everybody was staring at the figure in black.

They all knew who it was – Bro Jim McCall – who for the past few months had disappeared from view and was only ever spotted when doing duty in the latrines (this is usually considered to be penitential duty). Everybody knew that appearing to be doing penance was just another ploy of his, part of some private agenda.

What a turnabout! First of all Bro Hans surprising everybody with his confession of doubt and temptation to disbelief. Now Bro Jim in sackcloth and ashes!

Bro Gerry told me that, in his last talk with Bro McCall, the man had been very upbeat, talking about the rosy future ahead; about how the next pope was going to come from the community; about the monastery becoming a great place of pilgrimage. He spoke about the inside workings of the Church worldwide; how he himself was influencing things in a great scheme of world evangelisation that would eventually lead to universal conversion. Bro Jim is famous in community for mystery and airs – everybody loves to have a good laugh and play the game they call 'what dark scheme is Bro McCall working on now?' Whenever a brother says to him, 'It's great that we hear you were a terrible crook when you were young. Killing people in wars, gun running, subversive operations in poor, downtrodden lands, blackmailing governmental and UN bodies in order to get your way, piling up vast riches which you now use to influence the pope in the Vatican – it is enough to make the devil envious. It makes everyone feel that there is a God when someone as bad as you can be converted', Jim will go very quiet in order to let you know that it is all true!

Well, now here he was acting real strange, because he was trying hard to say something and was having great difficulty in doing so.

Brothers were giggling. Others were hiding their faces in their sleeves trying not to laugh, or perhaps from embarrassment. He waved his fist in the air and eventually shouted out. The emotion in him was what had been blocking his voice. But we all knew that all this was for drama and effect; that it was just another act.

'Please do not condemn my friend, Joseph Fogelman. He saved my life once.'

Everybody sat back, waiting for the story.

'On one occasion, in the Middle East, I found myself in a tight spot. MOSSAD had set up an arms deal with a group of militants. It was a 'sting' operation. I was double-crossed. They were both after the hi-tech stuff! I was the one disposable. Then this stout fellow appears from behind the curtain in the room. It was Mr Fogelman. I recognised him as a long-standing stool pigeon of MOSSAD agents. Or so I had thought! They had had him infiltrate the main Islamic group as a Saudi agent. The idea was eventually to expose him and let them think that they had been thoroughly infiltrated. The best counter-insurgency method of all. He had discovered both double-crosses, however, and had concealed himself in the room. I noticed he had explosives tied around his middle. We easily made our escape (it was in crowded Cairo). The man is a hero who, to this day, has a high price on his head ($30 million US – Reward for the arrest of one Ishmael Ali).'

The brothers could not restrain their guffaws at this and their laughter continued for a long time. His stories get even more outrageous with each passing day! We think the reason he takes himself off to sulk is that he knows that his tall stories are no longer received with the credulity they once enjoyed. But this is the first time that the brethren have openly showed their disdain, emboldened perhaps by his late descent into eccentricity, as illustrated by the penitential black garment.

As for the many stories about the rabbi. It is common knowledge that Mr Fogelman first came through the gates a year or so ago somewhat exhausted and dishevelled and in the company of Bro's Hans and McCall. It was after one of those early-period outreach *forays to the capital to 'bring hope to the destitute'. It was soon being put around that his down-and-out appearance was a charade; that he was, instead, somebody important. The fact that he was seldom seen publicly only added to the intrigue. The country was full at that time of foreign traders, unqualified journeymen, swindlers, financial 'advisors', holders of false credentials, embezzlers and so forth. It was during the period known as the 'encouragement of free enterprise' that also saw the winding down of the drugs trade in 'certain quarters'.*

Many of these fellows called in to pay us a visit. Fogelman was seen at first as perhaps another of those entrepreneurs. In fact, the take-off in our peanut enterprise was, for a time on the grapevine, put down to his business expertise. It was speculated that he had obtained, through contacts, a better deal for the community in the markets. Now there is another story going about. It is said that he is a sage, a deeply spiritual person who is able to counsel and encourage doubting or troubled monks. Since he has been appearing openly, brothers have been sneaking in to visit him and to speak to him. His words are passed around almost as new scripture! This, in turn, has led to all sorts of discipline problems and the latest, most serious accusation that he is a religious charlatan.

Jim spoke earnestly in his defence, dropping for the first time his usual tone of one-more-knowledgeable-than-thou. This time everybody was listening to humble Jim. The issue of the rabbi has become the latest 'great controversy' in community. It seems there always has to be one!

'I am speaking the truth, brothers. I admit that in the past I did not always talk straight. I am now appealing over the heads of our beloved superiors to you, my brethren, that he be accepted as one of us. He has told me that he desires to remain here a little longer. He can fulfil his own vocation by serving his Lord from this place. That is, until certain other arrangements are made and it is time to go. I am not saying he is a candidate for baptism. He has never mentioned the subject — but he does not make a big thing of religious differences. I propose that he be given some sort of 'associate' status in community —

a position that could incorporate some legal protection as well as responsibility.'

    Fr Sang was staring at Bro McCall, his expression more angry than ever. Hans looked flabbergasted. 'A Jewish rabbi on the governing board of a Christian monastery!' was probably his thought.

Paulo's diary did not record Sang's reflections, but was correct in observing that the man was extremely angry. If he had succeeded in deciphering Sang's thoughts he would have written as follows:

McCall is taking liberties with his power and is intent on taking over from me. Ever since Humility Day things seemed to have gone from bad to worse. Through a supposedly harmless liberal experiment, I have let loose the forces of anarchy in a community that previously, whatever its inner tensions and unresolved conflicts, had put forward a uniform face of brotherly love. Giving free rein to the forces inherent in every heart has only caused the community to indulge in blasphemy, uncleanliness, heresy and devil-may-care. It is strange how holy impulses are nearly always twisted to become their corresponding vices.

    I now realise that our very success has become the crux of our problem. The virtue of hospitality has allowed a charlatan to enter the community. The strict rule of never turning away anyone in need has allowed entry to a pernicious influence, not to mention the coming prospect of violent criminals living within our very own compound.

    In the not-too-distant past, everything had appeared to herald the New Jerusalem – the healing of the sick, the discovery of truth by those lost in superstition and heresy, positive theology, the reconciliation of enemies, the bold challenging of the powers-that-be; the wise and efficient service of Fr Hans, always producing positive results as he guided us through the intrigues and pitfalls of politics and finance.

    But now I have become suddenly aware that I can rely on no one. Not even Hans, who has probably become part of our Achilles Heel. Lately, I have heard old rumours again that previously I dismissed. I have begun to wonder how much he is to blame for some of our major problems! He has an inherent, if suppressed self-destructive streak that I had once viewed as a sort of invalid's gift, capable of bringing down blessings. Now I see it as a suicidal impulse that involves not only periodically placing himself in danger, but also putting the fate of the whole community at risk.

Sang bitterly reflected that it was Fogelman himself who had appraised him of Hans's real nature. Indeed, Fogelman seemed to have an intimate knowledge of Hans's psychological makeup, as well as comprehensive information on his deputy's adventures outside the monastery.

Did Fogelman have a file on Sang himself, too?

Sang knew that he was slipping into cynicism. He had initially not been keen on inviting back Dr Wesley and his criminal associates. Perhaps, he thought now, it was a good idea after all. The challenge, and tribulations, that the presence of the outlaws in their midst would inevitably cause would also enable him to regain control over his wayward monks. The brothers would look to him to do something when these fellows began to get on their nerves. The job of converting the wild ones, of getting them into 'little chats', the inevitable outbreaks of violence, perhaps some assaults, serious injuries or even deaths would mirror the early days of community when all was fraught with uncertainty. In those days everyone came to him for fatherly advice.

It was a bit cynical – but name a ruler who never used such methods of divide and rule?

'Send him away,' Obnoxious shouted.

'No, he is a father to me,' said another.

'And to me.'

'And me.'

'Out with him, he has been here too long, he's more trouble than he's worth,' others cried.

Hans intervened – with an immediate call to prayer. (What a cunning fellow! Paulo noted. Prayer solves all problems! It is a tactic that in the final analysis prevents this place going up in smoke.)

The call to order through compulsory prayer was a sure sign that Sang was worried that dissent was fast becoming revolt. The problem with the brothers was their idealism. So intense were they that often their ardour for even minor (sometimes the more minor the better) causes carried over into sporadic acts of petty violence (such as the breaking of plates, or the trampling of a shrubbery), which they saw as expressions of holy zeal. It had become a common saying with Sang and Hans that sloth and indifference were virtues worth cultivating in any society.

Now there was another cry.

'Why you stop coffee? Not even tea we get now!'

'Yea,' they chorused, 'who stop tea and coffee?'

Sang spoke at the top of his voice. 'Brothers, I have been meaning to speak about tea and coffee. I am very sorry that both have been taken off the menu. I was left with no choice. The sisters threatened to withdraw their labour if we did not get rid of *all* intoxicating drinks. Sr Jane, in particular, is adamant. Sometimes it is the stronger and braver thing to give way. Think of the advantages this offers. Once our bodily systems are clear of the last remnant of intoxicant substances, we will feel better. We will be new men spiritually. We will come to look upon tea and coffee as the enemy. If in days to come you see anyone drinking that stuff, it will make you sick. You will feel really cleansed.'

'We want coffee!' a few chanted.

Capricious spoke. It was unusual for this brother to complain. Everyone listened.

'Sr Jane is a big nuisance in the hospital. She tells me what to do all the time. Even when I do things *right* she corrects me. I always have to say – that is how I *am* doing it!'

'Those women have the wrong attitude,' said Obnoxious. 'Sr Josephine likes to see that the sick have much suffering. She prefers a long-drawn-out death. Jane and Josephine fight all the time over which of them is to take charge of the worst cases. We would all be better off without the sisters.'

'We do not need those women!' someone else shouted.

'They are our sisters!' said Sang. 'And they have many valuable skills. Who will take charge of female patients when intimate matters need to be dealt with? Who will do all the washing and cleaning?'

'Gloria was over in our quarters again,' said Obnoxious, 'looking for Bro Gerry. Bro Alfredo had to take her back. He broke the rules when he laid his hand on her. These sisters are a temptation to sin!'

Another chant began from the section of brothers who called themselves the 'militants'.

'Out with the sisters! Out with the rabbi! Out with the brethren who stand in the way of progress! March – against the backtrackers!'

There appeared now the prospect of a number of the brothers marching off to demonstrate, perhaps outside the rabbi's workshop, then through the gates and over to the convent. It had happened once before, when they had formed an orderly line in twos and singing hymns had circumnavigated the compound in support of chicken soup.

They were in a volatile state of excitement again. Sang wondered at how quickly they forgot their reverence for him, and how ready to disobey at the first prompting. How easily the very best of people could become a fickle mob.

'Brothers. Listen to me. Where are Eamon and Dan? This is the second time they have not shown up for general assembly. People tell me that as soon as breakfast is finished, they head off for the hills, figuratively speaking.'

Loud laughter changed the mood immediately. It was almost as if all the controversy of just a few moments ago had been discarded and forgotten at the mere mention of those two.

'Brethren – eccentricity is one thing. Serious breaches of the rules are another. We cannot afford to have some out there doing their "own thing". I am delegating Brother Alfredo to go and look for them. I expect they have forgotten their promise and are gone out on the river fishing. Brother Alfredo; you must ensure that they do not come to any harm through their own devices. Do not let them bully or browbeat you, either. Be firm.'

'Yea, massa.'

'Alfredo ...!'

'Sorry – Fadda.'

Quick thinking was working.

It was time to present the brothers with a new challenge. To get their minds on to other matters, to keep them on their toes. 'Brethren – I need your advice on a matter of conscience. It is incumbent upon me to make a decision – whether to open our hearts and our home to the worst sinners in the world. We have been asked to give refuge to a band of murderers and robbers from the slums of Kingstown. They are the most wanted men in the country. They are pitiless malefactors of the worst order. I am told by psychological and other experts that such people can never be reformed. What am I to do, brothers? Turn them away, or welcome them into our bosom, even if it means we put our lives at risk?'

Sang fell silent. They sensed that a humbled, powerless Sang was imploring them – and heaven – for help. Embarrassed, the brothers took pity on him.

There was a sudden quiet as the muttering stopped. Someone asked, 'Does it mean that some of us may get killed?'

'Yes,' replied Sang, still looking grim.

A loud cheer went up.

Sang spoke quietly. 'I know that you would gladly sacrifice your lives for sinners. But have I the right to ask this of you? Martyrdom is not martyrdom if it is involuntary.'

'It is voluntary, it is voluntary,' they cried, all the previous controversies now completely forgotten.

Even as he thanked them, he knew that he had committed perhaps his first serious sin in many, many years.

There were dramatic events taking place on the perimeter. Armed subversives were sneaking one by one into the compound under the supervision of their commander-in-chief, General Wesley. He was togged out like any old ragamuffin bush guerrilla, earphones blaring rebel music in his ears, grasping his revolver as though it was his 'mainstay'. Hans was later to say that it was amazing how grubby and iniquitous respectable intellectuals look when kitted out in the attire of a poor man. This fellow now had all the appearance of a starved ghetto youth, as if all those years of privilege, indulgence and achievement had never existed.

He settled the ghetto lads down in their new, earthen quarters. He bossed them about, taking advantage of the fear that he had put in them by his stories about the brothers, exaggerating the monks' baleful reputation as holy men and making funny, cryptic signs at every mention of them. He increased his hold over them by relating the story of his previous visit to the monastery – and how he had tricked their wicked leader into giving him some of their 'secrets'.

A little later, General Wesley, Colonel Dagga, Lieutenant Dog and the 'regiment' sat listening to Eamon, with fellow apostle Dan at his side.

'I know seven divils. Da first divil ya never see. He makes ya born in da wrong world.

'Da second divil comes to visit you when you are a baby. He looks like a man but he has a wolf's head and he comes and says: I robs ya of yer fadder and mudder. So ya never see yer ma and pa again.

'Da third divil – ya never see him. He hides around the corner, so dat when ya do something he sneaks in and changes what ya do. Dat is how he takes away yer good name and gives ya a bad name.

'Da fourth divil ya hear but never see. He whispers all the time. He tells ya lies about the world, so that he makes ya believe the opposite of what you see. He tells ya dat the world is a wonderful place. He tells ya dat you are alive. He tells ya dat those ghosts who ya see every day and who look human, are just people just like yerself.

'Da fifth divil is more evil dan da first four. Ya wake up in da morning and dis divil is dere. He is not just playing tricks for fun. He is out to torment ya. He, too, appears as a human. He wears special clothes different to other divils – these clothes disguise him as a policeman, a soldier, even a holy man or priest. But ya know he is a divil because he breathes down yer neck.'

'Yea, yea,' said Dagga and Don.

'He chases ya here and dere, round da trees and backyards and everywhere ya go. If he catches ya, he will kill ya unless ya give the spell.'

'Him no catch me yet – me too fast,' said Dagga proudly.

'Well, he killed me once. Da spell is what I will tell you later. Sixth divil makes ya *do* things. He is a little fella who gets inside yer head. He is da fella dat makes ya whistle when others talk; cry when others laugh, laugh when others cry; quiet when others are noisy; he makes you grit your teeth for no good reason except to make people laugh. He makes ya clench yer fingers tight when a person talks nicely to ya; and makes ya do backside noise when everyone is peaceful and happy. He tell ya to do dis or dat and it will make everything fine. Ya do what he sez, and den ya find yerself in worse trouble.

'Da seventh divil worse than number six and all da others, because he makes ya like himself. He makes you become his pal. Ya don't know he is dere, dat ye are *him*, and he *you!*'

'Oh no, no,' said Dagga, horrified; 'me hate to be like that.'

'Well, he got into me a long ago time. I had to be exorcised.'

The admiration in the gang's faces for Eamon shone like the

sun in the morning.

'Yo teach me de spell,' said Dagga, 'for me know de last devil is on mo tail.'

'You keep those monks away from here?' asked Dog.

'Do not be afraid,' said Eamon.

For the first time in his life he felt ... he couldn't put a word to it; in fact he wasn't really conscious of feeling this ... feeling. It was a sense of responsibility for these frightened fellows.

'If the brothers give you any trouble I will stop dem. Dey are afeared of me. Why do you have dose guns? Dey are not allowed here.'

'They need them as protection against evil spirits, which they fear greatly,' interjected General Wesley. 'They are not for use against other human beings.'

Dagga stared at Wesley, quizzically.

'What I mean is, Brother Eamon, Brother Dagga and his band of brothers are learning more peaceful ways to reach salvation. Long ago the devil taught them his ways; now they are learning God's ways. I will soon be sending them out as new men, to spread the gospel of salvation through the villages and towns. They will be known as Liberation Fighters – and when they triumph, peace will reign over the land. Dagga – your brothers must put their shooters out of sight.'

'There's a monk coming!' cried the lookout, in a state of high excitement.

'Quick, everyone, back down the hole,' ordered the general, and they all disappeared. Eamon and Dan went outside and hailed Alfredo, who was slowly and warily approaching the ruins.

'Brother Alfredo. What brings you over here? Eamon and I are praying with the spirits,' said Dan.

Eamon, who had never before spoken so much in his life as he had in the presence of the outlaws, now reverted to his silent self.

'Who in there? I can smell them,' said Alfredo grimly.

'You smell the ghosts,' said Dan.

Alfredo took a step towards the ruin; thought twice about it, and stopped. 'The boss wants to see you two,' he said.

As he walked off, he muttered 'brother smelly ghosts'. It was not clear to whom he addressed these words.

The new novice, former Archbishop's assistant Jaime Da Souza, walked through the gate late that afternoon. He was escorted in by Brother Solemn, who always took great pride as the breaker of the 'bad news' to new recruits.

This test of vocation often had the effect of making aspirants turn back even before they reached the inner enclosure. The 'bad news' was varied by Hans to suit the aspirant's likely persona and psychology.

'There has been a change in how the noviciate is run,' said Solemn, solemnly. 'The strict routine, that has always been so enjoyed by newcomers, especially for its contrast to the lax, corrupt lifestyle in the outside world, has been discontinued. The isolation of novices from the main body of brothers is now seen as giving one a false perspective on life here. You will begin work tomorrow morning as Brother Obnoxious's assistant (Obnoxious had been moved back to ceremonials).'

It was this isolation and strict discipline that, in fact, Jaime had been most looking forward to.

'But I must prove my suitability for the ascetic life.'

'You are a brother first, and an ascetic afterwards, if at all.'

So relieved was he to be here that he soon overcame his disappointment. He stopped and sniffed the air, a big smile breaking out all over his face.

'It is better than I thought. I can't wait to get stuck in. I have always envied the way the brothers are involved in the real problems of people. I have spent years talking to thin air, preaching to the converted, achieving nothing. I am so happy. And I no longer suffer from loose bowels. I was cured here.'

Srs Josephine and Jane were having a confab in the convent office.

'The brothers insist on having coffee back,' said Josephine; 'or else there will be trouble.'

'If you give in, it shows weakness,' replied Jane.

'What is wrong with weakness?'

'The sisters back me on this. They say you do not demonstrate leadership. They call for strong leadership.'

(Many sisters were upper class Kingstownians, who approved of Jane's no-nonsense attitude.)

'That shows they are very weak,' said Josephine.

'You waste hours with the dying, they say, while ignoring those who might recover. They call you the American hippy.'

'There were some very nice, agreeable hippies. Jane, I know that you have had a hard life. But do not impose your misery on others.'

'The sisters say that Gloria is a disgrace and that she should be sent back home.'

'"Home" is a misnomer. There is nowhere for her to go.'

'She disobeys instructions and continues to trespass in a male monastic enclosure. Excommunication is normally the penalty for that. And – I know men. They do not *need* any encouragement to unchastity.'

'She believes that God has joined her to Bro Gerry in the indissoluble bond of a mystical marriage, and divorce is not possible. It is their custom.'

'Mystical marriage! In my day it was called shacking up. Chastity meant abstaining from illicit sexual relations.'

'Illicit – that is the key word. In any case, Bro Gerry has no desire to continue any relationship that he and Gloria may or may not have had in the past. He has given his word to Fr Sang. I, too, have been reassured. However, don't denigrate the mysticism of the Jah. Who knows but that there is a spiritual bond between Gloria and Gerry – a bond fruitful of blessings for all. Even in the gospels friendship is praised as a blessed state.'

'Ever hear of "giving scandal"? A grave sin.'

'Gloria is just a big joke with the brothers.'

'Oh, I'm sure she is! They call themselves *monks!* They are a bunch of thieves, impostors and ruffians. There's a group of them – those so-called Jah men and women – who will only lift a finger to help when *they* decide to, and on *their* terms. They remind me of the scandalous drinking crew whose acquaintance I once had the misfortune of making in Ireland, long ago. Bro Dan was one of them. They all came to a bad end. As will that lot over in the monastery. Especially the Jah people. I don't give the monastery – or our United Church – much chance of survival. When the day comes and we are all unceremoniously wound up, I for one will be saying – "I told you so".'

'Don't live in the past. The future is exciting. Just think – in a few years time we will be dead! Isn't that wonderful?'

Jane did not reply. Instead, she grimly faced her superior. 'Mother Josephine. I think it would be better if you handed over to me. For a start, the sisters would be a lot happier. I have promised them that as soon as I am in charge, we will set up our own hospital. We will no longer have to set foot in male quarters. The chance of a bit of privacy – and to do things their own way – is a wonderful prospect to them. They have been through a tough time, with no evidence forthcoming of that equality of treatment that they were always promised "when circumstances allow". They still have to do all the unpleasant duties. And that so-called hospital is a death trap. How it ever managed to pass a Health & Safety inspection I will never know!'

'Despite the atrocious state of the building, people are brought back to full health there. It is the power of love at work. The zeal of the brethren overcomes every obstacle. It would be a bad day that saw an over-concern with obtaining "better facilities" or "improved working conditions". We would lose that enchanted, trusting touch that is producing results and sending spiritual reverberations around the country – and soon over the whole world.'

'The power of love! Is that what motivates the so-called Jah brethren? They beat up two of their own kind only the other day. Nobody understands what they really believe, or even what they are talking about. They overuse, and misuse incense. Their mantra greeting – *love all* – is ungrammatical. They are not even confirmed in the true faith!'

'It is the presence here of those whom some would see as new pagans that gives us the edge over other religious foundations. Not even the rascally Franciscans ever accepted the roughest sorts of no-gooders who are the heart of our community. They are "the treasure that we leave all others to find". They have not yet had long centuries of opportunity to pollute and betray the gospel, as Christians have. We have with us again the early Christians – so ready to receive, to suffer, and to impart the light.'

'Gracious! I have never heard such nonsense. I told Fr Sang that you were too much of a dreamer to be able to make proper decisions. That you were not happy in a position of responsibility and power. That nostalgia for the days of the rebellion of youth is probably the cause of all your problems. And do you know what? He agreed.'

'Sang agrees with everything everybody says to him. It's his technique. But it is true. I do not relish authority or power.'

'You are not happy in your job, are you?'

'No.'

'Well, hand over to me.'

'If it is the will of the Lord, I will.'

Josephine felt two emotions at her open acceptance of failure; an extreme disappointment, and also relief. Disappointment at no longer being in a position to change the world and its institutions. Relief that, as it was all meant to be, the next phase in her life, perhaps death itself, was that one step nearer – perhaps around the corner.

Within days, the handover had been put into effect. When rumour of the coup reached the monastery the following day, the first reaction had been – what next will be taken off the menu?

(What the mood was in the convent nobody knew – for there was no more secretive, impenetrable place on Earth.)

'Uh, ut's yu,' said the rabbi as Sang walked in, interrupting a session of woodcarving.

'What are you carving, Rabbi?'

'Ut's thu Tuwur uf Bubul.'

'Does that have any particular message for us?' asked Sang, for he realised that this man always had some lesson up his sleeve.

Fogelman said that he was trying to understand why people built churches with roofs, steeples and towers so high that they were completely out of reach. Is it ambition? Is it pride? Or the search for God – the God in the sky. He is not there. He is here.

'Oh! And have you been thinking over what I said?'

'Yus.'

What are your future plans, then?'

'Tu luvu.'

'Leave? Well, rabbi, it is the case that we are getting some-what overcrowded. There are new aspirants due in any time now. An unruly lot, I am told. I don't know if they'll make it as monks. I have spoken to the brothers about you. You may congratulate yourself that they speak very highly of you. They can see that you are a religious man first, whatever your past. You can leave here with the happy thought that you have inspired many of the brethren.'

'Um vury fund uf thum.'

'Bro McCall in particular seems very fond of you. I am cur-ious as to how you first came to know him. He tells a story about you and him in Egypt. We are never sure what to believe with Jim, sometimes.'

Ho ho ho. He had heard that story. Jim tells many tales about imaginary friends. He had been a friendless man. All he had ever wanted was a friend. But he would not open his heart.

'Where did you first meet?'

He said that, at the time, he had been a rabbi on the Kingstown circuit. He had come across Jim in the bar of the La Cucharacha Hotel. McCall was alone, drinking, hiding his deep anxiety. He had often seen him there, acting the hard man. He went up to him and introduced himself. Jim made it clear that he didn't wish to talk. Fogelman told him that he knew all the important people in Kingstown and had contacts with the 'people at the top'. If he needed help (he sensed he needed help), he would most certainly be able to provide it.

Then, apparently, Jim had a change of mind, perhaps realising that his unwanted companion might, indeed, be useful. Jim explained that he was in some trouble with regard to a business contract. He and a partner had been using a small aircraft to move large amounts of foreign currency out of the country. What his 'employers' did not know, at that moment, was that some of this money had gone astray. Jim suspected his partner, who had also gone missing.

'Well, we all know that Jim used to be a bit of a colourful character,' said Sang, sighing.

Everybody in town knew that too, Fogelman said. He had told Jim that the whole financial sector was aware that Umberto was moving large sums of money out of the country. There were no secrets in that town. Leave it to him, he said, he would speak to the very man himself about what had happened. He need worry no more.

Jim broke down, cried. For some reason, he began to feel that everything was going to be OK. It was the stress of pent-up emotion he was releasing now. He proceeded to open his heart to this stranger.

They went on to have a great talk. That was when Jim said

that he wanted to change his life, to become a 'new man'. He asked Fogelman many questions about the meaning of life. Why was he born? Was he a bad man? Was there really a God? What is the world for? He couldn't stop asking questions. The words kept flowing, like a man who hadn't spoken for years.

They discussed the answers to all those questions. They spent the whole night talking. In the morning, McCall had smiled again for the first time, he said, in twenty years. Fogelman could see his face wasn't used to it, for they were a strained, heartbroken smiles. McCall said that he had got it all off his chest. He felt that he had a clear conscience.

He said that he would return the money that he had taken from the aircraft, and put some of his own money in as well, and give it all to the poor. (McCall, Fogelman said, had some initial doubts about this later, but eventually he fulfilled his promise.)

He, also, now believed in God.

'That must have been about the time he first came to see me,' said Sang, as much to himself as to Fogelman.

He wondered now whether in fact he was giving shelter not to one, but to two master criminals.

When he had tried to do a check on Rabbi Fogelman in Kingstown, nobody on the religious circuit had ever heard of him.

'What did Mr Umberto say?'

The Prime Minister, he said, had no choice but to leave Jim alone and bide his time. Fogelman had assured him that he would say nothing, but leave it to his (Umberto's) conscience to return all the money to the people. Since then, Umberto had been using various machinations to cover himself. Eventually, word had come to him (Fogelman) that he had overstayed his welcome in town. But before he had even begun looking into the question of where to go, he was informed that there was a stop order out to prevent him leaving the country.

'That makes it even more imperative that you leave the monastery as soon as possible. Fr Hans will make arrangements.

He is a safe pair of hands.'

Sang was restless. This man knew too much. He could even be the cause of the downfall of the United Church.

Ho, ho, Fogelman had laughed, Fr Hans a safe pair of hands? It was as if it were some huge joke, and it caused his giggles to continue for some moments. Yet Sang thought that his laughter was also a little bit bad tempered.

Yes, of course he would leave at once. He was sorry for laughing about Fr Hans.

'Hans likes to think people can rely on him,' said a curious Sang.

Yes, he knew that Hans was a brave, honest man. But he had a compulsion. Gambling was a psychological compulsion, im-possible to cure. He had to take risks with everything, even – esp-ecially – with that which he valued highly, or loved the most. It was the worst psychological affliction a person could suffer.

Sang thought back, tried to run Hans's life and deeds through his mind in one sweep. He began, at once, to see everything in a very different light. (Later, when he had reached a proper, fuller understanding of Hans and his life, he would find that, for the first time ever, he felt a little *fond* of the man.)

'There is one last thing you could do for us, Rabbi Fogelman. The brothers need to "cool down" their misplaced fervour. I must teach them that overzealous behaviour leads to fanaticism and destruction. Their rage knows no bounds. They can be very scary. The brethren see you as an expert on religion. I want you to declare that you were in no position to have advised them on spiritual matters. Say that your advice was poor. And order them to listen to me.'

Fogelman said that he could not predict the effect of his words on the brothers. Sometimes they took him literally and sometimes they took him to mean the opposite of what he said. They were so honest and keen for the truth that they sometimes believed that they could even read his secret thoughts.

'But yu, Fr Sung, huve nut uvun sturtud ulung thu puth uf humuluty. Prugrus, urdur, cuntrul, puwur, succuss ur yur guds. Whuy dud Humuluty Duy ful? Yu shuld nut huv duclurud uh Humuluty Duy. Yu yursulf shuld huve bucum humbul fur uh duy unstud, und guvun thu bruthurs tum uff tu rust. Thut us humuluty.'

'Rabbi, I am a Christian. You are a Jew. Never the two shall meet!' said the exasperated Sang.

'Ut us tru thut uh um nut uh Chrustun. Thu nume uf Juw hungs huvuly un mu und un mu puple. Thu nume uf Chrustun hungs huvuly un yu.'

His words affected Sang deeply, in a manner that was inexplicable. But he suddenly could understand how the brothers had been so affected. He heard his words not only as possibly justified criticism, but as an expression of a deep sorrow and regret that spanned the ages and activities of man. This person did not speak as an individual, but as the spokesman of something, or someone, sacred yet vulnerable. He felt sorry for his own loss of temper. He took a step nearer Rabbi Fogelman and placed a hand of friendship on his shoulder. He thought, for a moment – although he may have just imagined it – that the rabbi flinched.

chapter
eight

The bodily cures and healings continued apace at the hospital. Innumerable folk, through the medium of little chats, also continued to be relieved of the mental burdens that had so handicapped and tormented them, even up to the very last moment before they entered the room. As the cured departed through the gates, clutching the standard gift of a bag of premium peanuts, they encouraged others coming in 'not to worry', 'health and well-being are guaranteed', and 'they give you a bag of peanuts for free'. They usually gave the impression of being a bit drunk. Their most distinguishing characteristic was their jollity and broad smiles.

Few of them (and not even many of the brethren) understood the nature of their healing, putting it down to some miraculous power possessed by the monks. Most thought it was down to the sheer intensity and power of their prayer. Every brother and sister was exhorted to pray hard and not to take the 'gift of healing' for granted. Praise and thanksgiving were constantly on everybody's lips; extra prayers were continually added to the daily quota and increased amounts of incense were dispensed in the hope that the 'power' would continue to be bestowed from above. They believed that if there was a cessation in prayer even for a single moment, or any reduction in the intensity of prayer, this wonderful power would most certainly be withheld – and failure and disaster would follow.

They did not realise that it was nature at work, helped along by liberal doses of faith. Fr Hans knew this; that as long as they had faith, miracles would never cease. Because he knew this, he also knew all the pitfalls and dangers. He knew when to call a halt and when to let things go; when to act and when to pray (which was why Sang gave him his head on most matters).

More respectable, reputable clients were now coming in. Professional people, wealthy landowners, even some politicians who went to great lengths to disguise themselves, were appearing at the gate. These people were in the prime of health, and positively glowed with well-being and prosperity. Hans was for turning them away, concerned that they had been drawn by the monastery's reputation for miracles, that the community's mission was becoming tainted with sensationalism. But Sang insisted that they too could be classified as poor.

'Isn't their wealth and success a terrible burden?' he asked.

Initially, these 'burdened' folk felt much guilt as they contrasted their good luck with the state of the poor around them. They soon saw, however, that the poor received not only a cure but a share of the prevalent happiness – of what came to be called 'divine love power'. They were envious, even bereft, at the sight of the joy on the faces of these wretches – happiness that they believed, at first, only the poor could ever possess. This 'happiness' or power, which seemed to be everywhere, as 'free as the wind', manifesting itself in the ignorant and malicious as well as in the innocent and good-willed, infusing the very buildings, grounds and the air itself, was unavailable to them. They suddenly felt, indeed, extremely poor. *They* were now the poorest of the poor!

Most then opted for the little chat. In this they had to justify their application for a share of the so-called 'divine love power' that was apparently so freely available to the 'chosen people', i.e. the poor and sick.

'We were made to *crawl*,' said one (this was the only time anyone ever revealed details of what had happened in a little chat).

Yet during that later period of 'outreach to the rich and powerful', not even one of those undeserving mighty, influential, respectable, ambitious or authoritative visitors ever left without displaying the 'look of divine power'. The cures had begun to take second place to this new phenomenon of 'spreading happiness'; indeed ordinary, miraculous healings were now seldom being commented upon at all.

News of the curative powers of the monastery had long since spread throughout the region. Now there were reports that the brethren had come into possession of an even greater power, that was more wonderful than the power of healing, indeed than of any power previously known to man. It was said of this 'power without a name' that it conferred happiness. Different accounts of the 'look of divine power' spread far-and-wide. Stories and rumours went beyond the shores of Jaman to faraway, more sophisticated lands. There, in some quarters with inside information, they began to talk about a new Third World revolution. Seemingly, this would take the form of all the people rising up together through the agency of this new power and taking 'responsibility for their own affairs' in a bloodless revolution, the likes of which would never before have been seen on Earth.

The power had strange, paradoxical qualities that only added to its mystique. Its presence, that was so obvious and transparent to the fortunate recipients when they first received it, soon displayed an elusiveness that instead of diminishing it actually added to its value and authenticity. It became extremely hard to qualify, quantify or be specific about the feeling once the recipient had left the monastery grounds. This made it all the more attractive. Its ambience and lack of definability added both to the bearer's and the new power's reputation. Its mystique grew with each recipient's inability to remember what it (or the experience) had been all about.

Some cynics, when they commented on the fact that the people always appeared drunk at the time, received the riposte that this only made it more genuine, as the true drunkard always regretted his over-indulgence, whereas these people only ever celebrated their lost 'inebriated' or 'hung over' state and longed for it back again.

The 'power' had affected a change, also, in the Jah brethren. They had previously been so taken up with internal debates and their own esoteric form of worship that their input at the workplace had been minimal. Now they were hanging around the farm and hospital all the time, helping when they could and no longer decrying work as 'slavery', or arguing that it was beneath their dignity to come under the orders of 'the Man' (Babylon).

In the past they had particularly abhorred little chats. Their tradition held that private discussion, or even 'confessing' were irregularities that Orthodoxy used to corrupt and control the weak and unwary. In their tradition, discussing (reasoning) and confessing always had to be done in the open – in full view and hearng of all. In that infectious air of happiness, however, there was a new liveliness to their stride and a new interest in and acceptance of monastic institutions. Some found themselves wandering in the direction of the little chat rooms. Soon, one or two were to be found hovering near the doors, or even trying to look in. It seemed that they had had another change of heart. For one eventually braved it and went in for a little chat.

The others keenly discussed with him the results when he came out.

'Is jus' talk,' was the first, guarded comment.

'Why yo look so happy?'

'I dunno, I dunno.'

'They trick yo!'

'Maybe so, maybe so!'

This response only increased the interest and encouraged more to decide for a little chat.

Meanwhile, Eamon and Dan were the given the official job of looking after the new, hooligan-aspirants, and received a blessing from Sang on their evangelising of these dangerous misfits. By restricting them to a remote corner of the compound, Sang was hoping to keep them out of trouble and harm's way. He did have doubts, at first, about tolerating a 'no-go area'. He justified it, eventually, by reclassifying the ruins as a 'second hermitage'.

Sang was quite proud of the fact that the two 'wild' brothers were now so committed to preaching the gospel! They had been written off by many as hopeless cases when it came to matters of spirituality. Indeed, their unofficial 'role' in the community had been to act as catalysts whereby the brethren were spurred on by the sorry sight of the two brethren to apply themselves ever more conscientiously to the task of their own perfecting. This 'gelling' of different, contrasting personalities in community was one of the success stories that Sang often lauded in assembly, sometimes referring to it as 'carrying the crosses of others' – a phrase whose meaning most of his listeners could guess at, though a few never understood it at all.

After a few days, it appeared that the newcomers, too, had 'gelled' – at least with their two 'soul' brothers. The rest of the brethren would glance curiously over towards the spot where 'the gang' were now appearing openly, sitting obediently in a circle at the feet of Eamon and Dan. Each monk tried to think – but could not imagine – what might be the subject of conversation.

Sang was starting to feel a little happier as some things, such as the Jah's new co-operative spirit and Eamon and Dan's sense of responsibility, appeared to be improving. He was feeling again a semblance of control. He began to dismiss the rabbi's criticisms as at best woolly thinking, at worst unwarranted interference.

He was relaxed enough to be able to return to his favourite escape – prayer of the eastern type – a meditation on 'nothing', fingers crossed and deep breathing absorbing the pressure of all suppressed worry and stress. He called up now the quality of indifference – particularly as to what might happen with regard to the blackmailers, Fogelman and Wesley. He felt prepared now – and commenced to engage in a struggle with his inner demons. With, if necessary, that Devil who was on the premises!

He sat for some time transfixed – in a near hypnotic state – on the tree stump, his eyes and ears taking in the birds, the wind-blown leaves and clouds, the hyperactive biosphere on and und-erneath the earth, the sounds of silence, all present and yet not present to his conscious self.

Hans came up and spoke to him.

'We never do talk much together, do we Fr Sang, when you think about eet, during the course of the days, weeks and months. We are always shouting instructions at each other across a room or yard. Always busy with somebody else's problem. We should talk a little together more.'

Sang woke brusquely from his reverie. He appeared to be in a state something similar to shock, but which actually was an even higher (or deeper) consciousness than that which he had just been roughly shaken out of by Hans. It was that state which few peop-le (not even the experts) ever attain – the twilight zone between ecstatic revelation and reality, the eerie experience of seeing both sides of existence. He spoke quickly, as if disclosing a revelation, or expressing a long-held, troublesome thought, his brief moment of happiness suddenly gone.

'Religion is the cause of all our trouble. If only we aspired less to perfection and the world of the spirit! If only we could accept sin! And the sins of others. Without worrying about it, or sweat-ing over whether our judgments are correct. How easier our lives would be … if we didn't give a damn.'

'What do you mean?'

'Why do I have to worry about the brothers, rules, what others think, or what will happen with those guys over in the ruins. Or when will Fogelman *ever* leave?'

'Do you think a nice little holiday might help?' asked Hans helpfully.

'When I leave this place, I will be dead. Indeed, it is already so.'

'That ees a strange thing to say.'

'Many things I say and think to myself would sound strange to you – a Western mind. It is why I so much look forward to those periods of mandatory silence – which unfortunately "progress" has enforced us to limit or reduce. It keeps me from having to think as you Westerners do. For instance, I know that whatever is going to happen will happen. There is nothing I can do about it.'

'That is what is called a tautology. It is a truism that has no relevance to religion or philosophy.'

'There we go again – arguing with words. It won't stop it happening. Will it? Why don't we all just ... shut up? To hell with it.'

'Oh Fr Sang! Please do not talk like that. Everything ees going so marvellously well. More and more people want to come! The Papal Nuncio is due on Tuesday. He is attending the retreat I have long planned for a group of top Kingstown professionals. The nuncio says we needn't worry too much about the Archbishop; that the next time he is in Rome he might recommend us to the Pope! Isn't that wonderful? How can we fail? We have the *spirit.*'

'Retreat?'

'The retreat I told you I was planning for some of the most wealthy, powerful people in Kingstown. It is entitled Unworldly Ways in a Worldly Environment. Bankers, judges, top police, business folk, even a few politicians – incognito – are coming. The dregs of society een other words.'

'We are pushing our luck. Especially with regard to the "power". There is still a flaw in our system. We haven't cured Winston yet.'

'Oh, Winston.'

Winston was their one black mark. He was the man they could not cure. He had come in with three diseases (a biblical number, someone had pointed out), and he still had three diseases. Brothers could not bring themselves to mention him now. He was pushed to the back, provided with an excess of nourishment and forgotten about. No visitor was ever brought to his corner.

'Ah, Winston will be cured sometime. He ees there as a sign. Some of our victories are invisible.'

'Oh, I suppose so. I am too glum at times.'

'And Bro Alan's people are happier now,' said Hans. 'Ever since they had that to-do with Bro Orbeck they seem to have gone very quiet. They are waiting for "something" to happen. The past and future no longer matter to them, I heard one of them say.'

'If they had attended one of my Scripture lessons they would not have needed to wait years to find that out.'

'Bro Orbeck apparently described to them a vision of heaven in which he saw many white figures. There was much debate over this. They have now accepted the fact that all humans may reach Paradise, even if some are not of Africa. They have even dropped the requirement to be African in order to join the Jah. Alan, in his last talk with me, said that he now forgives me and the Church for our past sins against his people. He put his arms around me, which was dramatic! Considering that their rule clearly states that they should never "touch the sinful man", i.e. someone not the same skin colour. He now says that their old beliefs were down to the obvious fact that God punishes people by giving them a different skin colour. The worse the sinner, the more the spiritual goodness is drained from their skin. That means that the whitest person is the worst sinner of all.'

'It might have some truth in it,' said Sang.

'Well, it gave them a bit of a problem explaining the yellow man. I once asked him about that – he said that there was nothing in their holy book – The Holy Piby – about it, but his private belief was that it was worse than being white. He said that God at creation didn't just withhold the goodness, but actually injected in a punishment-substance to mark out these yellow people. Alan says that his people are "coming along" with him and Orbeck in their new, progressive beliefs.'

'Now that you mention it, I did notice that one or two greeted me today with "Good morning, Brother". That's not their usual style, is it? Usually it is that raised, two finger salute that is so ambiguous.'

'We are getting there, Bro Sang.'

Looking at Hans with a sardonic eye, Sang said, 'You won't be playing poker with your retreat friends when they come, will you?'

They both laughed.

After another session listening to a prostrate, tearful Obnoxious reeling off his list of latest sins, then having to sooth the fellow with the assurance that in Heaven there would be a place for the likes of him, Sang needed to recover. He was considering finding a spot that even Hans wouldn't find, and returning for a good long while to that deep meditation disturbed earlier.

There were dangers in the way he contemplated, he knew. Its epistemology was not mentioned in Christian texts – placing the imagination in the void and draining all words and thoughts of any meaning whatsoever. A study he had once made at a theological college had resulted in his discovering that it was condemned as 'empty deformulising'. It was probably why St John of The Cross had been locked up by the Inquisition. Such un-Christian experiments might, it was said, encourage the Devil to enter.

The Devil – now there was a fellow! He was here already, in person. He did not need an invite! Sang mused on the fact that his technique was the exact opposite of Gerry's 'method', the latter being so steeped in Church practice, doctrine and imagery that it was carried to the point of absurdity. Still, even that touched on nothingness in the end, for one soon discovered that all that effort and concentration also led to the void. Gerry had probably realised this by now. He was pushing reality to its utter limits, as all madmen do. And it certainly did not calm down the same, hyperactive brother.

In fact, the only brothers who ever approached to something near this advanced form of truth realisation were Eamon and Dan. Even if they only got there by roundabout means – and were not actually aware of their own high state of consciousness. But who could say for certain that they were not aware? It would be just a question of setting them certain questions, put in very simple terms, and interpreting the answers metaphysically. He might even try doing that with them when he got the chance. Oh, wasn't it strange how all the activities of the higher faculties, in every culture, come back to the same thing in the end. Everybody got to the emptiness by different means. Was *that* truth?

Meanwhile, back to reality. Obnoxious had by now raised the decibel level of his cries and was (again) pounding the floor with his fists.

'Heaven is full of all sorts of people,' Sang assured him, calling up all his reserves of patience. 'You would be most amazed at who gets in there. It's not for nothing the Lord said there were many mansions. It's not only to keep incompatible people apart – but also to house all those awkward people you will find anywhere in the world. To say there is no place for you, Bro Obnoxious, is to say that there are limits to how far God's ingenuity can be taxed.'

'Oh, I suppose so,' said a sorrowful Obnoxious, 'after all, you have studied far more theology than I have. That is my problem. I should have studied more theology.'

'It might have helped,' said Sang, preferring to tell a small fib than make Obnoxious even more unhappy with the truth. Winston was not their only failure. Both Obnoxious and Snitchus were brothers who were still completely impervious to the new 'power of happiness' in the community.

Sang had settled himself under a cotton tree in a corner of the large peanut field not a hundred yards from the ruins, faced the east and prepared to meditate. At that moment he was interrupted by Bro Solemn, who these days was possessed of a continuous smile. He had brought a sealed envelope, a communication from the convent next door, he said solemnly, the smile temporarily back in storage.

Sang thanked him cordially and dismissed him with a blessing. He opened the envelope gingerly, for this was not the usual means of communication between him and Josephine. It had always been one-to-one.

'By ... Sr Jane has taken over! Josephine has surrendered.'

He immediately took himself back to the main building and found Hans.

'What does it say exactly?' asked Hans, wide eyed.

'It says: "Dear Brothers-in-the-Lord. It is with both joy and regret that we announce the unexpected resignation of Sr Josephine as Mother Superior. Sr Jane has taken over the post temporarily until the General Chapter election.

'"Joy – that Sr Josephine can now achieve her wish for a peaceful, contemplative life in the Lord. Regret – that Sr Jane now has to bear the burden of all the challenges and problems that have remained unresolved for so long in community. We ask for the prayers of our brothers, as we seek the will of the Lord regarding our future course. It has been forgotten in recent times that 'male and female He made them'. It has always been a source of unease to us that we have been forced into a subordinate role in the Lord's vineyard.

"'We call to mind, also, inappropriate emotional ties, the eternal problem of 'particular friendships' in at least one instance, that have marred an otherwise generally productive partnership with our brothers. To ease this period of painful transition, I have decided to permit the limited number of five sisters to continue working daily at the hospital. The rota will change every day, so that no sister will feel tempted, or trapped, by ties of a practical or emotional nature. Hopefully, by the start of the next ecclesiastical year (next month) brothers and sisters will be in a position to work independently within their own buildings. The challenge of the future fills us with joy.

"'Signed: Mother Jane, Superior.'"

'A coup d'état in the convent!' said Hans, astonished.

'Not a mention of any consultation, with us or even her own sisters. It goes against our joint constitution,' said Sang, continuing. 'Well, there is no question of appealing to outside bodies, or the Congregation for Religious Orders in Rome. We will keep this an internal matter. I can't say that I know Sr Jane very well as a person. But I do not believe that she is simply power-mad. Perhaps she has some logical explanation for this. I will adopt her tactics, send a written reply and ask for an immediate meeting.'

This usurpation of power and rule by a tyrant was the first of the 'signs' that were later to be interpreted in hindsight. There would come a time, in the not-too-distant future, when they would look back on number of such important signs that were not understood at the time, but whose meaning became quite obvious later.

For instance, there was a strange sighting over at the peanut shed. This was a building with a flat roof, constructed of bamboo overlain with coconut palm leaves through which the air and elements could flow freely. The roof was for drying out the peanuts (those destined for the retail trade) after harvesting. They were tied in bunches and laid out for days or weeks depending on the weather, until they were shrivelled and ready for roasting and salting.

A few days previously a brother had reported seeing the figure of a man lying motionless on the roof. When they went to check, nobody was there. They said it was a heat mirage. Yesterday another brother had reported the same thing – the outline of a man lying on his back among the peanuts. Again, when they had gone up to check there was no one there. Now today, a group of brothers and patients saw, broad as daylight, the same thing. For some reason they were hesitant about going over to check, so Sang was notified.

He did not have any time to deal with such a minor matter, he said. He was in a rush, and had more urgent things on his mind.

Later, these sightings would be seen as having been a forewarning – a version of John the Baptist's crying in the wilderness.

Other 'strange' happenings began to 'make sense', later. For instance, there was that incident when intruders were found inside the perimeter. Bro Alfredo gave them short shrift, but not before they had offered a puzzling excuse for their trespassing. They had seen a 'burning light' where there had only ever been darkness before. They had seen it on a number of occasions, over by the ruins, and eventually their curiosity had led them to follow it. Much later, that piece of information, that had been of no particular interest at the time, also came to be seen as an omen. These men had been goat farmers – shepherds who had been watching their flocks by night – who had come because they had 'seen a great light'.

Then there had been the visit by the Health & Safety inspectors. Nothing remarkable was noted at the time, apart from the fact that they had come dressed in garments deemed inappropriate in a community dedicated to poverty-of-life. The two men's suits were of the finest foreign material, their bow ties and pocket kerchiefs rather flamboyant. The woman had come 'dress-ed to the tee', smelling of the most pungent perfumes. However, it became clear, later, that this dress-sense overkill was part of a larger picture. It was an epiphany, that was to have all the resonance of the visit of the Three Wise Men.

At a certain moment in the future, each brother would try hard to remember many more such 'things', most too insignificant to have merited attention at the time, that had assumed new meaning. All those events and 'things' then became subjects of intense, excited conversation at recreation, during readings, reasonings and sermons.

Gerry, meanwhile, in a state of high intellectual excitement, believing he was on the very verge of cracking the inner nature of God, went around annoying everyone.

It had suddenly come to him that, if he knew God's name, it might give him the clue he needed. This search was the culmination of a task that he had first set for himself when he was wandering in the North Country bush after losing his job. He had much time on his hands, which he had spent looking at butterflies, birds, plants, flowers and communing with nature during the course of long weeks and months. He had forsworn alcohol for good. His mind was in a vacuum. He had then suffered attacks of extreme boredom while doing nothing, just relaxing and feeling somewhat nauseous in the sweltering heat. He was in that conscious state of which no other known to man is more conducive to revelations. That was when he had suddenly first visualised All-Being.

All-Being satisfied certain metaphysical requirements, but it was not personal enough, he was later to realise. It lacked empathy, even a moral dimension. He told himself that all the other names for God that different people had used throughout history were not correct. This was shown by their continual arguments over it – even up to the present day. He would have to find out what it was for himself.

When he became a monk, he had tried all the conventional religious techniques to discover more. This had eventually culminated in his unique 'method' co-joining the cerebral and the emotional paths to the divine. However, he had recently had to come to accept the limitations of this when, as a result of one particularly prolonged and physically destructive session, he had found himself enforcedly put into the isolation section of the monastery hospital. It had taken all the strong-arm efforts of Bros Alfredo, Capricious and Malicious to subdue and carry him to the unit. His cries of 'Judases' and 'shame' were heard all over the compound, prompting an outbreak of 'sympathetic' shouting and disruption by the other patients. Fortunately, the 'power' intervened to restore peace and happiness all round, and in no time Gerry was back to his normal self.

So he had given up on his 'method' and had considered dropping the whole matter of God's name altogether. Then there was a surprising, unexpected breakthrough. It was just a thought, a suggestion, a simple idea that came to him out of nowhere. He knew, however, that simple ideas that appear as if they had come out of the blue are frequently the fruits of germinating genius. They are the highest form of knowledge. Something that had always been there, just below the surface, yet for long inaccessible to ordinary men. There are hints and suggestions in dreams and 'mad' art and – lo and behold – when the sleeping genius awakes – there it is!

The idea had come to him, even as he was still bewailing the humiliation he had suffered because of what Hans had insultingly referred, to his face, as his 'breakdown'. It was that if God existed, he would want to be very close to his creation. He would not want to stay 'far out' or 'up there' where he couldn't influence events. That was common sense. He would indeed want to hide himself, to allow people to have a modicum of freedom, while at the same time surreptitiously manipulating things. So he had to infiltrate the world like any good intelligence agent. The only way he could do this – 'get into the act' or 'be here' would be by taking a human body. That was the meaning of the Second Coming. But the Jah were wrong; *he* had been right all along. There was no *Second* Coming. He was already here. Anyone, anywhere or at any time in any part of the world could look out for him, and he would not be too far away.

He also realised now that he probably already knew one thing about his name. It would be a name that encompassed the Trinity.

The task now would be to identify him. Watch for the critical signs. Such as people's names. He began a process of talking to, checking out and scrutinising every single person – brethren, patients and visitors alike. He increased his time in the library checking directories, as well as going through the telephone book. He devised a series of simple, straightforward questions that were technically structured, though subtle, to seek out the sign – suggesting that here was God.

'Brother – what is your name?' were the words with which he greeted everyone now.

The riposte was frequently just another question, such as 'Why do you ask?' Often it was the case that he had asked the same person the same question a number of times.

Gerry soon realised that many people were strangely loath to state their name, even in response to a direct request. That surely meant something; perhaps an unconscious humility over their name, with the realisation, perhaps, of just how far from reflecting the divine it was.

Then there was the brother who replied: 'What – surely you know it already!' This had sent him on a false trail for a while, researching the fellow's history in the files, until he discovered to

his great disappointment that not only was there nothing remarkable in him or in his background, but that his baptismal name was
Patrice, an unremarkable name. It had been popularised by a
historical personage who had tried heroically, but failed to convert a backward people on a remote island that lay on the very
edge of the then known world. Bros Eamon and Dan were products of that same land – so there was no question of the name, or
its bearer, having any special qualities, he concluded in sorrow.
He learnt many more interesting facts about people and places;
also about his colleagues, and not a few 'scandalous' facts. But the
trail had gone dead. His other recently acquired, annoying habit,
that of giving everyone lectures on the meaning of their names,
had become so tiresome that he was now forbidden by Fr Sang to
converse with brethren for a period of six months, an unprec-
edented punishment in community history.

He changed tack. He began looking for other signs.

The clues he looked for now were: an unusual physique,
verging on the magnificent (nobody fitted that description).

An excessive humility (humility, apparently, being an essential attribute of God). None of those pathetic efforts at humility,
such as allowing themselves to be covered in muck, or that of 'deliberately making myself unpopular' that some monks indulged
in, either out of genuine humility or sheer pig-headedness, was
anywhere near satisfactory.

A face that bespoke deep peace, wisdom and creativity. For
the purposes of this research he spent much of his time (even
during meals) closely scrutinising the faces of his brethren.
Visitors and patients were also given the silent, close-up look
treatment.

Someone bursting with joy and holiness. There was certainly
an atmosphere of increased joy and happiness in everyone. But if
he was ever alone with a brother, or succeeded in manoeuvring a
brother into a place where there were alone, he noticed a definite
fact – that happiness always vanished from the brother's face.

A special mark, or wound on someone's body. But after a time, and much secretive scrutinising, he was able to state for certain that nearly everyone had a scar, birthmark or ugly blemish of some sort on their body.

He listened carefully to the speech of everyone (for the ability to speak in tongues); he pursued the delicate but necessary task of touching everyone (for the 'power' in the body); even smelling brethren (to detect the aroma of sanctity). It was hopeless.

God was not here.

But he knew that He must be here!

Jim McCall, no longer in the black garment, was sitting alone in the office. He had been there all morning, working on the printouts that would go into the files under 'LIST OF ACQUISITIONS FOR MONTH'.

Food & mineral juices: individual items:

Tea & coffee	0
Flour	$1560
Sugar (grade C)	$1320
Oatmeal	$1320
Chicken feet	$1600
Fish heads	$1300
Cooking oil	$187.50
Salt	$125
Oranges	$1100
Potatoes	
Vegetables	$11000
Miscellaneous	
Rice	$11000
Artificial mineral juices	0
Additional food & milk from farm, items not costed here	

Hardware – items listed as follows:

```
Canvas sacking                                  $1460

Public utilities:
Electricity                                     $1989
Telephone                                       $1526
Gas (fuel for community minivan)                $1857

Miscellaneous:
Bus fares for travel                       $277
```

He found himself double and treble checking every item, an assiduousness that he had never possessed before. Every minute detail had acquired immense importance. Fr Sang entered and said that he had to draft an urgent letter to Sr Jane. He had decided that a formal approach was the wisest thing.

'That letter that came from the convent this morning was from Sr Jane, informing us that she is the new Mother Superior. It's come as a surprise to me, Jim.'

'I take no interest in such petty matters,' Jim replied.

'There hasn't been a telephone call from the convent, has there?'

'No, Fr Sang. None at all. None since before yesterday, anyway. That is when their line went dead.'

'By ...!'

'Do you want me to type it?'

'Yes, please. Address it: "Mother Jane, Love All! We are sorry to hear that Sr Josephine feels she is no longer able to bear the burdens of responsibility as Mother Superior. It is a surprise to us. The last time I spoke to her she made no mention of any serious problems, or of any intention to quit. Perhaps we over here could have helped out with a little advice and moral support. It is not possible to phone you, as there appears to be a problem with the line. Please let me know at once what help you need, practical or otherwise. Yours in the Lord, Bro Sang."

Jim had jotted down the note in his indecipherable handwriting, prior to typing it out. How he managed to type a comprehensible letter based on what was clearly a mass of scribbles and blobs was a mystery, probably even to himself.

'Ask Bro Alfredo to bring it over.'

It was always necessary to take special precautions to ensure the safe passage of message and messenger between the two establishments. Even though the distance was a mere half mile, there were any number of dangers in between, the worst being, not the occasional bandit who was happy to grab what he could, but the competent beggar who easily inveigled the charitably disposed to part with everything, and to promise even more. Bro Alfredo never had any trouble.

'Certainly,' said Jim, adding, 'Don't worry about anything, Fr Sang. It's all foretold.'

'What ...? What do you mean?'

'In the Book.'

'What is foretold, Jim?'

'"From now on a family of five will be divided, three against two and two against three. Fathers will be against their sons, and sons against their fathers; mothers will against their daughters and daughters against their mothers."'

'Jim, I have noticed a change in you lately. Are you sure you are OK? It's not like you to be quoting scripture.'

'It is not I who quote scripture. It is scripture that quotes *me*. Prepare the way of the Lord.'

Sang sank down on the office meditation cushion with a gesture of despair.

'Not you too, Jim? They are all giving me a hard time.'

'You must read the signs.'

'Look, Jim. Enough of this. It is time you and I had an honest talk. I was a bit affronted by the way you came into the meeting and interrupted the proceedings. Your contribution went very much against the grain of what I was trying to impress on the brothers. I have a question to ask you. What exactly is the relationship between you and Fogelman? I am not suggesting anything inappropriate. Your pal is just a bit of a mystery to me. That is all.'

'There is no mystery. He became my controller. All intelligence agents had one. That is all. It was all part of a—'

'Jim, stop it! I can always tell when you are off on another of your ridiculous stories. Hiding from reality. It is time you faced up to the truth about yourself.'

'The truth about myself?'

'Wait a minute.'

Sang went to the door and hung out the sign that said, 'Do not disturb.'

He came back in, kicked the meditation cushion to one side and sat down in a reclining position on the wicker chair, his feet up on the desk, facing Jim McCall.

He proceeded to give a prolonged yawn, mouth open as wide as possible, stretching his arms and then clasping his hands behind his head.

He waited for what seemed like minutes before speaking, all the time looking around the room at this and that object, which were obviously supposed to be of much more interest than McCall. McCall sat looking at him, nonplussed.

He spoke eventually, in a sharp, bored voice that McCall had never heard him use before. 'I hear from various sources that you saved the world.'

The sarcastic tone was not lost on Jim, reminding him, nostalgically, of one of his old bosses who, when he was a young man, had often tried to overawe him with just such a voice. He did now as he did then – pretended to be impressed.

'Some say that I did.'

'Saved the world ... Like shit!'

Even Jim was surprised by Sang's choice of words. He had never, ever, expected to hear the man use abusive language.

'I was involved in many sinful enterprises. You would be surprised at who were my bosses at various times. Even the Church.

Or at least the Vatican. You name an illicit business – I was in it. I had enough inside information to sink a thousand ships of state.'

'My God, McCall – sometimes I think you even believe it yourself.'

'I would expect some acknowledgement that I gave every-thing up for a better way of life. I have confessed my sins.'

'Have you confessed the correct sins? You are here under false pretences. You are hiding things from me. I keep you here only because of the continuous, desperate pleading of your family in Boston. They have paid us not to throw you out! So much for a holy vocation!'

'I know they have contributed to the work here. There is nothing wrong with that. I have been proud of their generosity.'

'Except that you didn't know the real reason behind it. You must have made a holy show, a major embarrassment of yourself to a lot of people! I class your presence here not as a vocation, but as the giving of refuge to a homeless fugitive. And it is as much to protect the fugitive from himself as others from him.'

'What do you mean – I am hiding things from you?'

'Don't tell me, McCall. Don't tell me.'

'Don't tell you what?'

'That you nurse ambitions of running this place. Of taking over the show.'

'I sure don't!'

'Look. They all do. You can be quite open about it. No grudges. It's natural.'

'What makes you think that? Isn't it down to a democratic election at General Chapter? Doesn't everyone respect you as our father?'

'Isn't Josephine a foundress? What difference did it make in her case? There is no loyalty any more. You have been taking electoral soundings of the brethren. What else explains your mel-odramatic entrance at the meeting?'

'Fr Sang. I am going through a bad time. I am sincerely repentant of my past. I know, truly, that I have been the medium of death, injury and trauma to others – in the cause of serving the powers of this world. I admit that I am an accomplished liar. Lying, you could say, has been my bread and butter. I met Fogelman in Kingstown. He recognised me before I had recognised him. It took me a while to focus and recall the past. He spoke of times, people and places that I knew. He was able to bring up things I had long forgotten. Many scams and scrapes of the embarrassing sort that I had put completely out of mind. I was more than discomfited, thinking, who is this guy? What is he up to? I thought that he was going to blackmail me.

'You see, the professional confidence man is able to tell you many accurate facts about your past. It is down to his training, as well as the law of averages. He can tell, from age, present status, one's location in that particular place at that moment in time, more than enough about one. It is the same here with you. By looking at you in that chair, assessing your age, likely history, present predicament, I could more or less give you a full account of your life, past, present and to come ...'

'Spare me the heroics, Jim.'

'It is not a miracle that he was able to relate to me all my past. I played along with him, waiting for him to show his trump card. I deduced that he realised that I vaguely recognised him (but couldn't put a finger on the when or the where). Of course, being a spiritual advisor to his own people in Kingstown, he claimed that he had all the inside information on the latest scandals, especially the financial wheeler-dealings. But a claim to such knowledge is the old, reliable safety net for any good conman. I never figured out how he knew about my bank account at the time, though.

'Still, that was probably one of the easier things for him to access. I could see that he, too, was very embarrassed that I should meet up with him again in that house of ill repute. And he was the one in the position now of having to ask for help. He had to ingratiate himself with myself and Hans. He needed a bolthole, or an escape route. His bank, or the bank of one of his friends, had found itself immersed in a major embezzlement scheme that was being conducted on behalf of the Prime Minister, Raul Umberto. Head office overseas was asking questions. He himself went to Umberto, acting the innocent about who was the king nib, and confronted him with the evidence. It was the worst thing he could have done, although one has to admire his guts.'

Jesus ...! thought Sang, realising that he was more out of his depth here than he could ever have imagined. Immediately regretting his impious exclamation, he went on to convert it into a prayer, *help me.*

'Why are you so anxious to keep him here?' he asked McCall. 'It is not the right moment, yet. He tells me that the storm clouds are gathering; that his enemies will soon come for him. He assures me that he will cause no trouble for us.'

'It sounds to me, McCall, that your buddy is passing himself off as a prophet these days! You, of all people, should know better! Unlike you, I know the history of religion, and these are the worst frauds. He plays up his Jewishness, which gives him a lot of kudos with us ruffian Christians. And – perhaps you should leave along with him.'

'I do a good job in the office.'

'So did Judas. This reputation you think you have with the brothers – with the likes of Gerry, in particular, who once loved to talk about how great a man you are – they no longer believe it. You are a laughing stock now.'

'Let them laugh.'

'I don't laugh at you. I fear you. When are you going to show your true colours? To put it bluntly, McCall, you are a fifth column. For whom I am not sure.'

'I never guessed that you held those opinions of me. It comes as a shock. So, are you giving me my ticket?'

'And have you living off the boast that the brothers had to

throw you out? No, Jim, you will just have to voluntarily walk out of here, as a proper failure.'

'Cruds – I won't do it! You will have to throw me out.'

'Never,' said Sang, laughing and hitting the table in glee.

He had won a victory – the nature of which, however, was mysterious.

Even Jim McCall was a little relieved to see Sang a bit happier for once. He just could not see what he was so happy about.

He had always doubted his own vocation, too. He remembered how he had come up to see the brothers, on hearing of their newly established set-up in the north, after that first talk with Fogelman.

His conversion had not been overnight. It was mainly, at the time, a curiosity about how the monks made their living, and he also had a business proposal.

Religion had never been a factor in his life until then. Metaphysical questions had never entered his head until Fogelman had set his thoughts moving in that direction. There was certainly the strain of living a life filled with various risky financial schemes that might at least partly explain what ensued. These ventures were usually given euphemistic social or pseudo-religious labels to allay the risk of being spotted for what they were. They depended on the good will and confidence of well-lined partners. If one out of six of these schemes even partially succeeded he was above water.

He made his proposal – the growing of *cannabis sativa* on an industrial scale, with his good self taking care of all the arrangements and accepting all the risks. When objections were made on grounds of illegality and immorality, a strong case was made by him, giving (somewhat cynically) biblical references for believing that such a scheme might be blessed by God. He had already begun to take an interest in these passages from Scripture.

He was invited to stay over, while assessments were made of his proposal. Days grew into weeks, weeks into months. He began to like his surroundings. He felt in no hurry to leave. When Sang or Hans assured him that the matter was being dealt with, he assured them that there was no hurry. He took part in all the services and ceremonies, helping even to dispense the incense at 'High' services as conducted by the Jah. He developed a taste for peanut soup. He couldn't understand how he had ever eaten meat, and said no whenever asked if he'd like chicken feet for a change.

When, finally, the day came and Sang asked him into the office and informed him officially that his proposal had failed to get approval, he was not disappointed. He said that there was 'something about the atmosphere' in the place that made him want to stay. He had tried his hand at praying those last weeks. Despite his doubts, these prayers were getting somewhere. He felt that God, or at least somebody, was listening. Didn't he hear a voice whispering one night in his cell, although there was no one else there? He had felt so comfortable there. A feeling of peace deep inside and of ... acceptance. Acceptance by him and ... of him.

The moment when Hans told him he could stay came back to him. He could not stop his tears then. Or now. He looked up. Sang had left his chair. He was coming towards him. He was now placing a fatherly hand on his head.

'General' Wesley had decided it was time for the revolution to begin. He knew that, as with all decisive events in history, there was a limited 'window of opportunity'. If he missed that moment when all is possible, there was no second chance.

They were here as 'guests'. Hans had been very impressed – 'edified' was his term – by the humble yet desperate demeanour of these self-loathing outlaws as they had sneaked their way into the monastery. Wesley had convinced Hans that this was the only way to get them in – by assuring them that they would remain incognito, safe from assault or arrest by the security forces. This was to be the new, secure base for their future operations – operations and tactics that many of them might still believe would be similar to those of the past.

Hans thought the plan was brilliant – just the sort of madcap idea he would have loved to have come up with himself. For, as every Jesuit knows, education can only be carried out in stages, drawing on what is already there, leading the initiates to fresh pastures. Negative energies and thoughts are redirected so that they are productive only of good. When Sang had expressed misgivings, Hans had offered to take sole responsibility, along with Eamon and Dan, for the education of these rascals.

This hesitancy and apprehension was because Sang had not been trained as a Jesuit, he told Wesley.

They were to be treated as simply the latest batch of novices, so unruly and unprepared that they had to be quarantined. As far as anyone on the outside knew, if they should come across them, they were just more of those queer monks. It was the most unorthodox recruitment scheme ever used, Hans triumphantly told Wesley, 'and that ees saying something'.

Wesley proudly replied that it was he, single-handedly, who had persuaded them to give up their life of crime and ungodliness in the first place. Or at least to call a temporary cessation to hostilities. He and Hans, despite their ideological differences, could work closely together, he said. He felt honoured to be working with a real Jesuit, a representative of a system that he not only had many differences with on ideological grounds, but one to which his own ideology was directly opposed. Yet in the fertile ground of their conflicting beliefs a new world might emerge.

'We call eet Liberation Theology,' said Hans, 'and the Pope disapproves of it.'

This statement was meant to reassure Wesley.

They would both work together to produce an advanced political education programme that utilised a new methodology called 'channelling'. The thieves and murderers channelled their most base instincts into new fields; but these must not appear, at first, to be so totally different or divorced from the past as to cause unease, suspicion or a sense of alienation. Thus, it might still be necessary to allow them to keep their weapons, for instance.

Similarly, their lack of social training meant that they did not know things taken for granted by even the crudest brother, such as sitting down for meals, going to the toilet as an act requiring privacy, obeying simple instructions from anyone who is more knowledgeable or wiser than oneself, or concealing aggression when happening to come across other people. All the normal, accepted values – such as are acknowledged by most of mankind – are either unrecognised or rejected by such people. It was a challenging task to put oneself into their frame of mind – but the educator had to think in exactly that way, if he was to succeed in his task. It was incumbent upon the educator not just to 'take on', but to fully partake in the pupil's mental pathology.

Hans knew all the techniques – within days the education process was in full flow with Wesley (dressed in that scruffy 'get-up' of jeans and baseball cap that he called a uniform) acting as the 'pupil'. In this way he was able to learn the techniques of Hans, and also anticipate (and experience) their effects on the 'subject'.

After two days Wesley was thinking – and acting – like a full-blown Jesuit.

Simultaneously, Hans was acting, speaking and behaving as a guerrilla/revolutionary leader might.

'Get into hees skin,' was his constant exhortation to Wesley.

After a time, Wesley was taking the training workshop so much to heart that, when Hans mentioned the upcoming retreat for the Kingstown top brass, Wesley fell to his knees and prayed loudly that they, too, would 'see the light'. As the tears came to his eyes, and as Hans ranted on about the necessity to exterminate such 'scum', Wesley found himself pleading for understanding and forgiveness for those who had been 'led astray'.

This 'emotionalism' of Wesley went on for so long, seemingly with no sign of ending or diminishing in intensity, that eventually Hans had to shout at him and bring him back to his senses.

'Do not, ever, let your emotions get the better of you,' he advised; 'that ees the best piece of advice you will ever get in life.'

'Hans, you are a great man,' Wesley sobbed.

Of course, by nightfall Wesley was regretting his emotionalism and rueing the many things he had uttered, seemingly involuntarily in 'stream of consciousness' mode, during the course of the day. Forgotten utterings – words, sayings and statements that he knew he had said but that he just could not remember – played most on his mind. He kept going over what he had said during each day in his head. It was as if there were something in those words, that he had uttered so carelessly, that had the potential to cause great harm existentially. Troublesome psychological genies had been released, a Pandora's box of suppressed emotions opened. He found it difficult to go to sleep. Throughout the night the worry caused him to shuffle and turn in an uneasy slumber. Yet in the morning he could not remember what had caused him to have such a troubled night.

As he ate the daily ration with Dagga and the rest (the food was brought over by Eamon and Dan), he found himself full of questions that he *had* to ask Han. He felt a strange excitement as he listed all these questions in his head (eventually having to write them all down to ensure that not one was left out).

The big discussion this day was Liberation Theology. Wesley had to admit that he had never heard of it, and was surprised that the church could have come up with such a concept. It had the sound of a bit of a con, he said. It was, admittedly, a great thing in its favour that the Pope had banned it. Not quite banned it, said

Hans, but had demanded redefinitions here and there. It parted company with those liberationists who espoused strict Marxist analysis, and those clerics who partook in politics. It rules me out then, said Wesley cynically. No, said Hans, this is where you come een. You can help me, the church and mankind get through this misunderstanding. We must develop a whole new liberation theology acceptable to everybody. Except the powers-that-be, of course.

'Sounds good,' said Wesley and then, looking extremely perplexed, asked, 'How am I supposed to be thinking today?'

Hans looked at him kindly and asked, 'You are thinking the same way you have always been thinking.'

'But ... am I still the person I was yesterday, or am I someone new?'

Hans patted him on the back enthusiastically and once again assured him that he was making spectacular progress.

'And there ees also no doubt about it – you make an excellent Jesuit! After your time here, the sky will be the limit. The country will be yours.'

Wesley beamed and then turned serious. 'How shall we make this liberation theology acceptable then? How can we get the church – and the respectable people who can turn things for us – on our side? And without their knowing it!'

'By dropping the name. At least temporarily. Think up a new one. I'm sure you can come up with something creative, Dr Wesley. We can always change eet back to liberation theology when we are successful. It's what all successful politicians do when they run for election – only the other way around.'

'You are such an insightful man, Fr Hans. You should have been in my game. You are wasted on the church and religion.'

'It ees you who is teaching me!'

'Ah, no!'

'How are your men?'

'I was going to mention them. Dagga is getting restless. They have got over their initial fear of the monks and have settled in, thanks to those two proletarian brothers. They keep them entertained with fairy stories all night. They send them to sleep with those Irish lullabies. Meaning no disrespect! But now they want some action. They are wondering if they might be let out for an evening to go sightseeing in the local vicinity.'

'Sightseeing! It is some good social-action they should be getting themselves involved een. Could they not go out in the daytime?'

'They have a bit of a problem with the daytime. But I like the idea of their doing social work. They will have to carry their guns with them, though. They will be under strict orders not to use those in any circumstances. They will conceal them on their persons.'

'Great. The Lord's disciples concealed their swords. I know some places they could visit and perhaps do some good. The people of the countryside are having a problem at the moment with thieves coming out from Mobby Bay and stealing their coconuts and bananas. Sometime even chickens and goats disappear overnight. They tell me, een fact, that the problem has worsened of late. Your boys could guard the fields. Thus they will still feel they are powerful men of the world, and also help liberate the poor from fear.'

Wesley's eyes and mouth opened wide and he shouted, 'Liberate from Fear! That is what I will call them. The Liberate From Fear Army.'

'That sounds real good, Dr Wesley. Explain what you mean.'

'The boys have been asking me how we should name the 'army', as they now prefer to call themselves. They first suggested names such as Vengeful Squad, Death Crew, Extermination Posse and others perhaps too crude to mention. They are the Liberation From Fear Army! Everything we do from now on has the objective of liberating people from their fear. We could not ask for anything more inspirational. It will appeal to the browbeaten masses. No longer will they be terrorists who, even if they had exhibited respectable revolutionary names such as Revolutionary Justice Front, People's Militia, the Radical Expropriation Party and so on would still send a chill up the spine. It is the message of love (that concrete, practical love that you told me about) that we want to send out. Every conservative peasant and worker will welcome an organisation with that new name.'

Hans was nodding as Wesley continued, 'The new liberation theology will work like this: the rich fear the loss of their surplus wealth, so we show them that the loss of unnecessary possessions is a liberation! Similarly with political power. We show those in power that losing power is the one sure way to save not just their lives but their self-respect and dignity – what we could call their souls. The Church cannot but give its blessing to such a programme of political and social action that has as its aim the relieving of rich and poor alike of their burdens. Our "anti-terrorists" will hit every street and highway, every village and town, every field and plantation with the full force of their war cry – liberate from fear!'

Hans was pleased. He could see that Dr Wesley was making excellent progress. Creative ideas were flowing. Sang need not have worried. The dangers of having a group of armed men on the premises was counteracted by the definite prospect of these same conscripts soon becoming willing servants of the Church, valuable 'spoils of holy war'.

'Today, General Wesley, you are the Commander-in-Chief of the LLFA, an anti-terrorist force dedicated to liberating the bodies and souls of the rich and powerful. You are the guru of a new philosophy that renders redundant all the old political programmes of Marxism and capitalism. You are establishing a new programme that accomplishes all that every revolutionary ever dreamed of – by giving people their freedom, rather than taking it from them, by giving them more wealth than they ever had before, rather than simply taking their material wealth from them. Your boys, once so taken up with evil, are now the vanguard of all the progressive forces, political, social, religious in the world. They are entering into a mysticism more pronounced that that ever conceived in the Communist Manifesto – that of the perfect, loving society.'

'Put it down that General Wesley is the new, compassionate Napoleon, Paulo.'

Hans had called in Bro Paulo to record these penultimate stages of the educational programme, with a view in mind of workshops, seminars etc. later.

Paulo had recorded the discussions between Hans and Wesley in minute detail. His impersonal literary style was to cause a calamitous misunderstanding some weeks later when Raul and Erico Mauris Sr read his account in the cabinet room. One particular passage received their fulsome condemnation and gleeful wrath.

Bro Hans and the great intellectual from Kingstown, Dr Wesley, locked horns in a dramatic showdown between these two Goliaths of the modern world. The priest and the atheist traded argument and counter-argument, two armies dug into their impregnable trenches. Total war was declared. The priest launched a heavy salvo of fire and death. The responding fire of salvos of love from the atheist gave answer. The priest knew no limits to the violence of his attacks on the country's establishment and prominent capitalists. The atheist drew on the unfathomable depths of love and healing. Death to Raul Umberto, death to his lackey president and all the whores of government, cried the priest. Peace be upon us and them, answered the atheist.

'At last,' shouted Umberto, 'direct evidence that the monks are planning the violent overthrow of the state. Wesley is a pussycat compared to them. What ... this monk is even proposing my assassination!

'Call in the Chief of the Security Forces. Phone the Director of Public Prosecutions. We will have a meeting first thing this afternoon. We have all the evidence we need. We can now enter their den, kill the leaders and lock all the rest up. The Lord be praised!'

chapter
nine

Bro Gerry looked up and knew at once that there was something different about the sky. There was a streak of golden light in the middle distance that did not belong with the orange hue that marks the tropical dawn. There was something not quite right, in fact, about the whole scene. He couldn't put a finger on what it was, and he became a little disturbed.

He had taken himself outside to a wooden bench facing the nearby mountains. He always found the mountains the best focus for morning meditation. The sea, to the north, aroused in him a sense of isolation; it also reminded him of other, less hospitable lands beyond the horizon from which he had been driven out by his enemies. He might always be considered something of an oddity here, but at least it was home now. However, even the sight of the mountains, glowing in the sharp, early light could not calm his mind. As he looked at them they seemed to be moving slightly, as if breathing. They were twitching in their chains; he could have sworn that he heard them grumble. His eyes were drawn back to the golden gleam. He became transfixed; he struggled to look away at something else. He was filled with an unnameable expectation.

To calm himself he took out his notebook and pen. He would

write a poem to express his feelings. Paulo Costello, the traitor, was no longer at hand to record his observations and theories. His old pupil had gone over to the enemy, and was now working for Hans and company (writing up the minutes of working parties and sub-committees). He had insulted Gerry, saying that he had come to realise it might be better that he (Gerry) stop thinking for a while. That his brain needed a rest. Well, who needed him, anyway?

He himself had already given up on theology and all this 'identity of the messiah' business. He would send no more missives to Rome. He had lost faith in everybody. Even in Jim McCall. That guy had gone over to the enemy, too. He had met him yesterday and his old companion-in-arms had acted totally out-of-character. He had become all-friendly and chatty, took him aside and told him that he was praying for him! Gone was that old familiar distance, that imposing indifference. As if he needed McCall's prayers! As if God would ever listen to Jim McCall – who was here under false pretences. If Bro Jim McCall had gone over to God then that would be the greatest betrayal of principle he had ever come across in his life. That climb down would just about ... sum the turncoat up.

He wrote what was on his mind:

The mountains ... are braver,
Than Jim McCall,
They never fall down;
The sky ... is more honest,
Than Jim McCall,
Not filled with empty boasts;
The Sun fire ... burns forever,
Not like Jim McCall,
Whose fire has gone out.

The moment he had written the last word, bursting through

the paper with a too powerful full stop, it happened. The golden streak of light had once again drawn his attention. He could scarcely believe what he was seeing. His uneasiness was still there, but now it was joined by holy fear. The curtains had parted and at the farthest distance he saw a magnificent chariot of golden fire drawn by four magnificent white steeds, driven by a glorious angel blowing a trumpet and waving a lash triumphantly in the air, coursing in an arc, up and down as it came ever closer to Earth. He knew, somehow, that when it arrived that would be the end of the world.

He was so overcome with amazement he did not feel fear any more. All of his surroundings had now taken on a golden, orange, pinkish glow. He heard choral singing, of indeterminate sex, subdued but beautiful, and intermingling in an unexplainable way with the colours. Soon the vision faded somewhat; becoming a blend of intermixed, confused colour. Now it was impossible to distinguish the heavenly chariot from its surroundings, as the vivid scene dissolved into the sky, mountains and sea. There was an eeriness as though all creation was saying goodbye, a soft, gentle glowing kiss encompassing all that lived. He felt empty. The experience, already, felt so distant, so long ago. What did it all mean? Time, perhaps, was short? He sat there in silence, comatose. Eventually they came and had to arouse him. At first his body was rigid, so that they had to lift him into a standing position.

'Nobody has ever seen anything like it,' he enthused, 'not Orbeck, or Sanctus, certainly not you, Hans and Sang!'

They didn't believe him of course. They said it was all in his mind. A dream. Hans picked up the poem and showed it to Sang.

Meanwhile, that same day some other monks were showing similar signs of emotional, if not religious instability. The two superiors now wondered if they were not witnessing the onset of another unknown 'craze'. For the phenomenon of uncleanliness among the brethren had taken a new direction in at least two cases. Sanctus had begun claiming recently that the wearing of clothes that covered the whole body was against certain passages in the Bible. Clothes were a hindrance to living the 'real life'.

It was noteworthy that, of late, his campaign for Jah rights had fallen rather flat, considering that the supposed second-class citizens were now claiming to see orthodoxy as 'the light' and their old ways as abominations. At least this was according to their spokesman Alan, who had by now come back in an attempt to regain control from the same Sanctus. Sanctus had taken some rebuffs from his brethren and endured some high profile slights in the last few days, a real testing of his new principles. At last, perhaps, he was seeing the beginning of a decline of his false, religious 'nous'. Nevertheless, Sanctus continued to insist, now, that wearing the habit was a 'vestige of sin' and should be discarded. Both he and Bro Asissy had appeared that very morning in nothing but shorts, their bare bodies greased with mud to fend off the worst of the sunlight. Mercifully, they had taken themselves off to the farm, well away from the hospital where more prudish eyes might see them.

It had also been announced that morning at breakfast notices that the convent had broken off all relations with the monastery, with the sisters declaring that henceforth they were going to be totally independent of 'oppressive structures'.

The news had come more or less as a total surprise to them (although there had been a rumour going about that Sr Jane was now in a position to stop fruit juice on Sundays). For few brothers had been aware of any rift or major inter-community problem, although they had noticed that the sisters were scarce on the ground the previous day. The official split in the United Church was now formally declared by Fr Sang, who expressed his great sorrow and warned the brothers that the devil was doing his work. They were to watch out as he was succeeding in 'working in them' as well. Let it be a warning to all that they could take nothing for granted. Splits and divisions were his means. But it was by initiating *little* splits and *petty* divisions that the evil one began.

Sang had finally succeeded in gaining an interview with Sr Jane the previous day. It had taken some time for her to respond to his written request for an appointment. Then he had to wait a further day before she was able to find a gap in her busy schedule to arrange an appointment time. He was shown to the office by the deposed Josephine, who grabbed his arm as they walked along and whispered to him that she was 'so glad and relieved to see you, Lee'.

It was all she could do now to stay on Jane's good side, she said. She lived in fear of imminent expulsion for some minor offence. It was much too late for her to start another career in life. She had not heard from her family for years. She was on the FBI's blacklist, and would not even be allowed back into the States.

'My dear!' sympathised Sang.

'Tell me, what's happened to the phone line?'

'It's dead. She says that there are no phone technicians this side of Kingstown. She won't have the last lot back anyway, because when they were here they chatted up the younger sisters and the line was worse after they left than it was before. What do we need a phone for anyway? she shouted at me! I tell you, she has deliberately cut the cable behind her desk and has concealed it with that big dieffenbachia pot. She won't let me mix with the other sisters either. She keeps me working in the office like a personal servant.'

Now *that* lie-down-and-take-it attitude was so unlike the old Josephine! She – who in her hippy-nun days smoked and drank with the best of them and enjoyed the company of every sinner in town – afraid? This fearless nun of the avant-garde of the people's church – succumbing to the dictates of an old-style, despot harridan? He would sort it all out, he promised her, placing his hand on her head in blessing.

'After all, it is questionable whether the convent is an independent entity, legally, anyway.'

Jane was in the corner of the room when he came in, polishing the top of a filing cabinet. Her back was turned to him and she replied 'just a minute' when he greeted her.

'Dust, dust everywhere. You'd imagine it's a virtue being dirty.'

'We are all made from dust, Jane. It's a holy ingredient – stardust – as the song goes.'

'That's the sort of rubbish one used to hear in this place all the time. Maybe that's why your monks are so unclean. Have you seen the muck and filth on them lately? The state of the hygiene over at your place is unbelievable. It's a wonder my sisters haven't caught some plague by now. And the walls and roof of that building ...! It's another miracle someone hasn't been decapitated. And please address me by my proper title. It's Mother Jane.'

'It's not just about dirt and untidiness. It's about healing body and mind, and saving souls.'

'I am pulling my girls out of there altogether. I'm sure that we can do just as good a job on our own here. For one thing, we will save on all that time that is wasted walking between your place and mine. I have made up my mind and that is it.'

'If you read the title deeds you will see that all property is in joint ownership. You cannot secede without our agreement.'

'I thought you might say that. Well, I have a serious accusation to make. Your place is no longer a Christian institution. The sort of people one sees going in and out of there ... smoking, swearing, some of them obviously drunk, men looking unchastely at the sisters ...! You cannot tell these days who is a monk and who is not. Furthermore, your brothers were encouraging Sr Gloria to go over at night time, breaking every church law there is. Does the Lord not make a special point of monitoring every single thing that goes on in his monastic institutions? Why else would a naïve, ignorant, poor soul, who knows no better, venture out at night just to subject herself to all the indignity of a common criminal being returned to jail – if she was not receiving some encouragement?

'Now what would any objective, sensible person conclude from all this? There is no smoke without fire. The facts speak for themselves. I hesitate to say it myself. The word "encouragement" perhaps says it all. I am considering whether the Archbishop should be told about what has been going on.'

By ... thought Sang, she is blackmailing me!

He took a deep breath and sat down on the floor (there was only one chair in the office). He manoeuvred himself into a meditative position, his legs turned inwards, his hands clasping his knees. He began breathing deeply, while Jane fiddled with her rosary beads. It was Western, medieval Christianity against Eastern, new-fangled 'interior' Christianity.

After three deep intakes of breath he said, 'Gloria, as you already know, sees herself as the chaste wife of Bro Gerry. All the brothers accept that she is "married" to Gerry. It makes an interesting comparison with that romantic relationship between St Clare and St Francis. Perhaps, if every brother and sister had a spiritual "mate", there would be less scandal. In fact we are considering whether we should set aside a small part of the monastery where Gerry and Gloria might live together. All with the approval of the church, of course.'

'What! I will ignore what you have just said. Perhaps you are a bit mad too. Men have dominated this church for too long. It is why things have gone downhill ever since the Ascension. If women had been in charge there would have been none of the scandals – all the wars, Inquisitions, corruption. There would have been none of the cruelty with which religion has come to be associated. I am going to declare our convent an independent church.

'Furthermore, I have heard of a schismatic bishop who is willing to ordain women as priests. Rome can do nothing about it. We will be just as true a church as they are! It will be a women's church. Just like you men have always had your men's church!

We will be the first woman's church in the world. It will put all your trendy, flower-power hippy experiments to shame. There is no such thing as equality. Women are superior! There will be no church like it anywhere. We will recruit more than half of the population of the world. What can Rome do about that? Most likely, because we are women they won't even show the slightest bit of interest anyway. They will leave us alone, content that we are out of the way. We will be free to get on with the real work.'

'What do the sisters say?'

'They are with me. They know me to be a no-nonsense pers-on. They don't even question my plans. They all agree that hav-ing their own church is a good idea. They also agree with me that it should be called the Women's Catholic Church.'

'Ah. How can it be Catholic if it's only for women?'

'Men will be welcome. But they may not be ordained, or hold the highest positions of authority. They may join us as brothers, where their service in doing the heavy work will be celebrated as a most wonderful, precious gift to the church.'

Sang had to admire her logic as well as her determination. Perhaps some good would come out of it, he thought. He decided to take a non-confrontational approach. After all, it was just an-other experiment. All is possible – so the Lord said himself.

General Wesley was giving a mission briefing to the mightily im-patient troops of the LFFA.

'Brothers of the Liberation From Fear Army – the hour has come to see if you are ready for war. In the darkness of night you will take yourselves out to the fields around the village of Don'tlookback, which is a half hour up the road past the bamboo grove. There you will hide yourselves in bushes, trees and anywhere else you can find. You will hide like a good guerrilla army. Nobody must know that you are there at all. You will not even see each other. Proper guerrilla fighters blend into the landscape—'

'Blend ..?'

'You make yourselves look like bushes and trees and things.'

'What do we do if we see duppy?' asked Cockroach, a small, rather timid killer.

'Fool,' Dog laughed at him. 'Eamon an' Dan say we now have power o'er duppy.'

'All de same, we mus' mek sure duppy doant see us neither,' said Dagga.

'Stop this fool talk,' ordered Wesley, alarmed lest his brave soldiers lose their nerve and change their minds. A few days ago there had been a demand from some of the ten for a return to 'sweet home' in Kingstown. The presence of Alfredo and other monks near the gate had prevented a full-scale exodus, their fear having been increased by a new terror – their sighting of the bodies of naked monks covered in war paint. An Obeah man had told one of the comrades, once, that that was how their invincible ancestors had presented themselves for battle. Most of them still feared the monks more than ghosts or devils; they were further unnerved by the monks' war chanting early in the morning and late at night, which had apparently become a lot louder lately. They were unable to sleep easily while it was going on.

'Mek sure gun hide in pocket. Dey no use anyway 'gainst duppy or devil. Yo mus' not kill dis time. Only warn!' said Wesley.

He saw them slink off into the night, feeling a little proud of how far his men had come in such a short time.

Don'tlookback was a village of twenty homes, only one of which had electricity. The venerable village chief, Mr Davis, popularly known as Mr Big Stuff, had addressed the other tribal elders in his house (the only one lit up) that evening. Dressed in a multi-coloured head-cover made from sheep's wool that rose like a tower above his head, with a technicolor robe concealing a vast bulk of well-fed stomach that would (if visible) have totally destroyed his authority and sense of dignity, and plain rubber sandals, imported spin-offs from the oil industry of Trinidad, he looked the piece. The magnificence of his turnout outshone all others in every way, for there was to be no competition with a chief like Mr Big Stuff. Indeed none would dare attempt to be so well dressed, for to do so would be a direct challenge to Big Stuff's authority. After a ritual sharing of the communal pipe and a song in hoary voice to a bongo drum, he made the village committee be silent and listen.

'Yo all know how we suffer from thief. At first dey tek banana an' coconut. Den dey come for chicken an' goat. Nex' dey will come fo treasure crop – de lamb's breath – holy herb.'

'No, no, no, save us, Lord.'

'Yeh – it true. An' dey big men kill wid guns. We country folk have no chance. Bud de Lord step in fe save us. De brother from de monastery come fe tell we dat he send ten new monks fe tek care of thief. Dey come tonight!'

'Lord be praised! Praise, praise.'

'Warn nobody go near cultivation tonight! Turn off all fire an' whole village stay inside home an' mek no sound. Lord be praised fo' holy monks.'

'Lord be praised fo' holy monks.'

'Dey save us from disease, poverty an' death.'

'Dey save us from disease, poverty an' death.'

There was no sign of the village whatsoever when Dagga and co. arrived in the vicinity. At first they believed that Don'tlookback must have been spirited away.

(Whatever modern science might say on the matter, it has been known for not just individuals but whole villages, towns and even cities to disappear overnight in such lands.)

Gradually, as the clouds shifted and faint moonlight appeared they could just about make out the huts entwined in, and almost covered by the vegetation. They made their way to the field that lay between the village and the river. Here they concealed themselves in the undergrowth. To pass the time, each man counted to ten an innumerable number of times on his fingers. Each one imagined that if every ten was a million dollars, how rich he would be at the end of the night, and how many things he could buy and nice places he could visit. The moonlight did not last very long and then it was all dark.

In the morning Big Stuff and the elders approached the cultivation warily. During the night there had been a terrible outcry followed by the sound of gunfire. Now as they came to the ganja plot they saw a number of bodies on the ground. But it was not this that first caught their eye. It was the empty ganja field. The crop was all gone. The ruthless thieves had killed the new monks and fled with the whole herb crop!

There was no doubt in anyone's mind now but that the Lord was coming.

Fr Sang himself, who had once accepted whatever fate might bring with total resignation, and always condemned what he described as the obsequious childishness of Western Christianity, was now looking up at the sky and asking for help.

His old philosophy could be summarised in a well-remembered, notorious sermon he once gave in Kingstown cathedral, broadcast by Kingstown radio over the whole country, causing consternation and scandal even at that early hour of a Sunday morning.

'Brethren, give up religion! Praying and pretending to be holy is getting you nowhere. What do you get when you ask a big favour – nothing! You pray for this and that and when your prayers are not answered you tell yourselves "it's because I didn't ask properly" or "I asked for the wrong thing". When the hurricane hit a few years ago, it was either "God is punishing us" or "we didn't pray hard enough". Did you really expect it not to happen again, just because you spend hours in church every Sunday? Did you really believe that? Well, there was another, worse hurricane last year! Two thousand years of Christian preaching has produced your infantile religion. Let me give you the wisdom of the East. You have to be an atheist before you believe. You have to be bad before you are good. You have to curse and swear before you can pray. You have to ask before you can give. So brethren, go out today and be bad. Curse, swear, get up to no good. Tell everyone that you do not believe in God. Laugh at the religious hypocrites. Above all – hate!'

Here was this same, wise man now pleading, 'Lord, I know I am worthless. Please save us. You know there is nothing I can do. I have never asked you for anything before, Lord. Just this once – help!'

He had started patrolling the compound, trying to work out where the Devil was hiding. Of the destructive presence of the Adversary he had no doubt. His own people had their effective methods for driving him away; smoking him out, making a lot of noise such as banging lids or pots, crying and shouting. These Westerners, who were so foolish, were actually scared of the Evil One! That is what gives him his power! He was not scared of the Devil. It was the Devil who was scared of him. Why else did the fellow hide? It was the sneaky, malodorous effects that Satan worked that worried him. He did not cause earthquakes, hurricanes and all those accidents that killed millions of people. His job was just to create a nasty smell in the vicinity. He left it to humans to do the rest. Every day, in the course of the last few months, he had been detecting the malevolent presence.

This was why he had started to take walks around the area at randomly chosen moments, day and night. At each spot Sang did his smoke-out-the-devil test. He carried with him a dispenser for this purpose, from which incense poured forth as he gave blessing. He visited the workers at the farm and hospital. He visited the new arrivals in the ruins, who had greeted him obsequiously, having been warned that he was the 'chief of the monks'. Wesley had sung the praises of the unkempt lot for defending the local village so effectively and bravely, but Sang appeared strangely distant and did not comment. After drawing a blank everywhere else, he had thought something, at least, would show up at the ruins. But even more intense prayer and extra smoke was to no avail here, either.

He went on to the hillside. Eamon and Dan dropped their tools and fell to their knees at his approach, their heads on the ground, not daring to look him in the face. Both had an exaggerated sense of awe and respect for Sang, based on the knowledge that this man could, with a single word, send them back to where they came from. He thanked them for all their fine work with the new aspirants, commended them on their agricultural work, and gave them a blessing. Once again, dispensing plentiful incense produced no good effect.

He went back towards the main building, wondering who else he could find to bless. Then he thought of the rabbi. Now why had he forgotten all about him? Must be psychological! Of course the guest would not want a blessing, but the room and the workshop could do with one.

As he approached Fogelman's room he felt a strange sensation at the nape of his neck, as if someone were blowing on it. He turned around and saw nothing. He put it down to the wind. He knocked on the door. No answer. He must be in the workshop. He blessed the door before he left. The workshop was just across the path. The door was open. He could see the man inside, busily carving as usual. He knocked.

'Cum un,' he heard, 'yu ure wulcume.'

'I was wondering, Rabbi, whether you had noticed anything unusual about the place. Any bad smells or anything?'

Fogelman gave him what Sang thought was a knowing look.

'Uh guts bud smulls ull thu tume. Uvury kund uf bud smull! Ut us nut unusule un thus pluce.'

'I mean ...'

He felt humiliated. It was so unseemly. He – a sophisticated, experienced cleric whose life had been spent sorting out other people's problems – was now making a complete fool of himself in front of this rabbi. What must he think? How could he explain himself? He would try as best he could.

'There is a bad influence in the community, which I am trying to track down. It has been here for some time – I cannot remember exactly when I first noticed it. But it is badly affecting the brothers – and sisters. Things are going screwy. My leadership is apparently of little use against these new ... fashions.'

'Fushuns?'

'Everybody wanting to do their own thing, for starters. Hans will not listen to my advice. I tell him we need to get a firm grip on the brothers, before they go completely off the rails. He is not paying any attention to administration these days, busying himself running seminars for all kinds of undesirables. He tells me he is determined to undo all the mistakes of the past – and have a truly loving, open community that rejects nobody. I tell him he is bringing dangerous people into the community, who will turn around and destroy us. He says that argument is exactly how tyrants and persecutors justified mass murder in the past. He cannot distinguish friend from foe. Your pal, Jim McCall, meanwhile, has turned all holy, which is the most inexplicable and ominous thing of all.'

There was bitterness in his voice.

Rabbi Fogelman said – at least Sang thought that he said: 'Hans will find his peace.' That he himself (Fogelman) might be responsible, or partly responsible, for some of the bad influences about the place. He realised, certainly, that being who he was and where he was 'coming from', might inevitably cause adverse reactions in a Christian community. He was very sorry. He (Sang) was not imagining things or overreacting at all! He had a responsibility, as the father of the community, to act whenever trouble appeared. He knew exactly what he meant by a 'bad smell'. It was not the product of an overwrought imagination. Things always 'created their own environment'. He would take himself off the premises shortly. In fact, Hans and he had had a discussion only a few hours ago about a likely destination. And Bro Jim McCall was going to contact a relative who owned a fast boat.

Fogelman sat down on a stool and commenced to speak in a resigned, relaxed way.

He offered to leave all his woodwork behind as a gift, hoping that it might be of some use to someone. As a small token of gratitude for the risks that had been taken in putting him up, he had taken a liberty and completed fourteen small carvings depicting what is called the Stations of the Cross. One day, perhaps, they might find a home on the walls of a place of 'spiritual refurbishment'.

'Where does Hans suggest you go to, then?'

'Hu suys ut wud bu sufe up wuth thu Jusuits un Bustun.'

He paused and looked at Sang. Did Bro Sang think, he asked, that Hans was anti-Jew, or anti-Semitic as they called it these days?

Sang was surprised. Such an idea would never have occurred to him. The subject of Jews, per se, never came up.

'I don't think so. I have never noticed anything like that. He hasn't said anything to me. Have you any reason for thinking that?'

Fogelman said that he felt that Hans was always uneasy in his presence. Hans would look at him oddly, as if he were 'another species'. He never looked him in the face, most times. They would have eye contact for less than a second, if at all. Then Hans would look away as if embarrassed.

Sang wondered. Hans would certainly not have thought that it was *Fogelman* who felt uneasy when they met. He said, now, that nobody was more capable, more intrepid and less hidebound than Hans. He said that he would trust Hans with his life. On one condition. That there were no bets involved. Hans liked to gamble. It might be okay to risk material possessions, but a life was too precious to gamble with. Hans had put his own life in the balance a number of times, but he had never come across an inst-ance of his risking the life of another. He assured Fogelman that he could trust Hans with regard to the travel arrangements, but that he (Sang) would double-check them, adding, 'I would think that it is safe in Boston.'

'Thunk yu.'

Fogelman, when asked, said that he could not show him the Stations of the Cross yet as it was still work-in-progress. But he produced a figurine of somebody he called, intriguingly, 'the monk' for Sang to admire. It might have been his imagination, and Sang didn't want to ask, but he thought that it bore a resemblance to – of all people – Hans!

He said that he hoped he didn't mind but that he'd like to bless the room. The rabbi could step outside while he did so. Fogelman said that he didn't mind and went outside. This time Sang prayed very intensely. He had a strong feeling, now, that he was near to something. He filled the room with incense, so that he was finding it hard to breathe. Then he came outside with the smoke all around him. Fogelman was chuckling, in a pleasant sort of way.

'Us ut dune?'

'That's it, all done,' smiled Sang, feeling rather chirpy for no good reason.

He walked away, and that was when he met the Devil.

The breathing on the back of his neck had returned, and this time he knew it was not the wind. The stench was out-of-this-world. He felt nauseous – as if he was being suffocated.

Angry, aggressive, hateful thoughts went through his mind. He thought of what he would do to turncoat Hans, to 'Mother' Jane, to those louts over at the ruins who were up to no good, to that Wesley fool who thought he was God Almighty. In part-icular, he thought of what he would do to the rabbi. He was a charlatan! He was a bad man! He was a corruption of what an up-right, religious person should be. He would put an end to ... the Jew. Death was too good for him. He would call in the police. He would call in the much-feared Special Branch to deal with him. He was coughing uncontrollably, felt even more sick – as if all that smoke was going to detach him from the world altogether. With great effort he struggled to reject the malign thoughts. The vengeful feelings. With further, even greater effort he looked behind him and through the smoke saw Fogelman standing in the far distance, as though a thousand miles away. There was nobody else there.

He realised something important now. That he would never see the Devil. That the fellow hid behind people's backs. So close up that no matter which way one turned he would remain out of sight. That was why it had been so hard to find him.

As he got out of the range of the smoke the ill-feelings sub-sided. He no longer felt vengeful. Gone was that vile hatred.

Within a minute or two he was asking himself what had come over him, and how on earth he could have entertained such thoughts!

The hospital, once described by an unsympathetic observer as an 'accident waiting to happen', was a place that defied all the logic of modern science. The least of the unscientific events that took place there were the so-called miraculous cures. One of the more impressive mysteries was the non-outbreak of any epidemic of in-fectious disease. There were so many diseases already there in their critical and chronic phases, and a lack of the normal facilities of hygiene, that it was more like a big party to which every dang-erous bug and hazardous material in the universe was invited. The tropical heat and frequent high humidity would have been the nirvana in which the germs and bacteria might have been given additional encouragement and a bon voyage to multiply by the multiples of zillions in every miniscule cavity and on every surface. A further cause for concern might be the custom of familiarity and love as expressed between patients and workers. Much hand clasping, kisses on cheeks and close breathing on one's fellow patient or helper ensured free trade of all bodily elements.

Yet nobody seemed to suffer any additional ailment, or experience a worsening in their own condition, and the brothers and sisters themselves remained in the best of health. It was this 'closeness' between man and disease that some held to be the medical reason for otherwise inexplicable cures – that the sheer superfluity of microbes in juxtaposition with competing micro-organisms worked as some sort of immunisation that explained it all.

Such was the basis of an involved theory put forward by Professor Man of the Boston Medical Bureau, in the renowned medical science journal *Under the Knife*. His proposal for ending the Third World medical crisis by eliminating HIV, AIDS and malaria through certain 'exposure methods' that he had researched in the Third World aroused great interest. This discussion was soon taken up by the world health bodies, then by the political, commercial and other scientific interests. Its many intricacies, controversies and spin-offs preoccupied the medical debate for years. It made Professor Man into an international expert, with a reputation for original thinking, a commodity rare in his profession.

But on the day he called into the monastery his attitude was anything but approving. He had stopped by (he was over for an important hemispherical golf tournament), as a result of reading various negative newspaper articles about the United Church in the American press. He said he had heard of the notorious reputation of the place and, being a medical scientist, just could not resist the opportunity to pop in and see how bad things were for himself. He did not believe that medicine and religion 'mixed', pointing out the harm done to the poor and ignorant by the strictures of various sects that either forbade various treatments, encouraged harmful treatments, or discouraged treatment altogether, asserting that disease was God's righteous punishment on Man.

'Oh, we don't believe that here,' said Malicious.

'Then where the hell are your doctors, surgeons, x-ray machines, radiotherapy unit, and basic plasma facilities?'

'Give us the money, and we will get them!' laughed Capricious.

'Heck, I have never seen anything so medieval. I will have to have a word with the director of this institution. And the Ministry of Health, if there is one.'

'Would you take a look at Winston for us?' asked Malicious quietly, finding the man's criticism tame stuff compared with what Jane often directed at them. 'Nobody has been able to cure him.'

The opportunity to nab the expertise of a real doctor was too good to be missed.

'Winston? What is wrong with him?'

There was a touch of nervousness in his voice. He thought – it must be bad if *they* can't deal with him.

'If we knew what was wrong he might have been cured by now. His body is totally lifeless. He smells like a corpse. He does not talk and it is hard to detect his pulse, or even his breathing. His body has an unnatural purple colour. There are many more things wrong with him as well.'

He was brought to the end shed and the smell of rotting flesh came to him before he had even got near the place. He felt his stomach retching. He took out a handkerchief and held it to his mouth and nose. His legs felt like lead. Clamminess made him feel faint. He regretted coming to the monastery.

'Brother Winston. Brother Winston. Can you hear me?' shouted Capricious, gently prodding him.

A faint noise was heard, interpreted as a 'yes'.

'There is an important gentleman here to meet you. He is a doctor. A real doctor! He might be able to help you.'

Another noise was heard.

Dr Man called for surgical gloves, a face mask and barrier apron, and after coming back in after an intake of fresh air, went over to Winston and opened an eyelid. He felt for a pulse. He straightened up and shook his head as he walked quickly away.

'There is no hope for him. Without blood tests, x-rays and a lot more, I cannot say for sure what is wrong with him. Your miracle cure certainly hasn't worked in his case!'

Dr Man was almost triumphant. He said he was now going over to the office (he just had to get out of that area) as he had a meeting with the 'director'. He promised Capricious and Malicious (in order to get away from them, for they were holding on to him tightly), that when he got back to Boston he would arrange for some medical supplies to be sent over.

Meanwhile, Sanctus had gone to visit Rabbi Fogelman, full of emotion at the prospect of speaking again with the man who had changed his life. For Sanctus, the rabbi had certain qualities that other religious people did not. For one thing, he did not have to obey any of the rules about fasting, silence, thinking charitable thoughts, or undergo the bodily strictures (self-punishment with the discipline was the one he hated the most) that he and his brethren did.

He thought that there must be something superior about a religion that indulged its adherents. Sanctus felt that no matter what shortcomings and failings he personally had (and sometimes making a list of them felt only like an exercise in pride), it didn't matter a bean to this fellow, who had a totally different set of rules. From what he had heard, this man's religion, although emphasising rectitude, allowed everyone to enter heaven providing that they obeyed the one true God. He had also heard that his religion had no comprehensive range of dogmas as such; no long list that a failure of belief even in one, or part of one, meant instant excommunication and eternal punishment. His religion sounded more loving, more forgiving. The only problem was: you had to be a member of the Chosen Race to join! That was an impediment, for which Sanctus had come to him for an answer.

'Rulus!' he chuckled, 'yo shuld suu thu rulus wu huve! Thuy full whule buks. Und thu Chusun ruce must untur untu huvun furst.'

'So dere is no hope fo us?'

'Uh dud nut suy thut. Tull mu – huw us Asussy?'

'Him better, man. After talk wid yo he more cool. Every day he more cool dan day before. Now he wear very few clothes an' muck himself up! Me think o' doing dat, but liddle voice tell me no.'

'Und ull thu uthur bruthurs?'

'Bro McCall really pray now. An' he such mighty big man once! Bro Gerry, him stop pray altogether. Fr Sang don't control brothers like he used. Fr Hans still organise retreats fo' sinners. Him only brother who never change one day to next. Sisters dem broke away from we. Dey no longer come here. So awful lot happen in past days. De sick still ged cure, except fo' Winston, and many, many come fo liddle chats.'

'Wunstun hus nut bun curud yut?' he asked, sounding surprised.

'No. A doctor from America saw him today and said that he was incurable.'

'Nubudy us uncurublu. Huv u pruyud?'

'We pray all de time fo' Winston.'

'Yu must shuw thus Umurucun! Hu must nut gu hume wuth buluf thut pruyur dus nut wurk. Nu, nu. Yu pruy thu wrung wuy. Yu must du ut prupurly.'

'Proper ...?'

'Uftur Jum McCull, yu pruy thu bust. Gu uvur und ... Nu,

gut Asussy. Tull hum tu cum hure.'

Asissy was hailed by Sanctus and he sprinted over as if he had been called to a big party in his honour. Fogelman proceeded to instruct the muddy, sweaty happy monk over the next two hours in some of the Jewish ways of prayer. He told him that he must have complete faith. Only that would work. Here was a chance for him to shine. If it were Sanctus, nobody would bother, but if *he* should get a cure ...!

Sanctus and Asissy went over to the shed a few hours later. They went to Winston without speaking a word to anyone. Sanctus told him to stand up. There was no response. Winston was helped to his feet by both brothers and, with Sanctus holding him up, Asissy clasped him in an embrace and kissed the many sores on his face.

Asissy prayed – as Fogelman had instructed – to the Lord and *demanded* that Winston be cured. It was a long, heartfelt prayer, agonised, yet with a sure belief that good was going to be done. When he had finished they both let Winston gently back down on his bed of pain. As they left, they noted a look of peace on Winston's face. Fogelman was at the door. Obviously he couldn't resist coming over and having a look at how his pupil was doing. He told them now that the success of the job would be apparent in about half an hour. Asissy had never felt so pleased with himself in all his life.

Sang, Hans and the American rushed over when news of Winston's cure hit the monastery. Ten minutes after Sanctus and Asissy had left, the brothers had heard loud arguing and swearing, mixed with copious mutual racial insulting between the patients in the open ward. When they went in, who was at the centre of the ruckus? The new Winston, merrily laying in and giving as good as he got from the others. It was perhaps not so much a new Winston as more likely the old Winston, but it was certainly a Winston they had never before seen in the hospital.

A way was made through the crowd of excited and argumentative spectators for Professor Man, so that he could get a full view of the cured patient. He could not believe that this was the same man he had seen not more than two hours earlier (the time in which it had taken him to complete a leisurely 'working lunch' in the Admin office). He produced again the notebook in which he had been writing down his criticisms of the place. Now he proceeded to detail as many facts about Winston as it was possible to collect (estimated weight, height etc.), asking questions of everyone. He interrogated Winston himself, both questions and answers being interpreted by Sang. An account was drawn up of Winston's medical history; a quick check was made of the hospital filing cabinet (despair evident in the brevity of the notes; he also noticed a death certificate, all ready for completion) and a document from the Kingstown General Hospital was found relating to the twenty-four hours Winston had spent there.

It was a happy professor who left the monastery that evening and went back to his hotel. He had enough information to produce a comprehensive scientific dossier on 'cure by infection'. Nearly a hundred photographs of the hospital facilities were taken; of every broken down, out-of-place item, every overcrowded area, all the faulty or primitive equipment. He took many more of Winston's body, now rapidly losing all its unpleasant sores and colouring. He cursed himself now that he hadn't taken a photo of Winston before the cure. That would have guaranteed him the Nobel Prize. Even the golf competition had slipped his mind completely.

Sang and Hans watched him go, feeling very pleased with themselves. The last thing they had wanted was for the professor to go back to a media-dominated world with more news of the 'invisible power'; and worse still, proof that it actually worked. Every shark in the world would be on his way – and the 'power' would remove itself elsewhere. The world was far happier believing that such miracles somehow *might* be true, while at the same time dismissing the supernatural with mocking comments and sceptical smiles.

When Winston was suddenly cured, with their visitor there to observe it, they had become alarmed. Fortunately, he was a non-believer. All they had to do was feed him a plethora of medical facts about Winston and the good professor would find a natural explanation. When Winston said that he was cured after Asissy kissed him, Professor Man knew for certain that he was on to a new, amazing method (the interchange of germs between disease ridden bodies) of curing the incurably ill.

When he asked Sang if Asissy was a dirty fellow, Sang revealed that he was not only dirty, but that he had not washed for a very long time; that he was full of germs and that in some ways their brothers were 'sicker' and more infected than their patients. Hadn't he noticed how untidy and dirt-splattered many of the monks were? Some didn't even bother to be decently dressed. Man nodded knowingly.

Their secret, hopefully, was safe.

The retreatants set out for the monastery from Kingstown in the early morning. They were travelling together in Luis García's air-conditioned Mercedes minibus, and were looking forward to the long, though scenic journey through the twisting river valleys of the Blue Mountain, helping themselves to their host's on-board supply of food and drinks.

'Hans's poker games, in the old days, were grand occasions, the social events of the poker season,' Luis was saying as they settled in. 'It will be good to play him again. He owes me a few dollars.'

As well as Luis, on the bus were two government ministers (Raul Umbero Jr and Erico Mauris Jr) travelling under the assumed names of Ron and Rick, the Papal Nuncio, Monsignor O'Delly, Superintendent Ivor Williams of the Fraud Squad, two of the country's leading industrialists, a high court judge, the US ambassador and the professor of Criminology from the university.

Despite their looking forward to the visit, all were aware that moves were afoot in certain quarters to investigate the monastery in the near future. The end-result might even be the arrest of the leading figures there. But that was for another day. Each was determined to make use of the time left for their private, personal purpose; for each was very curious about this place and its personnel.

They had a long-standing invitation from Hans to come up to 'recharge their batteries' and perhaps pick up a game or two of cards. All were poker aficionados and they could think of nothing more exciting than a game up there in a lovely setting away from the pressures of job and home. They laughed now to hear Luis and the Superintendent recount stories of Hans when he had lived in town.

'I always put him down as a little bit of a fraud,' said Superintendent Williams (proving once again that there is no more successful unmasker of the fraudulent than the experienced policeman), 'when he was putting a religious angle to everything while he drank rum and anything else that was going, playing cards and using swear words, it used to make me think. I suppose as a cop I am that little bit suspicious of everyone (even myself-ha ha). I studied him carefully. I checked his words with my own little "truth tests". Something about him was phoney. One thing was the accent. I asked him what accent it was. He said Dutch. I knew immediately he was lying. No, I won't tell you how I knew! I wondered why he loved to gamble. He doesn't just play cards for the love of the intricacies of the game – it was the gamble that he was addicted to. And most especially of all – there was his unwillingness to have a woman at his side. That is what got me. How could he stand it? They were the most beautiful women in Kingstown. Many were the times that we left temptation in his way; but he would only laugh about it later. No rise in him!'

'I remember,' said Luis, 'that you nearly brought tears to his eyes once. Do you remember? The only time he lost his temper.'

'We saw the other side of him. We were talking about war criminals who had come to live here in the Fifties and Sixties. They were all old men by then, who people laughed at as they shuffled their way about the hardware stores and bars. I said to people that few knew that these old white guys were all racists and murderers. They showed no sorrow for their past. I said that somebody must be protecting them. How else were they allowed to remain free? I said that their protector must be very powerful; that he could only be the Devil. Hans flared up. We might have done the same if we had been in their shoes, he said. How do we know for sure that we would have acted differently. How did we know that they weren't sorry and so on. It's the only time I ever saw emotion in him. His face was red. Here was this supposedly holy man of God, who always talked about morality, launching a defence of mass killers!'

'A sympathiser,' said Rick with disgust.

'Some of my best friends are ...' laughed Luis, trying to lighten the mood, for there was no need for unpleasantness while on a holiday.

'Hey, it's mango season,' cried Ron.

They stopped at a roadside stall and helped themselves to the best of the mangoes. The stallholder, an old woman, found them difficult customers. At the end of their haggling, she had found her stall lightened by about twenty mangoes (she could not count exactly how many they took), with the price in her hand for ten. Yet she knew that she shouldn't complain or feel bad, as she had been honoured (she was informed) by the custom of some of the most important people in Kingstown.

'That land they have up there,' said the High Court judge, 'it must have been greatly improved by cultivation. If it was me I would continue growing peanuts. They hold a steady market and are good for the country.'

'It would make a good dairy farm,' said Rick.

'A papaw plantation,' said the Superintendent, 'the demand from the tourist industry outstrips supply.'

'You are a bunch of vultures,' laughed Luis.

'You are very quiet,' said Ron to Monsignor O'Delly, the Papal Nuncio. 'I suppose he's asked you up hoping to charm you and get into the Pope's good books?'

'No, I'm going for a rest. Just to get a change of locale and some fresh air. Mind you, I will have to look into some of these stories I've heard. A nice game of cards is just the setting for a relaxed, frank discussion. So I might join in.'

'Don't bother unless you have some money,' said the Superintendent in a serious voice.

They were accustomed to socialising with the Nuncio, his roly-poly figure and jovial personality encouraging them to see him as sort of harmless, toytown diplomat who represented a powerless, pseudo-state with no economic, military or political clout. He was a good mixer, full of humour and, most importantly, never showed shock or surprise at any scandalous comment or revelation he heard over the dinner or card table. In fact, they loved to have him at their parties, for they felt that by his presence all their private misdemeanours and sins somehow had the blessing not only of God and the Pope, but of the devil as well. O'Delly, aware of this subtle power, used it to good effect, in particular to pick up all sorts of information.

He listened to the chat with interest. He was glad that at last he had managed to arrange a visit to the monastery. Ever since Archbishop Da Souza had lambasted Sang and company he had been deeply interested in this place. He had come across these charismatic movements before, elsewhere in the world. Yet none had obtained such a bad reputation for themselves, in such a short period of time, as the United Church. This, in itself, was a matter of curiosity and most likely bespoke powerful work taking place. Then there had been that 'draw' that had taken the diocesan administrator back to the monastery.

His own 'spiritual antenna' – that invisible 'diviner' which automatically came into use whenever highly significant but obscure, intricate situations needed sorting out, was being prepared for the task ahead. (One method was by a series of rapid, short prayers done with his eyes closed and breath held, while retaining the ability to hold a normal conversation with others at the same time.) As much as a professional chore, it was a visit of personal importance to him. He had by now had enough of the diplomatic life. He was looking for something more meritorious with which to end his days. He wanted to expunge all those accumulated venial sins garnered from a bohemian lifestyle. He wanted to become an ascetic of sorts, and end his days in the Lord's good books.

He admired those who lived a life he would have been unable to bear – the hard life. In particular, he wondered about something that he knew existed – for he had seen it in others – and of which he was greatly envious, even though he had never experienced it himself. This was joy and happiness. He had seen it in Da Souza's assistant when he had departed for the monastery. It was not that O'Delly ever considered joining the community – that thought had not even occurred to him. But he felt that, if only he could get near the source of this 'joy' or happiness, some of it might rub off on him. Just a little bit of it would be good enough; it would surely satisfy him for the rest of his life! It might even give him the motivation to look for a more useful, satisfying job outside this so-called diplomatic service.

'We never encourage these sort of communities in the church,' he lied. 'The Jesuits in particular gave us a lot of trouble in the past. In South America they once even tried setting up an alternative state. We had to move in the heavy guns and forcibly shut them down.'

'Oh God, I know all about them,' said the US ambassador. 'The CIA had to use all their tactics to get them out. Assassinations. The evil of it was that they used religion as part of their propaganda to justify revolution.'

'Oh ...' said O'Delly. 'I was talking about three hundred years ago.'

'What? They were at it then, too? As long ago as that? Well, I guess they probably caused the French Revolution too.'

Luis added his piece. 'Everything should be under the authority of the pope and his representatives in the country, which is you, Monsignor, and the Archbishop. Then there would be no trouble.'

'Fr Hans is up to his neck in revolutionary politics,' said Superintendent Williams. 'We have a transcript where he talks about a plan to shoot the Prime Minister. That is confidential, mind you. Off the record.'

'Ordinary people, everywhere in the country threaten to do the same thing every day. It doesn't mean a thing,' said O'Delly, becoming a little alarmed at the way the conversation was going.

'They've got guns hidden away,' said Ron. 'Some monks are even allowed to carry them with them when they go outside the monastery.'

'I'm sure we will find an explanation,' said Luis; 'In any case, what does it matter? They will soon be locked up, or expelled from the country from what I hear. Let us enjoy ourselves while we are there. I'm sure their hospitality is second to none.'

The university professor and the two industrialists (a term the latter used to describe themselves as 'any upstart could claim to be a businessman these days'), had been busily discussing card moves during all this conversation about the monks. They had no axe to grind with anyone, except to mutter a little about the fact that Hans had told them that they would all have to partake, not in religious services as such, but in what he called exercises that would reflect the best of relaxation therapy. It sounded good, but also worrying. The professor said that he had heard that a colleague of his, Dr Wesley, had partaken in some course at the monastery. He hoped to hear from him when next they met, and gauge his opinion on the work of the community.

Rick and Ron laughed when they heard this and said that they knew all about Wesley's visit there. The poor man had been trying to 'get' religion. Having failed in the political field, he was now hoping to use religion to get the support of the masses, who always admired the religious guru. He would learn all the correct vocabulary, talk about his conversion on the radio and so on, and put himself over as the new, loving Dr Wesley. He had also homed in on the organisational success of the monks, to see what he could learn there. Not a bad strategy at all, when one thought about it.

The Superintendent said that he would find out from Hans what Dr Wesley's plans were exactly.

'As long as he doesn't suspect we are government ministers,' said Ron.

'How do you know he won't recognise you both?' asked the monsignor.

'They might recognise our fathers, but I hear that they ban newspapers, radio and television at the monastery. So as junior ministers it is unlikely that they will have any idea of who we are,' said Ron.

'Well, just play ignorant about the political and economic affairs of the country,' said Superintendent Willams, sarcastically. His jibe was lost on the two ministers.

Another riposte came to O'Delly's mind, but he held his peace. Love, hate, humour, mockery were all very finely balanced in life – as they were with this jovial lot in this fine, speeding vehicle.

'I must say,' he said, keeping up a positive note, 'the government has done a great job in improving the roads of this country. We haven't hit one pothole yet.'

'Don't speak too soon!' laughed Luis, and the whole carriage burst into uncontrollable laughter. The rum was having its effect, and even O'Delly was able to forget for a while the venial sins of his own bohemian lifestyle.

The vehicle came to the inevitable cop roadblock.

'I will have that man's badge,' said a now drunken Ron at the sight of the approaching police constable.

'He's only doing his job,' said Rick, burping.

'Shut up, men,' said the High Court judge, almost shouting, '*never* rub a cop up the wrong way.'

'G-men,' said Luis, gesticulating over his shoulder.

The policeman looked into the vehicle and recognised the son of the Prime Minister.

'Just a warn. They are bad men 'round north. Don't stop for any roadblock.'

'Thanks,' said the judge, 'we appreciate the warning. You are doing a good job. Keep it up.'

'You hear that, sir? Don't stop for the next road block,' the cop repeated.

The warning had a temporary sobering effect.

'Tell me,' said Luis after a while, bringing up the subject of religion and catching O'Delly by surprise (for it was the one subject they never discussed on social occasions), 'is there a God?'

'You are asking the wrong person. Ask the monks. They are religious.'

But he soon realised that he was not going to be allowed to sidestep the question. For Luis asked it again, more adamantly. O'Delly wondered to himself what Luis was up to.

The judge joined in, his voice bullying. 'You should have some opinion on the subject. You are a priest! What sort of priest are you?'

The others went quiet and stared at O'Delly. He saw in their eyes various emotions – surprise, disappointment, subconscious fear that there might be a God after all, and genuine anger over not receiving some sort of existential assurance from a cleric, who was professionally paid to provide exactly that.

He felt in a bit of a spot. Where a jokey answer might have worked with sober men, it wouldn't with this lot now.

'A bad one, I'm afraid.'

'All I'm asking you is ... how do we know that there is a God?' asked Luis, irritably.

'Yes, of course there is a God,' O'Delly replied brusquely, hoping that a bold affirmation would be the end of the matter.

'Where's the evidence?' demanded the judge, whom O'Delly knew to be a cynic and agnostic.

'There are five proofs ...'

'Stop. I am not asking you for a speech. I am asking you for *evidence*.'

O'Delly could not quite work out this vicarious mood in his fellow passengers. Were they really serious, or just playfully serious, or even taking the mick? The latter was most unlikely, going by their faces. It was just like one of their poker games, he suddenly realised, when there was a really high stake on the table and 'jokes' were made, usually very near the mark or just spot on, about opponents' characters or reputations. Indeed, he often wondered how much real friendship there was between these people, and how much concealed enmity and hate.

'Are you saying, monsignor, that you are a fraud? Are you admitting that you have lived a lie all your life?'

The judge certainly knew how to put the boot in when he wanted, O'Delly noted.

'All those people you have led astray!' said Superintendent Williams. 'It must be on your conscience. Telling lies in the name of God.'

'Leading the ignorant astray,' said the judge.

'So you don't believe in God ...' said Rick heavily. 'Well, that takes the biscuit.'

'I never said that,' O'Delly replied.

'You sure don't look or sound like a man who believes in God,' insisted the judge. 'If it was down to me and a jury, the verdict would be guilty.'

'And the sentence death,' said Superintendent Williams, with a cold laugh.

O'Delly looked harshly at Luis who, he noted, was not saying much now although he had started the whole thing off.

'Why did you ask me if there is a God, Luis?' O'Delly asked him in a hurt voice. 'Are you really that ... bothered?'

'Just testing you out,' laughed Luis.

It was the master poker player at work. He wanted to get me all worked up, O'Delly thought. Luis was already working on all the others there, in his own, quiet way, preparing them for the big meal at the poker table. As the cardinal rule in poker was –never let emotion or ego influence your calculations, it was a sure bet that Luis would benefit from such subtle tactics. Well, the thing now was to let him continue to believe that he was more than just a little upset.

'Ha,' he laughed. 'Look at us. Fat, vain, greasy, gluttons pretending to be bothered about whether there is a God or not! I don't think that there can be a good, omnipotent God at all, if he has made the likes of us!'

He cursed himself. It had all come out completely wrong. He had not meant to say that at all!

The others went silent and sulked.

They were now about three-quarters of the way there. The drive was going smoothly. They were passing many villages and small towns with large numbers of unemployed, idle youths who glared and shouted at the passing Mercedes. As they went through one particularly noisy, unkempt little town, for some reason the judge said, 'We would be in trouble now if we got a puncture.' At that very moment they heard a bang. Luis with a great effort succeeded in pulling the vehicle to a stop.

'Tyre burst!' he shouted.

ten

After Winston's cure Sang was more jolly again. He was made to concede by Hans that, despite all that had gone wrong in recent times, the 'power' was still there and if anything its effects were being felt even more. Asissy was healing people! Even the latest rumour – that illegal cannabis plants had been detected ('smelt' was the word) within the compound – did not take from the air of satisfaction.

Hans and Alfredo were charged with the investigation. They approached the ruins cautiously, whistling and calling a warning of their approach to give some confidence to the hesitant Alfredo.

'Is Bro Wesley there?' called out Hans from twenty yards.

'General Wesley come,' Wesley shouted.

He met them in the open, greeting them with a comradely hug.

'My men said a prayer this morning,' Wesley said proudly. 'You would not believe that only a month ago their main interest was in going out robbing and shooting. The LFFA has already carried out its first engagement, and a very successful one it was too. They have cleared out a drug gang that was terrorising the neighbourhood and confiscated their contraband. I am so proud of them.'

He brought them in and showed them the cache. His men were in the tunnel, for they still feared to openly face the monks.

'There! Take it. Burn it. Just do not give it to the police.'

Hans was mightily impressed. Alfredo's eyes were as wide as his head.

'I told you, General,' said Hans, 'that nobody is impervious to good. But it ees to you that I give the credit. Your conversion is even more impressive than theirs.'

'I do not wish for any praise. I have no personal interest in power. It is the liberation of the masses that is our objective. I am irrelevant and dispensable. I am only a tool.'

'Humility! It always shines like the sun.'

'Could you lend us the minibus?' Wesley suddenly asked.

Hans went silent. That was a step very far, indeed.

'Where are you going?'

'I'm taking them to Kingstown for the day. They are still a little homesick, although I must admit they are now beginning to adjust much better to life here.'

'OK,' said Hans, 'but drive carefully. We can't afford expensive repairs.'

'It will be a training exercise in which, hopefully, after all they have learnt here, they will be able to see their old community through new eyes.'

'Alfredo, get the handcart, take this stuff away and burn it.'

Alfredo, in carrying out these instructions obediently, showed that he, too, had totally shed his old ways and was a new man.

'That golden chariot you saw,' Jim McCall was saying to Gerry, 'interests me greatly. Describe it again.'

Gerry, concerned at a seeming loss of control over his thoughts and imaginings (he had been informed that his face had taken on a fixed, wild look), had gone to Jim out of desperation. He was looking for a way out of religion now, hoping to escape soon from this place. Jim was still his best hope for sound, worldly advice.

'It was a great, big, fine vehicle, being driven by a very expert charioteer. It did not follow a straight-line route, but kept swerv- . ing and going up and down. It was heading here very fast, and seemed to be getting nearer and nearer, until it sort of faded.'

'Very good, I think I know what it means. Somebody significant is coming to pay us a visit. Or is, even, already here.'

'Anybody I know?' asked Gerry, dumbly.

McCall laughed.

'You don't get it, do you? It's the end of the world. Everybody else around knows it. Brother Orbeck, Alan, the rest of them – they are all prepared. That is why you don't hear a squeak out of them now. Everybody is having visions. All except Sang and Hans – for it is natural for those in power to be the last to know. It is the reason the sisters have pulled out. Providence has arranged it that way, to save them from the terrible cataclysm that will shortly take place. Winston's cure was the penultimate sign.'

'Penultimate ...?'

'There is to be one last sign. An attempt will be made to murder the Messiah's Forerunner.'

Gerry suddenly saw everything with great clarity. He must be the only sane person in the place. He had heard of such scenarios before. They were all fanatics! They were going to blow the place up, along with everyone in it. They were going to start a war with the government! He should have seen it coming! The signs were there, all right! The excited crowds. The cutting of telephone lines. The noisy movements by night of men and materials. The talking in code and the double speak. The shutting out of the sisters. The gunmen and dynamiters holed up in those ruins over there. Part of the monastery off limits to all except the inner circle!

He felt offended! He seemed to be the only one not being taken into confidence by the revolutionaries-to-be around him.

'Jim, don't do it. Don't let them do it.'

He had shouted the words at McCall. He turned and walked away, his feet taking him at a faster pace than that to which they were accustomed. He stumbled and fell. He pulled himself up and looked back to see if Jim was pursuing him. McCall was walking away, in the opposite direction.

The Jah met, as usual, in the open area in front of the admin block. It was a regular, scheduled 'reasoning' and they sat in a large circle around Sanctus and Alan. The two had agreed to put on a united front for the forthcoming 'big event'. They produced the three bongo drums and began a nyabingi chant. They were joined, quietly with no undue fuss, by Orbeck and to the surprise of everybody, Sr Gloria.

'Look east, he come from the east,' intoned Orbeck.

They all positioned themselves to face eastwards – to where the mountains 'ran down to the sea'. After prayers and hymns, Sr Gloria stood up and gave a 'fill-us-I-ing'.

She had 'run-I-way' to escape Sr Jane and her tyrannical rule. The heretical sisters were 'breaking from Home Rome'. They were setting up their own church and Sr Jane would soon be calling herself Bishop Jane, Head of the Church of Women. There was going to be a ceremony, conducted by someone who, Jane had said, was a bishop of the 'Church of the Anti-Apostate Pope'.

Gloria said that she wished that they could have the old days back when women knew their place and were privileged to do all the hard, unpleasant work so that the men could run the world. However, it didn't matter too much now, as it was end times.

'I am waiting for him, now,' she said in a resigned, sad voice, 'although I do not believe that he will come.'

'What?' demanded Alan, 'you are unbeliever?'

'No! I believe! I believe more than yo, cheeky boy!'

'What you mean?' asked Orbeck, intervening to calm the situation.

'I believe that he may, or may not come to me. He will not come from the east.'

'Not from the east?'

'No. Gerry come to me from over there!' she shouted, pointing west towards the monks' quarters. She stood up and turned to face the opposite direction, sitting down again with that characteristically stubborn, bold look in her eye.

It was time, Wesley was saying to his men, to start the war. 'The revolution does not wait for anyone. Those who are not with us are against us.'

'Where we go?' asked Dagga.

'Good news! We go a Kingstown!'

'Eeeh!' they cried, delighted.

'We go on what is call 'daytrip'. We go in real style in monks' minibus,' said Wesley, 'For we no longer sneak in and out through tunnel. We free to go in an' out main gate.'

This was good news to them. The tunnel had become problematical. In fact, it had become something of a serious danger to health. Every snake, rat, scorpion and 'hundred leg' in the region seemed to have come to live there. It was wet, stifling for lack of air if they had to stay there for any length of time (as when that army helicopter had circled overhead for at least an hour). The wooden beams supporting the roof were sagging.

'What we rob?' Dog wanted to know.

'We don't say "rob" word no more. We *liberate*. This time we liberate police station in de swamp village.'

'Police ...?' they shouted, astonished.

'How you expect liberate country if police still boss? Every day they go mash up shanty town. We teach them lesson.'

'OK, you general. You lead us. We have lucky charms now.'

'An' new gun,' Cockroach added, holding the second brand

new H&K MP5 loaded submachine gun that Wesley, as a confidence building gesture, had brought in earlier.

'Yo fool man! Tek dat t'ing away! It bring bad luck. No police or army bullet can kill we now. We immortal!' shouted Dagga.

'Did Eamon tell you that?' asked Wesley.

'Yea, man. He say w'en we wear these t'ings, police can no kill we. Bullet bounce off.'

'He say,' said Dog, 'dat if bullet kill body id cannot kill soul.'

'Yea, bullet bounce off,' Dagga repeated.

Bro Eamon had provided each 'soldier' with a large cross to put around his neck. Each also had in his possession a blessed medal and a phial of holy water. He was told that these would provide him with protection from the devil and even from fear, providing that he also uttered a prayer.

Their holy 'lucky charms' meant more to them than any new gun. Wesley was taken aback to hear Dog as well as Dagga now pronounce that there was no need any longer for such 'childish things'.

The men were collected at the ruins in the minibus, driven by Wesley. As they drove out through the gate, the brothers came to wave farewell and to shout prayers for their safe return. The general's men could not believe their eyes and ears. The monks were their friends! They had been told this many times, but had not seen any evidence for it before. They weren't there to put curses of spells on them but to give them blessings! The monks were smiling, laughing and waving at them! The brothers came over and grasped their hands through the windows and open slide-door. There were tears in the eyes of the general's men as they returned the gestures of love and shouted back 'peace an' love' as they exited the compound.

'Oh, Lord, me wan' stay,' said Dagga.

The men spent the journey looking out the window, shouting greetings at bystanders and crowds flocking the roads, excitedly

arguing over every feature of each passing scene. It was as though
they had been away for years, rather than a month. They were
seeing the world for the first time, with refreshed eyes. Wesley
couldn't get over the change in their attitude and behaviour. He
noted, and wondered about the fact that they were paying no attention to the weaponry at their side or to the job ahead of them,
vague and dangerous though that mission must have sounded to
them. They had lost all interest in what was actually going to
happen when they reached their destination.

While Wesley was somewhat surprised at the dramatic
changes in his men, he appeared to have no awareness of any
change in himself. As far as he was concerned, he was still General Wesley, Commander of the Liberation From Fear Army, a
newly established revolutionary armed group that was going to
cause mayhem in the country, terrorise the ruling class, and facil-
itate the long-hoped for takeover of government by himself, sup-
ported by the poor and oppressed. Yet here he was – admiring
this totally incongruous, fresh new outlook in his men,
sympathising with their newly acquired respect for nature,
scenery and even, possibly, other human beings.

The change had come over them when Sang complimented
them on their 'rescuing' the village from the out-of-town gang.
That praise, although it had confused them at first and they
hadn't a clue at the time what he was talking about, had given
them a pleasure that they had never experienced before. They had
been even more chuffed by the extra praise that Sang heaped on
them for bringing all that confiscated contraband back to the
monastery, to be harmlessly disposed of, when they could just as
easily have hidden it away to be utilised at a future date for their
own benefit. Such praise overcame all doubts that they might
have had about things.

He was even more confused by Dagga's words now.

'So, General Daddy Shaft,' Dagga said exuberantly, 'we go
visit police station and teach dem lesson. Dis gun teach dem good

lesson. It give dem big fright. But we can give dem *bigger* fright ... We need no gun now.'

'Right,' said the others.

'We need no gun. We have lucky charms!' said Dog.

'More powerful dan gun or anything,' said the formerly doubtful, now convinced Cockroach.

Wesley was bemused. He had already realised that the revolution was not going to take precisely the form that he first had in mind. Originally, there was to have been an onslaught on a quiet, undermanned rural police station in which the (usually) dozing sergeant and possibly one constable would be slaughtered (rather than an urban police station that would have heavy armour and probably a detachment of soldiers in place). Plans, ideas, tactics, motivations even, had all undergone much change since his long discussions with Hans. Of course, Hans, while knowing of their strong desire to change society radically – he had praised them for it – had not been aware (to the best of his knowledge) of their proposed tactics.

All that had changed now. He was going along with that 'fluidity' in things and events (changing as the milieu changes – an idea of Hans's not found in Marxism). What a foolish revolutionary he would be if he did not adapt some of the successful Jesuitical methods for his own use. It was this adaptation principle, without which any revolution would be doomed, that had inspired his 'conversion' to a new methodology. So he would go along with these changed tactics. They had emerged socio/organically after all. If the worst transpired, they still had their guns.

Yet even now he found it difficult to contemplate, or even to look at those guns. There was something about them that seemed to stand in the way of a triumphant, proper revolution.

Wesley suddenly realised that perhaps his men were not that stupid. Might not the use of the lucky charms be, after all the better, more sophisticated tactic?

'General Daddy Shaft ...?' Dagga began.

'Jus' call me Daddy,' said Wesley, to his own immense surprise.

He had no idea why he had said it. He felt embarrassed. A thin red streak appeared on his cheeks. He realised now that he was proud of 'his children'. He had no children of his own. He was too busy changing society. Yet here he was, having what he could only interpret as fatherly feelings for these 'vulnerable young people in his charge'.

He was using the language of Hans! He had been thinking and using Hans' concepts without realising it.

When the bus passed the First Class bar in the west of the city they were all singing the most popular Nyabingi chant.

As they approached the outskirts of the main shanty town, they observed a great crowd and commotion. Police and army vehicles were lined up in the middle of the road, and the occupants were arguing with the women, as the children contented themselves in removing light fittings, tyre valves, number plates and any other removable objects from the armoured cars, trucks and tanks. A number of men were held in a line up against a shop wall by soldiers, who were kicking their legs in an attempt to get a 'straight line'. Somehow, the minibus managed to get past the road block and enter the shanty along the rim of the main gully. Ahead of them they saw soldiers firing away – at what no one could see. The rest of the male population was nowhere to be seen. They pulled to a stop.

'Criminals gone to raat it,' shouted the head cop, 'bumboclaat army scare dem 'way.'

'Teach them a lesson,' the army colonel was saying to his captain, 'so that we haven't wasted our time. Level the illegal squatter shacks.'

'Teach them lesson time,' shouted the captain.

The army detachment recommenced firing left, right and centre as other soldiers poured gasoline over the nearby huts.

These were being set alight as Wesley and his children disembarked from their vehicle.

The sight of this strange crew, submachine guns slung over
their shoulders, crosses dangling from their necks, calmly approaching them made everyone stop shooting and cease the fire-set-
ting. Wesley strode up to the colonel, who had been talking with
the police chief.

'What the raas ...?' said the police chief.

'General Wesley of the LFFA, sir. I have been sent here on
an official mission to save these poor shanty people. Tell those
soldiers to put down their guns immediately. Or my children will
unleash their vengeance upon you, and upon all the wicked.'

The two security chiefs eyed the MP5s and the strangely
garbed interlopers.

'Come here, man,' said the police chief to Wesley, and turning to the colonel, said, 'Hold your men up until I have a word
with this chap.'

'That army upstart treats me like shit,' he said to Wesley in a
whisper. 'This is a good opportunity to teach *them* a lesson!'

'They are massacring innocent people. They are driving
women and children from their homes,' said Wesley in disgust.

'That is nothing compared to the way they are treating us
police!'

'My children will fight on your side, if it is necessary to do so
to save the poor children of the shanty,' said Wesley in a firm,
confident yet uncharacteristically soft voice.

A part of Wesley told him that he didn't know what he was
saying, or even doing. This was not why they had come here. To
help the police! He felt like one of ... those monks. He thought
that he wanted to die, right here and now. To give his life for the
poor people of the shanty. But that was foolishness, wasn't it?
What use was a dead revolutionary? Yet, it seemed that it would
be the right thing to do at that moment.

Before they knew what was happening (they had thought that

the additional weaponry was about to be deployed on their side) the soldiers found themselves facing the guns of the police and the LFFA.

The crowd had now surrounded the raiding parties, and were trying to get a closer look at Wesley and his men, keeping a safe distance at the same time. They had lost interest in the security forces, who were now in a stand off against each other. The men who had been lined up had also come over to stare at the strange gunmen.

Somebody noticed the 'lucky charms' and cried out, 'Dey got spells! Dey monks! Nobody can kill dem!'

'Yea,' shouted Dagga, 'Fire yore gun at me, soldier boy, an' see what happun.'

The colonel took aim at Dagga's chest, on which hung the cross. As a man who frequented his church with his family on major social occasions, and who thus considered himself respectable, there was no way he would shoot at that thing. They had been outmanoeuvred here. They would have another opportunity to show the police who was boss at a later time. He did not even feel angry, or humiliated. In a way, he was glad the raid had ended like this. He would have a good excuse for not 'cleansing' the area when he got back to face his bosses. Those blasted monks came between us and the criminals. There was nothing we could do, this time. Yes, they had guns. How do we know they were monks? The name 'United Church of Jaman' was written on the side of their transport. That is how we know.

And what's more – they use witchcraft.

'Robbed everything,' said Luis to Hans as the retreatants disembarked from the police lorry inside the main gate, 'minibus, cash, chequebooks, watches, mobile phones, shoes, jackets, the lot. Only left us our pants.'

'How are we going to play cards now?' asked Superintendent

Williams, depressed.

'Ah, the cards doesn't matter. We'll think of something else to pass the time,' said Hans.

They were taken to the meeting room, given refreshments (which included coffee) and after a good wash in a cold shower put into monks' habits. They were then taken to their cubicles in the brothers' sleeping quarters. Here, they picked up a prayer book and, incongruously, a small slab of chocolate.

They were told that they would join the brothers for the evening meal. In the meantime, they were free to just walk around in the garden and recover from their long journey and sorry ordeal.

O'Delly observed everything around him with a keen eye. He sensed that something important was happening, or about to happen in the place. In the distance he could see the Jah all gathered together, seated on the ground and facing in the same direction. Various other brothers went rapidly hither and thither, obviously running important errands. His 'antenna' was working overtime. It told him – there was revolution in the air. The actions of every individual in the next few hours would have permanent repercussions – for himself, perhaps for the world. This was his opportunity to do something positive for once in his life. It was the moment to do something that one had always dreamed of. To act on the spur of the moment. To put a long-held thought into action. He would be part of the revolution. He called for Hans.

'Those idiots who I brought with me don't believe in God. They are the biggest apes it has been my misfortune to meet in a long time. They seem to think that they can talk down to anyone and everyone. They even treat an ordained minister of the Church with contempt. They have been insulting me ever since I came to this country. You would not believe how rude they were to me on the journey here. I enjoyed seeing them robbed. It made my day. Do your worst with them, Hans. Get your brothers to beat the living daylights out of them!'

'We don't work like that here, Monsignor, despite what you

may have heard. We use gentle methods.'

'Well, it was good enough for me when I was a stroppy lad. It is what they need. A good shaking up.'

'They have received that already. They will receive love and care here. And they will be given the "power".'

'What do you mean?'

'You would probably say – they will see the light.'

'Oh. Ah. Ha ha, I understand! Ha ha ha. That is good.'

For once in his life O'Delly felt part of something.

Prime Minister Raul Umberto Sr had got his jet and had 'amalgamated' the police and army. Orders had already been received by all the senior officers in both forces. The tricky question had been which senior officers in which force got the few remaining jobs. It was to be the army. Senior police would be given temporary positions as advisors to the army on matters such as crowd control, traffic regulations and all the legal niceties. The main body of police would be sacked to allow the essential economies. Raul had even decided on the uniform that would replace both army and police attire. It was to be khaki, and the new force would be called the Presidential Guard. The army would love that as it had the sound of a higher status, even a political role. One day, hopefully, it would be Raul's own personal guard.

And at this very moment of one of his greatest political and personal triumphs, the Minister of Internal Affairs, Erico Mauris Sr, came to him with a report of the kidnapping by the police of unknown government ministers and some top Kingstown people. What was more, the police were in cahoots with the mad monks of the north, and they had taken their hostages to their fortified, well-defended monastery.

They already knew of the foray of the monks into the swamp earlier, where they had caused fire, death and mayhem using a variety of means.

They had entered into some sort of Satanic pact with the police, who had connived with them in all their actions and given them 'safe passage' back to the monastery.

'Magic icons, poisonous substances, devil-markings were used by them alongside the most advanced of modern weaponry to frighten the crowds. Even my soldiers refused to fire on them,' the colonel had said to Erico Sr.

Erico Sr now called on the Prime Minister to make a national broadcast.

'Will the party and people support me?' he asked, already knowing the answer (those reports from the field were almost too good to be true) and thinking, *It's as if God, too, is on my side.*

'The nation will march as one behind you, Raul.'

The Prime Minister broadcast that evening in the slot between the commentary on the last race at DaCosta Park and the cricket results. Consequently, most of the nation did not hear it. He addressed the people in solemn tones, apprising them of the revolt by the whole police force against the legitimate organs of the state, in collusion with the well-known devil-worshipping, foreign sect. There was a hostage situation, with the cream Kingstown society, a holy, proper cleric and some of his own ministers being held prisoner. He called on the army to act immediately, to put down this treasonable revolt with all the means at its disposal. 'Pray the Lord for guidance and fortitude in this hour' were his signing off words.

The Presidential Guard, with the colonel now promoted to Major General and appointed as the new Chief of Staff, set out from President Eddy Barracks in a long convoy of tanks, armoured cars and lorries full of soldiers. These men fired off their guns every now and then in a celebration of their new prestige as the sole law and order enforcers of the country. Every time they passed a police station they laughed, jeered and hurled insults at the 'lady police dem'.

Sang got word of the impending 'search party' coming his way in a phone call from Archbishop Da Souza;

'Is Monsignor O'Delly with you? Let me speak to him. He must not become involved in all this. Can you send him out the back gate?'

'The monsignor is involved in a very important spiritual counselling session at the moment. He cannot be disturbed.'

'What do you mean? Look. I have no power to stop you all getting shot. They have done this before – in Central America for example – so you will get no sympathy from anyone. Certainly not in the media. They hate martyrs. Do you want to be dead? Do you want to be losers? Surrender. Play the game. There is still a chance – if you give up. Say that you are coming under me, Da Souza. It might help. Whatever you do, don't let any police in there, for whatever reason they might give you. They are all rebels and have been disbanded. I told you this would happen if you kept on going the way you were. You didn't listen to me.'

'Your Excellency. Do you know who we have here?'

'No, who?'

'The Lord Jesus.'

'Stop kidding me, Sang. Do you think this thing is a joke?'

'He is here in person. I should have recognised him before now. No harm can come to us. We are OK. The Lord is with us.'

'Sang, man, it's all right. I will telephone Raul straight away and explain how it is. You will not be harmed. I will see to it. What have they done to you, son?'

Sang looked into the meditation area and saw the Kingstown lot doing their relaxation exercise under the supervision of Hans. Also with them were the policemen who had brought them in, and who had joined in the meditation. Hans came over to him and said, 'We are ready. On the last day every person should continue doing what he would normally be doing at that time.'

Sang met Gerry in the annexe.

'Gerry, the Lord is here. Be ready to meet him.'

'Yes, OK,' said Gerry abstractedly. 'I see a level plain, and a great meeting of two armies, under two banners, at the head of one is Satan, and at the other is the Lord. They are ready to join battle ...'

Gerry was still talking as Sang left him. The man was living in his own world now, wherein all reality came through symbol and mystic vision. (He was to become renowned – and end his days – as the doorman of the monastery.)

He went over to Jim, to apprise him of the security situation. 'They are on their way. We are ready. Bro Jim, I am sorry for everything. Why didn't you tell me before?'

'I only realised gradually. I was thinking, at long last here is someone who I can talk to, who has a modicum of intelligence. He was smart. I ... was able to unload all my problems on to him. This led me, I don't know why, into asking him questions about life, religion and so on. Things I had never thought about before. I was wondering about him – how he had this effect on me. I was wondering if I was in a bit of a mental loop. I realised who he was in ... the brothel. He had not gone there, as we had all thought, to pray for fallen women. He had gone there to save ... us!'

Jim choked back tears.

'Then I watched him bring back Winston. Everybody still thinks it was Asissy. But he was standing behind Asissy all the time. He was up so close to Asissy he was breathing down his neck. But nobody noticed him. It is always the person you least expect who is the star. Humility personified.'

'We don't have to worry about anything now, Jim. He will tell us what to do when the time comes.'

Sang went over to Orbeck (who, being in the company of Alan,

Sanctus and the Jah was breaking hermitage rules again). Sang addressed the whole group, who had not moved from their positions seated in the middle of the grass area for the past twenty-four hours.

'Babylon is coming. The Beast expects us to put up a fight, to use the Man's way. We shall not. The Saviour has come. He is here to lead us to the Promised Land.'

'Is he African?' asked Alan, in a low, sad voice, as of one who had come to accept the inevitable. Sang's answer surprised him and gave Alan and the others great joy.

'Yes, he is of Africa.'

'Praise, praise,' they shouted.

'Even if He only liddle bit African, He will do,' said Alan, anxious to assure Sang that his conversion to Orthodoxy was genuine. 'Nobody say He mus' be All-African.'

The others shouted agreement. They were tired of waiting. Either He came now, or He never would.

A number of police cars drew up outside the gate. It was four o'clock in the afternoon. Sang had already been standing there for quite a while. He knew exactly what he had to do even though, consciously, he had no idea of what was going to happen, or even what it was he was going to do. It was like being inspired; he felt that anything he did could only be right. He had no doubts. No more of not being in the right place at the right time. General Wesley and his men, unarmed, and a collection of brothers were also at the gate.

A policeman got out of his car and came over. He said that he and the other senior officers with him had heard that the monastery provided sanctuary. He said that they had spotted the army convoy outside Mobby Bay. It was proceeding slowly and cautiously in their direction. They knew that they themselves were going to be arrested and charged with rebellion. They would most likely be shot. But they also knew that they would receive protection in the monastery. They had heard about what the brothers had done in the swamp. Monks were more powerful than soldiers! The police cars were guided in and the relief on the faces of the officers was evident for all to see.

They heard a loud noise in the sky. It got louder, until everyone was staring up. It was that helicopter back again. The one with the military markings. The Jaman Defence Force. This time, instead of continuously circling the compound it hovered at about 450 feet. The door opened and two military personnel appeared, holding something between them. It was obviously a heavy object and they heaved it out. The airmen stood back, watching it fall, as the helicopter climbed skywards. The object fell to the ground between the workshop and Fogelman's room. Jim McCall was standing there. There was a bright flash, followed by a loud bang and the sound of shrapnel smashing into walls. Bits and pieces of what had been McCall were flung all around the place.

In the meeting room they heard the bang and commotion outside.
'What is that noise? Can you not get them to quieten down?' asked Luis. 'I'm enjoying this ... meditation.'
'Yes,' agreed all the others.
'This is really something,' said Superintendent Williams. 'I'm even glad I lost all those material possessions that Hans says are such a hindrance to happiness. It is true. It feels just like he says!'
'I'm afraid,' said Hans, 'that the monastery is about to be attacked by the forces of the state. The army is on its way here. They are fighting the police, and we are to be the scapegoats for everything. Our Prime Minister is behind all of this. He is a tyrant, a dictator in the making. Nevertheless, let us carry on.'
'That is my pappy you are talking about,' said Ron, upset that

all the others were now looking at him, as well as the reminder, just at that sacred moment of becoming aware of a new self-worth and precious companionship, of the machinations of politics in the grubby, outside world.

'Can you get me to a telephone? Those robbers took my mobile. I will talk to my pappy.'

'There is a phone over at the desk. I will set up the call for you immediately,' said Hans, bouncing about with joy at this unexpected opportunity hopefully to influence the Prime Minister of the country.

Hans got to work contacting the Prime Minister's residence. He was soon talking to the telephone operator at Government House. He put on a stern, overbearing voice and demanded to speak to the Prime Minister immediately. To tell the PM that his son, Raul Jr, was in serious trouble. Soon he was talking to Raul Umberto Sr.

'It's Fr Hans here, from the United Church of Jaman. Your son is up here with us, benefiting from a much needed spiritual retreat.'

'Who's that? What's this? Who the hell are you? Where's my son?'

'Your son is hoping to turn out to be a different person than his father. A better person. That shouldn't be too hard. To think that one time, long ago, you were a reformer and a socialist!'

'Who is the fool boy with?'

'He is with Luis, Williams, O'Delly, your High Court place man, your two biggest business associates, the ambassador and the country's top criminologist. They are here learning how to be human beings again.'

'The army are on their way there. Let me talk to my boy.'

'Sure. He is right here.'

'Hey, pappy, what's going on?'

'That place is under an edict. What the hell are you doing there?'

'I was invited up for the weekend for a bit of fun. Erico Jr is with me. That's all.'

'Hear that, Erico? Your boy is there too. Get your backsides out of there right now. It is going to be bombed and burnt to the ground along with everyone there.'

'Ah, pap, you can't do that! They are nice people here ...'

There was a commotion as someone came into the room.

There were cries of recognition and greetings from the Kingstown folk.

'Hey, Rabbi!'

'What are you doing here?'

'Hey, we heard that you were run out of town.'

'There were so many rumours!'

Without a word Fogelman walked up to Raul Jr. He put his hand out for the phone.

'Wait, pappy. There is somebody here who looks like he wants to speak to you. A bearded gentleman. No, I don't know who he is.'

He handed over the phone.

'Ut's thu rubbu, Fugulmun. Thu mun whu spuku tu yu abut umbuzzlumunt uf tuxpuyurs' munuy. Ut us tume fur yu tu stund duwn und udmut yure crumus. Gut uff thu puple's bucks.'

'It's you! I should have known that you were behind all this. It was you who put them up to it! Don't you dare repeat your scandalous libels in public, you hear me? In any case, I have destroyed the documents and moved my bank account. You are an enemy of the people, an enemy of the country. You are a foreign shit. Nobody will listen to you.'

By this time, all the visitors and a good many more were standing nearby, listening to the conversation. As is customary in monasteries, it is possible for the telephone to be switched on to the public address system (for a variety of reasons). Somebody had already done this, and every word said by Umberto Sr was being followed with avid interest.

'Yu must lut thus puple gu.'

'Don't you try to blackmail me. I don't give a shit about my son. You hear me? He can die with the rest of them. And those other so-called friends of mine – they can die too, and good riddance. To hell with the lot of them. Goodbye.'

'And that goes for me too,' shouted Erico Sr down the phone, 'You can't use my son to blackmail me! He can go down the chute too.'

The phone was put down.

Everybody in the meeting room stood looking at one another. Not a word was spoken.

Raul Umberto Jr, alias Ron, was the quietest of them all. As the others eventually began a low hum of conversation, he remained silent. A deep anger was beginning to build up inside him.

By now the military had parked their tanks and vehicles all around the perimeter fence. The newly promoted Major General, standing up inside his tank, used a loud hailer.

'You have seen what will happen if you resist. Our air force is ready to go again. Our infantry is ready to go. Our artillery is ready to go. Tell Mr Sang, his administrative staff and all his men to come out here with their hands up.'

Dagga, who with the others had been watching through the wire, now casually made his way to a bin. He pulled out his new H&K submachine gun, went over, placed the muzzle through the wire and commenced firing.

(It was at this point that the new Aspirant, Bro Jaime Da Souza, who was also at the gate watching events, felt that old familiar panic at the pit of his stomach and his bowels loosen. If it happened, it would be that disaster worse than death. He would have no future in the monastery. It was to his immeasurable relief and joy that his bowels held and he recovered his composure. He had passed the major test. The cure was for real. *It* would never happen again.)

The soldiers ran for cover and the Major General ducked down inside his tank. The same tank blasted a shell that went through the monastery gates without doing any apparent damage and sped harmlessly on its way to the hillside behind which it failed to explode, the only sign of it being a small cloud of dust. (Afterwards, the body of Alfredo was found in the rough area on the other side of the compound, clearly having taken a direct hit from this shell, the impact of which had carried him there.)

Dagga's next shots ricocheted off a number of tanks and vehicles. The Major General, thinking it was safe after a few moments to put his head up for a second, received a single bullet in the head just as it was completing the last leg of a long journey around the assembled military armour. The Major General fell dead. Panic hit the soldiers. There was no second in command, this being an appointment that the Major General had not considered necessary.

The appearance of the LFFA members dancing and whooping in front of them unnerved the soldiers even more. Most had already heard about these 'witches'. Meanwhile, some police officeers, a little bolder than their colleagues, who had earlier shed their uniform and were dressed in hastily requisitioned monks' habits, now came over to the gate. At their head was Superintendent Williams. He called out to the soldiers for a ceasefire, and asked the next highest ranking military officer to step forward. At least thirty men came up to the gate. Williams went outside to join them.

'Where is the radio man?' asked the Superintendent, exasperated. 'Get him here.'

The signals corporal eventually appeared.

'Put me in touch with whoever is giving the orders over the radio.'

'It's the Prime Minister and the Minister of the Interior. They are asking if we have captured the place yet. I'm afraid to tell them the army is on strike.'

Williams went to the radio jeep. After introducing himself, and informing Umberto that his army and their attack strategy was a shambles – and that the Commander in Chief was dead – the Superintendent was surprised by Raul Umberto Sr's next command.

'Williams, I am appointing you full General and Commander in Chief of the Presidential Guard. Now here are my orders.'

It was a totally unexpected development for Williams. For a moment he considered his conundrum. Should he remain in that ridiculous monk's garb and lose all prospect of career advancement, as well as the respect of his family, friends and colleagues, or take up the PM's offer and become the second, if not the most powerful man in the country? He hastily had the uniform removed from the Major General's body, went behind a lorry and attired himself anew. He tore off the 'Major General' bars. He called over a sergeant, who was leaning against a tank smoking a cigarette and thus appeared more in command of the situation than anyone else (Williams' leadership skills were already showing). He appointed him his deputy, promoting him to colonel on the spot.

Sang now asked him what he was going to do.

'Arrest all you lot. Secure the premises. Report back to the Prime Minister.'

Hans took him aside and spoke quietly. 'You were saying only a short time ago that it would be a pity if they shut us down. You said that you were enjoying the meditation. Why have you changed your mind?'

'Turn down the biggest opportunity of my life? I'd be a fool.'

General Wesley came over. 'Hi Superintendent, it's me, Dr Wesley. I am known as General Wesley here. Ha ha ha.'

'I knew that you would be somewhere in all of this. You will be shot for impersonating me, for one thing. You will also be shot for taking part in an attempt to violently overthrow the state, for another.'

'Address me as General, if you don't mind, General. This is a war situation. Your men have no chance against mine. They're scared out of their wits at the sight of the LFFA. There will be no need for violence. We use peaceful means now. Watch this. Lieutenant Dagga, put away your gun.'

Dagga threw his gun on the ground.

'See!' said Wesley.

'Everybody to their stations,' shouted Williams, a little more hesitant about how to proceed, and the gates were closed once again, the mass of the policemen still inside and now cowering again behind whatever they could find.

There was an intense discussion between Wesley, Sang and Hans. They called on all the monks and all of the LFFA to line up in front of the gate. This they did, in all their varied attire, body painting, tattoos, dangling medals, crosses and ornaments. They were all unarmed and there was no aggression, only peace and love in their smiles.

The soldiers were, once again, transfixed on the spot, unable to obey shouted commands to open fire.

A standoff had set in. After an hour, they were all still standing there. General Williams had no choice but to inform the Prime Minister and Internal Affairs minister of the continuing existence of the monastery.

Unobserved, Fogelman had gone back to his room after his conversation with Umberto. He now appeared again, this time in the open.

They could not make out what was wrong with Fogelman. He walked heavily, a slight stoop to his bearing. He stumbled along rather than walked. There was something else about him now. In the bright sunlight. That no one had ever observed before. For some reason, they had never been able to scrutinise his face and bodily features up close. Now, whether or not it was due to his lying in the sun (some said later that it was he who had been up on the roof) or some other cause, the features that they scrutinised were as dark as those of the Jah. His bronzed features gave him an impression of majesty. His dreadlocks danced ecstatically in the wind, with a beautiful, golden brightness. Even his awkward walk added to his splendour, his body having the bearing of a colossus, moving along like the earth.

At that moment a great cry went up from Orbeck.

'He come! Look. He come!'

A great outcry broke out and they ran and fell at his feet, some scrambling to get branches, bits of bush, even leaves to throw before him as he came up to Sang.

He bowed respectfully to the Superior of the United Church.

'Cun uh huve uh wurd wuth yu?'

'It's a mess here. You can't get out right now,' said Sang.

Fogelman said that he had hoped to have been able to stay there, but it was not to be. Would he send a message to Umberto immediately, saying that he was willing to give himself up? He would walk out and hand himself over to the soldiers without resistance. Furthermore, he would accept the blame for everything. He would admit that he had been behind the whole insurrection – the witchcraft, the scheming to 'convert' the nation, the instigation of dissent and subversion in the monastery, the brainwashing of people into believing in their own invincibility. He would confess to all this, and announce his guilt publicly over the radio if necessary. He would, also, publicly absolve Umberto of all guilt, if he so wished, even for the missing funds. He was sure that ways would be found to provide restitution.

Sang knew that the standoff was over. This brilliant tactical move by Fogelman would solve so many problems. It was exactly the sort of self-sacrifice that was to be expected from the Messiah.

The terms of surrender were acceptable to the government.

They said their goodbyes. Hans was in tears as the past came back to haunt him again and he watched the now upright, confident Fogelman prepare to leave. Sang wondered why it was that, even though he knew he was in the presence of Jesus, it all felt so ordinary and normal, an everyday thing.

Then came that unexpected, irrational, inexplicable, even macabre request from Fogelman that was to puzzle them all for ever afterwards, and which gave rise to a whole new theology of evil. He asked that it be Hans who should take him across to the waiting lorry.

Hans walked him over holding his arm. The eager soldiers took Fogelman from a speechless, bewildered Hans. They had already been informed that their prospective prisoner was the cause of all the trouble, in the monastery, in the country, indeed in the world. They believed that they were going to be doing everybody a great favour now in punishing him with the harshest treatment for all his crimes against the people.

Sang took Hans aside after they had all left and put a fatherly hand on his head. He said that he knew how he was feeling. He thought that he knew the answer to Hans's anguish. He no longer felt that the Eastern, detached way was the best. The Western philosophy had more love (as well as hate) in it. He was happy to consider that he belonged to the West, too, now.

'It gives more meaning to what you have just done,' he said, 'to look at it in black and white, good versus evil.'

'I don't understand.'

'It is a good thing that it was you, and not some poor innocent, who had to be the instrument of a dark deed. At the end, good always comes out. There is no grey area.'

'I will think about that.'

'Do you know what poor Jim told me?'

'What?'

'The graffiti slating our peanut business. He knew who it was.'

'Who? How did he—'

'Rabbi Fogelman. He admitted it to Jim. He said that he was worried that we were getting too caught up in the whole business side of things. It would destroy our work eventually, he said. He also apparently said that he loved writing cryptic comments, anywhere and everywhere he could, casual remarks and jokes for people to read. He had always used such means, over time, for the edification of people and even as a form of humour. He said that graffiti art was the best of all.'

This led to a lively debate between the two, which Hans, loosening up a bit, enjoyed immensely, suggesting that they bring up at the next community meeting a proposal that they have regular debates on Fogelman and his teachings, with the subject of graffiti as the first topic for discussion.

He is looking and sounding better already, thought Sang.

O'Delly now knew what it was that made people happy. He had picked up a little bit of it today, just as he had hoped. He knew, now, that his job *was* worthwhile after all. He had not wasted his life. Hans had invited him to become an Aspirant. It was music to his ears. He was acceptable! That was enough. He would go back to his dry, stale desk job and feel that every minor, seemingly futile task he applied himself to was worth its weight in spiritual gold. As long as he had the power. For wasn't that all that the monks did all day long – ordinary, mundane, repetitive jobs. There was no mystery at all about the place, its residents or their work.

Mother Jane was ordained a priest of the new Church of Women. Josephine, on Hans's advice, had reconciled herself to the new situation. She hoped, by her assiduous loyalty to Jane and the new church, eventually to bring about a reconciliation with the

Church of Rome. The sisters were abuzz with excitement at all the new ideas being discussed. Apparently, there were a vast number of encouraging messages coming in and large sums of voluntary donations from an amazingly wide and varied range of sources around the world.

Gloria had said to Sang that she did not want to become a part of a women's church. The Lord had come; He was that funny little man in the strange clothes. But he had left now. His room was vacant. Sang said that the Lord had given her His room as one of his last acts before He left. She would be happy to know that they would find her some menial jobs to do.

Luis the banker, Raul Umberto Jr, Erico Mauris Jr, the judge, the two industrialists, the ambassador and the university professor met Sang and Hans at the gate. They were ready to leave now. They had worked everything out in very fruitful sessions with their spiritual advisors. They knew what they had to do to restore the country to its rightful owners. Accompanied by the now plain Mr Wesley and his small group of friends (the latter to be inducted shortly into the restored police force), they left in an army wagon under heavy guard provided by a breakaway group of the old, now defunct Presidential Guard. It had been sent 'to ensure their safe passage' by General Williams, now the head of the anti-corruption squad that was leading the drive to rout the old government, establish a new, reformed police and army and clean up the country.

'I would not like to be in this government's shoes right now,' said Sang.

Everybody in community now made it a regular part of their time of recollection to go over their personal experiences of meeting or meetings, conversations, small chats, even just perhaps a brief nod and 'time of day' that they had had with the Lord in that short period time that He had spent with them. They understood many things now. They did not have to wait any more. He had come and restored the world. The Conquering Lion of Judah. The power would never leave them now. Their only question, doubt, misgiving, was whether their own, personal response to the Man had been generous enough; or good enough; or why had they been prejudiced; or not listened with more care to that difficult accent; or even sought him out more.

But it was the big question that tormented them. The question that they could not satisfactorily answer:

'What was his message?'